VISITOR

C.J. CHERRYH

THE FOREIGNER UNIVERSE

FOREIGNER	PRECURSOR
INVADER	DEFENDER
INHERITOR	EXPLORER
DESTROYER	CONSPIRATOR
PRETENDER	DECEIVER
DELIVERER	BETRAYER
INTRUDER	TRACKER
PROTECTOR	VISITOR
PEACEMAKER	

THE ALLIANCE-UNION UNIVERSE
REGENESIS
DOWNBELOW STATION
THE DEEP BEYOND Omnibus:
Serpent's Reach | Cuckoo's Egg
ALLIANCE SPACE Omnibus:
Merchanter's Luck | 40,000 in Gehenna
AT THE EDGE OF SPACE Omnibus:
Brothers of Earth | Hunter of Worlds
THE FADED SUN Omnibus:
Kesrith | Shon'jir | Kutath

THE CHANUR NOVELS
THE CHANUR SAGA Omnibus:
The Pride Of Chanur | Chanur's Venture | The Kif Strike Back
CHANUR'S ENDGAME Omnibus:
Chanur's Homecoming | Chanur's Legacy

THE MORGAINE CYCLE
THE COMPLETE MORGAINE:
Gate of Ivrel | Well of Shiuan | Fires of Azeroth | Exile's Gate

OTHER WORKS:
THE DREAMING TREE Omnibus:
The Tree of Swords and Jewels | The Dreamstone
ALTERNATE REALITIES Omnibus:
Port Eternity | Wave Without a Shore | Voyager in Night
THE COLLECTED SHORT FICTION OF CJ CHERRYH

C. J. CHERRYH

VISITOR

A *Foreigner* Novel

DAW BOOKS, INC.

DONALD A. WOLLHEIM, FOUNDER

375 Hudson Street, New York, NY 10014

**ELIZABETH R. WOLLHEIM
SHEILA E. GILBERT
PUBLISHERS**

www.dawbooks.com

First Printing, April 2016

1 2 3 4 5 6 7 8 9

DAW TRADEMARK REGISTERED
U.S. PAT. AND TM. OFF. AND FOREIGN COUNTRIES
—MARCA REGISTRADA
HECHO EN U.S.A.

PRINTED IN THE U.S.A.

To Jane.

Table of Contents

1

The lift slowed and shifted sideways. The indicator above the doors showed their approach to the change-point, the crossover, where the human side of the station met the atevi side and did face-to-face business. A schematic to the right of the door showed a second lift, outbound from the docking bay, destined for the same stop.

That lift bore a very welcome envoy from the Earth below.

On the Earth of the atevi—humans did not predominate. But on the station—it was supposed to be a treaty-set balance.

It had gotten out of balance. And that was only *one* problem he needed to solve in the near future. The *very* near future.

Bren Cameron kept a precautionary grip on the safety bar—not being a citizen of the station, not being familiar with the route, he remained wary of surprises from the lift system. He wore court dress for the occasion, as a lord of the atevi aishidi'tat, which he was. Not that the arriving party would care. But the occasion called for dignity. Respect. For him that meant brocade and lace.

Around him, his atevi bodyguards, black-skinned and golden-eyed, towered a head taller, armed and watchful. Wherever he went, they went, black-uniformed, constantly in contact with atevi authority, who could amplify their small force considerably on short notice.

Banichi and Jago, Tano and Algini—that team of four was the heart of his own household. Two more of the Assassins' Guild attended him on this occasion, one man from the aiji-dowager, who was in charge of the mission; and one from Lord Geigi's bodyguard, as a guide through station systems and a personal gesture of support from Geigi, who had been on duty shift after shift as atevi stationmaster in Central—control of which was supposed to rotate between human and atevi every two shifts, and pass politely between the two authorities.

That rotation had happened like clockwork for years . . . until—God, what was it? Five? Six?—days ago, when outside events hurtled the world toward a meeting they didn't want under the best of circumstances. The alien and extremely dangerous kyo had arrived insystem and were now heading toward the inner solar system, presumably for a visit.

Presumably being the operative word. The kyo were already at war. Not with them, but with someone, and it *was* a concern—on two fronts. They *hoped* it was actually the kyo visiting them and not the unknown Someone. And they had aboard the station five thousand survivors from the other human station—Reunion—which had run afoul of what was indisputably a kyo attack. The kyo had had second thoughts afterward. They had allowed the evacuation of the survivors and promised peace.

One truly hoped that understanding had held up.

And with news that the kyo were inbound, the Mospheiran-born stationmaster, Mikas Tillington, had gone berserk, locked down the Reunioner sections of the human side of the station, and refused to release control of Central to atevi on their regular rotation. Mikas Tillington had put himself in sole control. Mikas Tillington had determined he was *not* going to turn decision-making over to his atevi allies, not with this emergency bearing down on them, and he had emphatically refused to trust the Reunioners, who had come in as outsiders and a problem to his organized station operations, even to be free to walk the station corridors.

The Reunioners hadn't been treated well by Tillington's administration, and they were now panicked out of all reason.

Well, Tillington could lock the Reunioners into their sections, but not even he had dared lock the atevi shuttle out of dock. And that atevi shuttle had brought up not only Bren Cameron, human translator for Tabini-aiji, head of the atevi government, but also Tabini's grandmother the aiji-dowager, and the aiji's nine-year-old son, with staff and security, who brought the certain word that atevi intended to be in charge of contact with the kyo—and determined that they also would be in charge of the station, given the meltdown of the human-side stationmaster.

Once aboard, Bren, armed with a mandate from the Mospheiran President and the support of two of the four *Phoenix* captains, had walked into Central, ousted Tillington, and shifted control to the atevi control center.

Tillington having refused to negotiate at that point, Bren had locked Tillington in his own apartment under house arrest and set the atevi-side stationmaster, Lord Geigi, on watch and watch with his crew, all this pending the arrival of the shuttle bearing Tillington's replacement.

Also in custody, now, given a rapidly worsening situation in the locked sections, was the self-appointed leader of the Reunioners, one Louis Baynes Braddock, the former Reunion stationmaster, currently the primary troublemaker among the refugees. Braddock was Pilots' Guild, which in the distant past had run the ship. He claimed authority, he had ruled Reunion for over a decade, and, with Reunion lost, he had delusions of taking command here—a command that might never have gained followers, had it not been for Tillington's hate campaign against the Reunioners.

With the kyo approaching and the Reunioners in a state of panic, Braddock had made his move—and landed likewise under arrest.

It was not a good time for a civil war.

And with the four *Phoenix* captains themselves split two and two—two having backed Tillington and two vehemently opposed—it was time for the two powers of Earth to step in and

inform the authorities in space what *they* intended to do about
that rapidly approaching ship.

Two powers controlled the planet: the aishidi'tat and its
leader Tabini-aiji, who owned all but one of the shuttles that
kept the station going, and the President of the island of Mospheira, where humans had found refuge from the original quarrel that had split colonists from ship-folk—and where they had
lived and built for two hundred years, below a dead and mothballed station in orbit, never expecting *Phoenix* would return.

Never expecting *Phoenix* would have created another human
station in another species' claimed territory.

Certainly never expecting that a ship from that species
would be coming in on *Phoenix*'s trail with a purpose yet to be
determined.

Tabini-aiji had sent Bren Cameron up to deal with the im-
pending visitors by whatever means he found necessary. Necessity thus far had included the forceful removal of Tillington
from Central, and the arrest of Braddock and his followers.

The President of Mospheira was also moving fast. He had
quickly launched Mospheira's only shuttle and sent a replacement for Tillington, a unilateral appointment, with no reference to the Mospheiran legislature.

A good thing, in Bren's opinion. He *needed* help, someone to
take the reins of the human-side operation, Mospheiran *and*
Reunioner, because the *Phoenix* captains weren't in a position
to do it, the atevi authority *shouldn't* do it, and *he* had his hands
full with what was coming in on them from outside the solar
system.

The current time was first-shift, a fact completely irrelevant
to Bren's sleep-deprived body. The crisis of the moment had
determined his schedule ever since he'd come aboard. He was
currently operating on three hours of sleep. He'd had tea and
toast for a breakfast, issued a few housekeeping orders, cleared
small details left from yesterday, slipped into a good coat, and
set out, desperately relieved to know that the shuttle was here,

and to know that Tillington and his authority was officially and indisputably replaced, not by his hands alone.

More, he knew the replacement. Dr. Virginia Kroger. Gin. Robotics. Systems. And experienced in management. He'd worked with her. So had the captains. So had Geigi. And he was beyond ready to shed the problem of the station's unrest and take on what he was here to do, which was to deal with the incoming ship—to take up where negotiations with the kyo at Reunion had broken off, and lay the groundwork for real communication with the people of that incoming ship, far beyond the handful of words they'd established the last time they'd met. He needed to find out exactly why the kyo were here and what they wanted, beyond their enigmatic pronouncement back at Reunion that they *would* visit.

Most of all he had to bring the negotiation to a point that didn't lead to them joining the kyo's war, or seeing the kyo's enemies turn up here. And he had to do it without accidentally triggering a kyo attack on Alpha, the way the kyo had taken out Reunion Station.

The situation with the kyo was delicate and moment to moment already. There was no way to predict when the polite echo, station to kyo ship and back again, of the kyo's last transmission, *Prakuyo come*, would change. If it did, when it did, atevi Central would buzz him, asking him please translate and come up with a response that wouldn't send the entire encounter spiraling out of control.

He needed, badly, to leave all station politics in the hands of sane people, and withdraw to his apartment, get a full night's sleep, and wake with his mind fully focused on the kyo problem.

Please God that Gin could keep the station quiet.

And that he could come up with answers.

One had to be very, very quiet getting up this morning. Great-grandmother was resting in her private rooms in the apartment. Cajeiri, aged fortunate nine, dressed with the help of two of his bodyguards, while his guest Irene, who had slept apart, dressed with the help of his other two.

It had to be yesterday's clothes for Irene: that was all Irene had brought away when she had escaped the Reunioner sections. But staff would have cleaned her clothes during the night, everything taken in stride. From some source, last night, one of the servants had provided Irene a rather too large sleeping-robe. And his own bodyguards had provided her a proper place to sleep.

Irene's hair, which had been gold, now was not. She had cut it right at the roots, so now it was very short, black, curly, and just showed random gold tips all over, which made, Cajeiri thought, a really pretty effect.

Shortly after nand' Bren had arrived on the station, she had done that to her hair, put on atevi clothes, stolen a key, slipped out of her mother's apartment and gone straight to the ship-folk door guards, speaking only Ragi, which of course they could not in the least understand.

The guards who barred her way might have suspected she was not atevi, but atevi dress was not something humans could easily lay hands on, so it had been clear she was somebody. The guards had had to ask authority, and their going to authority meant that word had gotten to Jase-aiji, who was the third-highest of the ship-aijiin. Nand' Jase had immediately taken Irene in hand and brought her to nand' Bren. The very topmost ship-folk authority, Ogun-aiji, had declined to stop Jase-aiji doing that—because everybody knew that those three human children, who had gone down to Earth to visit the aiji's son, were under the protection of the aishidi'tat.

They had always agreed, Cajeiri and his young associates, that if there was ever any trouble or they felt they were in danger, they should all get to the station maintenance tunnels and go straight over to the atevi half of the station and ask for Lord Geigi. So when the news had spread that the kyo were coming and Tillington-aiji was locking down the Reunioner sections, Bjorn and Artur and Gene had done just that, but that move had only gotten them trapped in the tunnels as *they* locked, so they had been stuck where they were.

But Irene had never gone to the tunnels. The Reunioner stationmaster, Braddock, who was causing all the trouble, had taken up residence in the apartment next to Irene's, and Braddock's people had locked Irene in, trapping her, as he'd also hoped to trap Bjorn and Artur and Gene, so Braddock could hold them to negotiate with in the emergency, all because they were under that special protection.

So Irene, being both brave and clever, had made a second plan. She had kept her atevi clothing that she had worn home from her visit to the world, and once she was sure from what Braddock's people said that nand' Bren was on the station, she had waited until people were asleep, then taken scissors and cut her hair, put on the clothing she had kept, *and* taken her mother's master key, *and* walked right up to the ship-folk guards like a lord of the aishidi'tat.

Then she had told nand' Jase and nand' Bren exactly where Braddock was, and *that* had let nand' Bren and nand' Jase move to capture Braddock and take control of the Reunion sections by way of the tunnels, without anyone getting hurt.

It had been a brave move on Irene's part. If the ship-folk had returned her to her apartment, she would never have gotten away twice, and her mother would have been very angry. But Irene had not lost her nerve, and even if the guards had been sure she could not be atevi caught on the wrong side of those locked doors, she had kept using names like Lord Geigi over and over, and saying that she was under the protection of the aiji in Shejidan—which she was. So even if the guards were absolutely sure she was human, and even if they might not have understood what she was telling them about the aiji in Shejidan, everybody on the station knew Geigi's name, and the guards had certainly known those clothes were not station clothes. Everybody definitely knew three Reunioners had been to the world and back.

So the guards had *had* to ask somebody what to do about Irene.

Now Irene's mother and Braddock were both under arrest. They were locked up for security reasons, but they might get out again someday. And if they did, they probably would find out who had told nand' Jase where to find them. That might make life very unpleasant for Irene.

One could not, would not, let that happen. Not to Irene and not to any of his human associates. Cajeiri was resolved on that. They would never, ever be in a position where Braddock could threaten them again.

Gene and Artur and Bjorn and Gene's mother had all been found safe, rescued out of the tunnels. Then atevi security had gone in to get Bjorn's parents and Artur's out of the closed sections, because they might be in danger from Braddock's people. They were not safe to be put into Mospheiran residency—because Mospheirans and Reunioners were at odds. There was certainly no place for them among the ship-folk. So all of them were guests on the atevi side now, under Lord Geigi's personal protection. They had spent last night just down the hall, in Lord Geigi's guest quarters. Things were still very desperate in the Reunioner section, and the big section doors were still shut and guarded, but this morning Gene and Artur and Bjorn and their parents would all be waking up safe, to a good breakfast, right down the hall from Great-grandmother's apartment. And they owed Irene thanks for all of it.

But for the same reasons, Irene had no mother able to see to her now, because her mother had taken up with Braddock's people. It might be politics that would never change, though sometimes people took positions for safety's sake, and he was sure they would find that out, if that was the case—but he suspected it might go deeper and darker than that, because Irene did not want to see her mother, even if she got out of arrest, and expected her mother did not want to see her, either. Ever.

Cajeiri understood, or tried to, knowing that humans did not have man'chi as atevi had. But they certainly had feelings *like* that feeling, and if Irene said whatever loyalty she had to her mother was gone, he was sure something like man'chi was broken, and might never be able to be fixed.

So it had pained him to see Irene sit there last night in Lord Geigi's apartment, with everybody else happy and relieved to be safe, and everybody sitting in company with their parents. Gene's mother would have taken her in, and Artur's parents might—they had seemed concerned about her. So maybe she should have stayed with other humans. But she had set herself apart, and only tried to be happy.

So he had asked Irene to come with him last night, and she had done that.

There had been one small difficulty in the invitation. He had not asked Great-grandmother before making it. His bodyguard had certainly explained to staff, before they even showed up in Great-grandmother's foyer, but he had not told Great-grandmother personally, because Great-grandmother, mani, had been asleep when they arrived.

Mani was not in the habit of patience with untoward surprises. She was very strict, very proper, and she was not often kind. But he had done justice in bringing Irene home with him, because Irene was how all his guests had been able to escape, and how authorities had been able to catch Braddock.

Besides, mani had said this was his suite, this little set of rooms inside mani's apartment. There was a bedroom and two rooms for his bodyguard, so there was a bed, Veijico's, that Irene had had to herself, while Veijico and Antaro took Jegari's and Lucasi's beds, and Jegari and Lucasi had slept in his room. Staff had helped without any argument—and staff would tell other staff closer to mani that everything had been quite proper in their arrangement, so that mani would not find fault there. He was sure of that.

He would wear his third-best today. He had had mani's staff do all they could for Irene's clothes last night. They were country clothes, and not quite the thing she should have in mani's apartment, but necessity was ahead of fashion: that was what nand' Bren would say. Irene would look proper enough for a country estate, if not the court, and mani would understand that the informality, certainly, was nobody's fault.

Today all sorts of things were going to change. Gin-nandi was coming onto the station, and nand' Bren would have *her* there to take care of all the upset Tillington had caused, so nand' Bren could concentrate on what he had to do, what all of them had to do, soon, which was to talk to the kyo and make that meeting turn out all right, so the kyo could go away and the world could just go on with no problems.

There was a war elsewhere, involving the kyo. He had seen something like a war, which his father told him was something atevi had not tended to have nor ever wanted to have again. It took very large problems to unite as many clans on one side of something as on the other, which meant a quarrel beyond what even the Assassins' Guild could settle. There had been the War of the Landing, which atevi had fought against humans, and won, but that was a long time ago, and generally, until the whole South had fallen under a bad influence, one just did not see people turning up with mortars and such awful things. The South had brought them from the coastal defense, where they belonged, and so the aishidi'tat had brought others in, and people had begun to forget the rules, and fight for themselves, without the Guild. And terrible things had happened, that still gave him nightmares.

That disturbance was over now, due in no small part to nand' Bren, and now nand' Bren was here to make sure the Earth did not end up involved in somebody else's war.

What the kyo had done at Reunion—he had seen that, too. That was war the way the kyo fought, which was a lot worse than artillery and mortars. He had seen the result, which had not even looked real, it was so terrible. His guests' parents had lived through it. Bjorn had been alive when that had happened, but Bjorn said he only remembered the dark—he had been scared of the dark ever after, though he tried not to admit it. Irene had been a baby when it happened. Gene and Artur were born after. But very many people had died. Thousands. And the kyo had done it.

Because, nand' Bren said, of a misunderstanding. That was a very scary thought. It was hard *not* to have misunderstandings with people who did not speak the same language. The misunderstandings that had caused the War of the Landing were the examples everybody used. And that had killed very many people, before they had thrown the big weapons into the sea.

Well, they just had to make certain that no misunderstanding happened. That was why he and mani had come up here with nand' Bren, because back at Reunion, he and mani had been able to help nand' Bren to talk to nand' Prakuyo, which had helped make peace and get everyone safely off Reunion.

There was a very good chance it would be nand' Prakuyo on that ship out there. But whoever it was, they had very quickly arranged to come up here, and now that Tillington was out and Braddock was locked up, that ship out there was going to be mani's concern—the kyo, and the fact the kyo could blow up the space station if they said the wrong thing. So his having an unescorted girl for a guest in his rooms last night was a very minor problem, and mani would probably not distract herself to consider it, on a morning when they were *about* to get a new human stationmaster, and finally get to concentrate on the reason they had come up here in the first place.

He did not want to lay a problem on mani's plate first thing in the morning. That was never a good way to start an explanation.

Maybe he should order breakfast for just him and Irene and his aishid, and not explain anything. Yesterday had been stressful, even if it had had a happy ending, and mani might want to rest.

That also meant he had to keep all the human guests very

quiet and not pose even the slightest problem for mani or nand' Bren while they dealt with the kyo. That was *his* job as much as it was Lord Geigi's, and he was trying to do just that: keeping the presence of his guests quiet, so they could both rescue his guests from the Reunioner situation, and not have trouble with the Mospheirans, and keep the kyo peaceful and happy all at once.

It would all work out. It had to.

2

The lift doors opened, exhaling cold fog around the arrivals—a short, bundled figure, Gin Kroger, foremost of the five. Gin was first out of her cold suit. She dropped it in the designated place by the lift, and left her escort, walking forward to offer a hand.

"Gin," Bren said. "Good to see you." The bow was almost instinctive by now, but he reached out to shake an ice-cold hand. It might have been a hug, except for witnesses and dignity. Their association had been that of fellow travelers, colleagues, allies on two years of voyage and two hellish crises in the middle. "Hot drink and a sit-down?"

"God, yes." Back in gravity, chilled to the bone, and probably as sleep-deprived as he was, she would want that. There was a small room adjacent, part office, part acclimatization lounge, here at the interface of human-side and atevi-side, in an area mostly used by freight personnel and visiting shuttle crews.

Gin was exempt from customs, being what she was . . . although her last transmission had mentioned not knowing where to send her baggage. Tillington still occupied the official stationmaster apartment.

But Gin would manage. Gin knew the station inside and out. And she had the authority to move walls. Literally.

She was no bit changed since she and Bren had last parted company: an average-looking woman, gray hair clipped short, wisping out of order, thanks to the static of the hooded cold suit. Makeup wasn't Gin's style, either. Her usual kit was a stretch tee and pants that might be plaid or floral, but today—today, on assumption of office—it was a brown suit and a travel-rumpled blue blouse.

The lounge afforded an instant tea dispenser, a box of tissues—noses tended to run, in the change of atmosphere—a round table, and moderately soft chairs for gravity-stressed bodies. Chained to the side counter, next to the tea service and water tap, lay a thick, well-worn manual of freight requirements, shipper and customs contact numbers, with a list of major station rules and regulations on the cover.

Gin merited a pass on those. She'd written no few of them.

They owned this little room for the moment: Bren's bodyguard had the door, proof against any chance intrusion. Gin's staff was handling the logistics of her move. Gin had asked for a conference with him on arrival, a fast one, nothing conspicuous, and this room was the most convenient.

Bren started to draw the tea himself, but Tano, of his bodyguard, silently took over, and delivered two utilitarian cups to the table.

"Good trip, considering?" Bren asked.

"Smooth, compared to the goings-on here," Gin said. "Are we secure to talk?"

"Secure," Bren said, "as long as Geigi's holding Central. And he is."

"I've read the Central log up to the point you transmitted it." Gin took a careful sip of tea, cradling the warm cup. "Tillington's created us a real mess, hasn't he?"

"With no small help from Braddock. It's going to take time and trustworthy change to straighten out."

"It's my impression," Gin said, "that Tillington's senior techs in Central may be reliable. I'm not so sure about his administrative staff. My own staff will be shadowing the lot of them, and not just to come up to speed on procedures. Two of my team are intelligence. If we find sabotage, we'll deal with it.

Expeditiously. We can manage more shuttle seats on the next downbound if we have to."

"Good." Bren nodded. "I'm fairly sure of Mr. Okana's character. I don't have as much experience of the other man, Brown. On the other hand, there was a general sense of relief in the room when Tillington was arrested and your appointment announced. Control of Central has been an ongoing issue in one form and another ever since the news about the kyo went public and the panic broke out in the Reunioner sections. Tillington exhausted his crew, mentally as well as physically, but they've had a full cycle and more to recover. They should be ready to take over, now they've got a sane individual in charge. Still, Geigi will keep Central in his hands until you officially request the handoff. His staff has been working double shifts since he took control. Necessary, considering the Tillington problem, and they'll hold on, no worries. But they'll be very glad to hand off."

"I appreciate that. Sincerely. I'm going to unpack, get my staff situated. First off, I'm going to talk to Ogun. He and I aren't strangers, and he called me, en route. He wants order restored. We're in complete agreement on that. He *has* asked that I keep the section doors shut."

"Under present circumstances," Bren said, "it's a good idea. But understand—the conditions in the Reunioner sections are not comfortable. Some of the apartments, as I understand, are more like cubicles, with temp paneling, not even real walls, no water tap, no secure storage, just a fold-up cot to sit and sleep on. And two or three roommates not necessarily of your choice. Bath is shared by sixteen apartments and food service is four or five kitchen counters to serve an entire section. The situation can't go on. Maybe we can't improve the living conditions right off, but we can give these people news, some hope that 'better' is coming. We can improve the food, hell, that at least. And *com* service needs to be restored, once we're sure Braddock sympathizers aren't using it to coordinate disruption. If we *don't* restore it, we're going to have *more* Braddock sympathizers. The Reunioners are afraid, and not just scared that the kyo might blow up the station without any reason. The kyo's arrival was the trigger, but not the core of the problem. Ten years of surviving on rationing after the kyo blew hell out of Reunion, then we come along with brochures advertising the good life. Freedom. Abundance . . . and they arrive to a second-class citizen reception from Tillington here at Alpha. They've *no* reason to trust us. Not now. Tillington's done a *lot* of damage. The Reunioners aren't sure they won't be handed over to the kyo on demand. That's crazy. I don't think that's remotely what the kyo want. But rumors don't have to be rational."

"Agreed," Gin said, and drank a gulp of tea. "Tillington's definitely on the list to ship out, and that's going to be on the next shuttle, if there's room. I expect there will be others going with him. My staff will be reviewing, auditing, and interviewing, but I'll compose the final list. *We'll* rout out and eliminate the problems in the human sector. *You* concentrate on the kyo, Bren. You just deal with that problem and trust me to manage this."

"I have every confidence in you. Needless to say, you'll have my backing, as well as the aiji-dowager's and Geigi's. Anything you need that we can supply, you've got."

She dipped her chin, sipped the tea. "I understand you have custody of the three kids plus one. And their parents."

"Their parents minus one," Bren said. "The girl's mother is in custody, along with Braddock and his aides. Captains' Council wants to keep it that way until there's time to consider the cases."

"*Are* they under charges?" Gin asked.

"From both sides. They're in atevi custody at the moment for endangering the kids who were under the aiji's personal protection. Irene's escape, her testimony regarding Braddock's attempts to control the kids, gave Ilisidi the absolute freedom to go in and rescue them in her grandson's name, and to arrest Braddock and his aides without involving the Mospheirans."

Gin gave a quick nod, complete understanding of the tangled

politics involved . . . and the reason it wouldn't be good, at the moment, to have Braddock sitting in Mospheiran *or* ship-folk custody.

"On the human side, Braddock's open to charges of threatening station integrity," Bren continued, "insurrection and attempted kidnapping, under Mospheiran law, which is enough for a start on keeping him and his staff confined, but I assure you the atevi charges are quite as severe. Irene's mother is being held primarily as a material witness at the moment. Ship security thinks she may have heard things of interest in Braddock's prosecution if the ship-folk get their hands on him, which is a whole other nest of troubles. Right now the dowager isn't interested in prosecuting her, but she's not handing her daughter back into her custody, either. For my part, I don't know what duress may have been involved with the woman, or whether she may come under charges herself from one party or another, but one thing I can't forget. When she was arrested with the others, with her child missing for hours, and as atevi enforcement and ship-folk were hauling her and Braddock away—there was no point at which she protested her daughter was missing or asked where her daughter was. *That* bothers me. To this hour, it bothers me. I'd wanted to give the woman a chance for Irene's sake, but at this point, I don't know."

"It bothers *me*," Gin said. "How are the kids now? How are the parents taking their new situation?"

"Everybody's been housed on the atevi side—they're all guests in Geigi's apartment, and they're glad, I think, to be safe, out of the Reunioner sections, and well-fed, though naturally they have concerns. Their kids' attachment to the young gentleman makes them all a special case among the Reunioners *and* on the Mospheiran side, and it's possible Braddock's not the only one wanting to take hostages, especially now that Braddock's set the possibility in everyone's mind."

"What a mess. Those kids have made a breakthrough in atevi and human relations, and that idiot turns it sour."

"True. On the other hand, the mess got that idiot into custody, *and* makes an important point. Right now and forever, the kids are under the aiji's protection, and under atevi law, that includes their relatives and associates, so far as the kids choose to maintain the association from their end. Which is convenient. I don't *want* the parents to go back to the Reunioner sections. It's not safe, political pressure is inevitable, and frankly, and above all else, *I* can't afford the worry right now. I need my head free to deal with the kyo. Where they are right now, they become Geigi and Ilisidi's problem. I haven't asked them their preferences, because if they run counter, I'm not going to listen."

"Works for me. What about their stuff? I understand looting and theft are still a problem in the Reunioner sections."

There *had* been that problem on the voyage, dealt with as best they could. House survivors in a damaged station for years, and need began to trump ownership in more than a few instances. Whether it was a problem that would persist once they assumed something like normal lives was something for future authority to sort out.

"Geigi's hard-locked their apartments, and Ilisidi will consider the aishidi'tat's credibility involved, should anything happen to them or their belongings."

"Excellent. —Regarding the Reunioners in general, the President is taking the position that the new meds mean the Reunioners can successfully acclimate to the planet, and that means they can integrate into Mospheira. He says you back the idea, therefore the aishidi'tat will back it."

"I do back it. I think Tabini will. Likewise, I think, the captains; it gets the problem off their deck. With the situation we have now, it's the *only* solution that's going to work. Trying to expand the station to accommodate them is not going to erase the differences between Reunioners and Mospheirans. Living on a planet—is its own logic."

"Logistically—"

"A slow, slow process. I know."

"Maybe not as slow as you think. We could use the petal sails. Not for passengers. But for cargo."

Petal sails—like those that had brought the first Mospheirans down to Earth. *Jase* had made his first, terrifying trip down by parachute. Likely Jase still had nightmares. But the technology was so old, so primitive. Chutes had failed—lost people, lost supplies, landed in the sea and sunk. The hazard was legendary, a scar on the Mospheiran psyche.

But using landers to bring down *cargo*, and reserving the shuttles for people . . .

"We *know* weather now," he said. "The old landers were tin cans dropping blind, but as I understand it, Geigi targeted his chutes, dropping his relay stations."

"He crashed one," Gin said, "what I hear, pretty spectacularly. The others landed soft enough."

"Might not have lost that one, if he'd been able to work directly with the Mospheiran side of the station."

Gin shrugged, a side-tip of her head, and took another sip. "I think we can do it."

Geigi had had no paidhi to translate between him and humans, during their absence on the Reunion mission. When the coup that unseated Tabini and grounded the shuttles severed him from his own government, Geigi had immediately secured communication with Mospheira's university linguistics department, which was, itself, tightly connected to the Mospheiran State Department, which talked directly to the Mospheiran President.

For two years, Geigi had told the University scholars what he wanted—from Tillington, ironically enough, on the other side of the station wall, then had to wait for an answer relayed down to the ground and up again. Geigi had traded materials he had stockpiled for the atevi starship to get cooperation from the station, and had set up, via satellites aloft and his petal-sail landers on Earth, a communications network that had kept data coming in from the mainland and from space.

Geigi's landers weren't the desperate, cobbled-together efforts of the early settlers. Geigi had had the benefit of advanced robotics design. His landers had had the ability to move and defend themselves on the ground, and to collect data in their immediate areas. They'd also scared hell out of the districts where they'd set up shop.

Use *that* tech for dropping Reunioner baggage? Cut the time-frame in half with no special construction? *Hell*, yes.

"Certainly sounds possible," he said. Shipping and cargo were not, these days, his problem. He didn't think about such things routinely. But, God—

"Absolutely possible. We can carry passenger modules on every flight, and carry fragile cargo down in baggage, our object being to take *people* down, just people, no heirloom china, no wardrobe."

Relief hit, hard and welcome. Sometimes you had to shut down politics and talk to the engineers. *Every* flight reducing the political pressure up here. And Mospheira was about to bring another shuttle online, and start construction on a third. They *might* get to the long-promised flight a week. Currently, it was short of that. Considerably short, with mechanicals, and docking delays, and delays for inspection and maintenance.

But did they truly dare restrict the flow of cargo? Two years of Murini's shutdown of the space program had left them continually running to catch up. Everything, every plan had been thrown off course. Of course, bleeding away the jobless population of the station, the need for cargo going up would ease proportionally.

How long *would* it take? The largest passenger module could handle fifty-one people in relative comfort. More, if packed tightly. Infants . . . God, babies. His felt the tension returning. Pregnant women. Infants. Women who had bred with abandon on the return flight, free at last, or so they believed, of the restrictions of the past ten years, and destined for peace and plenty. They'd extracted 4,043 individuals from Reunion. Released 4,149 to Alpha. How many were there now?

He shut that thought down, concentrating on the purity of numbers. Figuring forty-three hundred total by the time the last flight . . . round figure: eighty-five flights.

Eighty-five.

"We'll need *all* the shuttles . . ." Gin's voice provided welcome relief from a sudden wave of panic.

"The aiji has already agreed to allow the Reunioners to land on atevi shuttles."

"But not to settle in atevi territory."

"That, no."

"Settlement is going to be a hot issue on Mospheira," Gin said. "The damned Heritage Party is going to squawk. Loudly. Lot of history there."

"Just what *is* the political temperature down there? I haven't been able to ask the President his situation. *Can* he push this through?"

"Mixed. He's already claiming, in principle, that the Reunioners come under Mospheiran law, which makes them a Mospheiran responsibility and subject to Mospheiran decisions. There'll be those who don't like it, on both sides of the shuttle run, but no one down there, *no one*, is remotely interested in the Pilots' Guild gaining an independent foothold anywhere in the system."

"No argument there . . . from anyone other than Braddock."

"The President plans to start the relocation process by decree, an emergency declaration. He'll make it soon, let it play second to the headlines of the kyo visit, which is going to dominate the news every step of the way. I suggested, in my last communication with him, that we land Cajeiri's three young *associates* first, along with their parents and relations, and not just to satisfy Tabini-aiji. This business with Tillington and Braddock is *going* to go public, no way not. Those kids are innocents, pawns in the affairs of three governments. They're bright, they're charming, and they'll play well to the cameras. Getting them down first puts *their* faces instead of Braddock's on the Reunioner presence. It'll remind Mospheirans they're dealing with people needing a home, not Pilots' Guild plotting a government takeover." A slight smile. Another sip. "Even better for Mospheiran consumption would be an image of Braddock being carted off in cuffs. Tastefully, of course."

The engineer wasn't damned bad at politics. She never had been.

"So," she said, "the first Reunioner landings will be a minor issue. Kyo will be the big news, and *you* get to explain that."

"Happily. By comparison. I hope."

"I'm asking the question—just for my personal consumption, mind: I promise I'll never quote you— *Are* you that confident we're going to come out of this encounter all right?"

"Hell, no," Bren said, on a humorless laugh.

"How are you reading this approach?"

"I can't. It's exactly what the kyo did at Reunion—but slower, at greater distance, with more communication. I'll tell you frankly what worries me more than any question of whether or not the kyo want real estate. We both know the kyo are at war, which is a fact we've deliberately kept need-to-know. The last thing we want to do is get entangled in the kyo's military problems. We don't know for certain where their enemies lie—or who's winning, or even why they're at war. It's possible they're looking for an outpost or even a refuge, and we *don't* want either in this solar system."

"Understood. Agreed. But your estimate is that they're here to talk? That that's Prakuyo out there? Are you optimistic?"

They'd used to share a brandy on occasion, aboard the ship, when Gin had had her quarters down the corridor from the dowager's door, and his; and in dealing with Gin on that voyage, he'd been able maintain a sense of what was human. At least, Mospheiran human. They had been able to share jokes, share frustrations and worries, of which there had been no shortage, in two years of voyaging, half of it in eerie isolation, in the depths of the ship; and half of it in a ship overflowing with unscreened passengers.

Gin had been there, waiting for word, when they'd dealt with the kyo the first time. She'd shared those hours with the rest of the ship, the fear of the kyo changing their minds and attacking, the fear they'd have to choose who to save and who to leave to die. If they hadn't raided station stores and gotten those supplies aboard, there'd have been no way to save the majority of the people. They could have saved a few hundred . . . at most.

Dark hours, those.

Gin wasn't asking for reassurance, or promises now. She was asking, *Bren, what's your best guess?* and he answered with a frankness he wouldn't give to many.

"My optimism," he said, "centers on the fact they chose to talk at Reunion, that they *initiated* communication from the moment we came into range. They *chose* to talk. Why they chose to attack the station that first time remains a mystery, one I'd *very* much like to solve before meeting with them, but when Ramirez left a damaged but still inhabited station behind, completely at their mercy, the kyo chose to leave it alone. I believe they chose to sit and watch, waiting to see whether the ship would return, and with what reinforcements. I'm encouraged that, after four years of silence, they chose to send over a shuttle rather than blow the place to hell. I'm not totally clear on what they were doing or what prompted it: an attempt at communication, maybe; or a team trying to investigate. And when the station blew up that shuttle, after another *retaliatory* strike—if in fact it was their action—they still chose to leave the station operational, and sit back and wait for six more years, until we showed up. Then they *still* chose one more try at communication before attacking. It doesn't explain the waiting. It doesn't explain a lot of things. My experience says not to imagine I know the answer. My experience says we're not dealing with our language, our concepts, our culture, our laws, *or* our instincts. But the little history we have with them shows an inclination to talk. That's what they *seem* to be doing in their approach. I take that as encouraging. I hope for it—since there's damn-all we can do if they start shooting. —And that's about the total of the wisdom I have."

Gin just looked at him for a moment, then: "You can do this," she said quietly. "I have every confidence, Bren. Just trust me for the human situation and don't worry about it."

"I do."

"You're frowning."

"God, Gin . . ."

"Trust me."

"Just—I'm sorry for what I'm handing over to you. I had no desire to lay hands on the Reunioner question at all when I came up here. Now I have a tall stack of china, as my atevi associates would say, on a very weak table. And I'm afraid I set it all up for you to sort out, for good or ill, with no great amount of forethought."

"I at least recognize the serving pieces," Gin said. "And you acted when and as you had to act, with nobody getting hurt. Your getting Tillington out of Central and getting Braddock contained solved a huge problem. I'm truly grateful for that little assist. I also have the Central log, and while I'm sure Tillington's spun the record seven ways from Sunday, he *couldn't* doctor what happened when he shut the section doors on fifteen minutes' notice. We had injuries, we had people seriously affected in one way and another, while people with serious and valid fears regarding that incoming ship were locked in place like fish in a net, waiting for slaughter. It's no wonder there were riots. And thanks to his extremely vocal campaign to settle the Reunioners at Maudit, we have a situation with the Captains' Council *and* the terms of the atevi treaty that we're not even going to mention until a proper moment. Overall, it's not going to look good for Mr. Tillington's management skills. Whether or not he's actually done anything illegal is another matter. But the President will have more than enough cause to put him under wraps and keep him there for a long time to come."

"I hope so."

"I have another question for you."

"Ask."

"I'm wondering whether to tell the Reunioners about the prospect of landing at this point. I'm hoping you have a better sense of their temperature right now than I do."

"Best not to disturb them too much, in my opinion, though you'll soon be in a better position to judge. They've had so much bad they won't believe good. In their view, they've been lied to by just about everyone. Trust, in anyone, in any promises, is nonexistent."

"And the section doors? Senior Captain Ogun insists we keep them shut."

"Much as I regret what Tillington did, both to feed the resentment and to trigger the explosion, I tend to agree. The Reunioners have been pushed to the limit. Support for Braddock is grounded in their lack of options, not respect. We need to get information flowing—their com's been shut down even for news—and rumors are our greatest enemy. Let them know what's actually happening. Open up the private channels, at least a certain number of hours a day. Let them contact their friends and relatives. Assure them those four kids and their families are all right—the kids are available if you need to talk to them. Which leads to another issue of distrust, this one of our own doing. We interrupted all the door locks inside those sections to get in there to get the kids . . . we called it a malfunction. It kept masses of people out of the corridors. Kept people from getting hurt. Injuries were minor. And the system is fixed now. All the locks are back to normal. But the amount of unease it left in people's minds, even with the malfunction story—I worry about that. A part of me thinks we need to explain it in full. The other part wonders how people will react, knowing they can so easily become prisoners in their own homes."

"My problem, Bren. Good to know, but let me deal with it.

—What's the kyo time frame? How much time before they get here?"

"Unchanged in their approach," Bren said. "Their messaging began with pings. Then, right after we came aboard, they shifted to voice and began requesting the dowager and the young gentleman and myself. We advised them we're here and kept that message cycling. Yesterday a voice that sounded like Prakuyo indicated they want to talk. I told them come in, and that invitation and their response, *Prakuyo come*, have been cycling back and forth ever since. That's the limit of the exchange. We're expecting them to arrive in three days, last calculation at their current rate of approach. But that's subject to change and the kyo's intention. And we don't know whether they'll dock or expect to link with *Phoenix*, which is currently standing off from the station under Captain Riggins' command. He's a new man. I don't know him, but Ogun appointed him and I assume he'll take Ogun's orders."

"The shuttle picked up the kyo transmission and played it for me. Scary feeling, being out there in that speck of a shuttle, knowing that ship was bearing down on us. Gives you a whole new sense of perspective in the universe. And makes you sympathize with the Reunioners. You say *sounded* like Prakuyo. Straight answer again, Bren. Are we sure it's the same kyo?"

"Straight answer, I'm *not* wholly sure. We don't know even if Prakuyo is a name, or a title. Whoever's in charge, they know our names, they know enough to communicate as if they *are* the ship we dealt with. Prakuyo an Tep, or someone claiming to be him, requested a meeting. I invited him to come aboard. And the Prakuyo voice accepted it."

She cast him a wry glance. "Let's hope it *is* him, then."

He winced. "Gut instinct said it was, and gut instinct extended the invitation."

"So far, your gut's been pretty smart. I trust it. Final question: what's your sense of what they'll be looking for? What's their interest in being here—if it's not warlike?"

"If they aren't here to establish a base, I can only speculate. They'll wonder what sort of resources we have, whether we have a large presence in space—which we don't—whether we're armed—which we aren't—and whether we pose a threat to them, which we also don't. We hope we live too far apart to be a threat or even a relevant fact to each other, even in trade—but what they call too far may differ from our concept. All I can say is, so far, so good. I *am* encouraged. Let me stress that. But I have to be careful of the other possibilities, and I can't say they won't exist."

"Fair enough."

"There's something else, something I'm going to try and clarify before this meeting, and not just because it's important to understanding the kyo. It's also one of the keys to the unrest between the Mospheirans and Reunioners. Tillington has led the Mospheirans to blame the Reunioners for attracting the kyo's attention and getting blown up."

"Blowing up the kyo envoy's ship will do that."

"True, but that was four years *after* the first attack. Among the ship's crew, which you know as well as I do, there's a suspicion that Braddock himself did something to touch off the kyo the first time. They believe he must have *done* something to bring an attack down on Reunion. To this day there's no substantiation for that. Braddock being Pilots' Guild doesn't make him popular with the ship, but we still don't know, as an issue of pure fact, what the trigger was."

"Ramirez was sticking his nose where it didn't belong. He got caught snooping, and tried to run away. He tried to run a diversionary route, but the kyo didn't bite. Instead, they traced *Phoenix*'s backtrail and took a shot at what they found. When the station failed to respond in kind, they backed off to watch what might happen next."

"That's certainly what we've pieced together from the few records Ramirez left accessible, but the question remains: did the kyo know about Reunion *before* Ramirez triggered that response? Had they been watching, possibly for decades, until he intruded just a bit too close for comfort? *Did* they follow the ship's backtrail? Or did they already know where Reunion was and just decide to go in? Did they truly attack without warning, or did they signal first? It'd be useful to *have* that information out of Braddock, but there's no way we can trust anything he'd tell us. We know now that those flashing lights are their way of initiating contact. We know from his log that they flashed lights at Ramirez, and he ignored them and ran. We know that four years later, at Reunion, they flashed first and Braddock blew up their envoy's ship."

"Now they're signaling us. Here."

"I have a notion it's a similar situation. There's been a lot of heat on Sabin for leading the kyo here, but *Ramirez'* backtrail was there—ten, twelve years ago."

"You're suggesting they followed Ramirez here?" Gin said. "That they've watched *us* for years as well? Watched the space program develop? The station come alive?"

"I'm saying it's possible."

A moment to take that in, then: "Optics," Gin said. "E-M signatures. Once you know *where* to search, there are ways to search, without being spotted yourself."

"*Phoenix* spotted the kyo this time *before* they started to signal. They've got the instruments, but how'd they know where to look?"

"I suspect the ship-folk have been watching their own back-trail since we left Reunion. My suspicion is that they spotted the ship on entry."

A moment of silent consideration, then Bren ventured: "Or maybe when it started to move."

"That *is* a possibility," Gin said somberly. "Distances. Distances we're not used to figuring. We don't know where the kyo star is. Even if we did know where to look, it could be so far away we could be seeing it as it was fifty, a hundred or more years ago. For them to be checking up on us since we got back from Reunion—they'd have to get within the solar system, for anything current. What we're watching could be a ship that's *been* out there for a year. Maybe a lot longer. But they're talking to us, the way we exchanged messages at Reunion . . . which means a ship from Reunion has to have come here sometime in the last year to pass that information on. It *might* be Prakuyo. It might not be."

He wasn't used to figuring time the way spacers did. He'd had conversations with Jase about looking back into time and racing forward into it, how optics and communication were limited by the speed of light, but ships weren't—how everybody stared into the past when they looked at the sky, looking at stars dead of old age long before *Phoenix* had ever flown. Jase's reality could turn his mind inside out. But he couldn't waste time now speculating into such things. He hadn't time. There *were* certainties within his reach. There had been, somewhere out there, in a time definitely relevant to them, one venture of the ship that hadn't gone well, another that had gone somewhat better when they'd met a kyo ship at Reunion, and a kyo ship now was coming toward them. So it was above all likely that, despite the vastness of the universe and the trickiness of space and time, they had a cause and effect on their hands. Two motes in all that space had bumped into one another, and become involved, and had to figure each other out.

"Whoever they are," he said, "however long they've been out there, whether they've known about us for a hundred years— they turned up at Reunion, and evidently they *are* going to engage with us in a very few days. Maybe they tracked Ramirez a dozen years ago, maybe they followed us home, maybe we're a question they now find it important to answer. And we're not an easy answer. We're two species, one of which isn't native to the planet. Ramirez was nosing about where they didn't want him, but even *we* don't know what he was up to, and he took that secret to the grave—so to speak. If they have to come close just to look at us, they *don't* know the fine details of who we are. And if looking at the stars is looking at the past, they can't know the detail of what's going on beyond *us*. Can they?"

"They can't," Gin said. "That would be true. Unless they've been there, they don't know."

So, unless they'd gone and looked, for all the kyo knew, Earth and Reunion might only be the tip of the iceberg. For all they knew, there was a vast human and atevi empire out there.

It echoed conversations he'd had with Gin and Jase on the voyage home, idle conversations at the time. So many conversations. So many strange things. So few solid answers.

He'd not liked to think too much into the strangeness, while it was going on around him. Now . . . it was a distraction.

"Why they do anything at all is still a wide-open question. But I'll be trying to get a face-to-face meeting even if it's not Prakuyo. I know that's a risk, but so is carrying on a conversation in echoes. Every clue to their mental process matters. I'm lost in the technical business. But talking—if it's Prakuyo, I have a notion where to start. If I have to start with somebody new—I still know where to start."

"You've got my backing," Gin said. "Anything you need."

Bren sat back in the chair, increasingly relaxed in her presence and feeling a lessening of the shakes that came from a cold lift car and far too little sleep. For days. "I asked for Kate to come, but am I glad it's you? Yes. There's nobody better. You were *there*, you know what the Reunioners have been through, what they've come from—and you know something about the kyo."

"Not nearly as much as you know."

"Better than anybody else Mospheira could send. You may not have dealt with Prakuyo, but you were there for the decisions."

"Maybe. But out of touch with everything for way too long." Sip of tea, nearly the last. "It's been frustrating. The lot of us got home—sent down soonest they could organize a shuttle flight. Decommissioned with honors. Extended leave. Our pick. A reward, they called it. Company headhunters lost no time. Great pay. No damn power to intervene up here. I've been worried about the Reunioner problem, but once I left the station, I've had no information and less input. Tillington's reports were all 'everything's fine.' Kate took the initiative nine months ago and tried to communicate with Ogun. She got a long formal answer that said absolutely nothing. Then Kate and I wrote to the President and laid out our concerns, our *opinion* of what needed to be done." Gin took down the last of the tea, then a deep breath. "Maybe we were a little impolitic. We got a 'We're doing the best we can.' And: 'We share your concerns.' Form letters, damn it all, from some harried secretary to a Presidential aide. Last I knew, Kate was still fighting the good fight. You—you had your problems on the other side of the straits. I just settled into my high-paying industry job and tried to do some good there, waiting for a chance to get transferred back up here. All I got was— 'Transport is limited, no options, wait for the Mospheiran program to fly.' I did propose landing the Reunioners, in our letter to the President, and I proposed it to anyone else I thought might have some influence in the situation. I proposed the option I gave you, regarding the parachutes. The answer was, 'There's no decision yet.' Every bit of funding was poured into the Mospheiran shuttle program, and the companies involved weren't turning loose of their finance and *their* prospect of commercial shuttle traffic, hell, no, no interest at all in any cargo landing on anything *but* the shuttle. —I'll tell you, Bren, you put this in my hands, give me a good cooperation with Lord Geigi, and cooperation from the captains—"

"From Jase and Sabin, guaranteed. Ogun—promise to get the Reunioners off the station and out of his concern and you may be able to sign him on."

"I'm going from here to Ogun. Directly. I've dealt with him before. I can promise him a solution. I can also inform the President that five thousand Reunioners delivered in small groups make fewer ripples than five thousand up here, destabilizing the treaty with Tabini-aiji. I hate to say trust me. But trust me."

"You've got it," Bren said.

"You just keep the kyo happy."

"Two, three days," Bren said, "until we're fully engaged with the kyo. After that—we go as long as it takes. And I can't predict how long that will be."

"Whatever you need," Gin said.

"Just give me peace—on the human side of the station. Solid support from human Central. Geigi has a standing agreement to notify me immediately, at any hour, of any change whatsoever in that ship, or the message."

"You've got the same from me. At any hour. If they wobble in the least, I'll be *in* Central and talking to you."

"Appreciated. Understand, granted the kyo will dock, atevi will be the sole agency dealing with them. If we meet face-to-face on this deck, we do it in an area atevi will manage. Best interface, original interface—there seem to be useful points of similarity between kyo and atevi, concepts in common . . ."

Gin waved a hand. "I swear to you I'll be content if I can just find concepts in common on the human side of this station. I leave the kyo and the linguistic technicalities to you. But working with Lord Geigi . . . I do look forward to that."

Geigi and Gin. Two of a kind. Straight-forward, get-the-job-done. Tinkerers.

"If you'd been here when Geigi was setting up his landers, God only knew what they'd have done. They'd probably have *walked* to Shejidan."

"He did that design himself. Didn't he?"

"Help from the workers and techs, the Archive and the University, but, yes. He did."

Gin's eyes fairly sparkled. That was Gin. Pure and not-so-simple.

3

Cajeiri had ordered breakfast for just himself, just Irene, just his aishid . . . which he had not intended to involve the dining room—or any great commotion.

But staff came back to say that Great-grandmother was also awake, that she was aware he had a visitor, and that they both should come to *her* breakfast.

That was a scary prospect. And Irene had heard all during her visit to the world how particular mani was, and how one had to walk quietly and stand straight and never fidget. Now she looked worried, and put hands on her coat and her shirt.

"I am not proper."

"You are perfectly proper, nadi." He was a *little* worried, but if mani was angry, she was angry at him, not at Irene. "It is a perfectly good country coat, and mani mostly prefers the country anyway. Come."

His aishid would *not* join them at table if mani was inviting him. They would take breakfast by turns, in the kitchen, which was the ordinary way bodyguards managed their comforts, and they would not go wanting.

He went first to the door, Irene following, and he waited for her in the wide hall, so they could walk together, his aishid about them. Mani's dining room was the middle of the apartment, and of course next to the kitchens. Back in the Bujavid mani regularly had breakfast on the balcony, with the wind and all; but here it was a moderately large room, a table reduced by half the size it could be, and to his chagrin, mani had arrived before them, and waited.

He bowed. Irene bowed. They sat down, as mani's servants stood ready to seat them, on opposite sides of the table, with mani at the head.

"Good morning," mani said. "And a *surprise* this morning. *Good* morning, young woman."

"Nand' dowager," Irene said very faintly, and with a bow of the head.

"Well, well, eat what you fancy, young woman. The green bowl contains the one dish you should avoid. The rest are safe. The paidhi-aiji has breakfasted with us and has survived. We shall not ask if you slept well—it would be a wonder—but we trust you have been comfortable."

"One is comfortable, yes, thank you, nand' dowager."

"Eat."

Irene reached for toast. So did Cajeiri, quickly, to have something other to do than stare at Great-grandmother, who spooned preserve onto fish, and for a little space there was gratefully nothing to do but eat.

"Nand' Bren is up and about," mani said, in the way of gossip, "and has met with Gin-nandi, who is in the process of displacing Tillington permanently, to our great satisfaction. We have had no change in the kyo message. Lord Geigi is still holding Central, valiant man, and once he turns its operations over to the humans, he will doubtless wish to retire to his apartment and rest undisturbed."

"One wishes," Cajeiri said, "to pay courtesies to Lord Geigi's guests, very quietly, before he arrives. As a courtesy, mani-ma."

Mani did not look at him, but she did not frown. "You may do so. There are delicate matters which need addressing. They are your guests. You may see to them, but do remember there will soon be other demands on your attention."

His guests. He had not been prepared to hear that. He was not unhappy to hear them described that way.

And mani said, not, "See to them!" but "You *may* see to them." That was, he was sure, only because there was company at the table and she was talking to him as a grown-up.

He was also grateful for that. "One understands, mani-ma."

Talk moved on to trivial matters, proper at table, the menu, the doings of staff, the observation of how the apartment had changed since mani was last in residence.

But after breakfast, in their departing, mani said,

"Are you, Great-grandson, capable of making sensible and secure arrangements for your other guests? And can do you do so adequately *today*, since we cannot rely upon the future?"

"I shall try, mani-ma." He was surprised, a little dismayed, utterly caught without ideas. "How shall I do this?"

"Ask staff. One understands your young guests have wardrobe in storage. You may retrieve that. The parents may have concerns about property left behind. Reassure them on this point, but make no promises regarding any return to their residences. You may, however, order clothing and some food and items of their preference, which will have to come from the Mospheiran side. Lord Geigi's staff will likely know how to arrange that, and you may assume that they will remain Lord Geigi's guests for some time. Do not, however, leave this restricted hallway under any circumstance, nor send your staff or bodyguard outside this hallway. Rely on senior staff for any errands which must be run, and if they cannot, refer to Cenedi. Otherwise do as you must, stay as long as you wish, but do *not* disturb nand' Bren and Lord Geigi, who may wish to rest when they return."

"Yes, mani-ma. I understand."

"If you need assistance in any matter, ask Cenedi. Do what you can within the resources of this section, and refer all simple requests to staff, all security questions to Cenedi. Do you agree?"

"Yes, mani! I shall do that."

A motion of mani's hand dismissed him. He bowed. He went to Irene, who stood aside with his aishid.

"We have permission to get your clothes from storage," he said, "and everybody else's, and that will be easier than sending to the human side. We shall have to ask Lord Geigi's staff to bring them. We shall make up lists of what everybody needs besides. You will sleep here again tonight, since mani has not said otherwise, and mani says everybody else will stay with Lord Geigi."

"I stay here?" Irene asked. Sometimes she could keep her face as quiet and proper as could be, but when she talked to him, she let things show. And she was very anxious to be sure she understood.

"Yes," he said. "Yes. At least tonight. Maybe tomorrow night. You are *my* guest, now. Mani will not let anything happen to you. Lord Geigi will protect everybody else. You will not have to go back to the Reunioner sections and you will not have to go back to your mother. Nand' Bren will say so, to the ship-aijiin and to everybody. You will not have to go back to her."

It was a temptation, Bren thought, a sore temptation, once he was safely in the lift, within the atevi half of the station—to head back to the apartment and go back to bed for at least two more hours. He wished to do nothing thereafter but eat, sleep, stare at the ceiling and assemble the vocabulary and the connections and clues he had from the last meeting with the kyo . . . until it came time to use them. He wanted no more distractions.

But there was information he needed. He had potential sources. The Reunioners he had at hand—the parents of Cajeiri's young associates—were not the ones apt to have that information. But there were others—people he was not anxious to deal with, but had no intention of turning over to the ship-folk. Or to Gin. Not yet.

He could ask Jase to interview them, but he couldn't be satisfied with secondhand information. He'd think of questions

Jase might not think to ask, questions that might well need asking at the right moment, not after the fact.

There was no getting around it. He had to talk to Braddock.

Sleep first. Just two hours. That was all he needed.

He had already understood from his aishid, who kept abreast of details with other staff, that there had been a change in one of the situations he was tracking. Irene, and only Irene, had gone home with Cajeiri last night. Whatever had happened to suggest that relocation was a worry, but he thought he understood, and it was a sad business, a kid whose situation was not a happy reunion, and who might have been realizing it all too well. Geigi's staff would allow whatever the young gentleman wanted unless the dowager countermanded it . . . and the dowager had been asleep when that move had happened.

He was sure that situation was already handled, however. The dowager's staff would never permit an impropriety on the dowager's premises, so he was confident that things involving the dowager's premises had been done as properly as need be. He was also sure the dowager would have *not* brought down the weight of her displeasure on a guest this morning, when she did find out. She had *probably* found out by now.

No, the dowager would definitely not reprimand the girl, though what the dowager's real opinion was, Cajeiri would surely find out privately. And so would he, Bren was quite sure. He was prepared to go smooth that over if need be. He should do that, at least, before he settled into his own apartment and took hold of their more threatening problems.

"How has the dowager received the guest?" he asked, while the lift went through its changes.

There was a delay, while Banichi consulted via pocket com. That was usual. The length of the delay, however, suggested more to the answer, and more to the answer—

Was not good.

It was not necessarily good when Banichi made a second call

for information, and *that* conversation involved, he gathered from the name referenced, Lord Geigi's staff.

"Nadi?" he asked, in the not unlikely case Banichi was reluctant to distract him with another problem.

"The young gentleman has brought Irene back to nand' Geigi's staff. And there is some trouble which the staff does not understand. Gene and Artur have been translating, prior to this, and there is not an active disturbance, but there is distress of some sort."

"I should go there." If Irene was upset, if parents were upset, or if adjustments of some sort needed to be made in her situation, he needed to be involved. Geigi had offered to solve the human situation by lending his large guest quarters. Geigi, on watch and watch for days, and still due to wait for Gin, deserved to come home to domestic tranquility.

Nor did Irene deserve to have to explain herself.

"Is Irene moving back to Geigi's apartment?" he asked, and Banichi asked the question of staff.

"No," Banichi reported as the lift stopped. "The young gentleman has told staff she is a guest of the aiji-dowager."

Cajeiri would not hedge that fine point. So Ilisidi was aware, and had involved herself in the matter. That might or might not ease tensions. Not, was more likely.

"We shall go there," he said, hauling his mind back from problems of an oncoming alien ship and a new human administration, and back to the smaller politics of three sets of Reunioner parents, of vastly different social class, thrown onto the charity of an atevi lord and the earnest efforts of his staff.

Hell with the social class. He was on the side of the agreeable ones. And he was forming opinions.

The apartment door opened before they reached it, grace of his aishid's advisement to Geigi's staff that he was coming, and Geigi's major d' met him in the foyer.

"Be welcome, nandi. One is uncertain whether the problem need involve the paidhi-aiji, but the young gentleman being here . . . one felt obliged to notify the other staff."

"I am glad you did report it," he said. "What is the nature of the problem?"

"There is a request to return to the sealed sections, nandi, and we are instructed not to allow it. The young gentleman has arrived with Irene-nadi, and by our lord's instructions we have done our utmost to make our guests comfortable. But one person asks urgently to be allowed to return to his apartment, fearing for something left there."

"We are not surprised at that. Let me reassure them."

"Yes," the major d' said with relief, and led the way down the hall which brought them, in the traditional way, past the dining room and master's bedroom, past the bath, and to the door of the very large guest suite. The major d' knocked once, then opened the automated door, in the way servants of any earthly house would do.

The adults, likewise the eldest boy, Bjorn, were startled by the entry; not so, the three youngest, not so Cajeiri.

"Nand' Bren," the major d' announced him, "paidhi-aiji, Lord of Najida, Lord of the Heavens."

Bren walked in, bowed politely to Cajeiri, and to Irene, the dowager's guest. Artur and Gene stood up at once. Their parents and Bjorn rose uncertainly. Bjorn's father stayed slouched in a chair. Bjorn's mother stood by a guest-room door. And Banichi and Jago, Tano and Algini, took up position by the main door, and the sides of the room.

Atevi would not have been anxious at that move. The parents were. Bjorn's father straightened in his chair. Bjorn's mother came to stand beside it. Only Cajeiri stayed seated . . . and Irene. One did not miss that little move of Cajeiri's hand, bidding her, the dowager's guest, stay seated.

Manners. Manners that played out in a handful of seconds.

Manners which wouldn't govern the parents where *they* were going, but which would definitely govern three of the children, in the circles where they might move.

"Nadiin-ji," Bren said. There were two chairs unoccupied in the little sitting room, and he took one. Servants waited to provide tea, and as much tea as the whole company must have absorbed this morning, he signaled acceptance for form's sake. "Please. Sit down. We'll go on human custom, and I *will* answer questions frankly. I hope you've been comfortable."

The parents' anxious glances flicked between him, seated, to the four black-clad, armed Assassins' Guild standing solemn guard.

He understood their unease. They had been lifted out of one threatening situation and dropped into a world as alien to them as that oncoming ship. Their lives were in suspension. There were things they didn't know and no one had had time or fluency enough to answer—things regarding their future and their children's future.

Certain situations were still in flux. It was not an occasion to unbend and make extravagant promises that he would do this and that or that they could have this and that. He couldn't promise that their lives would resume a normal track. Nothing the Reunioners had experienced in the last decade had been normal, and their future involved changes, changes to everything they knew . . . changes in their own children. Some of those changes were already happening.

"News this morning," he said, "*Tillington* is replaced." That was good news for any Reunioner. Tillington had been the roadblock to any improvement in their situation. "I've just spoken to the new Mospheiran stationmaster, who is Gin Kroger—you don't know her, but she was on the voyage with us, she knows what you were promised, and she's determined to begin meeting those promises within the limits of resources at her command."

They did like that news. They were a little suspicious, and that was understandable.

"What about our situation?" Artur's mother asked. "Did you talk to her about us?"

"I can assure you that for right now, you'll be as safe here as anywhere on the station . . . more so than where you've been. Safe and as comfortable as we can make you. I can't say right now *how long* you'll need to stay here." A cup of tea arrived beside Cajeiri, and another beside him. "You know that there is a kyo ship inbound, they want to talk, and that we will be talking to them as extensively as they want, much as we did at Reunion. We expected this visit. We're not utterly surprised by it. We'll deal with it and we expect it to end as reasonably and quietly as our last conversation at Reunion, with their understanding that we've told them the truth and that we're peaceful here. Best case scenario, we'll make a solid agreement and all sleep better at night. But that means there'll be a time in which I'll be quite busy with that visit, and you'll have to rely on your young folk to translate to the staff for you. I've no doubt your young folk will manage to communicate at least as well as they did on Earth. Ask, and maybe they'll teach you the words they know. Staff is prepared to handle mistakes—they'll be charmed with the gesture."

Tea had now arrived beside everyone, and he picked up his cup a little before Cajeiri, who was watching his moves, not the converse that strict manners and protocol of rank dictated. "Atevi custom discourages serious talk during tea, understand. It's a way to ask that we calm our minds and speak quietly for the space of a cup or two, not quite on business, but let me assure you, conversationally speaking, that the new stationmaster is determined to fix things, and that your own host, Lord Geigi, who is right now busy with the arriving stationmaster, has locked down your premises in the Reunioner area to preserve them absolutely intact. Right now things are still a little too unsettled in the sections to go in after property, but be assured it's being safeguarded."

"We have business," Bjorn's father said unhappily. "We have jobs. We're grateful. But we have a lot to lose. Everything to lose. There's a notebook. All my notes. Family records. Two hundred years of records."

"Mr. Andressen. It is Andressen, am I correct?"

"Yes, sir."

"What records would those be, sir?"

"Private."

Bjorn's father—Mr. Andressen—was not accustomed to atevi-scale intrigue, or was baiting a trap.

"I do take note," Bren said with equanimity, "and whatever they are, they will be under guard, along with other property. Nobody is going to enter the premises until we can make a systematic recovery—no recklessness about it. If you have particular items, provide a list of what you want and where to find it, and I'll order it found and safeguarded. It may not happen in the next number of days. But it will happen. I take it, in your current situation, this is not a matter of medical urgency."

"My research."

"And you are?"

"A physicist. With *company* records."

"Excellent. I'll remember that."

"I have status on station. I have a position. Consult your own records."

"I'm sure I'll do that when we have time, but right now that ship is a priority."

"I don't need to be locked up over here. I don't need my wife and son locked up. I want to leave, I want to get to my bank, I want to find an apartment . . ."

"As I understand it, a very few Reunioners did manage to find employment, in consideration of patents and processes—would you be one of those?"

"I'm employed by a Mospheiran company. I have standing."

"Which company?" There *had* been a few such transactions. The companies' behavior was questionable in legality. The patent ownership, regarding things recovered from Reunion records, was questionable. All of the issues were very far from his current problems.

"Asgard."

Purification systems. "Interesting. Probably you've been robbed, Mr. Andressen, and the Mospheiran government may be interested in that."

"I don't care to discuss this on this side of the wall. I don't care to be here."

Questionable what Andressen had in his two hundred years of records, and whether it was in the Archive, which was common to anybody with University clearance to access, or whether it was something developed since the Archive, in which case there *still* might be ownership issues—in the chaos of a kyo attack and the evacuation of Reunion. Very many people had died. Ownership might be very much at issue.

"I'd advise you engage a lawyer, Mr. Andressen, when we do have this settled."

"I just want out. I want my family out."

"Mr. Andressen, take my advice. Say no more right now, and be content where you are. You're here now because your son was once part of the association the young gentleman made aboard ship, and your son was endangered by that association. That threat is still under investigation. Until it is resolved, this is the safest place for all of you."

"He was *endangered* by an unannounced shutdown of station systems!"

"Which was occasioned by a general atmosphere of tension between Mospheiran stationers and Reunioners—in which your former stationmaster made moves against the station systems. You ran, by what I hear, to Irene's residence, where Mr. Braddock was, at the time, asking whether your son might have been with her. Why was that? Why did you think she might know where he was?"

Andressen clamped his lips together. Then: "Because Irene Wilson *is* a friend of his. Because I was looking any place I could think of. And *hoping* the kids weren't in the tunnels."

That was reasonable. That was exactly where Bjorn had been. And Gene and Artur. It was where they had met on the ship.

Except Bjorn hadn't been allowed to continue that association. Bjorn had gotten into a station acculturation and education program, which Bjorn's father, employed possibly questionably by a Mospheiran chemical firm, had arranged.

And Bjorn sat there now, listening to every word, his increasingly worried look moving from his father to Bren and back again.

"Let me explain the situation," Bren said. "Your son *does* have the benefits of association with the young gentleman," Bren said, "which is the reason why former stationmaster Braddock was attempting to lay hands on all that group. Their being under the aiji's protection can make them targets for people with an agenda—as it did, then. But the aiji's protection is no small matter. The aiji has taken a hand in this situation and you are not, due to your son's association, to be released into the general population, where you could find yourself in harm's way. On the other hand, this is your choice. You can have a comfortable and productive life within the aiji's protection. Or you can decide to terminate the relationship and leave that protection when we can establish some hope of safety for you. But you may not decide for your son."

"He's a minor."

"We're not speaking of Reunion law. Or Mospheiran law, for that matter. His association with the aiji's son is his to determine."

"He's *human!* He's going to *be* human."

"Biologically, certainly. But he will make that choice. As all the others will. Bjorn."

"Sir."

"You understand me. You cannot undo the association. That exists in the minds of very many people, not all of good will. If you do leave the young gentleman's company, that is yours to choose. If your parents will not stay with you, that is *theirs* to choose. Your decision is for you to make, but understand that if you do leave the young gentleman, you will no longer have that association, and neither you nor your family will remain under the aiji's protection. Atevi will understand you're of no use as a bargaining chip if you choose that course, but humans might not."

"He'll stay with *us*," Andressen said.

"Your choice, Bjorn Andressen."

Whether Andressen had gone to Irene's apartment to talk to Irene or to talk to Braddock was a question. Braddock's people had been trying to lay hands on the children who'd visited Cajeiri. And while Bjorn had been invited to come down to the world with the others, his father's ordering him to opt out had made him far less useful to Braddock's scheme, at least in terms of public identification of Bjorn as part of that group.

But rather than simply admit to Andressen that he didn't have Bjorn, Braddock, who'd set up operations in Irene's mother's apartment and next door, had ordered Andressen turned away with no answer whatsoever.

All Andressen's actions pointed toward a man trying to minimize his son's connections to the atevi and get his family established on Alpha Station, which would not imply a willing association with Braddock.

Irene's mother, unfortunately, was entirely another story.

And how that all was going to sort out, he had no knowledge. He hoped Irene wouldn't ask. Not now. Not in front of the rest. And he was sorry to have had the discussion with Andressen in her hearing . . . but going or staying, with parents or without— was a choice they all had; everybody should understand the choices the youngsters *could* make, and he didn't have the time to sit down in private counseling with each of the families. They *would* be an association behind the kids—or they would not.

"The conclusion you can draw," he said, to steer the talk to a happier direction, while Andressen glowered in silence, "is that Bjorn, and Gene, Artur, and Irene, are all the personal concern of the young aiji, that everyone here is going to be protected, watched over, and eventually settled in a comfortable situation, the exact nature of which I don't yet know, but it will be comfortable. For now, please just settle in here. I know you're short of clothes and personal articles. We can supply those, part of the hospitality, if you will kindly make a list. If you have special problems, like your records, Mr. Andressen—" A little nod in that direction, a last attempt at conciliation. "We'll make every effort to preserve and protect them. Anything this staff can do for your comfort, they'll be happy to do. I'm also going to ask Central to provide the Mospheiran vid feed to this residency, in addition to the station's Ragi feed, so you'll have information and entertainment—the Mospheiran accent's a little different, but I'm sure you'll have no trouble with it. Just rest. Pick up as much of the atevi language as you can. Nadiin-ji." He changed to Ragi, for the children who understood it. "The young gentleman will be occupied with the kyo very soon and he will not be able to assist you, but rely on Lord Geigi. He wished to invite you to dinner when you arrived, and now he can. So enjoy your stay. Help your parents. And *stay here*. Above all else, do not go about in the tunnels again. We expect to deal with this incoming ship, and for it to go away, and then we shall expect to find you a good situation."

"Nandi," Irene said, and Gene said it, and Artur, all with solemn nods. Bjorn looked not to have understood half of it, but he said, "Yes, sir."

"Good," Bren said in ship-speak; and to the parents: "I just reminded them Lord Geigi has wanted to invite all of you to dinner. He happens to be the most powerful man in the aishidi'tat next to the aiji himself, so if you ask him something, understand who it is you're asking. If it's reasonable, if it's possible, he can make it happen. He's very pleased to have you here."

And to the children, still in ship-speak: "There's every likelihood that you'll get to show your parents trees and weather someday soon. Not on the mainland. But on Mospheira."

That created a little shock.

"Your children," he said, setting aside the cup of tea, "have an opportunity. A very great opportunity. Consider carefully the advice you give them. But remember it is *their* choice."

He left it at that, rose, bowed to Cajeiri, bowed to the gathering, and left, having promised as much as he could, committed as little as he could, and not said a thing about how or when or how long the interval would be. No one could predict that.

Cajeiri, wise in court ways, would not venture to amplify the promise he'd just made. Cajeiri might have his own intentions, some of them stretching well into the unpredictable future. Right now, and Cajeiri well knew it, his father made the rules, and the paidhi-aiji had already made all the promises it was possible to make, and made the warning to Andressen as plain as need be.

The boy was growing. The paidhi-aiji made, this time, an important bet on it.

4

"Jase-aiji," Banichi said as they walked the corridor of the residency, bound for their own door, "proposes to visit us. He is at the crossover now."

Jase was at the point where he had met Gin, less than an hour ago. Gin had gone up to ship-folk territory to talk to Ogun and now Jase had come down bent on talking to him. The two movements might not be unrelated. For a certain amount of time now, Ogun would be safely occupied listening to Gin, and Jase, closely allied to second-senior Captain Sabin, had left ship-folk territory and come down to the interface to find out whether it was a good time.

"Tell him come," Bren said, and that happened.

Jase, being third-senior captain *and* the ship-paidhi, had a certain protected status—being the *only* way Senior Captain Ogun could translate what the atevi half of the station was doing. But on his last shift, Jase had taken high and wide action getting the children and their parents out of the quarantined Reunioner section—not consulting the senior captain, who had been off watch and presumably asleep. So Jase had presumably spent the last several hours debriefing on the action with a senior captain not entirely pleased to have the third-senior conducting a raid on an area of the station the senior captain's orders had sealed.

The fact that they had simultaneously extracted the former Reunioner stationmaster, Louis Baynes Braddock, before he could take possession of the children and their parents and make his own demands in negotiations with the kyo—that had solved a major problem for Senior Captain Jules Ogun.

A very large problem, a problem that might have been avoided, had Ogun dealt with the lit fuse, otherwise known as Mikas Tillington, a long time ago.

Ogun had been reasonably content in Tillington's long stint as the human-side stationmaster: Tillington had taken care of business in which Ogun had little or no interest, while Ogun had technical emergencies on his hands. Ogun had trusted stationers to deal with stationers, and let Tillington take charge of the Reunioner refugees. Ogun hadn't intervened when Tillington had slammed the section doors shut and isolated the Reunioners in their residences—it had happened with a fifteen-minute warning, but fifteen minutes could not take Ogun totally by surprise: no, Ogun had taken Tillington's assessment of the Reunioners as risk, had let it happen, and to this hour Ogun wouldn't necessarily admit that the second-senior and third-senior captains had been right about Tillington.

Ogun might, in that light, not thank the third-senior captain for his unilateral move, bypassing any advisement and giving him no word of what was going on inside an area under seal.

But Ogun was smart enough to know that Tillington had gone a step too far with Mospheira and Shejidan, and that relations with the earthly powers, human *and* atevi, that supplied the station, which in turn supplied his ship, mattered far more to him than did the convenience of Tillington's cooperation.

As of an hour ago, Ogun had Virginia Kroger arriving as human-side stationmaster, he had the atevi government aggressively claiming ownership of the kyo situation, he had the fourth-senior captain, whom he had appointed, sitting out on *Phoenix*, not in a position to do anything useful, and he had Captain Josefa Sabin, his least favorite co-captain, in a position to say I told you so.

He really hoped Gin was pouring balm—or at least good sense—on the situation up there.

And he hoped Jase was not bringing trouble down with him.

Bren arrived in his own apartment foyer, shed his coat for a more comfortable one, and settled in for a brief bit of relaxation and checking of messages in his little sitting room, leaving the matter of informing the dowager to his bodyguard's contact with her bodyguard, in the interest of finding out what Jase had to say.

His apartment. His refuge. Not the place for grand state functions, this, but the extent to which Geigi had moved walls about, rearranging the human-designed linearity into the traditional relationship of rooms, rooms in an order that atevi found comfortable, with inner halls to let staff move about—that made it homelike, convenient, everything where it always was.

He was glad. He fit here. He knew his station staff did. Except for the modern panel near the door, except the air ducts and the fact the more massive furniture was bolted to the wall, one could believe there was stone and wood involved.

Tea arrived. More welcome, a plate of wafers. Distantly, half a cup and three wafers on, came the opening of the front door, and very quickly Jase turned up, a silent presence in the sitting room doorway.

Blue uniform—no bodyguards at the moment. Kaplan and Polano usually were somewhere about, but Jase walked in solo and simply slid bonelessly into the convenient chair.

"The offer of asylum still stands," Bren said, by way of opening, which got him a weak smile.

"Not quite yet. If I weren't apt to get another call from Ogun real soon, I'd take a brandy."

"What does the man want? We got Braddock out."

"I think deep down there's considerable gratitude for that. Sabin said to me— 'Welcome to the inner circle. Ogun hasn't expressed himself this bluntly since Ramirez died.'"

"Gin's still up there, I take it."

"Gin's arrival was a rescue." Jase tilted his head back, edged upward in the chair with a deep sigh. "Sabin's got ears up there. There's not a detail Ogun didn't ask. Three times. I think he's convinced, but I think he's looking for a way to space Braddock. I don't think he wants him to stay in atevi custody. I think the aishidi'tat is going to get a request. He hates Braddock. Personally."

Interesting—in the light of *what* had made the late Senior Captain Ramirez desert Reunion and leave the station at the mercy of the kyo.

Ogun had been second-senior when that had happened.

And Ogun hated the Reunion stationmaster with a deep, abiding passion, while Sabin, who had had no share in that decision, had been mightily upset, and blamed Ramirez and Braddock with equal heat.

Five thousand survivors? Ramirez, faced with a dice throw for the future of the human species in this end of space, had opted to run for their centuries-ago origin point and leave Braddock. And the whole surviving Reunion population.

What had Ogun known and when did he know it? Had he agreed with Ramirez' decision? If not, Ogun had had to live with the knowledge for ten years here at Alpha, knowing he'd had no choice but to go along.

Ramirez had been senior captain. And then Ramirez had been dead and Ogun had had to deal with the situation Ramirez had left.

Now, ten years later, a third-senior captain bypassed the protocols Ogun had followed, arrested the problem at the core of it all—and handed him to atevi authority.

Not a situation inclined to induce warmth and love within the Captains' Council.

"Is he exercised at us?" Bren asked. "The atevi *did* initiate the action."

"Initiated it with ample cause. Even he admits that. —I think he's actually happy," Jase said, and took the cup of strong tea a servant set beside him. He added four lumps of sugar, and stirred. "Most calories I've had since yesterday."

"Have a wafer. There can be a sandwich, if you want it."

"Let this hit bottom, and I'll consider it. —He's happy to have Braddock in custody, but I don't think he wants to let this go off entirely into atevi decision-making. I *think* he intends to try Braddock himself."

"You think he wants to open up all that history?"

"I'd swear not. I'd think not. But he's—are we secure here?"

"Tano's been over the place. Entirely."

"I think he wants the ship's record cast in a certain way, and a trial might be how he does it. Better yet, a plea and a statement from Braddock. I think he suspects atevi might be too easy on him."

"Atevi have charges against him—his aiming at the children, among others—that wouldn't go well for him under the aiji's law. But I can understand what you're saying. I can understand how Ogun might want the record clear."

"I think *all* of us want the record clear. He asked me directly how much authority you have, how much credit with either government down there, whether you can get the Mospheirans to take the Reunioners in, and he's no little dubious that the Reunioners are going to go along with it."

"They *can't* want to continue living as they have been for the last year."

"Ogun is convinced Braddock has support in wanting to build a station out at Maudit. That the Reunioners won't accept being sent down, they won't trust the offer and they won't want to be put under the Mospheiran government. I have an idea that topic may have come up between him and Gin by now. He *wants* it. It puts a real major problem at the bottom of a gravity well. He just doesn't think it's going to work. He thinks there'll be sabotage by the Reunioners, and that the Mospheirans won't accept them down there any more than here."

"Then he should have shut Tillington up."

"He knows that now, but the damage is done. Now we need to fix it."

Bren nodded slowly. "There *will* be problems, no question, especially if Mospheira expects gratitude and cooperation and the Braddock people don't see they owe it. But relocation to the planet is the only viable option. Maudit isn't going to happen without a huge commitment of resources from the planet, and neither government is the least bit interested in supporting it. Mospheirans won't share power up here and Braddock's people will insist they run the station, as long as one of them remains up here. Landing's the *only* choice that makes it absolutely essential they go through screening to get back up, like all the Mospheirans up here."

"Even if we claim guilt by association and pack the noisiest Braddock supporters down first, landing is a choice I don't think the Reunioners can even envision. They can't imagine dirt under their feet or a sky over them. You know Artur came back with a pocketful of pebbles. He was *fascinated* by rock you can touch. These people have no concept."

"There *is* no perfect answer when a group of people simply can't have the situation they used to have. But that's Gin's problem. It *must* be. As of now, I won't have a brain cell to spare for the Reunioners as a whole until we've met the kyo and dealt with them, something that might take years. Gin's got a plan for the relocation—a good plan—but it's not in my control. Only those four kids and their families are."

Jase nodded. "I'll relay that. I know Sabin will understand. If anything gets in your way—advise me, regardless of the hour. I'll try to handle it."

Jase didn't mention Riggins in any planning. Nobody did. The fourth captain, Riggins, did what Ogun told him, and right now it was to keep their one starship, *Phoenix*, slightly apart from the station, capable of moving to save itself, but not capable of protecting them if things went massively wrong.

If things went absolutely, massively wrong—Riggins and the

ship's caretaker crew might be all there was left of Mospheira *and* the world they knew, and then, only if they ran. If the damage the kyo had done to Reunion was any indication, such weapons as they had were primitive compared to the kyo's.

"Appreciated," Bren said.

"Did you get any sleep last night?"

"Not as much as I'd like. I'm going to become a little less available for a while—trust Gin to manage the problems, trust you to deal with the captains—and take the opportunity to write a few letters, now I can trust they won't be detoured into Tillington's hands."

"The man tried to exit his apartment this morning," Jase said. "Our people stopped that. No knowing where he thought he was going. Maybe to meet Gin."

"He really wouldn't have liked the reception," Bren said. "Thanks for the catch." And on a sudden realization: "Gin's going to be shipping out some of his personal staff as well. I don't know who's on her list, but it may create some security issues. Again—I don't know, and I'm not in a position to ask. But if you could track that—"

"I'll ask Gin. If people have to be moved into a restricted area, ship security can assist with that. Get them clear off the station until the shuttle's ready."

"I'd appreciate it." Asking Mospheiran security to deal with their own former high-level officials—had problems. There were problems, too, in using *ship* security to handle a Mospheiran problem, but in a station with dangerously accessible controls, physical safety trumped political considerations.

"I'll take that sandwich," Jase said after a moment. "If it's still offered."

It seemed like a good idea. Meals had become a matter of opportunity, the last two days. Or three. One took what one could, when one could.

At very best, one hoped for a snack, and then a session in the office, catching up on correspondence, and reporting to people who needed a report. Possibly a walk across the hall, to the dowager's residency.

That was days overdue, too.

"Aiji-ma." It was an offered session in the dowager's sitting room, and one had had altogether too much sugared tea. And a half a sandwich. That was all he'd managed, before the invitation from Ilisidi had arrived.

"We sent the young gentleman to Lord Geigi's to gather information on the needs of these guests. We have heard. We have given orders. We trust staff can provide."

"Indeed, aiji-ma. Clothing, food, all such. I have assured them their personal belongings will remain under lock—I arranged that with Lord Geigi. Gin-nandi has spoken to Ogun-aiji—we hope in a good exchange, taking place now or just concluded. I proposed to the Presidenta a need to bring the Reunioners down to Mospheiran territory, and he was most receptive, but logistics remained a problem. Fortunately, Gin has arrived with a possible means of freeing shuttle seats for passage to Earth with far less expense and delay than seemed likely."

"We are interested," Ilisidi said, and he explained Gin's notion of one-way landers:

"The landers themselves can be salvaged, aiji-ma, and a failure or two with those will not involve loss of life. We have always concentrated on fragile loads going *up* to the station, but grouping our cargoes differently, and using the petal sails as we can . . . we can provide many more seats in much less time, at much less cost."

Ilisidi thought on the question, eyes flickering. "Indeed. And shall we provide transport? And a landing for these loads flung recklessly down from on high?"

"Where safe, aiji-ma, and any human passengers on atevi shuttles would be flown to Mospheira immediately on landing . . . with the assistance of the aishidi'tat. No large mass of people at once. Easily carried on one of the smallest jets."

"And where would these people be settled, and under whose guidance?"

"By my will, aiji-ma, a scattered resettlement. Widely scattered, inconvenient for association, but with fair treatment and workable prospects."

There were analogous situations with atevi, the necessity for a disgraced clan to be broken up, divided, absorbed by rivals. That was the *resettlement* he used. And it *was* fully apt.

"We leave such details to the Presidenta," Ilisidi said. "What will these people think when they know their future, and when *will* they know?"

"One cannot say. I have cautioned Gin-nandi to wait until we have dealt with our visitors, at least until we've determined their intentions, but whether she will regard it, or whether circumstance will force her to tell them, one cannot know. Mospheirans and Reunioners are not quite the same in their thinking; and one foresees difficulties. Will there come a day when there is no difference? Or will five thousand Reunioners change Mospheiran thinking? I do not know. I do not know how that will develop. But sending them apart—that was never a good answer."

"There will be politics." Ilisidi gave a wave of her hand. "There is always politics. Let it be as it may. It will flow about these children. Let it *not* flow onto the mainland. The parents, particularly, should be cautioned."

"One will convey that, aiji-ma."

"We understand you *have* cautioned them."

"Strictly and firmly, aiji-ma."

"And Irene-nadi's mother?"

"One does not yet know, aiji-ma."

"The child will be wiser than the mother, we strongly suspect. We can keep the girl for a time. But when she goes down with the others, what part will her mother have with her?"

"Aiji-ma, that remains to be seen. We do not know what our choices may be."

"The child may *not* reside in our household permanently."

"Yes," he said, with no question about it. "I shall take the matter in hand, aiji-ma. There will be a solution."

A second wave of the hand. "You will not distract yourself with this child, paidhi. Nor with the vexations of the parents."

"No, aiji-ma." He was very glad not to discuss that matter. "I shall not distract myself even with a thought of them."

"So," Ilisidi said. "Go find us a solution for these foreign visitors. Advise them we shall speak to them. Arrange it so we shall speak to them inside the station, if you can. The ship poses inconveniences. But we shall bear them if we must. *Their* ship poses still more. We prefer to avoid that."

"Yes, aiji-ma."

"What is this agreement? You are most valuable when you argue, paidhi! Do not say yes to me!"

"I shall most strenuously object when you are wrong, aiji-ma. You have been infallibly right at least this last hour."

"Ha." Ilisidi set down her teacup. Click. "We are soon to find that out. Dismiss your other concerns, paidhi. We are extremely glad you were able to welcome Gin-nandi. We should wish to invite her to our table. And we are certain Lord Geigi would wish the same, but we are entirely disarranged by other guests not of our planning. The Mospheirans will be in some turmoil at her arrival: she will need to speak with them. The Reunioners are already in turmoil and *they* may need reassurance. But all these things must proceed without us. Certain things *must* remain in suspension, perhaps briefly, perhaps for an extended time, on the whim of our foreign visitors, and we are approaching the point at which we will not be able to deal with distractions. Is there any matter, paidhi, which perhaps should *not* remain in suspension?"

He had been running his own calculations—his own estimation of what he could deal with, what he *should* deal with. He had been paring them down, even in visiting the parents last night, and this morning. In meeting Gin. In making contact with Jase. One piece of business and another off his agenda, and out of his way.

But there remained one matter, in Jase's estimation. And in his.

"Braddock," he said. "Braddock."

5

The operational as well as official transfer of station power was imminent—not the usual shift for a handoff, but days overdue; and Bren came to atevi Central to witness the first official and orderly handoff of station control between atevi Central and Mospheiran Central to take place since the news of the kyo ship had broken.

Gin called from atevi Central, speaking Ragi—which was itself unprecedented. Gin didn't have that much Ragi, but she had enough to introduce herself politely and very impressively on com broadcast to the whole atevi control center, and to request, formally, that "things" now pass to Mospheiran hands.

"Excellently done," Lord Geigi said warmly, in ship-speak. "Welcome, Gin-nandi."

Geigi knew a little human language—not unnaturally, he had more of a ship-speak accent than Mosphei', and he scrambled two accents and a language inside five words, but he managed.

Never in the history of the station had the atevi stationmaster and the Mospheiran stationmaster exchanged impromptu words in each other's languages. Habitually, handoff had been a simple, prearranged series of button-pushes and button-push acknowledgments.

It was a psychological change in their offices, a change in very many ways.

The techs looked a little surprised, but not at all unhappy, and Geigi finished with, "Thank you, Gin-nandi," in mixed ship-speak and Ragi.

"One is pleased, nandi," Gin's voice answered, in Ragi. "Thank you."

And it was done. Atevi techs slid back chairs, relieved, after shift and shift and shift, hours on, and hours off only to snatch food and sleep a little.

"We shall keep the regular rotation from now on," Geigi said. "Honor to you all, nadiin-ji. You have done extravagantly well, and I shall list all my staff for the aiji-dowager's personal remembrance. Go. Shut down now. We are resuming regular schedule in all respects. You will return at the official time."

There were happy expressions, tired people contemplating a meal and bed, and a decent time to rest before the shift came back to them.

"The dowager bids me say," Bren said quietly to Geigi, "that you are to rest, yourself, and that when you have leisure she will be pleased to see you, Geigi-ji. Your apartment right now is full of humans, both children and parents, and should you wish to take your hours of rest in my small guest quarters, you would be very welcome."

"One is grateful," Geigi said, "But my staff will shield me, and I should pay respects to my guests, however briefly."

"I have one favor to ask in the meanwhile, Geigi-ji. I wish access to Braddock."

"Jase-aiji sends word that Ogun requests him sent to their security. I have referred the question to the dowager."

"The dowager has referred it to me," he said, which was the truth. *Do as you see fit* had been Ilisidi's word on that matter, in essence. And he had not communicated with Jase to give an official schedule, not yet.

"Indeed." Geigi gave a little nod. "Then, Bren-ji, I shall walk with you toward our unwilling guests. Then I shall leave matters completely to you, whatever you do with Braddock and his associates. We have attempted to make the woman in particular comfortable, since her daughter is a guest and under the aiji's protection; but she remains quite angry and defiant toward us."

One took notes on that, certainly.

"We have kept all of them separate from each other," Geigi said. "Two of them have thrown bedding onto the floor and one has attempted to dismantle the plumbing. We would be quite glad to send all of them to Ogun-aiji. But we are not glad, for the child's sake."

"I shall call on the woman first, then," Bren said. "I shall at least make an effort."

"One wishes you success," Geigi said as they walked the hall.

Calling on Irene's mother was what he had sworn he wouldn't do. Braddock might have necessary information. Braddock— knew things he might want to know. He had no reason to believe Irene's mother was in any sense well-placed in Braddock's counsels. He had sworn not to be distracted by the children's situation.

But—one couldn't take the woman for granted, either. What her credentials were, who she actually was, what her connections had been, he had declined to ask Irene, and it was doubtful they'd get much from what personnel records Sabin had managed to extract from Reunion records before destroying the station's memory banks.

Sabin's people had spent much of the voyage going over what they'd gotten, looking primarily for information on their more troublesome passengers, and details regarding all contact with the kyo.

The Reunion citizen rolls, as it turned out, proved uninformative at best. They hadn't gotten their judicial files, hadn't gotten their educational records, or their council records, and the personal files they had were fragmentary, covering individuals a hundred years deceased more thoroughly than the survivors, giving them little to no information on a significant number of persons they'd taken aboard.

In an attempt to build their own files, they'd conducted interviews during the voyage. The problem was, any random person among the survivors could claim to be a nuclear physicist, a trained mechanic, or a medical doctor, with no proof to the contrary, necessitating an exhaustive system of cross-checks. If the interviewers had gotten three unrelated Reunioners to swear to a claim, it was indicated to be truthful—pending the individual's performance on an ever-expanding series of tests. A few individuals had had the foresight to bring actual records and badges with them—or company documents and research, as Andressen had done; but most had crammed necessities and sentimental items into what they could carry, and boarded in extreme haste.

Braddock . . . was Braddock. He was indisputably what he had been, and, also indisputably, not what he still wanted to be. Head of the ancient Pilots' Guild, at odds with the ship's officers, bent on becoming master of *some* station—he'd been campaigning to be given resources to build a new station, but Mospheirans, who had a centuries-old feud with the Reunioners' ancestors, were worried about Braddock's leading a riot and taking over the human side of the station, a fear Tillington had done nothing to settle. It was that fear, in fact, which had prompted Tillington to slam the section doors shut at the first remotely justifiable opportunity.

Hostage leverage—much as Braddock had used against the kyo for six years.

That . . . was the one thing they knew regarding Reunion's interactions with the kyo. According to Jase's report, no information relating to either kyo incident had turned up in those records. One feared those details had been buried in levels they hadn't been able to lift, in their haste to destroy all records from which the kyo might extract information.

Braddock had been in charge of the station from long before the kyo's initial attack. It would appear Braddock had buried all files associated with the kyo deep into some archive only he could access. If those records existed at all, they were on Re-union. Presumably Reunion no longer existed. But that was not guaranteed: the kyo might still be going through it for small bits and clues, itself a worrying proposition.

Braddock . . . was Braddock. And Braddock, from current ev-idence, had never ceased *being* Braddock. Whether the kyo's arrival or that lockdown had initiated them, riots and looting had indeed begun, and there was some evidence that Braddock had already been plotting a breakout, and had already had a notion of using the kids, who were under Tabini-aiji's protec-tion, as currency in the bargaining.

If Braddock hadn't personally and willfully triggered those riots, he'd certainly been preparing to take advantage of them, once they began.

Irene's mother? He hadn't asked Irene too closely about her mother's involvement with Braddock and Braddock's lieutenants—who, well before the lockdown, had repositioned themselves to her apartment and the one adjacent—apartments which not only contained one of Braddock's intended hostages, but also just hap-pened to be within shouting distance of the section doors, the thin line that held Reunioners out of the sensitive spots of the station.

Braddock had, according to Irene, moved into the apartment next door, but he'd spent nights in her mother's apartment. He suspected it wasn't an unwilling relationship. Jase had warned him about the connection when the kids had come down to the planet.

He certainly hadn't wanted to put any pressure on Irene, but if he did send Braddock and his lieutenants to Ogun for prose-cution . . . did he include Irene's mother in that package? Or did he establish some special status for her?

Did he try to reunite Irene with her mother, and include her in the plan to take the children and their families down to the planet?

Not enthusiastically. No. He didn't.

He didn't want to be in a position to decide that question. He didn't know what was right. But he also had to consider that woman's child had been invited to come under the dowager's roof, under the dowager's personal protection, with all the politics *and* prestige that went with it.

So he headed now toward the very interview he'd most wanted to avoid and maybe, just maybe, he'd learn something useful—before he talked to Braddock.

It was not Guild who stood watch over the Reunioner prisoners: it was Geigi's own non-Guild security, individuals who simply stood there to lock what needed locking and to settle small disputes. Such regular security would still be able to deal with a great number of situations once the Guild itself moved in, as the Guild was in process of doing. And they were adequate for what needed doing now. They saw to it that Ms. Williams and the others were fed, gave them clean clothes—and made certain they didn't have contact with each other, or do harm to themselves or others.

Which meant, as it turned out, that they kept them in separate small rooms in what was by design a small and little-used detention facility. They fed them three times daily, and simply kept the doors shut.

Was there danger of an escape? Not likely. There was nowhere to go, on this side of the station. Argument, with no commonality of language, was not going to affect the atevi guards in any way. And atevi being generally a head and shoulders taller, and commensurately stronger—physical force was no threat, either.

Ms. Williams, by the empty tray that passed him as he approached, was awake . . . and in good appetite.

He knocked as simple warning on the door before security unlocked it, and found Ms. Williams sitting glumly on her atevi-scale cot, which was all the furniture the barren room afforded, besides a sink and an accommodation.

He walked in. Banichi and Jago took up position on either side of the open door, while Tano and Algini stayed outside with the regular guards.

She glanced up, stared, then got up in a hurry. "Help me," she said, breathlessly, desperate. "Please . . . help me."

"I'd like to, Ms. Williams." Tell her that her daughter was safe? The woman had never yet asked about her daughter, that he had ever heard. "But you've landed yourself in some difficulty."

"I've done nothing. I've been taken captive and held here for no *reason*—"

"You're being held, Ms. Williams, because there are some serious questions about your associations, and the part you played in their actions."

"I've done *nothing.* I'll tell you anything you want to know!"

"Then we should get along quite well. To start with, can you explain what Mr. Braddock was doing in your apartment, or why you refused to help Mr. Andressen find his son, or even just to tell him you didn't know?"

A rather blank blink. The second might not be the question she expected, perhaps. The first—quite likely.

"I—I had no choice."

"Explain."

Nervous flutter of the hands about her person, straightening her shirt. Actions instinctual, but not without intent. Ms. Williams was a beautiful woman, dark-skinned, dark-eyed, on the young side of thirty, with appeal in every line of her—human moves, setting off human instincts.

He lived in the habit of suspicion. He lived, he thought, *because* of his habit of suspicion. And he was not moved to think better of her for that manipulative body language.

Was there going to be an explanation? He waited. He simply waited.

"I was seeing Theo Verner. And Braddock . . . Braddock just showed up at the door and Theo let him in and said he had to stay because security was hunting for him."

"Go on." He wasn't going to give her leading questions, to help her shape her story. He just waited. And listened.

"So. So they moved in. And Theo stayed. And Braddock went next door, I think."

Not quite how Irene had described the living situation, but plausible. He still waited.

She twitched, uneasy with his lack of response. "Who *are* you?" she asked, somewhat belatedly, and without the breathless quiver. "How do I know you can help me?"

"Braddock, Ms. Williams. Go on."

And bit her full lower lip. Then, a bit sullenly: "There wasn't anything I could do. He was just *there*."

Innocent victim, was she? For Irene's sake, he so wished that rang true.

"So?"

"So these atevi came in with ship security and took us out into the tunnels, with no coats, nothing, and Captain Graham, he was in charge, he kept asking Lou questions."

Interesting. Lou, now. Not Braddock.

"I *told* him, told Captain Graham I wasn't part of it. *Told* him I was freezing to death, and he just handed me over to the atevi with the others and they brought us here."

"Where you're not freezing."

"I'm shut in this room and I can't talk to anybody!"

"That's sad, Ms. Williams. Is that all I need to know?"

She'd wound up to tears. They glistened in her eyes. They'd *been* glistening for some time. Then, like the flipping of a switch, thought took over—or tactics changed.

"You're from the planet," she said, voice and body turning overtly respectful. *"You're* the one that was coming—the one they were talking about."

"If I were?"

Would the tears fall? Would she finally ask, Where's my daughter? Would she say, I've been afraid to ask that? I've tried to ask that?

"You're *with* them. You're Cameron. You *can* help me, can't you?"

Evidently she wasn't going to.

"We can dispense with the tears, Ms. Williams. I'm immune. What were you doing with . . . Lou?"

Blink. Realization, maybe. And the tears vanished. The face was frozen, thoughts flickering fast in the look.

"I'm waiting," he said.

"What do you want?"

"What do you *suppose* I want?"

Hesitation, then. A slow intake of breath. A complete change of body language, from pity-me to reestimation.

Bren just stood there. Waited.

"Look. Look. I did what I had to do. I tried. I *tried* to stay alive. I did what I had to do."

"What *was* that, Ms. Williams? What did you have to do?"

Deep breath. Arms folded. Jaw set. "I don't know anything."

"What sort of thing *would* you not know, Ms. Williams?"

"Oh. Hell."

"You're in fairly deep. What do you expect us to do?"

Chin trembled. A little. He was almost inclined to believe it. "I don't know. I don't have a clue."

Almost.

"You know the depth of the game you're in. I understand you better than you might think. So let me advise you—you haven't got any better offers. You won't find any better than I can give you. And if you *ever* try to double on me, you'll have lost your last best offer. So I'm asking again. What's your relationship to Braddock?"

"Where's my daughter?"

He didn't let *his* face react. His aishid might read him. He didn't think Ms. Williams could. "Your daughter."

"My daughter. My daughter, who stole my keycard and skipped out into the tunnels. You know where she is."

Just a little edge to that question. And what happened to be a wrong conclusion. Irene hadn't escaped into the tunnels. She'd walked out the section door personnel access, escorted by armored ship security. "She's safe," he said.

Deep, deep breath. A little shaky, in that reaction. So perhaps there *was* a modicum of concern.

"Why did you let Braddock in? Why did you let him set up operations in your apartment? Why did you let him lock your daughter in? What *is* your involvement? This is a test."

The answer took a second. "I let him in because he wanted in. Because he wanted to operate near the doors. I don't know what he had set up, except Theo was running messages from there. I *protected* my daughter."

"I'm interested in your logic."

"I worked for Lou. Have for several years. I knew him socially. I survived the first attack on Reunion. I was pregnant. The father was dead. Half the people I knew were dead. I helped Lou set things up, get admin together— When Irene was born I set her on a pallet in the corner, and then went back to my station. I was trying to find people, find equipment, find supplies—I slept there, I ate there, *I worked,* and I put things together, and all the while we never knew but what that ship would come back and finish us. But we kept trying. And I kept us alive. Then they finally did come back. They came in, and we got that one hostage, and they went away. They didn't come back. And we just held on."

Not a tear. Not a wobble. But the woman wasn't lying now, he had that strong feeling.

"When everything settled, the first time, Lou—Braddock— gave me a place. With my daughter. Yes, we had a relationship. Off and on. It was what there was. We lived all right. I was—I was all right. We were doing fine. Others—not so well, maybe. But what do they say? 'Dead help is no help'? We had to stay alive. We were keeping admin running. We had to keep the station running."

"You had a kyo ship sitting there watching you."

"We didn't know that."

"So you weren't doing that well after all, were you?"

"We were feeding ourselves. We were rebuilding. It was getting better. When *Phoenix* showed up and said we had to leave, and get on board . . . we were scared, was all. We were scared. Lou said they'd hit us if we moved. They'd track us to the other station. They'd do the same thing. They'd wipe us out. And he was right, wasn't he? Now they're here. They've followed us."

It was a reasonable interpretation, given gaps in understanding.

"Can you describe the attack?"

"Which one? There were two. I was asleep when the first came."

"The second, then. *Were* you in a position to observe the lead-up?"

Shake of the head. "I was in admin," she said. Her voice was less steady. Her eyes flickered with other visions. "I don't know what happened, except there was a ship. We thought it was *Phoenix*. Next thing we knew, the alarms sounded. We went to emergency shelters. I ran. It wasn't that far. I took cover. We felt the shock. It went through you, through your bones, before you even heard anything." She shivered. "Lights went out. Fans stopped. People had hit the wall. We all hit the wall. Or the wall hit us. I don't know which. I woke up in the dark. With no fans. Just people moaning and crying. Metal pinging, the way it does. But we were still airtight. People didn't panic. We felt around, took care of each other the best we could. First the fans came back on. Then the lights did. We just sat and waited . . . I don't know how long . . . for an all clear. It was a long time."

He had to ask. "Where was your daughter?"

"Nursery. She was all right. It was a deeper place. Smaller. Better protection than we had. When we got the all-clear I went over there. Saw she was all right. Went back to work."

Spacer mindset. He knew Jase. He knew the thinking. He nodded. "You say they came in."

"They did. And we caught one."

"We."

"Our people. Our security."

"Did you see him?"

She shook her head. "Didn't. Never did. I saw vid once. That was all. We just held on to him. We figured, if they ever came back, maybe we could deal."

"You figured?"

"Lou said. That was what he said."

"Did he ever say what led up to the attack? Did he ever say anything?"

"He said . . . he said they didn't talk. Just fired."

The kyo had indicated otherwise, in a fairly straightforward animation of ship, station, and boarding craft.

"Did they signal at all? Did they do anything?"

Shake of the head again. "We didn't see them until the explosion. One of our service-bots. They just ran it down. Collided with it. Or blew it up. That's what I hear. Maybe they mistook that for an attack. All we saw was the explosion. But then the alarm came and—" She shrugged.

"Service-bot. Did Braddock say that?"

"No. Theo did. But he said he didn't know. Not for certain. Said something about the first attack and mining craft that got blown up."

"And you think they might have mistaken an accidental collision—for an attack, and retaliated. Twice."

"How would I know? That was Theo's notion."

"Let's go back to that first attack. Tell me about when *Phoenix* came back the first time and offered to evacuate the station."

She frowned. "Most people don't know about that. Lou kept it from them."

"Why? Why not give them a choice?"

"*Phoenix* came back and wanted to take people off. But we couldn't. The ship was in from a long run. Its onboard stores would be flat. We had all our food production, but we'd lost the storage units. There was nothing to transfer to the ship. No way the ship could take on and feed everyone. We couldn't. Lou said no, the ship should stay and defend us while we got production going."

Now that was interesting. "How long *did* it stay there?"

"Long enough to take in fuel. They talked back and forth like they were going to stay. And then they didn't."

"Who was talking?"

"I don't know. Lou, on our side."

"Did he explain the situation?"

"I don't know. I wasn't in on it. But they talked a lot of times. They were back and forth on the com. The ship wanted to re-fuel. They did that. The word was they were going to stay and keep us going till we *would* have enough for the trip. They finished refueling. They disconnected. And then they started moving off. We still thought it was just positioning the ship. Then they just left us."

Beyond interesting. A station with a lot of survivors. And no food for a trip with no assurances on the other end? *Someone* would have had to decide who could leave and who had to stay and take their chances. The lack of food supply was an insur-mountable problem in rescuing all the survivors.

The truth could have triggered stationwide panic.

It was no wonder Braddock had been just a bit reluctant when *Phoenix* returned, ten years later, with pretty much the same demands: fuel the ship and abandon the station.

But one look at the damage to the station would have told Ramirez the ship hadn't the firepower to protect it against those weapons. If the people refused to come aboard . . .

A hard decision. A spacer decision: save the ship, at all cost.

A unilateral decision. Sabin swore she hadn't known there were survivors.

So what *had* Sabin been doing while that had been going on?

Off shift? Supervising the refueling?

Ogun and Sabin.

There were more than thirty people on the bridge, on any of the four shifts. He'd personally been up there. He'd seen it. One shift had been held overtime, maybe. Maybe two shifts had cycled up there, in a position to know. More than thirty, maybe twice thirty people who'd been in a position to see and hear what was going on, more than a few who'd have heard the exchange between Ramirez, senior captain in those years, and Louis Braddock.

The ship had refueled. *Somebody* had been in charge of that operation. Somebody had known there were survivors on the station. God knew how much Braddock had told Ramirez, what Braddock had demanded, what he'd told Ramirez about their situation, their numbers, their food situation.

God knew, too, whether the kyo ship had still been there when *Phoenix* had come in that first time. Or if they'd picked it up. God alone knew *why* Ramirez had done what he'd done.

At *least* thirty people out of the hundreds native to *Phoenix* had been in a position to know something—or pieces of something.

But nobody had broken the silence until Ramirez, dying, had done it himself.

Ogun and Sabin, on either side of a ten-year silence, and a cadre of officers who weren't telling their shipmates, their fellow officers—what they'd known. And done.

Ogun—with a passionate hatred of Braddock.

And Sabin and Ogun . . . in frosty cooperation.

"Ms. Williams," he said quietly, "let me assure you, first, your daughter's with her friends and their parents, and she's under the lasting protection of the atevi government. I can't alter your personal situation right now. But I can keep you under atevi authority, and I can assure you no harm will come to you here. I may be able to make your legal situation better, once we're past the current emergency. Meanwhile I want you to be safe. I want you to be more comfortable. Is there anything you want, that I can bring in here?"

She shook her head, not asking a thing. Scared, maybe. Not trusting anything.

"I'll give orders, all the same," he said. "I'll get something to help you pass the time. And I'll tell your daughter I've talked to you. Is there anything you want to tell her?"

A second shake of the head.

"Are you angry at your daughter?"

Third shake of the head.

"I'll tell her that, then." He inclined his head, a little bow. "I'll order food be brought in from the Mospheiran side, while I'm at it. You may prefer that."

"Thank you," she said.

He left, with Banichi and Jago, and the guards outside shut the door.

"Instructions," he said to the guards. "Be watchful. Do not allow ship-humans access here without my specific order, no matter their rank, but avoid violence so doing. Lord Geigi will contact you and send certain things for this lady's comfort. We are in keeping of a woman perhaps more threatened than threatening, but she is clever, she wants out, and she is deceptive. Do not afford her a weapon or anything that can be made a weapon or do harm, nadiin, and be sure that word passes to all who stand guard here. Be courteous. But be extremely wary of this person."

"Nandi," was the answer.

And to his bodyguard, as they left. "Her information was interesting. I wish to do some study before I talk to Braddock. I am reconsidering transferring Braddock and his associates out of Lord Geigi's custody."

"She spoke of the ship," Jago said. "And events at Reunion."

"She did," he said.

Did he *believe* what Williams said? He wasn't sure. He didn't know the technicalities—didn't even know what questions he should ask to judge what she said.

But letting Williams believe he did believe her . . . that seemed the safer course.

What he was going to *do* with the woman—whether he wanted her in any wise associated with her daughter—that was a heavy decision, one that affected far more than Irene and her mother.

He wasn't sure. He knew more than he had known. But he was far from sure.

He was going to get a call—at any given moment—that the kyo had entered an approach. Or changed their transmission. Or needed a response.

God, of all things, he didn't need this woman on his hands.

6

First order of business, returning home, was a call—a very troubled call. "Jase. I need to see you, urgently. Don't ask. Please come."

And when Jase did turn up at the apartment, Bren opted for his office, a cubbyhole of a room, but private, even from staff. Even from his bodyguard, though not because of secrets, but for just the mood he wanted. "I shall see him there, nadiin-ji. I ask you be patient. Tell staff let us be alone until I signal."

It was Jase. It was a very close ally, in territory Jase could not exit without their leave. They still frowned, perhaps reading into the context of the business with Irene's mother. But they bowed and went back to their own territory.

He waited.

Jase arrived from the foyer with Asicho, who quietly let him in, then left and closed the door.

"Problem?" Jase asked in ship-speak.

"Deep apologies," Bren said. "I dropped in on Ms. Williams, on my way to talk to Braddock. She had a story. I don't know enough to figure how much is true. But her account had some details I do need to ask."

Jase sank into the nearest chair. "Ask."

"Since Ramirez. Since before we went out to Reunion, and after we came back, I've heard one story, that present crew didn't know any part of what went on between Ramirez and Braddock, they had no idea the station had survivors, but after

Ramirez said there had been, we, on our voyage, went back moderately prepared for the possibility. We understood the purpose was to destroy the Archive, to be sure the kyo had nothing usable—and if there were still people holding out there—"

"That's all true."

"In the way of a person who's not familiar with the operations of the ship, in the way of a person who, at the time, had very little concept what that might entail, I find a question I never have asked—a question which may have been too obvious for you to volunteer. I didn't ask into the time it took *Phoenix* to approach the station when it came in, how long to talk to it, to refuel. I did ask who *was* in command, who wasn't . . ."

"Ramirez," Jase said. "It was Ramirez all the way."

"I believe everything you've told me. I *believe* it, Jase. But Ms. Williams filled in a certain amount of detail from the other side—from the Reunion side—that possibly casts Braddock in a more favorable light."

"That their food stores were destroyed and we couldn't take all of the survivors on board?"

He was shocked for a moment. He *hoped* he wasn't about to hear there were deeper secrets.

"That's the gist of it," he said to Jase. "Ms. Williams indicated that when the ship came in, after the attack, there weren't sufficient supplies left to transfer to the ship to keep them alive on a long voyage, that they needed time to rebuild the station facilities, and that what Braddock wanted from *Phoenix* was the ship to stay there while they did rebuild that supply. There *were* certainly supplies to take when *we* arrived. We loaded them on, filled the tanks . . ."

Jase nodded. "It's what Braddock maintained all the way back here. That he'd had firm agreement from Ramirez that the ship would stay and defend the station while they rebuilt the tanks. So the station let the ship refuel. But Ramirez refueled and then ran out on them."

"That's fairly well Williams's story, yes."

"Honestly, *we* don't know enough to deny it. Having seen the damage to the station, *we* knew our weapons wouldn't stand a chance against whatever did that. Senior captain *must* have realized the same. If Braddock refused to accept that, insisted on *Phoenix* fighting an unwinnable battle . . . I can't say I wouldn't have made the same decision."

"Maybe. But there was another option, one *you* might have suggested, had Ramirez actually asked advice from anyone, especially the two individuals he'd specifically trained for the circumstance."

"Try to talk to the kyo?"

Bren nodded, and Jase sighed.

"I must admit, I have wondered whether or not I'd have thought of it. Whether Yolanda and I'd have had the skill to try it, young as we were. But we'll never know, so I try not to dwell. Ramirez was in command the entire time, and when the word came to pull out, we believed, we *believed* completely, that there were no survivors. Timing was what you might expect for a search for survivors and refueling. You've seen the log. Tapes of the rescue boarding just cut out, once they were in, and the senior captain's personal log is cryptic, to say the least. Thank God for that single reference to their flashing light contact attempt. Without that—"

Without that one key, he might never have made the connection between the lights with which the kyo ship had greeted them, and Ramirez' choice to ignore the same signal and run. It had given him his first insight into the kyo's actions.

"As for Braddock's claims the station's food supply was pretty well flat . . . we can't argue that, because we don't know. Braddock could have been lying, stalling to keep us there to protect him while he rebuilt the station. Not because the food wasn't there for a viable evacuation, but because Braddock wanted to preserve his little kingdom. There's no denying what Braddock did *this* time is exactly what Ramirez told the crew he did last time—he refused to evacuate. With the kyo right there, with plenty of food stores on the station, he refused to evacuate."

That much was true.

"If you're asking what I *think*—I think his motivations were the same then as now. I think he knew that if he boarded the ship he put himself in the hands of *Phoenix* captains. As noisy as he was about being in command of the ship, I think he knew the old Pilots' Guild, which was his *only* justification for his position, was going to die as a separate entity the instant he crossed the threshold. I think he was willing to hold those people hostage until he got concessions, primarily a continuation of his own power and prestige, in writing, first from Ramirez, then from Sabin, while we were sitting there with the kyo looming over us. I think that was exactly it. I think he knew that evacuation was inevitable this time, given our interaction with the kyo, the promise we made them to evacuate the station. I think he forced that boarding party on us because he wanted to know how many crew we had, and whether he stood a chance of seizing control of the ship. I think he didn't *want* his people or himself shunted off to the old colonist quarters of the ship, for which you can't entirely blame him—the plumbing down there's as old as the ship. However, he'd care more about the fact that the security locks would seal him and his people off from the crew areas. You recall—you had the old admin quarters, but you still had to go through keyed locks to get near the bridge."

Also true.

"That's not the situation he wanted," Jase said. "But we damned sure weren't going to allow him or any of his supporters up in crew territory, seeding doubt into the crew and who knows what into the ship's systems. So yes, I think he tried to hold the fuel hostage to avoid a repetition of Ramirez' actions, and insisted on Sabin's attendance in his office in order to 'negotiate,' even if it meant holding her hostage—we know now how fond he is of that tactic. But it didn't work. We got her back, got the fuel, and got the people off safe. And that's really about all I can tell you."

Things Jase said fell comfortingly into place. Maybe too comfortingly. He wanted to be sure.

"I tell you what still bothers me. Ms. Williams maintains Ramirez talked to Braddock—several times and over some period of time. That it got heated. Wouldn't the bridge crew know? At least that he was talking to *someone?* Wouldn't they talk? That's thirty people trying to keep a secret from family for ten years."

Jase frowned, thinking. "Communications doesn't go anywhere between bridge and the rest of the ship without the communications officer authorizing it," he said slowly. "And what goes on between chief at com and someone in a private call doesn't go all over the bridge. It's entirely reasonable, if the senior captain initiated that conversation from his office, that only *two* people on *Phoenix* were in a position even to know the exchange took place, let alone hear it—Ramirez, and the head com tech. Kalmanov. Who's dead, now."

"How long dead?"

"Six, seven years. Natural causes, what I know. People do die."

"Granted."

"Maybe Braddock did believe he had an agreement: with Ramirez. Maybe he concludes that the way he still says he outranks the ship's captains. I don't know. We don't trust him, plain and simple."

"We?"

"Ship-folk. *Phoenix* crew. And this is something maybe you don't know. The Pilots' Guild didn't go ashore. It was *put* ashore. It was put ashore at Reunion because its priorities had shifted over to Reunion Station, and the captains of that day just stopped taking its orders. From the foundation of Reunion Station, it ceased to be relevant to the ship. Braddock thinks it still is."

"Put off. Years ago. *Generations* ago. That's a long time to hold on to a fantasy job."

"He's Pilots' Guild." As if that explained everything. And perhaps it did. Except:

"And yet it took this long for the Pilots' Guild to hold the fuel hostage to the ship's actions."

"They had their little kingdom. We were the easy reason for the station to work and build, the reason for a Pilots' Guild to hold power. We were fine when we were gone, I suspect. A problem to the station authority when we were in dock. Likely we were always in the way . . . until they wanted something from us."

"And what they wanted—for the first time in the history of the station—was protection. So from the founding of Reunion, the ship came in, got fueled, and went out to explore the surrounding space . . . until Ramirez, as Gin put it, stuck his nose where it didn't belong."

It went to the heart of the kyo problem: how long had the kyo been watching? Not just watching Reunion, but the ship itself?

"Pretty much. Beyond that—beyond that, I just don't know your answers. To a certain extent, blind loyalty to the ship, adherence to its hierarchy, *does* drive us. We go where the senior captain tells us. Do what he tells us. Under ordinary circumstances, the why never comes into it much. What happened . . . made sense at the time. Once we knew there was more to the story . . . there was no one to answer the questions, because Ramirez never confided, not in anyone. The log has locked segments *only* the senior captain can access—which means Ogun, now—and it's possible it holds the keys to Ramirez' actions and has greater detail on the entire mess, but my personal feeling is it doesn't and Ogun doesn't know."

"Where was Ogun, when Ramirez was holding the bridge?"

"Sabin says he wasn't on the bridge at any time during the exchange, that he was handling the refueling. She said Ramirez wouldn't leave the bridge. Shift was held and held. Sabin was third on call, but Ogun himself never got the handoff until after we moved ship. We just arrived, fueled, and left. All under Ramirez. So the last few days, before you got here, when we had Tillington occupying Central shift and shift and refusing to budge, it triggered things. It triggered things, and Sabin began to talk about that time.

She'd been awake and trying to get contact with Ramirez during the refueling. She dropped that bit on me, when we were dealing with Tillington's holdout. She was mad as hell at Tillington. But not really Tillington. I'm breaching a confidence. But she didn't swear me to secrecy. There's still old heat there."

"Could the kyo ship have been there still? Could Braddock have believed it had gone away and Ramirez have spotted it? *Phoenix* knew the kyo were here before the station became aware. It has better equipment than the stations. It was *designed* to search out planets and analyze solar systems from a distance. Right?"

"Among other things, yes. And knowing what *we* know from our voyage—yes. It's entirely possible."

"But that brings us back to that secrecy within the crew issue. If *Phoenix* spotted the kyo, more bridge crew would have known *that.*"

"Not necessarily. Then, again, Kalmanov might have been the only one to know, and two *can* keep a secret."

Any distant signal, when no other human ship existed, when they'd already worried about pursuit, would have been reason for *Phoenix* command to panic.

Again.

The kyo had signaled with lights, and *Phoenix* had run. The kyo, rather than follow, had attacked Reunion and backed off. If they'd tried to contact the ship again, when the ship returned to Reunion, this time via com, and, once again, rather than respond, *Phoenix* had run.

Overall, a suspicious and confusing signal, even to him, and *he* was human.

There was no denying that when *Phoenix* returned, ten years later, and this time *did* respond in kind to that initial signal, the kyo had proven more than ready to talk rather than fight.

Everything would be so much simpler to figure if both Reunion and *Phoenix* weren't so dedicated to their own secrets and so obsessed with shifting blame.

Jase was the *only* one to play straight with him, but Jase had been, what? Less than fifteen when *Phoenix* first encountered the kyo ship. Jase hadn't been in a position to witness anything.

Jase was another of Ramirez' secrets. Jase was what they called one of Taylor's Children . . . born from lab-held genes, in the ship's storage. *Born* on Ramirez' order—along with Yolanda Mercheson. They'd been born on Ramirez' orders, and early in his time as senior captain, and taught, also on Ramirez' orders, a heavy course of human languages, widely varied ones.

While Ramirez was out hunting for another life-bearing world. Preparing to make contact with an alien species, or so they'd pieced together. And Jase was to be his conduit for contact.

So they believed. Chances were, they'd never know for certain, since Ramirez had spilled one secret when he died, but taken others with him.

And why in hell—if Ramirez simply wanted to contact an alien civilization—hadn't he just come back to Alpha Station in the first place? Was he that determined to work out of Reunion?

"I'm asking these things," he said to Jase, "not because I doubt anything you've told me, but to get your take on Braddock's story about Ramirez' actions back at Reunion. Is he lying?"

"I can't tell."

"The food business. Is that a lie?"

"First of all, they *had* supplies. Enough to survive long enough to effect repairs just as Braddock said they needed to do, and to get back in operation. Second, we could have taken what they had, added it to what we had, and even if they were way low, chances are we could have made it. It wouldn't have been a happy voyage. We'd all have gotten a lot leaner. But we could have made it here. The ship was designed to carry colonists. That means feeding them on the voyage. Stored food? That's for variety, not survival."

"Would the Reunioners be aware of that fact?"

"Hard to say. They're several generations removed from the

original settlers, who might well have been briefed. The fact the station here was mothballed when we arrived, the fact that everything was shut down—you'll recall we got the old machinery up and running in fairly short order, but we were never running wholly on that. Until we got the tanks functioning again, we were working solely on *Phoenix*'s own resources. We went on doing that, easily supplying our own people, while we contacted you and built a space program. Could we have prioritized differently—if we'd arrived here and found the station had been wrecked, even destroyed? Yes. We could have. It's within our capabilities. Whether the stationers understood that at the time, whether they believe it now, I don't know. Evidently not, if Ms. Williams believes the story. But we would *not* have boarded more people than we could feed—no more than this time, when we were completely surprised by the numbers. We were built, in the long ago, to be able to sustain huge numbers. Being conscious as we are of how fragile our species still is in space—we always maintain that capability. If the worst should happen here, if we can't make peace with the kyo. *Phoenix* can still run. We're not advertising that, but it can. And it will, if it comes to that. I tell you that in confidence, too."

Bren drew a long, deep breath. And was absolutely sure Jase Graham, whatever else, was telling him as much truth as he knew, regulations and rules aside. He'd bet lives on it in the past. He bet them now.

"The ship's run away twice already, and abandoned one manned station," he said. "If it should run a third time, that certainly wouldn't say anything good to the kyo."

"It's not *going* to run. *You're* going to get us out of this."

"Thanks. Thanks for the confidence."

"Trust *us*, too."

"I trust you like a brother. I somewhat trust Sabin and I have a notion what Ogun wants. I don't know Riggins."

"Ogun's man, entirely. Trained under Ogun. He'll stand by Ogun, at very least."

Split. Still. Right down the middle of the Captains' Council. And Riggins was out there in charge of the ship, which had weapons—not near what the kyo had. But tools that could be weapons.

"I'm disposed right now to make Ogun very unhappy," Bren said. "He wants Braddock turned over. And I have a strong feeling I should keep Braddock and his aides *and* Ms. Williams where I can reach them. They're the only command-level witnesses to the attacks on Reunion."

Jase smiled grimly. "Then Ogun will have to live with it, won't he? I'll give you another for free: If the kyo demand Braddock's hide, once the truth comes out, or if Prakuyo just wants payback . . . if it's between him and the rest us, *give* him to them. None of the captains will complain."

"We'll hope it doesn't come to that. A lot depends on how much I can get out of Braddock, when I talk to him. I *want* to know what, if anything, the station did to trigger that first attack. Ms. Williams claims that the second time, the kyo ship hit something. A service-bot is the popular story. Implying a misunderstanding could have triggered an attack."

Jase snorted. "Starships don't 'blunder into things.' Besides, the kyo themselves indicated they sent a slow-moving manned probe, that a fast-moving something from the station struck and exploded the probe. We know that at least one of the passengers, Prakuyo, escaped, only to be held hostage for the next six years."

That little animated sequence, part of the first real communication with the kyo, was only *one* of the questions he hoped the upcoming meetings with the kyo would clarify.

"Might some people have seen that initial explosion and that's the story that's grown up around the situation?"

"I think it a lot more likely that Braddock himself created the story to cover the fact that he fired first."

"My thoughts trend in that direction as well," Bren said. "I'll be curious to hear Braddock's story directly from him. The one thing I'm afraid we simply can't answer is whether Ramirez spooked out of Reunion mid-negotiations with the suspicion of a kyo ship on the horizon—or whether he made the cold-blooded decision to leave the instant the ship was refueled. To get out while the crew was unaware there were survivors, and maybe to come back once he had another base secure for the Reunioners to jump *to*. Maybe he read Braddock the same as you read him, and figured the promise of a new kingdom would get him to abandon the old. That plan relied on *this* station still being alive. Instead, it took ten years to get it operational, and not solely in human hands. And all the while Ramirez knew what he'd done. And when he died, the situation back at Reunion was his dying statement."

"Confession or warning, it was a hell of a thing to keep from us all these years."

More than a little bitterness colored Jase's tone. Fully justified, in Bren's opinion. But there was still something missing in the Braddock equation. Something very important. Blind ambition, the need for power, didn't wholly explain Braddock's reluctance to board. Given the conditions he claimed, it wasn't, bottom line, reasonable.

"Tell me this," he said to Jase. "And I ask because I need to understand. *Why* do you think Ogun's so very hot to bring Braddock up for trial? What does he possibly hope to gain by it? Is it that important to the crew? Does he want to stir all that up again?"

"Important to Ogun personally, maybe," Jase said. "I don't know. I don't know about the value to the crew, except as a demonstration of some sort of justice. I think Ogun's carrying a lot of anger about what happened—on Ramirez' behalf—or anger against Ramirez, I don't know. He was Ramirez' direct alternate, the way I'm Sabin's. He's the one person Ramirez might have taken into confidence. Or not. My personal suspicion is—Ramirez didn't. And Ogun had to find out with the rest of us what Ramirez had done. Ogun didn't want Sabin to go back there. But he didn't try all out to stop it, either. Maybe guilt. Maybe just wanting some reasonable explanation for why Ramirez betrayed him on such a scale. Maybe he just wants the truth out of Braddock, and wants to extract it himself, never mind Braddock couldn't possibly tell him what *Ramirez* was thinking."

"You think he's looking for a scapegoat?"

"In a word . . . yes. I'm personally not that anxious to see it happen. I don't think it'll help anybody. We need to deal with the situation that exists right now, not find someone to blame for the past."

"Granted. Still, I want to *know* the past mistakes: what happened, not necessarily why. I don't want to repeat those mistakes. I'm going in to talk to the kyo and I'm hour by hour finding out things that disturb what I thought I knew about what happened back then. I have to know: did *Phoenix* get *anything* off that station I don't know about?"

"No. And Sabin and I have personally had our hands on every file we did pull—if there was anything greatly surprising, I didn't spot it. The team blew up everything they couldn't lift. I wish we did have something on the kyo, on Ramirez, on Prakuyo's time as a hostage, beyond what we know and beyond what I've told you. We don't."

"If you think of anything, if anything occurs to you, if someone suddenly recalls something someone said ten years ago, I want to hear it. Immediately."

A short silence, then:

"Williams disturbed you. I don't think I've seen anyone do that. Not even remotely."

"I don't trust her. I don't think her connection to Braddock's operation is slight, and I find Braddock's former aide just happening to have an apartment near the section doors to be highly suspect. I read people fairly well. She's tough and she's smart, and when somebody I don't trust scrambles truth and untruth with some skill about it, I do get uneasy. The one pretense she's not that good at—is caring. She's like a mirror. She reflects the person she's talking to. Until I talked about her daughter, she didn't show any concern. I think she's taken reasonable actions to protect *herself* and protecting Irene was a byproduct. I don't think having her daughter involved with the aiji's household necessarily makes Ms. Williams our friend, and I think she'd use that association in a heartbeat to further her own position—I think perhaps she did use it to further her position in Braddock's entourage. But then—I don't always understand ship folk."

"She's not ship-folk," Jase said. "She's a generation of stationer you've never met, born to a set of rules you've never lived by. I find those rules difficult to understand at times myself. Rules are rules, no logic need be applied. The rules exist to control the station, to keep the machine running. Ship-folk, stationers, like atevi—we're born to a loyalty. Unlike atevi, there's nothing biological holding us there, only a conviction drilled into us from the time we're born, and there's no recourse if it falters. Shatter it and you shatter us. We *are* analytical people, but we don't ask questions that might disturb the people who make the decisions."

"*You* don't reflect like a mirror. *You* don't put on emotion on set cues. *Your* loyalty isn't blind."

"Mine? You mean me, personally?"

Bren nodded.

"You'd know that better than I, I suppose. But no. Certainly not consciously."

"And I can't claim I've never seen her type before, if I'm reading her correctly. Irene didn't *want* to go home, did you know that? She ran back to me, last thing before boarding, *begging* me to get her back."

"Was *that* what she asked? She wouldn't tell the boys."

"She's not her mother. I think she's fought harder than we can imagine not to *be* her mother. And if I can smooth her path to her own set of rules, I will."

"Turning some Reunioners into Mospheirans may only take a generation. Making Reunioner admin into Mospheirans may be a wholly different matter. And it won't be just Braddock and his lot who will resist."

"Damn." Bren closed his eyes, trying to shut down the analysis of yet another problem. "I *have to* detach, Jase. I have to stop thinking about it. Except as it produces information relevant to the kyo's perceptions of our collective actions. Except as it affects their intentions now."

"Of course you do. —Let it go, Bren. I'll keep the Captains' Council happy. I don't know how, but a short recitation of *Don't disturb Bren Cameron right now* may be reasonably effective. Stay away from Braddock. Don't engage with him."

"I have to."

"You *don't* know the technicals that can sift truth from untruth. Give *me* access. Give me the questions you'd ask him. I'm sure Ogun and Sabin can amplify them. I can judge the technicals he can throw out, and if I can't, they can. And I agree, I *promise*: he stays continually in atevi hands, until you say otherwise."

"Best offer I've had, I suppose."

"I'll relay your assessment of Williams, by your leave. There may be more questions for her, as well."

"I'll clear you with Geigi, and with atevi security. You *might* debrief also with the Guild Observers. Your ability to explain to them would take another load off my mind." He'd understood as much as he needed to, regarding the kids, who were underfoot, and the rest of human politics, which was going to be Gin's job, not his. "You might talk to Williams for a start, go in dressed atevi-style, court dress, the whole business."

"She'll recognize me."

"I don't doubt. But if you speak to her in that capacity, she *might* see you as different than other ship-humans, and say things she might not say otherwise."

"She might," Jase said. "She *might* be a little confused as to what I am, and where the relationships run, considering where she is. Which is only to the good. I'll consult. But you leave that to me for now, friend."

That word. That uniquely human word Jase used consciously, by choice. *Our* relationship. Lateral, not hierarchical, nor part of any hierarchy.

He wasn't used to that. He'd become less and less certain how he could relate to it. Trust me to make decisions, Jase meant. Trust those decisions.

He nodded. "Appreciated. I do trust you."

"Sabin asks how ready you are for this."

"On one level, as ready as I can be. On another, I don't know enough, haven't thought enough, haven't prepared enough. But some things I'm *only* going to get when I actually have to deal with our visitors."

"We'll do the rest," Jase said. "And by the way—a note from just before I came down here— Gin Kroger's told the senior captain she's about to address the Reunioners."

That had to be done. On a fairly urgent priority.

"I'll send you the clip, when it's available. Likely she will. Likely Geigi will. But just to be sure. And don't worry about it. Other people can handle these things. Even the whole planet. Just let us. We'll work things out. Got it?"

"Got it," he said. He had to smile a little. He knew his failings. Jase left, and he didn't have the responsibility anymore.

Not for Braddock. Not for Williams. Not for Irene. Not for any of the kids.

He had, for now, only one problem, inward bound . . . still inward bound. He had notifications of every message cycle. And his notifications had faithfully continued, he found, even with the handoff to Mospheiran Central.

Gin had seen to it.

7

"*This is Virginia Kroger, your new stationmaster. Many of you recall my previous tour on Alpha Station as we set up mining and manufacturing. Others of you will recall me as technical advisor on the recovery mission to Reunion. So I trust I am not, to most of you, a stranger.*

"*I am up here by appointment of Shawn Tyers, the President of Mospheira, to take command of Mospheiran station operations, not just during the kyo visit, but for a time afterward. I shall be cooperating with ship command, with the atevi stationmaster, Lord Geigi; and with the special delegation sent by the aiji in Shejidan. This is the same delegation which met the kyo at Reunion and peacefully secured the release of the entire Reunion population.*

"*I have every confidence in the delegation's ability to handle the current situation.*

"*It is not likely that the kyo visit will have any impact on the ordinary citizens of the planet, or on ordinary citizens aboard this station. But because we wish to avoid any accidental false signal, we are asking everybody aboard to be patient, do their jobs, follow established routine, and, above all, not to attempt to view our guests or seek any contact with them.*

"*We will do our best to keep you informed on this historic visit, within the limits of courtesy to our visitors. As you may understand, our energies have to be concentrated on the visit itself, and progress at first may be slow. Once we do have solid*

*information, we shall be forthcoming. You should know, offi-
cially, that this visit is a planned event, called for in our first
meeting. We met them originally in their territory. Now they
meet us in ours. Our visitors are here, we hope, to see that we
are as peaceful as we assured them we are.*

"We are aware that the status of Reunioner residents regarding station residency remains a question, and that this also
underlies recent disturbance on the station. We believe that a
year is far too long to have had this uncertainty going on. The
simple truth is, I can't fix everything this week, and some
things will necessarily be delayed as long as we have kyo visitors to deal with, but I promise you I'm already working on a
resolution, and Reunioners will see some immediate improvement in conditions, starting this hour.

"I do regret to say a small number of individuals attached
to the former Reunion administration have been apprehended
and charged with actions against public safety and with attempted kidnapping of the children who lately visited the
planet. Until we are sure we have identified and apprehended
all individuals involved in this attempt, we are maintaining
security at its current level.

"To explain definitively what happened and why, I offer the
following. Atevi authorities received an appeal for help from
one of the children. Atevi personnel moved to intervene, and
to arrest the individuals responsible. Reunion citizens were
told that there was a lock malfunction. This was a ruse covering the rescue of the children and their families and their removal to a safe place on the atevi side of the station. Atevi
authorities notified the President of Mospheira and the ship
authorities during the operation, cooperated fully with the ship
during the operation itself, and there is a consensus of all governments, first, that the atevi were within treaty rights, and
acted correctly, for the protection of the children, who have
been, since their visit to the planet, under the protection of the
atevi government. Secondly, the three governments agree that

Mospheiran and Reunion territory on the station should re-main separated for the next number of days, until a thorough investigation has been completed.

"This is for the safety of all individuals aboard the station. We have reason to suspect organization behind the recent riots and unrest linked to the individuals already in custody. To this end, we have set up a task force that will be both a clearing house for any information, and a source of protection for any who feel threatened. Contact information for this task force will follow.

"This does not mean a policy of perpetual confinement of Reunion citizens. It means protection of both Reunioner and Mospheiran citizens, both to be treated equally under the law, and neither should want for supplies or reasonable living con-ditions while we work out a better arrangement than we have. By authority of the President of Mospheira, I declare there is one human authority aboard this station, and I promise it will be evenhanded and fair to both Reunioners and Mospheirans. We have enough supply of food and necessities. Where we lack, we will get enough. And where there is unemployment, there will be, within the next few days and even before the kyo visit has concluded, jobs offered to Reunioners, within the Re-unioner areas, with station credit attached. We will be needing everything from manual labor to organizational skills to achieve our goal of better living conditions for everyone.

"To begin to make those changes, I am asking that Reunion citizens in each section and each residential block choose rep-resentatives. These will meet within the next few days, regard-less of activities involving the kyo visit. By secret ballot, these representatives will choose a director in whom they have con-fidence. This director will meet with me and with other Mos-pheiran officers, to work out a schedule for repair within the three sections, to appoint leaders for the construction, deal with resident representatives, and to work out an orderly pro-cedure for reopening the section doors.

"In the meantime, I am ordering Central to restore vid channels to Reunion sections, and to restore Reunioner com service to Central, so that residents can report any emergencies or problems in their areas. We will be working on full restoration of com service throughout.

"Among early priorities will be improvement of services to areas of deficiency, whether in the Reunion or the Mospheiran sections.

"In regard to the children removed from the Reunioner sections—the three the atevi government has declared under its protection, and one closely associated with them—the President of Mospheira will oblige the atevi government by providing a safe haven on Earth for them and their immediate families, as soon as the details can be arranged.

"Matters currently under discussion on Mospheira include a lottery for a limited number of Reunioner citizens to gain residency on Mospheira, to provide a constructive link between Reunion folk and Mospheirans in general. This is a very exciting and unique opportunity. We are all human. We have a great deal to teach each other, from our vastly different experience apart. It will be a case of signing up as individuals or families, and your names being drawn. There will be a limited number of such slots, a number flexible only in the sense that families will not be separated. Individuals and families who are chosen in that lottery will receive settlement assistance, including a residence and financial support during the first year. There will be emergency return for any persons who prove medically unable to adjust. I'll provide more detail about the operation as we work it out.

"Now let me speak to the Mospheirans under my administration. We will be developing a new program for freight handling that will free down-bound shuttle space for passenger seats and decrease turnaround time for the shuttles. While up-bound seats will always remain scarce, and, excepting emergencies, may require six months to a year on a wait-list, this *does give us a little more latitude for personnel who may wish to leave the station, particularly those who would wish to retire or leave the program. Such applications, however, necessarily depend on an extensive building campaign for unmanned heavy freight landers. I can promise you that jobs will not be lacking in Mospheiran areas, either.*

"I will provide a written copy of this message on the system, under my office information, and vid will re-run this message at the midpoint of every shift.

"I am delighted to be your director. My last tour of duty here was a time of building and progress. I hope to equal or exceed that record. I am confident of the stability of our food production. I am confident of supply. I am confident of the programs we are instituting, including the building of a Mospheiran shuttle fleet. I am extremely confident that we will pass the meeting with our kyo neighbors and get on about our own business.

"Thank you."

The screen returned to regular business, the schedules. News. Music.

A *lottery.*

Brilliant, Bren thought. A possible benefit . . . and a scarcity of seats.

A pilot program . . . random enough in selection to give a decent idea how Reunioners would adapt to the world; and generous enough to get attention.

A year's living. Safety. Reunioners couldn't even imagine living on a planet. If they were rounded up, forced aboard a shuttle, brought down to an open sky and inverse curvatures, told they had no choice—they'd do the human thing: panic and object.

Told there was limited seating and only the lucky few could *win* a ticket?

Absolutely brilliant.

There'd be sign-ups. At least enough to fill shuttle seats.

Enough for a small community here, a small neighborhood there.

Good reports from below would lure more takers into the next lottery.

If it went well, they'd have people clamoring for more and more lottery slots.

Diminishing the number of Reunioners aloft lessened the pressure up here.

Gin had it all under control. Or was headed there.

He sat staring blankly at the screen, at the channel that repeated endlessly, scrolling information past.

A message flashed up.

From Jase.

I've gotten into the recovered records. The only record on Inez Williams is that of her boarding with her daughter. She is listed as "clerical" and skills include "records officer."

It actually would tally with Williams' story about helping organize after the disaster . . . if one had a remote clue what a records officer did.

Lists no surviving kin. That's not uncommon, sadly so. Families that emerged completely intact from the kyo strike are less than ten percent of the Reunioner population. I'll keep the inquiry going, but I don't think we're going to find more on Williams. No surprises with Braddock. No surprises with his assistants. They are what we knew they were.

Brutal fact. The whole kyo encounter was a situation without remedy—it was what it was. There could be no "justice" where Braddock was concerned. Not for his decisions while in command of the station. Two species had gotten afoul of each other. Response had been extreme. People had died.

It wasn't the first time, and if they'd learned nothing else dealing with the atevi: why mattered. Why had the kyo fired on the station? Not the second time. The *first* time.

Mistaken identity?

Retaliation for a perceived wrong?

Wrong moves from the station?

Or simply a set of motives so far afield from human or atevi that they were never, ever going to make sense?

Even as he reassured himself that communication with the kyo was not only possible, but actively desired, he had cold moments of asking himself why, and what if, and exactly *who* he had been dealing with at Reunion.

In answer to that, he had the image of Prakuyo an Tep—which part was name, or title, or personal name, he never had figured out. An image of Prakuyo an Tep sitting quietly, gray, massive, immensely strong, sharing dainty teacakes with an atevi child.

Prakuyo an Tep, whose face showed no expressions that a human could read. But then—atevi could be as unexpressive. Sometimes. When they didn't trust a situation, didn't approve, or didn't want to commit to it. It was a control every paidhi had had to learn and one Bren found difficult to drop in recent days.

He wasn't sure Prakuyo an Tep's face even had muscles that delivered the full range of expression humans and atevi could exchange. Bone seemed to lie very close to the skin. Prakuyo had been quite thin, after six years of incarceration, but the other kyo they'd met had had a similar boniness about the face. The gray skin was crossed with wrinkles below the chin, around the mouth and eyes, and, very faintly, on cheeks and brow. The skin itself was interesting: normally smoothly gray as fine polished leather, sometimes showing a dark gray freckling, a web work that came and went. Was *that* emotion? A blush? A circulatory surge? Or a color change wrought by the skin itself?

The eyes blinked, the nostrils worked, the mouth moved. But the freckling appeared in moments of heightened attention. And once, once with what might have been a laugh. The kyo made resounding booms. Thumps. Was it laughter? Humming . . . that might have been sorrow.

So many differences. Individually, Prakuyo an Tep read as a gentle fellow, a reasonable fellow, understanding kindness, responding to sweet flavors, reassured by a child's innocence and curiosity . . .

But what in *hell* had made the kyo ship, which had blasted thousands of hapless humans into oblivion—send in some of its people? And after a human ambush of the kyo shuttle, with at least one of their own unaccounted for—what had made them sit out there for six years, waiting?

What feeling let Prakuyo an Tep, after enduring six years in a cage—gently respond to an atevi child?

Were they one and the same kind of decision? Did it make sense, that behavior? Were they that patient—after having run in and blown hell out of the station in the first place?

And the other side of the equation—what was the mentality of a Reunioner administrator—having suffered that devastating attack—who then sat pat and played power games with the only ship that could get him and his people out of there?

Williams' account might have made some sense of Braddock's refusal to board—if Braddock hadn't resisted removal a second time when the ship, under Sabin, came back for them.

Had Braddock been that certain he could get the ship to accept conditions?

As a negotiator, it was essential to his own job to calculate both sides of a chessboard.

Jase chided him for involving himself in the Reunioner situation. Jase was taking steps, researching records, dealing with Braddock as a human problem.

But the fact was, Braddock's actions were wound intricately into the kyo-human contact. The question remained *why* Braddock had done what he had done—twice. That *why* was a human problem. That *why* didn't matter for the kyo negotiations ahead . . .

Why didn't matter.

But it did matter . . . in order to find out *what*. What happened had happened because of *whys* on both sides. On one hand, the kyo did things they couldn't explain logically, because they didn't yet have the kyo logic upon which to base the actions. On the other, they had a human administrator and a senior captain who'd done things they *could* explain, based on human logic, but which of the multiple options actually applied was dependent on a relationship they couldn't figure, because one of the principal players was dead.

Maybe Jase was wrong. Maybe Braddock had acted for two different reasons, similar but different, that just happened to manifest in the same way. The first time made no sense, unless Braddock had been as ignorant of the food capability of the ship as Williams. But logic would suggest he'd have expressed that fear to Ramirez and Ramirez would have set him straight.

Which depended on him believing Ramirez, which in turn depended on him *wanting* to believe Ramirez, which would put them right back to Jase's assessment of Braddock's motives.

The second time . . . maybe after rebuilding and surviving with the situation for over ten years, Braddock had thought he'd won, that *his* station was going to survive. That any proposal to dismantle it and destroy all that work was insane.

Maybe Braddock had just spent too much, tried too hard, believed too much in himself and had no faith at all in the ship's captains . . . who, one had to admit, had run out on him.

Braddock had convinced himself the kyo ship sitting in the system for six years was an unmanned drone. Maybe Braddock had had his own notions of making a crazy, silent peace with the kyo—in which light he might have blamed the ship for actions that, in his eyes, had brought the kyo back and started the whole problem.

Phoenix had come back, renewing its order to evacuate, after the Reunioners' ten years of work and survival. From Braddock's point of view—possibly—the ship's presence might stir up the kyo again, who'd sat there peaceably and might be, eventually, approachable.

Or maybe Braddock had no trust of anything the ship wanted. No confidence, first, that he wasn't still, directly or indirectly, dealing with Ramirez . . . and secondly, not trusting the ship's motives with or without Ramirez.

Bren rubbed his temples, trying to think. Playing both sides of the chessboard had its drawbacks . . . one of which was that one might give a scoundrel *far* too much credit for good motives.

But it also, when overlaid on reality, pointed up where the problems lay in a given scenario. And primary among questions was the character of Braddock himself—trying to lay hands on four kids who could affect the relationship between ship-folk and atevi, making moves toward breaching those doors and possibly taking over the station—what had such a man done, regarding the kyo? Ramirez had been in command in the first encounter with the kyo. Braddock had commanded the second and third—the attacks and the actual face-to-face contact, once they'd taken Prakuyo.

Ramirez had died with *his* secrets. They'd get no more from him.

Which left Braddock.

So you were the leader of a trapped population who'd found out the kyo were barreling down on their new location—what *wouldn't* you do? What line *wouldn't* you cross, to make sure your people survived?

Spacers *could* make decisions that, to planet-dwellers, ran counter to instinct and emotion. Jase, in his turn, had been shocked . . . at the way planet-dwellers made decisions that could risk three men to save one. Irresponsible, Jase had called it: *emotional decision* had a bad connotation in his world. One always had to remember that, at some critical moment, he and Jase might not decide the same.

And maybe from Braddock's view, what *did* scaring hell out of four kids and their families weigh, against a ship that could do what it had done at Reunion and kill all of them?

Bottom line, Braddock didn't trust the captains any more than they trusted him. That relationship had gone poisonous long before any of this had happened.

Jase said that the ship could have gotten all the survivors off Reunion and back to Alpha—maybe with very short rations, but Jase believed they could have made it—and that was probably true.

The ship, under Ramirez, had indeed arrived at Alpha, at a mothballed station, without supplies or fuel. And they might *still* have been all right with what was there if they'd been carrying passengers. But because they *hadn't* had thousands of half-starved people to take care of, they'd been able to work that much faster, with no shortages. No internal politics slowing every decision. They'd made quick, autocratic deals with the aishidi'tat. Deals with Mospheira. The station had gone back into food production and building, and had no trouble gaining population, refueling the ship, keeping it and the station in good order.

The ship was everything to the ship-folk. The station—any station—had importance, but only in relation to the ship. That part he had gotten from Jase, very clearly.

Ramirez had died, command had shifted down the chain, and Ogun, *very* reluctantly, had let Sabin go back to Reunion. For what *precise* mission? He wasn't sure he'd ever heard the plain truth on that, and he'd *been* there.

The Captains' Council had been split and angry for years.

Ogun's position was not to disturb whatever was left at Reunion. Possibly Ogun himself had been in the dark as to what that was. Nobody to this hour was admitting anything, and Jase, close as he was to the situation, couldn't figure who had known what, either.

It boiled down to one person who *was* an outside witness. One person Ogun had wanted in *his* hands . . . for whatever reason.

He sent a message to Jase, personally, in Ragi. *One regrets, but one cannot exempt Braddock-nadi from questions. What I wish to know does not regard technical matters, but time, perceptions, and actions, which are relevant to the kyo mind. The*

*answers will involve more than words. I must see the answers
he gives. I shall apprise you of all these matters. Forgive me. It
is not lack of trust or confidence, and one asks you follow with
your own inquiry, but I must satisfy a constellation of my own
questions.*

Jase would not be offended. He was sure of that.

What Ogun and Sabin might be was another matter. But he
was not negotiating with ship command. Not on this.

No, he was not going to go into a conversation with the kyo
without accessing every resource he had.

And Braddock was top of the list.

8

Tea in mani's sitting room, a very subdued tea, compared to those they'd shared on Earth, for one thing *because* it was mani's sitting room (though mani was not present), but also because, Cajeiri thought, *Bjorn* was with them. Bjorn had not been part of the association on Earth, and besides being oldest, Bjorn had had to argue with his father just to come to tea. Maybe, Cajeiri thought, that was what made him sit so worried and quiet.

He had invited them, with mani's permission. He had gone down the hall and brought them himself, hoping they would talk more freely without their parents on the edge of the conversation, but Bjorn had turned glum and the others were clearly uncomfortable and making small talk around him. The three who had been his guests asked after Boji, asked after staff and people they knew, all such things as he could answer, and Bjorn just sat in silence that grew less and less comfortable, staring into his teacup, taking only an occasional sip, ignoring the nice teacakes.

The others talked in Ragi—they were here to talk in Ragi, and it seemed wrong to talk ship-speak in mani's sitting room; but for the most part they generally used little words, words surely Bjorn remembered, careful to keep it simple. At one point Gene directly asked Bjorn if he understood, and Bjorn said he heard. He knew.

He'd missed them, he said then in ship-speak, and looked a little wistful.

"Why don't you just tell him?" Artur asked, likewise in ship-speak.

"Tell him what?" Irene asked.

Tell him. There were secrets the boys knew and Irene did not, and Bjorn just sat there staring at his teacup, not even looking at them. Cajeiri had no idea how to deal with this different Bjorn. He had been hopeful when Bjorn had argued with his father to come with them. He had hoped this visit would help bring Bjorn back to them, but so far it was just . . . awkward.

"Bjorn?" Artur said, but Bjorn just set his cup aside, and said, in ship-speak, that he thought he should go back to his parents, that his father was upset and would upset Geigi's staff.

That much, Cajeiri followed.

"Antaro," Cajeiri said, with a nod. "Go with Bjorn."

"Yes," Antaro said, and Bjorn got up, said quietly, "I'm sorry. Artur,—my father's not—" There were words Cajeiri missed, involving, it seemed, Bjorn's reason, and his troubles with his parents.

Antaro stood ready to escort him. And without a bow, without any courtesy, Bjorn just went to the door, looked back at them with still no courtesy, looked at Antaro, and left into the hall. In a moment the outer door opened and shut, and they all sat in silence.

"He regrets," Artur said then in a hushed voice. "His father has trouble. His father took papers. Gave to people so Bjorn can study."

"So Bjorn can have a tutor," Gene said. "Bjorn's father took papers from his company, gave papers to a company here so Bjorn can have a tutor. Bjorn is scared. He thinks his father is in trouble. And his father always gets sick when Bjorn says no."

Bjorn's father had had heart trouble on the ship, Cajeiri remembered that. Bjorn's father had been with the ship-folk physicians for several days. But Bjorn had said he was all right after that.

Was he not all right, now? Was he still sick?

"Nand' Siegi might visit him," Cajeiri said.

"Atevi upset him," Gene said, and added, "We think he gets upset so Bjorn stay."

One began to understand. "But Bjorn's father is truly ill."

"*Maybe,*" Gene said.

"Bjorn *wanted* to go down with us," Artur said. "But he says now . . . Irene, translate for me."

Artur talked. They all listened, and Irene frowned and said:

"Bjorn says—he is almost grown up. Four years and he is adult. And he cannot make his father different. But he wants to make good place for his mother. He told Artur he wants to keep his study, but also keep association. Always keep. He learns this station. He learns Mospheira. Someday—he may be on the station, may be on the planet, but he will associate with us, help us, help you, Jeri-ji. He is grateful and he is embarrassed. One does not know what he will do, but future time, all time, he is our associate. He wants to say this to you, not to nand' Bren. He is scared for his father, thinks maybe he is sick. He protects his mother. He wants to keep association with us."

"Man'chi," he said. It suddenly, to him, seemed very simple. He realized he was fortunate in his own parents, in mani, in nand' Bren, in all his associations—they were all strong, strong enough to protect *him* when he had needed it and strong enough to protect themselves. But for all his angry shouting, Bjorn's father was not strong, and his mother was not. Her man'chi held her to Bjorn's father, both of them weaker than Bjorn. Gene's mother let Gene run free, and worry about her only a little. Artur's parents worried, but they were strong. Bjorn's parents were constantly pulling at him, and Bjorn could not leave them as they were and walk away. That was not the character Bjorn had, right now, though ultimately, when things were more settled and his mother was safe—it might be different.

"One understands," he said. "He will join us when he can and help when he can. Tell him we said so, Arte-ji. We understand. And he will still be our associate. He gets a pin. Tell him that. Make him understand."

There was a map in his little office at home, and they knew exactly what he was talking about. It had colored pins for every associate he had gained, each in their geographical place. He was not sure right now where he would have to put this one. It would be a separate color from the other three, perhaps. And he was not sure whether it would be somewhere on Mospheira, or on the station. He was going to have to get a new map for that, if it was the station.

But that pin was going to be there both to call on and to take care of—no matter how many years.

9

"**G**od. It's the traitor." Braddock had definitely aged in the last two years—lost weight, lost hair. He'd had, once upon a time, an angry, forceful presence. Now . . . delivered by Lord Geigi's security into a small room near the detention center, he looked uncertain. Angry, perhaps. But not like the man who'd stood off kyo and *Phoenix* alike. "I figured it'd be Sabin. But it's *you.*"

Bren held the seat at the end of the table. Banichi and Jago stood behind him, Tano and Algini held the doorway. In a room full of Guild, there was no sense of threat.

Besides, violence had never been Braddock's personal choice.

"Mr. Braddock," Bren said, gesturing at the chair at the other end. "Please. Sit down."

"You're responsible for *all* this," Braddock said, attempting to take the offensive. "*Your* people arrested me, your people and that Taylor upstart. What does *Sabin* say about it?"

Bren put on a pleasant expression. "Tea, sir?" And in Ragi, "Tano-ji, two cups."

There was a service on the sideboard, utilitarian, plastic. And prepared. Tano moved.

Braddock dropped into the chair at the other end of the table. "Skip the courtesies. What the hell do you want?"

Tano set a cup in front of Bren, provided another in front of Braddock, who swayed away, sending Tano an uneasy look. Bren picked his up and took a sip. Braddock pushed his away.

"I'm wondering," Bren said, setting down his cup, "what you actually hoped to do, in moving closer to the section seal."

"Who's asking? *Sabin*?"

"Do you have some lingering quarrel with Captain Sabin?"

A flicker of thought, perhaps reconsideration. "What do *you* think?"

Bren gave a gentle shrug. "*I* authorized the move to sweep up your group. It wasn't Captain Sabin. Captain Graham, who was the captain of record at the time, simply provided reinforcement, primarily to reassure the Reunioners with a human presence—and keep ship's authority involved. But I'm here because you've managed to cross the plans of the man who rules most of the planet down there, and you're verging on alienating the President of Mospheira, which is not to anyone's great benefit. I represent both in taking that action. I'm here, now, to explain the situation to you, and to give you a chance to recharacterize your actions, *maybe* to start over. That chance won't always be available. But Ms. Williams offered some information that might cast your actions in a better light. So I thought I'd ask you personally, at least, just to satisfy the record. My attention is fairly well occupied by the visitors approaching us. But I can spare enough time to figure out whether there *is* any reasonable explanation for what split the ship and Reunion. I met Ramirez, though briefly. I understand you and he didn't get along."

All along, that constant flicker of thoughts darting this way and that, a frown that grew darker.

"Who the hell *are* you?"

"We've also met, briefly."

"I know your name. That doesn't tell me who you are. *What* you are. Why you and these—" His gaze swept the room at an overwhelming atevi presence. "These *people* have any say in how this station runs."

Interesting view. Like Lord Topari, Braddock was having a little trouble with that word *people*. But then—Braddock's ancestors had departed this station when humans alone had run it, and back then, the ancient human Pilots' Guild had been in charge.

"Because, Mr. Braddock, humans never owned the planet, and human residents abandoned this station to go down to the planet shortly after you left. When the ship came back—*humans* didn't have the resources to get back to space. Atevi did. Atevi graciously *share* their planet with humans. They graciously *share* the station with humans, who until very lately used atevi shuttles to reach it. The atevi government very graciously transported humans back up here, and both nations of the planet jointly run this station. A treaty binds the Mospheiran government and the atevi government to share equally in that operation. Mospheira had a recent problem with Mr. Tillington, who wanted to believe he had more authority than his position warranted, but now the President of Mospheira has replaced Mr. Tillington, with instructions for the new stationmaster to fix what Mr. Tillington tried very hard to break. As for who I am—in the polite sense of your reasonable question—I speak for the atevi government, where they have to deal with outsiders. And I speak for outsiders where they have to deal with the atevi government. I've also been granted a fair amount of power to propose and dispose—so that things don't *annoy* the atevi government. The ship—is the ship. It docks here. The ship is the *guest* of the two governments of the world. Forget the balance of powers that prevailed here when your ancestors and mine were last on this deck together. That's ancient history, sir. This station is *not* governed by the Pilots' Guild *or* by the ship. So believe me when I say it is possible for you to have a fresh start here. You are not now dealing with the ship. You're dealing with an atevi official, who is asking you who *you* are."

"This is *our* station."

"No. It isn't. It contains a part of a station humans built, then abandoned, centuries ago, a part in which you were clearly not pleased to be contained. And you are not now in the hands of your own government, or even of the Mospheiran government. The ship *is* asking you be handed over. I can do that, if that would make you more comfortable. It would certainly make Captain Ogun happy. Or you can become accustomed to atevi presence for the rest of your life."

That was *not*, perhaps, what Louis Baynes Braddock had expected. Not in the least, from his sullen glance about the room, the uneasy shift in his seat, what he wanted.

Though admittedly, a contingent of Assassins' Guild on watch were not a lighthearted and encouraging presence.

"I won't say that the people behind you are my *friends*, Mr. Braddock, because that word doesn't translate in any sense that leads to good places. But four of them are my *family* in every good sense—I live with them, we take care of each other, we laugh, and we *trust* each other absolutely. Whether you can envision that for yourself—I don't know. You don't look as if you even believe it's possible. And that's a problem, sir. It really may be a problem you can't overcome."

The sullen look had cracked, given way to a general pallor. Braddock's hand curved around the cup, turned it, turned it. Maybe he was thinking of some entirely foolish move with it. Perhaps it was just the only source of warmth.

"Are you afraid, sir? I assure you—you're in a *different* place, where things will always be *different*. No one will harm you, granted you don't try to harm anyone, yourself. But to be happy, sir, you do need to accept that things will be different."

No answer. No answer at all. And no happiness, either.

"Here's my point, sir, and please listen to this very carefully. *Mospheirans* are different from you, too. Mospheirans are *not* the people you left here. They're not the rebels. They're not the colonists. They're people who've adapted to life here, and changed themselves in ways that will probably startle you more than atevi will startle you, because your tendency will be to *assume* they're like you. They're not. And you, and your entire group of survivors, are a very small number compared to the population of Mospheira. You wouldn't even constitute one small town, and Mospheira has cities, large cities, which vastly outnumber the population of this station. So believe me when I say adapting to people who look very different from you at least gives you fair warning that there will be differences . . . but adapting to get along with Mospheirans—as ultimately you must—means understanding that there will be differences between you and people that look just like you."

"Don't lecture me."

"I do apologize, then, for disturbing you. I'll leave you in peace. But I do hope you'll give it some thought. *You* aren't going to change things. *I* might. But that's your choice."

"You want something from me."

"Not if I can't trust you, sir, and I don't think I can. I have other things on my mind, and I'd better go back to them, since this appears to be a mutual waste of time."

"You're going to try to meet with the aliens."

"Yes."

"I gave us a chance," Braddock said. "And I was damned *right*. I found out what Ramirez was up to. I tried to stop him and he ran off and did it anyway. *We* paid for it."

"Now I'm interested." He set his arms on the table. "*What* was Ramirez up to?"

"The ship was set up from its origins to find life. It's got equipment the station didn't have. I got word that Ramirez had found a living world—not just living, but advanced. How advanced—he apparently wasn't sure."

"Timeline," he asked Braddock. "When and how did you hear, relative to the first attack on the station?"

"Prior to the ship's last trip out. The story got to me. I called him. I wanted to ask him about it. He was aboard the ship . . . he never left it but briefly. He declined to come to my office. He pulled all personnel back aboard immediately."

"All ship's personnel."

"Everybody."

"Who told you the story?"

A frown. A hesitation. "A doctor. Who heard it from a patient. Who died."

"Natural causes?"

"Heart attack. One of Ramirez' senior science staff— collapsed in an eatery—on our side. The ship wanted him back. He was critical and the doctor attending didn't want to shift him. The man talked about aliens, about going there—crazy-sounding stuff, how they suspected they had a find, they were going after it and the crew couldn't know what they were into. He didn't want to go there. He didn't want the ship to go." Braddock took a large gulp of tea, likely tepid, and set the cup down. "Ship's security showed up while the doctor was working on the man. Tried to pull him out. Station security sent for me. I came down there. I talked to the doctor, tried to talk to the man, but he wasn't able to talk."

It was interesting information. It fit what he already believed about the ship's activities. Braddock's account was not guaranteed to be completely accurate on any point. But it could be.

He waited.

"Ramirez," Braddock said, "wanted his man back before he died. I said there were medical reasons not to transfer him and I wanted Ramirez to come to my office, that I had some things to discuss. Ramirez didn't answer. Next I knew he'd issued a general board call with no warning, nothing. He just ordered everybody back aboard, and then backed the ship out of dock and left with *no* word where he was going. But he'd taken on fuel. He was out and away and there was nothing we could do about it. Ramirez' man—I tried to talk to him. But he wasn't capable of talking. Dead within hours. And the ship was gone."

If the truth, this information implied that Ramirez was *returning* to the system where he ended up triggering the entire chain of events. He'd been there, checked out the planet from the far reaches of the system, come back to refuel, then returned for a close-up investigation—maybe made urgent by the fear that one of his technical people had spilled what he was up to. Urgency—might have pushed him too fast, too far.

That move of *Phoenix* back to its discovery might well have set off alarms within any self-protective species . . . assuming the kyo had been tracking the human presence prior to that incident. How far into the system had he penetrated before the kyo ship signaled him?

"We just carried on waiting for *Phoenix* to come back." Braddock continued. "And no, I didn't spread the news about—I swore the medical team to secrecy. A year and two hundred eighty-two days after that—the aliens showed up. That's what we know. That's all we know. But it doesn't take a genius to add two and two. Ramirez went where he wasn't wanted and they retaliated. They came in, they blew up a mining craft, which tipped us off to their presence. We received the final transmission from the miner, scanned the area, and saw the ship, coming fast. I wasn't in Central when it happened. Central reported it was *Phoenix* on an out-of-control entry hitting the miner, but when they reported the velocity, I knew it wasn't *Phoenix*. *Phoenix* would never enter the system on that trajectory, precisely because of the mining operations, and its speed was . . . frankly, it was terrifying. We tried to talk to it. We instructed another miner craft to flash lights. Got back on the lag it had already been blown to hell as well. We tried to signal with the station lights—and they opened fire on us."

That was a suspect datum. The kyo's initial attempts to communicate via flashing lights was something the station had witnessed in their own encounter at Reunion. Braddock might be trying to embellish his own account, might be trying to take credit for that ultimately successful method, not realizing that the kyo had tried to contact Ramirez via that means long before it made that run at Reunion.

"Let me get this straight. *Two* mining craft were destroyed."

"At least two. Deliberately."

"Ms. Williams said the kyo ship hit them. Accidentally."

"Ms. Williams was never in a position to know. They were not on intersecting vectors."

"How again did you signal?"

"You're asking this because that ship's coming."

"I'm asking because it seems useful to ask someone who was in charge of Reunion's actions prior to the attack exactly what those actions were. Yes, it's still coming."

"We tried everything," Braddock snapped bitterly. "Frequencies up and down the range. Flashing lights. They ignored us, just kept coming in. *Fast.* I ordered the collision alarm, not because I thought it was going to hit us, but because I knew what it could be, and what had most likely happened to those miners."

Collision alarm meant get to small spaces, padded spaces, places to survive. So Braddock credited himself with the fact there *were* survivors.

It could be true. Such a general warning, if given, had to come from Central. And if Braddock had been there, he would have been the official in charge, the one who had to make the call.

"I'm at a point of decision, Mr. Braddock. I'm going to have to speak to the kyo. It's very likely the individual I'll be dealing with is the one you held hostage for six years. I'd like to avoid any mistakes that may have happened between you and them. Is there *anything* you did in that initial encounter that you wish you hadn't done?"

A lengthy silence. A grim scowl. "You think I haven't asked myself that?"

"I imagine you have. And what you know could be useful now."

"First of all I wish I'd known it wasn't *Phoenix* first off. I wish we'd had those two minutes back. I wish I'd given that collision alarm sooner. I wish I'd known it was going to fire specifically on section eight so I could have told everybody in that area to get the hell out and seal the doors. It's what I *wish*.

But *wishing* is damned useless. They came in on the attack. They hit us the way they'd hit those miner craft—with no transmission, no warning."

"Then they stopped."

Braddock took in a deep breath.

"You said frequencies up and down the range. So you tried to talk to them."

"Hell, yes. Didn't do damn much good, did it?"

"What did you say to them—exactly, what did you say?"

"They were plowing through debris of our mining craft! We told them to stop."

"Exact wording."

"How the hell do you expect me to remember?"

"It would be useful. You might well have said something that, to their ears, sounded like a challenge. I'd very much like to avoid those words. Now what, *exactly*, did you say?"

Braddock shook his head. "'Who are you?' or 'What are you?' I can't remember! I know I said 'Stop.' A lot."

None of those words sounded remotely like what he knew of kyo speech. God only knew what it had sounded like, if they'd even been able to hear it. They'd at least have noted there'd been a transmission.

"And they did stop."

"After blowing a hole in the station!"

"They stopped attacking," Bren said. "The question is why. What happened then?"

"They left. Disappeared."

"And then Ramirez returned."

"Too damned late. And then refused any responsibility."

"He did, however, offer an escape. *Why* didn't you want people evacuated when Ramirez came back?"

"Put every survivor into the hands of the hard-headed fool who created the problem? A fool who hadn't either the intelligence to realize or courage to admit he created that problem? Board that ship with *maybe* enough rations to get back to a station we had no proof still existed? Trust Ramirez even meant to take us there? For two hundred years ship command has been telling us there was no signal out of Alpha and now we're supposed to take everyone out of Reunion where we've got a chance to survive and go kiting off to Alpha in the hope we'd find something we could put back together before we ran out of supplies—at which point, who do you *think* would become the expendables? I told Ramirez: help us put things back together, give us an assist to rebuild our supply, and we'll send some people with you so you can go find out what's at Alpha. Ramirez agreed, but wanted to refuel first—fine. I trusted that lying bastard. I had to. And he left us. He just *left* us."

Assist in rebuilding. Manpower for the massive numbers destroyed in the attack.

"What about protection? Weren't you concerned about the kyo?"

"I told you, the aliens had disappeared. They'd retaliated for whatever Ramirez had done and left. There was no sense in running, so long as Ramirez stopped pushing where he didn't damn well belong."

Disappeared, or gone back to lurking. And the possibility still existed that Ramirez worried that ship was out there and knew the ship had no weapons to compare with whatever had slagged a whole section of the station.

"Did Ramirez say anything about them still being in the system?"

"Ramirez said a lot of things. They could have been. They could have been following *him*, for what we knew, watching *him*. It didn't encourage us to want to go out on a ship that could be a target."

"So, *Phoenix* left and you rebuilt. Mined. And then, four years later, the kyo came back."

"Yes."

"So, how did you first see them? Was it the same ship as before? Did it approach the same way? At the same speed?"

"How should I know? It looked the same, by what we could pick up. And the approach wasn't as fast, but still faster than *Phoenix* ever did, coming in. It flashed lights at us and we flashed back—"

"These flashes. What pattern did they use? What pattern did you use?"

"Pattern? There was no pattern."

"I see."

"What the hell do you think you see? You've no *idea* what it feels like. We couldn't escape, couldn't even shift orbit. We had no real firepower. When Ramirez deserted us, we had to come up with *some* kind of protection. And it worked. This time, when they shot a missile at us, we were ready, and we blew it to hell."

"Was that the explosion Ms. Williams mentioned? She said the ship itself ran into a service-bot."

"I told you, Ms. Williams was never in a position to know anything."

"And yet, that *is* a fairly widespread belief among the Reunioners. Were there two explosions? Or did you, for some reason, fail to tell your people the truth? I'd think you'd be proud to have countered the first attack. If you countered it."

"I'm saying we stopped it."

"Is it, perhaps, because it *wasn't* a missile? An honest mistake, perhaps, but firing on a small ship approaching slowly, in a peaceful way . . . might not be viewed quite the same way as intercepting a direct attack."

"It *wasn't* slow and it wasn't peaceful. It was a missile aimed straight at us."

"It carried crew."

"There was a second ship. That was the boarding party."

"Really?" Not according to the kyo it wasn't.

"The missile was aimed at us, probably to create a breach. The second ship was right behind it. We blew the missile, debris hit the manned craft, and it crashed into us. We caught one of them alive."

Not the way the kyo told it, either. The station had fired on a shuttle craft, plain and simple. Somebody was not telling the truth.

"Did you find him before, or after, the mother ship fired?"

Braddock's chin lifted. "After. Inside the station. He got that far."

"The ship *did* fire on that same section, as I recall."

"Destroying what was left of their ship. They didn't want us stealing tech. But they damn well knew we had one of the crew. His suit was sending telemetry."

"Till you stopped it."

"Till we stopped it."

"Did you find any others? Any remains?"

A shake of the head. "No."

"And the ship backed off."

"Left us."

"After one shot, destroying the ship and whatever remained of the crew, they backed off, again, and watched. This time, for six years."

"We don't know—"

"Please. You thought it was a robot they'd left out there. That's the story you gave us. But you went on holding that survivor hostage. And when we gave you a chance to board, you wouldn't cooperate, and you took a captain hostage."

"Not hostage. We were negotiating."

"Negotiating *what*, for the love of God? The kyo ship that blew a piece out of your station is sitting out there waiting, and you want to negotiate with a ship that's trying to get you out of there?"

"Because we *did* have a hostage. They left us alone, because they knew we had him, whatever he is. Six years, they made no attempt to get him back. Maybe it was a robot out there. Maybe he was watching us watching him. But we were *winning*."

"Oh, good God."

"We'd rebuilt. We were stocked. We *had* one of them. And

they weren't attacking. We were handling things. We stood a chance of them just watching and maybe just deciding we weren't worth another ship. Maybe eventually we could deal. Then *you* came back and want to depopulate the station. I'm not highly confident in *Phoenix* command. I'm not highly confident in giving up what we've got in favor of something a hell of a lot less certain. I've got a *Phoenix* captain wanting a refueling. How did that go the *last* time we trusted a captain's word?"

"You kept the kyo in solitary confinement, made no attempt to communicate with him or his ship, for six years?"

"I told you. We were fine. We were in control of our lives. Until you came blazing in to upset the situation and promise our people paradise here at Alpha. Look at what we got! Short rations, no jobs, and lies."

"That part's aside from my interest at the moment. The kyo. When your security took him into custody, did he resist? Was anyone hurt?"

"He was alone."

"Injured?"

"No. Moving through the wreckage under his own power."

"Armed?"

Hesitation.

"No."

"Interesting. Did you interrogate him?"

"You've heard the sound that comes out of him. What do you think?"

"Six years. Silence. Solitary confinement. Starvation.—"

"We didn't starve him. Everyone was on short rations."

"Curiously enough, he didn't seem to hate you."

"Hate *us*?"

"Why do you think his ship attacked?"

"I have no idea. You claim you talked to him. You claim you know what you're doing. You tell me."

"I talked to him. I talked to others aboard their ship when he rejoined them."

"How? Bloody *how*?"

"I'm a linguist, among other things. It's a very small, very basic vocabulary we worked out. But we did work it out."

"Why? What makes you so damn sure they're not going to do exactly the same thing to this station?"

"I'm not a hundred percent certain, Mr. Braddock. But we have talked, which is a step ahead of firing blindly at what's not like us."

Braddock scowled, unsure, perhaps, whether or not he'd just been insulted, and Bren didn't bother clarifying. Braddock was, indeed, an attitudinal man bent on control. Attitudinal, maybe ignorant, but not a stupid man within the limits of his self-set boundaries and his managing of the station. A man capable of lying to cover what could well have been a bad mistake, firing at the shuttle craft, which had drawn a measured response from the mother ship. Take any constructive approach with their hostage? No. Apparently not.

A man who defined himself by the power he wielded—Jase was correct in that. He wished he'd had this conversation two years ago, on the voyage back—with witnesses accessible. Two years to sort truth from Braddock and talk about the mistakes.

He'd *wanted* to talk to Braddock. Sabin had said no, don't give the man legitimacy. And then refused even to discuss it, which was not unusual for Sabin.

He trusted Sabin. Not the way he trusted Jase, but he trusted her to have solid reasons, even if she didn't share them. Security aboard the ship had been risky. He didn't blame her for wanting not to stir anything up . . . and somewhere in the mix was the fact that Braddock wasn't the only one who'd put a slant on history. Ramirez' lies, lies in the ship's records, orders given, truths withheld—the voyage back to Alpha with a cargo of Braddock and passengers who told one version and ship's crew who weren't sure of the tale they'd been told—no, he understood Sabin's reasons for not wanting to get into that sealed past.

Did he believe everything Braddock had just said? Braddock had had twelve years to think up a version of facts that cast himself as the hero.

But while the ship as a whole might be hostile to the Pilots' Guild, the real fight, the source of all the decisions bringing them to this moment, appalling as the thought might be— might have been a personal war between two men, between Braddock and Ramirez.

Ego. And two opposing visions of a human future.

It did raise a question:

"Did you talk with Captain Sabin about Ramirez, when she was aboard the station?" he asked. "Did you tell any of this to her?"

"No," Braddock said shortly.

"No, you haven't, no, you didn't want to, or no, she asked *you* and you wouldn't answer?"

"No, no, *and* no. I have *no* interest in talking to her."

"Having tried to hold *her* hostage—"

"I didn't."

"Assume she thinks otherwise. Would you tell it to Ogun?"

"Ramirez' right hand."

"So no interest in talking to Ogun."

"No interest."

"I'm even more grateful, then that you would talk to me." And before Braddock could respond one way or another: "I hope we'll be in a better situation this round. And your information is helpful."

A muscle jumped in Braddock's jaw. "We *had* it going. We'd *survived*. They were leaving us alone. So now we're here. And so are they. We're in the same damned situation, except now we've got a kyo ship bearing down on us, with Ogun and Sabin both in charge of it all. Am I happy with the situation? We were hell and away better off at Reunion."

"What would you say," he asked Braddock quietly, "if I told you that the same kyo ship that attacked you the first time had been sitting out there in Reunion space—all that time. Eleven years from the time of the first attack, and until *Phoenix* came back the second time?"

Braddock's expression went stone cold. Upset. Very.

"You think that?" Braddock asked.

"I strongly suspect that's why Ramirez left. I think he realized it was there."

Moment of silence. "They said so? These *kyo* you 'talked' to?"

"No. But their appearance was instant, for us, when we came in. I ask myself—why did Ramirez take out without warning? He never told the crew there was anybody alive at Reunion, so the crew wouldn't pressure him to come back. He said nothing to us until he was dying. His whole bridge crew apparently kept the secret, even from other crew."

"I hadn't heard that part."

"I think, Mr. Braddock, that there's a lot that various people haven't heard. Secrecy, the unwillingness to compare notes, has caused us all a great deal of trouble and unpleasantness."

"Lay that at Ramirez' door."

He said nothing for several moments until Braddock's defiant anger began to wane.

Then: "Tell me, Mr. Braddock. What were you going to do with the children?"

"What were *you* going to do with the children?" Braddock shot back.

"Protect them."

"*And* use them."

"Mr. Braddock, the children wanted a birthday party."

"Don't give me that. What were you up to? What does this have to do with anything?"

"Why," he asked, patently ignoring the question, "did *you* urge Ms. Williams to send her daughter down? And why didn't you do the same with Mr. Andressen?"

"Irene went down to get a look. To tell us what she saw."

"An undercover agent, then."

His lip lifted. "Yes."

"I see. And what was her report?"

"She liked it." Braddock didn't sound at all happy about the statement. "You poured every extravagance you could muster on those kids. Of course she liked it."

He could counter, quite truthfully, that Irene had also begged him to get her back. But he didn't toss that into the argument. It had come in the nature of a confidence, from an upset kid, who probably knew she was being used, and would be, and by whom.

"Bjorn Andressen didn't come down. Was that your doing as well?"

"Don't look at *me.* Andressen's obsessed with getting his kid into station admin. He believes that's going to happen. *He* was the obstacle to his kid coming down."

"So what were you going to do with the kids?"

"The same thing you're going to do. Play politics. Work out an agreement that *you* want. Don't deny it."

Braddock *could* have said *I wasn't going to hurt those kids.* But he jumped straight to his justification: *you're doing the same thing.* He sincerely wished Braddock's indignation had made him say *I wouldn't have hurt the kids.*

Braddock's attitude . . . would not play well with the atevi.

"Well, Mr. Braddock. Thank you. I fear our time is up. I'm being pressured somewhat to send you to ship security. I don't think I'm inclined to do that at the moment. I will assure you that you needn't be afraid to be with the atevi. They aren't part of the question. Unfortunately you've upset the Mospheirans, but Tillington's gone now, at least from any position of authority. His replacement knows the situation. She was at Reunion with us, and she *may* advise a changed position toward your people."

"Is this a threat?"

"Mr. Braddock, it's a simple statement of your situation. It would be a very good thing if you reevaluated your relationship to the Mospheirans. I don't know that it would have any effect on Captain Ogun's opinion, but it might. I leave that to—"

"What does it take to get *your* backing?"

"Mine?" A novel notion. "In what, Mr. Braddock?"

"I have five thousand people, who have skills, who can run this station."

"That's an interesting idea. What am I supposed to do with that information?"

"We can *be* good allies."

"I'll remember that, Mr. Braddock." He pushed back from the table. "And thank you for the discussion."

He rose, turned to leave.

Braddock snapped, "Just who the hell are you, Cameron? Who do you work for?"

He had to smile. Slightly. "For the atevi government, Mr. Braddock." He turned back to face Braddock. "*And* for the Mospheiran President."

"At the same time? How the hell does that add up to an honest job?"

"It used to be hard. It isn't now. They're very much of the same mind. And let me add another thought for you to ponder. In a few hours, I'll be representing the kyo as well."

Braddock's mouth worked then just stopped, hanging slightly open.

"Think about it, Mr. Braddock. Consider the fact that I, and my predecessors, have done this before, with, if you open your eyes to see, obvious success. Think about it and perhaps we can talk again after I deal with the visitors."

"If there's a station left."

"I prefer to remain optimistic on that point. Our survival, however, might well depend on my grasp of the truth regarding what's happened over the last twelve years. With that in mind, if anything occurs to you—things I might need to know, dealing with them—say my name to your guards. Ask to see me. But expect that after a certain time I'll be busy. You'll understand that."

"I *understand* that you better not make a mistake."

"I hope you wish me luck."

"I *hope* you don't get this station blown to hell."

"In that, sir, we are in complete agreement," he said. "Good day, Mr. Braddock. —Nadiin." He gave a nod to his bodyguard, and left.

10

His aishid didn't ask him what Braddock had said. He wasn't
ready to frame it in a form they would understand without
ambiguity . . . and if any of his associates understood when he
was deep in thought—they did. They asked nothing, said nothing
to disrupt his train of thought on the way back to the residencies.

They did hand him a recording of the session which, yes,
they had made, and which properly should be Guild business
not involving him—if this were on Earth. It wasn't. And he was
not at all sorry to have a chance to review the conversation.

Once back in his apartment, he immediately retreated into
his office, first to make a transcript of that useful record for
Jase, for Jase to use at his own discretion, and then to translate
it into Ragi, for his own staff, for the dowager's staff, for the
Observers, and for Geigi. The original went into secure storage . . . against future legal action.

Then he returned to the Ragi version, adding notes, some of
which were a page unto themselves, trying to explain— the
associated human thinking, human actions, and the technology
involved.

And not, he realized, just to his atevi associates.

Be aware that I may be mistaken as to any of this, he added
at the top. *Braddock-nadi and I are not of the same people and
Lord Geigi and his aishid would be a better guide regarding
what was possible for him to have done as stationmaster. Likewise Jase-aiji may have a very useful opinion.*

He sent it, to all parties involved, then took time for a much-needed shower and a change of clothes, before joining his aishid in the secure informality of the security station to discuss the sum of all his recent meetings.

"You have read the transcript," he said.

"Yes," Banichi said. "We have arranged to consult with Lord Geigi's aishid, and with Cenedi, personally."

"One does not trust Braddock," he said, settling in his usual place, on a cabinet corner, "and one does not trust Williams-nadi. But there is within these two stories—which a year aboard the ship gave them ample time to coordinate—the assertion that Ramirez found a habitable world by distant observation, and went back to investigate it more fully. We may take this to have been the kyo world, or *a* kyo world, and that the kyo objected to this return visit. This, we have inferred from Ramirez' own account of his first meeting with the kyo ship."

"Is it possible," Jago asked, "that Ramirez-aiji returned to Reunion Station to refuel with the intent of never returning? If he was looking for such a world in order to begin a new association, with himself as aiji, might not the discovery of such a world be the keystone to his plan?"

"A very good point, Jago-ji," Bren said, and one he should have considered on his own. Investigating a potentially viable planet might not have made a senior staff member, the man who'd had the heart attack, want to leave the ship, but permanently severing relations with the station . . . might. "Braddock states that the first Braddock knew of the kyo's displeasure was the arrival of a ship at high speed while *Phoenix* was absent. Williams indicated the kyo ran into a mining craft and took that for attack. Jase stated that such an accident was not likely. Braddock stated, today, that the ship deliberately destroyed *two* such craft as it arrived."

"Perhaps they believed those craft to be something other than mining robots." Banichi's voice revealed contempt. Mines were known to the atevi, but not with any positive association.

Honorable individuals simply did not employ means of destruction that were not specifically targeted.

"It is certainly possible. Particularly if their enemies use such tactics. Having taken out the mining craft, Braddock says, the kyo fired on the station once, then withdrew."

"An attack not resulting in the anticipated response," Banichi said after a moment. He said it in a Ragi way, which was a single word. A concept. "During or after."

Meaning—

One had to be Guild, perhaps, to know all that word meant. He saw the others thinking, soberly so.

"One cannot assign human *or* atevi interpretation to the kyo action," he cautioned them, "and one dares not conclude. But there is the chance that they sat there, silent, for more than ten years, with only Prakuyo's ill-fated contact to break that silence."

"One suspects they were indeed watching," Algini said. "Preserve and observe."

"Perhaps," Tano said, "they attributed Ramirez-aiji's intrusion to their enemies and believed they had found their base. They are at war. They attacked with no alternative explanation in mind, and when the station did not respond, they withdrew to observe."

It was exactly the scenario slowly evolving in the back of his mind.

It attributed restraint to the kyo.

It implied that Prakuyo an Tep's team might have realized the station was not what they thought it was.

Placing oneself in that unlikely situation—what *would* he report to superiors?

We just attacked another species.

With all the terrible facts that implied.

Was it human-centered thinking, to think the kyo would feel the same shock, and perhaps suffer political paralysis? Surprise was possible for a mecheita, a fish, a worm. Dismay was possible in any mind forming a plan and acting on it to unanticipated results.

Humans and atevi both experienced guilt. Having been a rider of mecheiti, he was not sure *that* species felt any such thing. And that was the highest third species he had ever dealt with . . . well, but maybe Boji. And he very much doubted guilt figured in Boji's greedy little mind.

But the kyo realization, beyond intellectual shock that they had been wrong about the nature of Reunion Station, would surely reach to dismay that they had acted on a wrong assumption, that they had damaged something they did not understand, and that the universe they thought they knew had just surprised them.

Realizing the other side would have a reaction to their action—perhaps a complex reaction . . . One couldn't climb very far up the technological tree without figuring out actions brought reactions. And the kyo built starships.

So, they damaged the station and realized:

That other species is going to react.

Which realization would suggest the next obvious question:

How is that species going to react?

Was *that* why the kyo hadn't gone in to extract Prakuyo an Tep, when that contact went bad? Not to provoke the situation further?

And from that cell—had Prakuyo an Tep been *reading* his captors?

Had the ship waited all that time, waiting so as not to bring the problem it had created back to their world?

Or had it been waiting all that time so as not to *miss* the reaction when it came?

In human or atevi understanding, the kyo should have reported. They should have communicated with their own people, warning them: *There's more than one non-kyo, star-faring species out here. We may have started another war.*

We're waiting to see what they do. Where they go. How many ships.

Not because they attacked us, but because . . . we made a mistake.

All this time, he'd been assuming the mistake had been on the human side. He'd allowed his impression of Braddock and Ramirez, their secrecy and their overbearing ambition, to color the events. He'd allowed himself to *assume.*

He'd had a year to go over his notes aboard ship. As it turned out, he'd heard everything about the incident except *how* the kyo had come in, a detail he needed, and hoped he had, in this interview with Braddock.

Fast. Hard. And firing at anything mechanical.

That conversation would have been useful, two *years* ago.

Yes, he'd wanted to talk to Braddock when they'd first brought him aboard, at Reunion. But Sabin had said no, and he'd been busy talking to the kyo. Then they'd been busy getting out. He'd assumed he'd get the chance. With reasons not to raise issues during the voyage, he'd assumed there would be a relaxation of attitudes when they got to Alpha Station, once Sabin *wasn't* trying to keep the lid on a pressured situation.

He'd thought he'd have time.

But he hadn't had it. When they reached Alpha, things had gone to hell locally and they'd literally run to board the last shuttle flying. He'd had to shut down all thought of the kyo and Reunion, and concentrate on staying alive and getting Tabini back into power.

So all his assumptions regarding Braddock and the events leading to the attack had crystallized, frozen where they stood, because he'd been too damned busy down on the planet to think about things aloft. He'd assumed, that dreadful, dangerous word, that there had been a mistake or an action on the *human* side that provoked the attack. He'd assumed that Braddock's moves answered everything.

He couldn't assume now. He had to know. Braddock might *not* have been responsible for the attack—he might in fact have taken reasonable actions and actually saved lives. Possibly

Ramirez had done something to provoke it, but it was also possible the kyo just opened fire without preface.

The kyo were at war, and if the kyo hadn't realized there was another species involved . . .

The attack Braddock described implied a complete lack of hesitation. They'd acted in confidence they absolutely knew what they were doing—and then what? Realized they didn't know what they'd done?

If that was the case, what else could one conclude? That *Phoenix*, entering a kyo region, had *acted* like an enemy ship, running when spotted?

Had the kyo followed such a lure before and run into ambush?

He became aware of a general silence, everybody sitting about the counters of the security station, watching him, nobody moving, nobody saying a thing, while his mind spiraled off into infinity. He was embarrassed. But they knew him. They waited.

"I think," he said, "you may be right. I think it's very possible the kyo attacked the station as an enemy outpost, then realized they had attacked a people unrelated to their war. They then had to know what those people would do about the attack. They stayed. They waited. They observed. We have no idea how many ships they have at their disposal. But if the mistake was on the kyo side, and not Braddock's—I think it would make some sense for them to observe the reaction, however long it took, and do as little as possible to provoke another action. It would make sense to advise their own people that there was an unknown species in the area. It would make sense to admit what they had done, and then to try to deal with it without widening the conflict. Sensible people would not want to take on a second enemy."

"They sat there as a sacrifice, perhaps," Banichi said.

So much of atevi culture was embedded in the machimi, the plays.

And there was, indeed, in the long ago, more than one instance of a clan acknowledging a mistake, prepared to accept whatever reparations the offended might demand, the honorable thing being the offender satisfying the offended.

Nothing had been off the table. Life. Death.

"One dares not assume their customs are ours," he said. "But I may have been mistaken in assuming Braddock was the offender in the encounter. Indeed he may indeed be an offender in every other of his actions, but not necessarily in this one. I think we have at least two competing models for what happened back at Reunion, but only one offers an explanation for the kyo's extreme patience, that being the one of mistaken identification leading to a retaliation far beyond what would seem reasonable. It appears that the station's response puzzled them, their attack on Prakuyo's mission offered nothing better, and after we arrived, the whole concept of humans coexisting peacefully with atevi—posed them an even more complex puzzle, without answering anything. I dare not assume anything or anyone is exactly the same as humans or atevi. But three actions stand out to me: the speed and pitiless destruction of their first approach. The strange patience of their watching for ten years, despite the station taking Prakuyo an Tep prisoner. And Prakuyo's attempt to board the station, unarmed. One has no idea whether Prakuyo an Tep has an official position, whether he is some sort of a paidhi, himself, or whether he is, possibly, the one who ordered that initial attack. All these things are possible." He drew in a deep long breath, and with it felt a settling, as if a few of the pieces that had been careening in wild orbit had just found a stable relationship, a configuration that let him surmise where more pieces might fit.

But one dared not trust it. All those pieces had to stay in orbit, nothing dropping, until he could say they were individually true, or false.

But at least, and to his relief . . . he no longer felt any need to deal with Braddock. Whatever insights he might have gotten from that quarter had been gotten. With luck it would help him ask the right questions to extract and understand the kyo side of those events.

"One has absolutely no idea what, if anything, about these two witnesses' testimony is true, nadiin-ji, but in their two reports, I have pieces to work with, possibilities which may well help us to understand the kyo's actions and the kyo's way of thinking, and I shall try my utmost. My absolute utmost. Let us hope Prakuyo's own account will provide a felicitous third, clarifying the details. Continue to consider the transcript and all else involved. Help me where you see *anything* I may have missed. I have sent a translation of the interview to the dowager, and I shall value her insight, but you have your guild's unique experience to draw on. Consult the Guild Observers where you will. There will be nothing secret from the aiji or those who advise him, so they may have all the information you deem good for them to know."

"Yes," Banichi said, and the others nodded solemnly.

11

Mani rested, reading some letter nand' Bren had sent—but that was not all mani had been doing. Cajeiri understood that. Mani had her staff arranging a dinner that well could have served a full table of guests, not for them to eat, no, but to send up the hall to relieve Lord Geigi's staff, who were doing their best to provide for people who had come away with no baggage, no possessions but the clothes they wore.

Lord Geigi's staff had pulled the several wardrobe cases from storage, one of which was Irene's, so it had come to mani's door, and mani's staff had pulled out the pretty clothes Irene had had on Earth. And Lord Geigi's staff, in addition to getting the crates from storage for Gene and Artur, had sent orders to shops on the Mospheiran side to get clothes for Bjorn and the parents. With help from Gene and Artur, they had gotten sizes, and requests, and nice clothing and all manner of small things were due to arrive before dinner.

"Go, go," mani said, dismissing them both. Mani mostly rested and read, besides giving the major orders. "You may assist, but make no troublesome suggestions that would entail more work for staff. Advise them that dinner will be sent, so they may rest. See that things have been done that should be done. And yes, you may stay for dinner."

"Yes," Cajeiri said, for himself and Irene, and back they went, with his aishid, and under constant watch from guards in the hall.

He and Irene had new things to tell the others. He knew, for instance, there were security people from Lord Geigi's staff busy packing up everything but the furniture in all their guests' homes in the restricted sections, and putting it in crates and moving it to secure storage, so that all their property would be safe. That would be good news for everybody, particularly Bjorn's father—except Irene said she wished they would send all hers into space so she could just start over.

"There will surely be *some* things you want," he said.

Irene shook her head. "No," she said. "Nothing, Jeri-ji. Nothing."

He could not imagine that. Every piece of furniture, every carpet, every ornament in his own suite at home, he had picked from storage in the Bujavid's underfloors, and it had been owned, a lot of it, by people a hundred years ago. Every carpet, every vase that Irene had so admired in Lord Geigi's house, and in the Bujavid, had a history, and hands had made it, and all the details like where it came from were recorded, even to what sort a glaze was, or who had gathered the clay and who had fired a pot. A piece like that, when not used, went to storage, to wait for some other person to want it. He felt very lucky to have found so many wonderful things. Even if his own mother had not quite admired his choices.

Throw it all away, Irene said. So she could start over.

That was just—wrong. So he caught the attention of Lord Geigi's major d' when they arrived and said, "Reni-nadi may tell you throw all her property away. Do not argue with her, but do not throw it away, either. Tell security save it in case she changes her mind someday."

"Yes," the answer came.

The new clothing came. There were also things like lotions, because the air was dry; and such personal things as toothbrushes and combs, and there were personal bags, too, so they could keep their belongings together—and everybody was happy with that. Bjorn *had* no atevi clothes, but he had gotten a number of sweaters and trousers such as Mospheirans wore, and he was pleased; and Gene's mother cried a little, but Gene said that was because she was happy with her clothes—one hoped that was so.

Irene went from one to the other, translating occasionally, mostly talking quietly to Gene and Artur and Bjorn, who at one point, when she seemed unhappy in all the confusion, patted her shoulders. Gene put his arms about her as if she were a child, which was a little shocking. But that was what humans did, and Cajeiri just stood aside and understood that for all Irene's strong denials—Irene was not calm inside, whatever she was feeling.

But Irene wiped her eyes and put on a cheerful face afterward.

Staff brought refreshments, and they had, with their new clothes, what was almost a party, despite everything going on.

And they, he and his associates, and Bjorn, sat at a little table apart from the grown-ups, and had a chance to talk. He knew he should not stay too long, and that when he did leave, he might not get to come back before the kyo had come and gone. So he sat with his associates and told them, quietly, what he knew about the kyo ship, and showed all of them the little book he carried constantly now, which was his same little notebook where he had written down human words *and* kyo, from way back on the voyage.

That was, amid all the other things, so strange—that all of them could sit in regular chairs and do what they had used to do in the tunnels, under bright light now, with hot tea and little cakes, in Lord Geigi's apartment and with the parents in the room—as if one world or the other was a dream.

Bjorn was one they had lost. Bjorn since they had gotten him back had been so quiet, and reserved, and clearly a little overwhelmed, and maybe feeling left out. Bjorn was the oldest. He had always been the one most clever about locks and accesses and systems. He had never been the one who knew least, and now that was how things were.

Bjorn asked, quietly now, in Ragi far from fluent, "Where we go, Jeri-ji? Where we go, all done? My father, scared."

Little words. Old words. Words from the tunnels. It seemed likely that Bjorn had composed that question by himself, struggling for words, and not asking anybody.

"Why Reunion?" Bjorn asked. "Why are kyo upset? My father ask . . . why now here?"

It was an old question, what the kyo wanted, one they had asked in the tunnels and never understood. He was much older than seven, now, and he had seen things he had not seen, the first time he had tried to answer that question.

Would he have been brave enough to approach Prakuyo an Tep now, the way he had done then?

Maybe he would not have been that brave. Or as stupid.

Artur said quietly: "Maybe they were scared of *us*. Maybe they're scared now. They're only one ship, coming to visit us."

"To do what?" Bjorn asked.

To do what was indeed the question.

"To know whether they were right to let us go," Irene said. "Wouldn't you want to know?"

"It does make sense," Bjorn said.

"Are *you* scared?" Gene asked.

Bjorn gave that tiny finger-measure, the old answer to an old question, the old joke, from days in the tunnels. And they all laughed a little.

Long day. Very long day. Bren's supper was past—sandwiches with his aishid before returning to his office, in what had become a full day's work, at variance with any regular station shift. A breakfast invitation had just arrived from the dowager saying, uncharacteristically, *At the paidhi's convenience, should he have the leisure.*

Breakfast, for the dowager, on her ordinary schedule, was far too few hours away and *leisure*, for him, was nonexistent. He had reports still to write, one to Tabini and another to Shawn, advising them of the mission's situation—and then there was the necessary memo to the Guild Observers, specially worded to explain to them how to interpret the situation. They were sharp, and they were in constant communication with Guild on station, including his aishid and the dowager's, but there were points they needed to understand, one of which was the simple fact that the paidhi was making the personal effort to keep them informed.

The difficulty was not so much the effort of writing those reports. It was nailing down what he *did* think, and what he *was* doing, which was in a state of formation, not finality—fluid as it had to be, until he had better information. He rested his head against his hands, wishing he didn't have to make Braddock and the situation with Ramirez make sense to traditional-minded Guild, when he wasn't sure it made sense to him. But the effort kept him grounded, so to speak, kept him aware that he did have to make sense, ultimately, to the legislature on the continent, and get it to understand how little the average Reunioners had been responsible for their own misfortune, and why Tabini felt justified in diverting the shuttles to Reunioner relocation.

Answering close questions for the Mospheiran legislature, and the inevitable committees—that, at least, was likely going to be Gin's job.

Part of him so longed to be at that breakfast tomorrow. He wanted to talk to Ilisidi, assure himself that she understood what he had learned—beyond that transcription he'd sent her—and hear her astute reckoning of all things political, because her insights were always thought-provoking and generally worth hearing . . . and because, on Earth, it was always his habit, like a touchstone. Whenever the dowager issued the slightest whisper of an invitation, he moved schedule to be there, not only because *At your convenience* had never really meant his convenience: it meant hers. It meant that he would find it more convenient than anything else he might have scheduled to hear what she had to say. It meant: *be there* and *be prepared to stay late.*

But here—here it had to be different. Here, the problems were human, the incoming ship was a puzzle not emitting enough clues, and he was, hand over fist, unraveling an incomplete record of human actions in which a human mind kept finding only logical gaps and more questions.

He had to believe the dowager, being wise, well knew what the paidhi was doing, or trying to do, and he had to assume for once the *if* really meant *if*.

But he still wanted to go. For one thing because he had not been eating on any kind of schedule. Bindanda had done his best to keep everybody fed, but mealtime had been a moving target since the hour his feet had hit the deck, with none of the ordinary time for reflection and reassessment.

For another, he had a *See me* from Captain Ogun languishing on his desk as of an hour ago, and Jase had signaled him that Ogun's message was about Braddock—a topic he was not, at the moment, interested in discussing with the senior captain.

Ilisidi's invitation did offer him an escape from that—at least as regarded where he had to be tomorrow morning on Ogun's shift. But that invitation might well bring up an equally unwelcome topic: Irene, who had been swept up into the dowager's household, not, one suspected, to the dowager's great delight. He did not want to be asked for a solution to that question tomorrow morning, or any morning until the kyo were a vanishing point in the distance.

Part of him wanted to turn off the desk console and lock his door on all those extraneous problems, and focus on nothing but the kyo. He kept trying, desperately, to get his mind *back* to where it had been a year ago . . . before that moment of freezing that situation and inundating his consciousness with Tabini's grave situation, a Guild conspiracy, a threat to the aishidi'tat that had developed because the ship . . .

No. He did not want to go there either. That causality was

not in his hands, not now, and the problems that had caused Tabini's problem might have to get worse, with the need to solve the problems up here.

No. He needed to go back, mentally a year, *two* years—back to when he first began grappling with the kyo grammar and making tentative structures. That was the moment he had to travel back to, a frustrating puzzle lacking pieces, a puzzle which did not do well with current distraction.

But every time he began to resurrect that mindset, every time he tried to imagine the significance behind a kyo word, questions regarding the events leading to his meeting with the kyo would rise and his thoughts would skitter helplessly back to Williams' story or Braddock's account of the attacks on Reunion and begin spinning over the same old problem.

He couldn't figure those two individuals out—and *they* were human. It was a shaky premise on which to imagine what the kyo side of the event was.

Tempting . . . so very tempting simply to assume the simplest explanation. To assume a species at war *had* simply mistaken who and what they were dealing with.

Expectations. Assumptions. Therein lay a trap. Kyo *might* in some points behave as humans would. Humans in some regards behaved as atevi would. But the limited exchanges with the kyo had given him no understanding of their instinctive behavior or their abstract concepts or their intentions.

Except . . . the kyo had no easy sense of *we*, at least as he'd tried to express it. Expanding a simple pronoun grouping of himself, the dowager, and Cajeiri to include Prakuyo had raised violent objections. Prakuyo, it seemed, was not and would not allow himself to be included in *we* without suitable consideration, which Prakuyo at that time had not been willing to make.

But *association*, it seemed, was not only acceptable, but, perhaps, inevitable.

Association. It was a key word in the atevi language. Prakuyo had sensed that significance and begun to use it, along with its peculiar pronouns, with a meaning Bren couldn't begin to guess. He'd tried to remember when it had first become an issue. He *thought* it had involved several stick figures and the terms humans and atevi. Groups, perhaps. Whereas "we" had been in reference to specific individuals. But one thing was certain, Prakuyo had used "association" to mean something Prakuyo understood, to a people for whom it had biologically ingrained connotations. That had become worrisome. Fortunately, the atevi involved in that meeting knew as well as he not to assume a mutual understanding.

There was one concept Prakuyo had tried to emphasize.

That association could not be broken.

But what, exactly, did that mean? That things that had met would—what? Be doomed to go on meeting? That the outcome would always be the same? That *this* association could not be broken. Or that their several species could never undo the contact—which had, at their parting, never been resolved.

The concept worked on a planetary surface where oceans and mountain ranges shaped the contacts one was bound to make, but space was not that way.

Unless one counted that star systems, which developed in clusters and strings, as Jase had explained in some detail once— with empty spots and dust like mountain ranges and oceans. Starships didn't jump into empty space. They jumped to the next safe and adequate point of mass, and set up bases— stations—at stars with useful resources.

The fact remained that Prakuyo had been determined to characterize their small group, which included three distinct species, male and female, young and old . . . with that term *association*. A group that sat around watching vids and eating teacakes. And laughing.

Where did one start, with that? Might its meaning to the kyo be something far more simple? Those who had met, could not unmeet? Perhaps it had an even broader scope: what was done couldn't be undone—

Kandana—major domo—opened the office door, entered quietly with a little bow. "Has the paidhi an answer for the dowager's staff?"

Do or do not. He had to decide. Now.

He *had* to stay focused, bottom line. Half of him was beyond curious whether the dowager herself had any insights urgent and helpful on the issues raised in that transcript, but he suspected she had not. He suspected that Irene and staff problems with the guests was the matter of the dowager's interest; and the body so wanted simply to plead exhaustion and sleep late for one, just one night's—

Running steps sounded in the hall, crossing from the foyer.

Running, in an atevi household, never heralded good news.

Kandana frowned and opened the door again—admitted Asicho, who bowed deeply.

"Nandi. Nand' Gin says—one cannot understand entirely—please call immediately. One wished her to delay but she hung up. She named the kyo. One does not know the detail."

A tick upward in heartbeat. "Thank you, nadi, nadiin. I shall manage." Asicho was *not* the most fluent of his staff where it came to dealing with humans, Gin had a little Ragi, if only on certain topics, but the message came through. Asicho bowed and left, Kandana followed, closing the door silently behind him.

The adrenaline surge stayed.

Bren swung his chair about, punched two presets on the desk console, one the video display, first of which tracked the kyo position and clocked the routine ping of their mirrored message.

The message wasn't due yet. The position showed nothing changed, not rate of approach, not direction.

Second preset was active Central, whichever Central was active, but preset number eight was one he'd established this afternoon, attached to Gin's personal com.

"Gin, Bren here. What's going on? Has something changed?"

He glanced at the clock: a little more than two hours before handoff to the atevi. Gin was not scheduled to be in Central at this hour. She had already had a long day, getting both shifts online and communicating with Ogun.

"We've got an off schedule transmission," Gin said. *"May be a graphic.* Phoenix *senior tech consulted me, making the same guess as I made. They're looking it over now. Should have an answer any minute. Are you at a console?"*

"My office, yes. I am." Thank God he was dealing, for the first time since his arrival, with a calm, resourceful, and helpful Mospheiran director. He had a mental image of the techs, the room. Gin was likely there at the moment, working in concert with *Phoenix* techs on a routine she'd helped work out in the first place—translating kyo graphics with good success on black and white transmission. Color had not, at last viewing, been quite as satisfactory.

"No verbal message?"

"No. Stand by. I'll window what I'm getting."

He saw a blank display pop up in the corner—he hadn't used the system in a year, and he faltered a bit, toggling over to half-screen display.

He saw tiny black lines. Saw the little bar that was the place-marker rip across and across and across.

It was going fast. Blank space did that.

White dot. Central of the line.

Calibrating? he wondered.

The white dot became longer, and longer with successive passes.

Became a long white bar growing line by line. Then began a thicker white bar under it. That developed downward as a thick white vertical.

Then a black dot appeared centered on the white.

Line after line, and both the relative length and proportion of the thin line and the white vertical, now developing a black arc—that touched off a supposition. A hope.

Another white dot appeared, off to the side, in the black. In a few more passes two images were developing simultaneously, and the black arc on the white vertical became a black circle.

He guessed, over time, what the white vertical might be. What that second object, at a fair distance—might be. He waited, not willing to prejudice Gin or the techs.

"I'm thinking that's the mast," Gin said finally. *"That's the docking mast. And I think that other shape is* Phoenix. *They've shortened the actual interval between the two by a third. They're deliberately including the ship as part of the question. Either-or."*

"I agree."

"They understand the station architecture, do you think, that being the docking port? God knows they had ample chance to observe it at Reunion."

"Prakuyo made an entry at Reunion, but I think it was through the hole they made."

"Deja vu."

"I hope not. They watched *Phoenix* lock onto Reunion. Probably they watched your shuttle dock this morning. At Reunion, the two ships locked to transfer Prakuyo. I'm thinking this is a query. There's two choices in this frame. *Phoenix.* Or the station mast. I think we send them the one we want them to use."

"We can do either." Calculations, metal and plastics and adaptation. Gin's department. She'd been part of the operation when they'd linked ship to ship with the kyo the first time. *"It's your decision which."*

The transmission was, over all, good news. The query about two docking modes removed one terrible possibility from the table—but immediately mandated he make decisions which had their own consequences. Offering a meeting aboard their own ship, using *Phoenix* as a base, would be comfortable for the kyo, and certainly secure. Offering the station was a more open, liberal gesture on their own part, though scarier and less comfortable for the kyo—who were born to a slightly greater gravity and whose version of room lighting was closer to dusk. But Prakuyo an Tep, at least, knew what the conditions would be.

If *only* they were dealing with him. Her. Whatever Prakuyo was.

The door opened. His aishid arrived quietly and lined the wall, aware that something significant was going on, probably listening all the while, and he was glad of their steadying presence. "The kyo seem to be proposing to dock," he said to them in Ragi, and reporting it made it more real. "Station or ship, seems to be their question. One inclines to prefer the station."

Solemn, silent nods from those whose advice he most trusted. Acceptance, just acceptance. Anything he chose, they'd go with.

"My bodyguard has come in," he said to Gin, in Mosphei'. "They're aware. I'm inclining toward requesting the kyo to come into the station. It gives us a base not dependent on ship command. And if the kyo are here to observe who we are, then offering the station seems more welcoming—given the situation that developed at Reunion."

"*I'd agree,*" Gin said. "*It's to be an atevi operation, top to bottom, once they come aboard, am I right? Having ship politics interfering in this, even in minor details, would not be helpful, and I am definitely not proposing my section of the station for the honor.*"

"Agreed. Our answer needs to be a graphic of just the mast. I think they'll ask more details as they get closer, technicals I can't give. I can translate them. But I can't come up with them."

"*I can,*" Gin said. "*And Jase can. I'll talk with ops, prepare them a suggested procedure. In graphics.*"

"I'll let you get to work," he said.

"*I'll handle it. I'll stay on in Central until it's done and received. If that takes some of Lord Geigi's shift, we'll stay and do it. I trust that's all right, if you'll explain it to Lord Geigi. We'll send everything past you.*"

"At any hour. I'll advise Geigi to wake me if anything comes in."

"*That'll be a good idea.*"

"Gin."

"*Yes.*"

"Thank you." Fervently. He could only imagine managing this with Tillington in charge and Ogun hanging over Tillington's shoulder. "Thank you, Gin."

"*No problem,*" Gin said, and there *wouldn't* be. He believed it so far as anybody on the station could assure him of anything.

He shut down, working his hands, which had gone cold, sorting his mind into Ragi. "The kyo have queried," he said to his aishid, "about docking, and we have invited them to come in at the mast. I have made the decision without querying ship command, but one has already made it clear to them that the choices in this matter are all atevi choices. One wishes to advise the dowager that this has happened, however I now fear I must decline her invitation for breakfast. I have to rest."

"Indeed," Banichi said. "You should. *We* should, Bren-ji."

It was the first time he could recall Banichi calling halt.

He nodded slowly.

"One gratefully accepts your advice, 'Nichi-ji. Bindanda has been trying to provide us a proper meal and you have more than deserved rest and a good breakfast tomorrow. Let the Guild Observers and the dowager's guard deal with what comes. As soon as I approve Gin's message, which should be in the next few moments, we shall sit and take a little tea, and then we shall all of us rest."

Even with the best intentions, however, there was no escape from the problems, and the time was short. The question now, if they were to have the kyo on the station, was *where* to put the kyo that would be both comfortable and secure, in all senses.

"I shall make a list of the kyo needs and ask Haiji," Algini said, on the second round of tea. Haiji was Geigi's Guild senior. "The gravity aboard the kyo ship was slightly greater, therefore they should be comfortable enough in that regard. One understands there are heated storage areas on another level within reasonable proximity of this section's lift system, which, once converted, could provide not only comfort, but security for the visitors, and ease of access for the aiji-dowager. One believes Haiji will suggest those—the chart shows large spaces, having all useful connections, and with lift access—freight lift, but one believes a simple reprogramming of the system controls what cars stop. Haiji might have that information."

Leave it to his aishid to know more about the passages and parts of the space station than he had ever needed to ask: the Guild made a point of knowing the layout and resources of any place in which they operated, as soon as possible, and to whatever extent they could.

"Do so," Bren said. "Excellent notion." And in one suggestion, that was a problem packed off, perhaps, to a good resolution. Haiji knew or knew where to obtain what they needed, and if Haiji did not, that information was surely something Geigi could find, and Geigi could move work crews required to make the necessary changes. Geigi had always said it was an hour's work to move a noncritical wall.

Time to prove that, it seemed. They needed a floor plan. A sketch, at least, of what the kyo needed. Atevi furnishings were large enough, at least the larger items. Geigi's operation could move it or produce it, for that matter, in very short order. It might not be wood, but wood, fabric, stone . . . it could look like anything Geigi's artisans wanted it to.

"The kyo will perhaps wish to refuel," Banichi said.

"They might, and we shall offer it, but in point of fact, we have no idea what their ships _use_ for fuel, or their efficiency. _Phoenix_ could not carry sufficient for a round trip, Reunion to Alpha, but that does not mean the kyo ship has the same limitation."

It did, however, raise a good question. If the kyo ship did come in needing supply—that suggested either malevolent intent to take it or peaceful confidence that they would get it, each of which answers posed certain other questions.

He shut that thought down. Fast. The kyo wanted to come aboard. They wanted to talk. Concentrate on that. Solve *that* problem properly and most others would resolve themselves.

"We do not know how many visitors to expect," Jago said.

"We do not. They've given no indication, yet, how many or for how long. We shall just have to manage as we discover the situation. Still, I doubt that they would be seeking a long stay, unless their dealings at Reunion have made them fugitives from their own authorities, which one hopes not to be the case. I do not expect more than a few individuals ever to leave their ship. On the other hand, they may insist we come aboard."

"Either way, we shall be ready," Jago said, and Bren felt another vertebra relax. Another concern successfully delegated. His aishid, Gin, Geigi . . . all the functional details were in hands in which he had utmost confidence.

There remained one individual and one concern he had put off—and now, with preparations starting, she did need to be informed.

Not a full meal. Not a discussion of human problems.

Arrangements. Actual preparations for her joining him, actively working with the kyo.

That trumped any politics going on in Geigi's guest quarters.

"Tell the aiji-dowager's staff, nadiin-ji, that one would take great comfort in a cup of tea tomorrow mid-morning, if convenient. I shall have a report to give her, by then."

"Such an invitation will come," Jago said. "We are assured the paidhi will have access at any request."

12

It was after a late breakfast in his own apartment, with one of Bindanda's most comforting concoctions of eggs and toast under his ribs, that Bren put on one of his good coats and slipped quietly—well, quietly for a man with four bodyguards—across the hall, where the dowager's staff showed him immediately to the vacant sitting room, providing him a chair and a cup of tea, advising him that the dowager would join him momentarily.

He had, he found on waking from a relatively sound sleep, one troubling question about his atevi allies in the upcoming meeting with the kyo, and that worry centered not around the dowager, but on the involvement of the young gentleman, and most particularly—on the young gentleman's division of attention between his young associates and the business at hand.

Specifically—and potentially delicate—there was suddenly a girl involved, in what sense a human was completely uncertain. There had been a threat to the young gentleman's entire circle of associates of similar age.

And there had been, Narani had informed him on inquiry, more than one instance of Irene or Irene and Cajeiri visiting Lord Geigi's premises to settle some distress from Bjorn's household. The young gentleman had been delegated to *solve* the guests' problems, which apparently continued. Andressen-nadi wanted communications. He wanted to contact his company, which, for whatever reason, had not contacted him. And communication on the Mospheiran side of the wall was one thing Mr. Andressen definitely would not get.

People had devotedly kept troubles away from him for a number of hours. They still were doing it. He didn't doubt the dowager's wisdom in asking Cajeiri to rein in his guests, and Irene helping Cajeiri was a reasonable arrangement. But Irene would soon be left to cope on her own, since Irene would definitively *not* be going down with them to the area they were setting up.

He didn't doubt the young gentleman's usefulness when he was truly focused. Cajeiri was every inch Tabini's son, at home in the court and in the affairs of nations. Cajeiri understood the give and take of diplomacy, having had the canniest set of teachers the world had to offer, and he had dealt with a scary lot of experiences that no nine-year-old, human or atevi, ought ever to have met. He could be uncannily practical and observant.

Excepting the distraction of his young associates, one of whom *was* female and without parental supervision.

He hadn't wanted to think about the Reunioners.

But with Narani's report—that concern was back in the middle of things.

No one knew better than Ilisidi what was currently at stake, both for her grandson and the future of the world, yet she had allowed this potential distraction to linger in her residence. There had to be a reason.

And Andressen, meanwhile, wanted to talk to a Mospheiran company.

A wonder any of the Reunioners were mentally stable, given what they'd endured over the last decade and more; and God knew the whole operation would have been in far worse shape if Irene hadn't been the brave, clear-headed kid she was.

Irene was also the fragile one, the one whose adults had all failed her. Of all the kids—*this* girl had turned up resident *in* the dowager's apartment, with, apparently, the dowager's blessing.

The dowager didn't make emotional decisions.

Well, not ordinarily.

At least not the soft-hearted sort.

So was there an atevi *reason* for the distraction, a reason lodged somewhere in the dowager's known biases . . . her protectiveness of her great-grandson, for instance?

The boy had had *one* association in his life with kids his own age, and those kids had been *these* kids. Cajeiri was at an age where he should be forming critical associations, a pattern of relationships that would not change much in later life . . . essential connections that *were* not friendships. Man'chi didn't wear out, change with age, or weaken with time and distance—one had figured that out over time. Man'chi was something else.

But it could grow strange and strained. It could, if neglected, rupture catastrophically. He'd seen that in more than the machimi plays. He couldn't, being human, *feel* identically with the emotion, but he could certainly feel an analog, and he didn't take any atevi relationship—including hatred—as transient. A breach of man'chi was serious.

And in the dowager's household, in *her* context, with Irene—he suddenly thought he *did* detect a glimmering of Ilisidi's reasoning. The one of the kids who was most threatened, the one who'd just had a life-altering breach with her mother— Irene was, in Ilisidi's eyes, a point of instability far more critical and dangerous to her great-grandson than Andressen could be.

So he *did* get it.

Come *here*, girl, be *here*, feel *safe*.

Conform. Enter, and cooperate.

God, of *all* people to attempt to shape a human child's relationships, *Ilisidi* was not the one he'd choose. But it was always and only Cajeiri she was protecting, damned straight it was. Ilisidi was going to shape her grandson's contacts, his associations, and his opportunities to attach man'chi. Irene, unattached, claimable, and shapeable, had gained the dowager's attention.

Things once associated, the kyo had said, were always associated. They'd said it as plainly as they'd said anything. Humans in particular had tried to construe it a dozen different ways, tried to figure out if it was friendly or threatening . . .

But a connection in atevi terms was neither. Friends didn't exist, and man'chi couldn't be shed, not without catastrophe.

He felt a little chill he hadn't felt in a long time, where it came to atevi. He'd failed to understand. He was preparing to talk to people who were truly alien, and he'd failed to grasp what was making frequent passage right past his front door, among people closest to him.

Would his aishid ever leave him, ever break from him? No. They *could* not. And he *would* not leave them. Therein was the difference between species. Could and would. Two very different things, provoking the same action.

The logic was there. They didn't do things the same way. The dowager didn't react to crisis by closing in and shutting out. She expanded out. She reached for what was loose, and instinctively secured it.

Things once associated are always associated. The kyo can't unmeet us. They can't undo the decision to attack Reunion. They can't carry on as if none of these profound things had happened. They want to nail it down. They want a resolution, not a problem.

Something to their advantage.

"Paidhi?"

He was not *that* unperceptive. He'd felt his way through situations with a tolerably good vision for a good path. Understanding the logic might take a while. But the path—

"Nand' paidhi."

Bang. The formidable cane. On the hard flooring.

For one brief moment, he was back in ancient Malguri, in the dowager's domain, sharing a cup of tea at their first meeting, and then . . . he was back. The dowager was, in vivid present tense, standing in the doorway of her sitting room, hands on her cane, having arrived at his request.

He stood up immediately, gave a proper bow, to which Ilisidi nodded, and walked in, not without curiosity. The dowager was never without curiosity.

"One begs pardon, aiji-ma," Bren said, chagrined.

"The paidhi-aiji was thinking," Ilisidi said. "One trusts it is a recoverable thought."

"It was a useful thought, aiji-ma. Your presence—has a favorable impact. Always." He stood until Ilisidi sat down, then settled back into his chair. Cenedi was with her—Cenedi was almost always with her, constant shadow, but Nawari was not, at the moment, which likely meant Nawari was talking to Banichi and the rest of his aishid out in the foyer, a routine sort of exchange.

"Flatterer," Ilisidi reprised, as the servants moved about, serving tea and little cakes. "A useful thought, you say."

"I have now firmly resigned worrying about humans or atevi, aiji-ma, or worrying over any difficulties that Lord Geigi can solve. I have begun to think concentratedly about the kyo. One is in process of planning."

"We hear they are now coming to dock at the station," Ilisidi said. "You have invited them to do so."

"It seemed more convenient than committing our mission to a junior captain aboard *Phoenix*, aiji-ma. Riggins-aiji is closely allied to Ogun-aiji, and we do not know him. The offer we have made the kyo to come to the station tests their willingness to trust us, if they will do so, and signals our willingness to admit them." His arrangement would also be safer and more comfortable for Ilisidi, but he gracefully omitted that consideration. "As to what I was thinking, as you entered, aiji-ma—I was considering that if they believe things once associated are always associated, they may have something of that motive in coming here . . . simply to examine what we are and to reach a certainty instead of a conjecture. Perhaps to *assess* the damage of our association to themselves, perhaps to discover what a continued association could mean—and in that light, it might well be the same ship and crew we met. That was my thought, among others."

"Indeed, a reasonable consideration," Ilisidi said.

"Does it seem so?" he asked. "At times, aiji-ma, I question my own reasoning. Particularly in this case. The variables are so many."

"How would Mospheirans deal, in their situation?"

If one gave information to the aiji-dowager, it stayed, for all future purposes, available to her.

"We are very mutable," he said, "and we would argue a great deal among ourselves about the composition of the mission, their associations, their instructions, and their limitations."

"Mospheirans would wish to continue the matter subject to debate even into the event, no matter the shifting nature of the information," Ilisidi said wryly. "One has occasionally observed this tendency."

"One regrets," he said over a sip of tea, "one finds this same lamentable tendency in oneself."

"So doing, you question your own reasoning, debating within your own mind."

"A factor, indeed."

"And yet, this mutability is a useful trait," Ilisidi said, "since you *can* change your footing more quickly than some atevi of our acquaintance. We spent two years dealing with the ship-folk *and* the Reunioners, at some small remove. Prakuyo an Tep, on their side, endured six years of Reunioner governance, so he may find dealing with atevi a relief. We *are* perhaps less complicated than the Reunioners."

"One would never call the aishidi'tat uncomplicated."

"Ah, but we do manage ultimately to make a decision. And in this, *we* have an objective—a reasonably simple one: to continue as we are, undisturbed."

"Indeed, aiji-ma."

"Human agility of thought, and slowness in decision. And atevi stability of thought, and quickness to respond. I have the impression that the kyo themselves are not without complexity. For that very reason, stability on some points is useful, else we slip off into confusion and assumption. Atevi and humans have *also* learned, from the War of the Landing, that even ancient certainties can change. We have lately been reassuring these western Guild, these Observers, for instance, that *your* judgment is reliable, when they have for centuries held that they cannot trust us Easterners. And they are about to trust *us* Easterners to deal with the kyo, and they will soon be asking *you* how far to trust these visitors."

"I deeply regret if I have challenged their trust in me."

"Your very presence challenges them, and they have stepped far out onto that path. They have seen firsthand the dangerous territory that exists up here between two sorts of humans, and they now observe the dangerous territory you have navigated for the aishidi'tat—to our benefit. They are impressed. They are not so confident in the Reunioner children, and they ask what influence these different humans may bring to bear on my great-grandson. Well, well, time *someone* dared ask such things. But they have seen the advantage my grandson derives from his human association in *his* administration, and they understand with some amazement that it is your intention to make Reunioners and Mospheirans one people."

"By no means a smooth road, aiji-ma."

"Yet the journey is begun, thanks to you, and the Observers have seen this and are in favor of your doing it. They have also realized that up here in the great heavens there are forces and numbers which must be dealt with, now that we have entered this territory. We must rule ourselves wisely, so as not to be ruled by others, and the aishidi'tat as a whole must rapidly form wider associations and make new alliances—as we Easterners did when we joined with the west. We did not lose by it. Nor did the west." A wicked smile stole forth, a twinkle of amusement. Controversy? Intrigue? Scandal? The dowager maintained her legendary orthodoxy while being a ruthless agent of change. "I have shocked these Observers, perhaps, but they have come here to be informed at all manner of things, and they take their advisements from Cenedi, from Banichi, and from Geigi's bodyguard as well. We are oil and humans are water. We do not need to be other than what we are to exist in the same vessel. Are the kyo yet a third thing? They seem so."

"One is glad to know the Observers are seeking advice."

"The Observers do ask politely to be briefed on the kyo situation."

"I shall definitely make that effort."

"And they *will* advise the aiji to accept your judgment on the Reunioner solution."

That was off the map. And not entirely comforting. "Aiji-ma, one hopes for review and advisement."

Ilisidi gave a dismissive flick of the fingers. "Oh, eventually we shall have an opinion. But our word to the Observers was that Mospheira itself will do quite enough debating on their own. We should not complicate it unnecessarily. We simply say that if the Reunioners stay up here we must match their numbers on the station, and that if they go down to the world, they will not settle on atevi land. Both things you have already said. We are also confident you will not work to the detriment of the Presidenta who has been so serviceable to the world at large, and you will make it very clear that good relations with the aishidi'tat are always to Mospheira's benefit, in this matter and others. We have every confidence in you."

He perfectly understood *that* argument.

"More," Ilisidi said, "and in that same understanding, we shall take care of our own young guests until there is *no* likelihood of any demand from any other authority to take them. See to it that all relevant people are aware of our claim. We will not be interfered with. And we trust that Mospheira will cooperate in this, as *we* will cooperate with them in this business with the kyo. We shall consider Mospheiran welfare and the welfare of the aishidi'tat to be linked, and we *shall* maintain it in its current balance of power."

Scarily blunt. "Yes," he said, "that is the Presidenta's understanding."

"Henceforth, where it regards the kyo, you will represent the aishidi'tat, *not* the Presidenta of Mospheira."

"Yes," he said. It *was* where he had to stand. Ironically, by Mospheira's own appointment, that was where he was always required to stand—even if, at times, he seemed to be taking his stand in a place utterly black and without any bearings. It was necessary. The immediate universe worked, because, at critical times, he did exactly that.

"We have read your account of the meetings with these two Reunioners. We place no confidence in the representations of the girl's mother, nor in those of the man who was taken with her."

She would not so much as say the names, and it was not inability to pronounce them. She certainly would not release the girl to her mother: she made that clear by declaring Irene under her protection, in atevi territory. Mospheiran sensibilities might experience a little twinge of guilt over the fact. But Mospheiran sensibilities were not now in charge of Irene Williams, nor ever would be while the dowager held her resolve.

"Yes, aiji-ma," he said again. Ilisidi might not personally keep the child. But Irene would be free of the influence of both those people—and seeing to that, where humans were concerned, would be *his* responsibility. He had no question. He understood, now, how it was.

Sip of tea. On both sides.

"How is she faring?" he asked, and Ilisidi pursed her lips.

"Well. Quite well. —Did we not just hear that you are divorcing yourself from such details?"

"Indeed, aiji-ma. You did indeed just hear it. I make a solemn promise."

"So, well. She is not your concern. She will, we believe,

choose to go back to the other children in Geigi's care so long as we are engaged with the kyo. We have advised it. *That* association, of all her associations, should not be broken."

For someone with no more knowledge of human children than she did the landscape of Maudit—Ilisidi surprised him.

But then, Ilisidi had gotten everything she owned by reading situations that others didn't.

Jase was back, quietly, without his bodyguard, and without advance notice. Bren heard it when he arrived back in his own foyer, and his first thought—not entirely unfounded—was a fear that his exchange with Jase about needing asylum because of actions taken in the Reunioner matter . . . might have become real.

Jeladi had shown Jase to the sitting room, ordinary enough procedure; and stayed with him. Not that one did not trust Jase, but Jase's actions were out of pattern, and yes, elderly Narani had also appointed himself to serve Jase tea and keep a close eye on their trusted ally.

Jase, who had had experience of great houses, stood up when Bren arrived, and paid a considered and respectful bow to Narani, as if to say—I know why you've been standing there. Narani reciprocated with courtesy—one knows you knew—and staff could relax, now that Banichi and Jago were in the room. Narani and Jeladi quietly left.

"Apologies," Bren asked in ship-speak. "Staff is worried. How are we doing?"

"So far, so good," Jase said. "The kyo ship is reacting, ongoing. They received the assigned path by schematic. It looks as if they read it more or less accurately and they're going to follow it."

"You're getting updates on their position."

Jase tapped his left ear, where there was a com plug. "Lord Geigi's assistance. I told him I'd be briefing you. Ogun sent me."

"Ogun." *Sabin* would have been his expectation.

"Cynically I think Ogun is convinced Sabin *would* have sent me and, if she had, *Sabin* would be the one getting my report. But that's all right. This way they'll *both* get reports."

"Gin's in the loop, too."

"Absolutely. She's interfacing with ship-com with no problems. Ogun's happy, Sabin's happy. I don't know about Riggins, but I'm happy. We're as happy as we can be with a shipful of unknowns barreling down on us. I hope there's no problem over here."

"Just worry about the situation," he said, with that feeling of all the china stacked, so, so delicately, and not wanting to disturb any arrangement he'd put in place. "Not enough pieces to finish the puzzle . . . and I've got a few that just don't fit."

But of pieces that did, he had his aishid, he had his staff, he had the dowager and her household. And Geigi and Gin.

Now he had Jase, sent by the senior captain to keep him informed. All involved administrations aligned to a unified purpose. That, he hadn't expected. But he'd certainly take it.

"I have the guest room," he said. "It's yours for the duration if you want to stay, and I can work you into the arrangements we're making for the kyo. I'd be relieved to have you close."

"Information and Bindanda's cooking thrown in."

"Exactly."

"How can I resist? I'll call for a few changes of clothes and my personal kit. But I'll need to keep myself tapped into ship-com from here. And there, understand."

"No objection at all. And I'll advise staff it's proper. Ship should know *exactly* what we're doing at all times. Your expertise with the technical issues will be an asset, definitely. But otherwise I'm going to be a bad host. I'll be working. My hours are odd and I can't do regular briefings. You'll have to rely on Narani to find out what's going on—he'll be talking to Banichi *and* Cenedi and Geigi—everybody who's likely to know anything. He'll keep you briefed. That's a promise."

"You do what you need to do as long as you need to do it and don't worry about me. I'll be available, I'll put no demands on the staff, but I *will* relay information up to Ogun as needed. Don't worry about him, not in this. Once he commits to a course—and he's only annoyed that he had no choice about it—he's committed. And he's put things in your hands. He just wants not to be surprised by anything."

"Understandable. And I admit to a certain relief at the cessation of background power games. —Get whatever items you need for a stay. Welcome. Move in Kaplan and Polano if you like. I'll advise Narani and Kandana you'll be here for the duration, with absolute clearance. If you can bridge to Geigi *and* the Reunioner guests for me and keep them informed and calm, you'll take one more thing off my mind."

"No problem," Jase said. "I'll do anything you need."

"Top priority in this household is going to be information, rest, and food, as much as we can get in any category whenever we can get it. We need to stay informed, and we need to stay able to make sane decisions at any hour."

"Understood," Jase said.

They'd worked together, been under attack together, time after time. He had no doubt at all that Jase understood.

Having Jase at hand, someone who could read the manner of the kyo approach, who could predict and advise in terms of ship behavior—was a great relief.

"What's your sense of the kyo's schedule?"

"Last report, they're blowing off *V*. We're watching that. They've seen us maneuver. We haven't seen them. We're assuming the same systems, but we're interested—technically—in their operations. Once they're rid of that energy, they'll lay down an approach course, fine it down, and by that time we'll have a reasonably accurate schedule, barring something unforeseen. They won't have large corrections to make, but there should be some. Their original course would blaze through real scarily near us."

Jase went on to explain the technicalities, which might have made sense, had he not had his brain attuned to his own technicalities at the moment. Information of that sort simply slid off nouns, verbs, aspects, and tenses like water off wax, substances impossible to mix. He nodded at appropriate times, and found Jase's features blurring in his vision.

"And this is the last thing you need clouding your mind."

He blinked, found an understanding look on Jase's face.

"Get back to thinking kyo, Bren. We're running out of time." And with that, Jase went off with Tano to talk to Kandana, and Bren sat where he was, Jase's final words ringing in his ears.

Running out of time . . .

God.

His heart began to race. He tried to push the urgency out. He had what time he had, nothing could change that, and he needed to make the best use of it, not waste time paralyzed with the ticking of the clock. And as if Jase's words, or perhaps his arrival, his assumption of responsibility for all the pesky communication problems had tipped some scale, triggered something deep within his subconscious, his thoughts grew fuzzier and fuzzier and his eyes drifted shut, though he wasn't sleepy. He recognized the state of mind, a thought trying to reach the conscious mind, a set of images, of impressions, bits and pieces bubbling up from the mental basement—widely separated elements trying to assemble into a meaningful whole.

He needed to lie down. Rest. Let his subconscious do the work a lifetime of work had trained it to do . . .

He was in the kyo ship, a dim, ornate interior. A complex of unidentifiable smells, rumbling voices no human throat could duplicate, Banichi's face, and Jago's.

He saw Ilisidi's amusement, floating globes, and swaying curtains of plants: *Phoenix.* The voyage out and the voyage home.

He'd had ample time, then, to think about the kyo's promise to visit. When his mind wasn't fuzzed with the transit.

He'd considered it in human terms, and in atevi context.

Things associated must always be associated.

Understandings once made should be kept vivid, never allowed to deviate into separate, potentially hostile states of mind.

Atevi managed it by clans, that intricate family structure that guaranteed stable situations, stable arrangements, and because of those relationships and links, personal safety. Man'chi—loyalty, attachment—needed not be identical, but it needed to remain compatible.

The kyo, a monoculture by all they had been able to determine in their brief contact, might well feel themselves at risk, being seen, visited by strangers—for all they knew, an intrusion into their native solar system.

The kyo were apparently at war with the only other intelligence they knew.

Finding a ship where it shouldn't be, the kyo had mistaken the terms, the nature, the identity of what they were following. They had blasted their way into a situation that was to them without precedent—a mistake that, if reciprocated in kind, might jeopardize their own world, their own existence as a species.

Suddenly, out of the chaos, a word surfaced: *reciprocation.*

The one thing they had established in their encounters with the kyo—was reciprocation. Reciprocation in the messages. Echoes. Signal for signal. Exact.

Things once associated were always associated.

Reciprocation. Echoes of messages, exact echoes.

To the logic of what motivated this visit, *that* possibly mattered. Were they establishing some sort of symmetry in the relationship? A neighborly return visit . . . bringing teacakes?

Was it—could it be—conceptually that simple? Did he dare—

He blinked. Blinked again, was sitting in a chair with Jago standing in the doorway, looking at him. Two seconds, maybe. He'd been two years ago and back again. But not all the way back. Not yet. He was still dazed. *Phoenix* and the kyo ship seemed more real than his own office.

The past was still trying to drag his attention to something urgent.

"Bren-ji, you were asleep. Will you go to bed?"

Blink. "Not yet, Jago-ji."

Asleep? No, though it might have appeared so. He'd not phased out like this since—since two years ago, when he'd last worked so hard on the language. It was like being drugged. The brain was doggedly trying to join two frayed ends of thoughts that just couldn't get together in any sane way, though he could feel his brain struggling, trying to force that union. The room kept shorting out, bright lights giving way to kyo darkness and the miasma of incense, deep tones that vibrated through the air, and went straight to the gut. Plants growing madly, tiny cars racing down a tiled corridor . . .

That was it. That was where he needed to be. That was the mindset he'd been seeking since he got the news the kyo ship was coming. But he couldn't stay long enough. Jago called him back . . . or he'd flinched away. He blinked back to his own apartment on the station.

He was afraid. He'd been afraid when he'd had to venture aboard the kyo ship, and Jase's parting shot had put him right back into that terror-filled moment.

Right where he *needed* to be, however, on that ship. That old hollow feeling was back, a feeling that he was trapped, bouncing helplessly between two places, two modes of expression that could white-out one's thinking altogether. He wanted not to leave the memory before he had the answer, but Jago was here, pulling him out. He tried to put a mental marker there, just in case. He *had* to come back to that foreign place, that moment.

He wasn't entirely certain he could. And that uncertainty— scared him.

"Will you have tea?" Jago asked.

Two blinks. "Glass of brandy," he said, desperate, aware of

Banichi and Jago, now Tano and Algini. And Jase. Jase had come back into the room. When had that happened? "One regrets, nadiin—nandi." He saw their worried faces, but they seemed to be in the dim lighting of the kyo ship, memory vividly painting over the bright light around him. "I am rather tired."

Exhaustion was not all the cause, not half. He recognized the fugue state, the brain persistently conjuring what was possibly relevant to a single lost and desperate thought battering its way up like a swimmer from the depths—and just not getting to the surface. The brain had finally let down the gates, because Jase and Gin and Geigi were all there, all taking care of those things that didn't, *couldn't* matter to him, and he could turn loose of all other worries. He could go back to that foreign ship, walk that remembered corridor, and see the kyo, every detail.

Massive folk, gray, robed in geometric patterns and shadows, expressionless to first observation—but not expressionless, if one had paid attention, while talking to the one kyo they knew.

He let the thought spread out like a chart: curiosity, suspicion, all those things at once. He recalled the kyo's expressions, detected one kyo's attention dancing between him and the dowager and a precocious child, *not* one species meeting another, but three species in face-to-face encounter, with the kyo trying to figure it all out at once.

A toy car on the table.

That was the instant that had opened the door for them: the gestalt of the visit to their ship was not a statement, but a question—who are you? What are you? A question coming from three sides and four. A child, and an elder, a woman, a man, and two species all stood connected in the same instant. Something was before them that the kyo hadn't even conceptualized. Everything was laid out—and nothing that either side had thought they understood was immediately understandable.

Prakuyo an Tep. The kyo they knew, years locked in a cell, the kyo that they had set free, that they had fed, and returned to his people—was there gratitude? Could one assume that emotion in another species? It was common to humans and atevi—but the underlying reasons were *not* identical.

Again that word surfaced: *reciprocation.*

We came to their ship to talk, he thought. *And we managed, from that risky beginning. Those were the pieces we had. That was the situation.*

Might this visit now be the reciprocation? The echo?

They'd offered the kyo peace. Understanding. If this visit *was* reciprocal . . .

The past . . . slipped away like oil, taking the fear with it.

Jago set a glass in his hand, the brandy he had asked for. He took a sip, tasted, smelled, felt the sip go down.

The shadows in front of him were not kyo. They were his people. The room was his room. He sat where he had always sat, feeling fragile, feeling exhausted—feeling embarrassed for the momentary lapse; but able now to conjure the memory of that ship, its sounds, smells, ambient urgently trying to overlay the sight of his own people, and the bright lights of a sitting room that was not his home on Earth.

If he let it.

"One had lost the thread," he murmured. "One had lost the beginning . . . not forgotten it, but lost it. Quite lost it." He was not sure how much time had elapsed just now—a few seconds, he thought. No, long enough for Jago to fetch a glass of brandy. But in that interval, one critical meeting had flowed through his head, and spread out in all its detail of color, texture, sound, smell, sense of gravity and light. Vibrations of kyo expression. He hadn't been able to remember the detail until now. He had needed to remember, and hadn't been able to, because he had lost that one essential connection. That moment of seeing the whole picture. "Dreaming awake, I think. I think I *am* tired."

Other images came back to him. An airport in Shejidan. The beginning of everything. Tabini's downstairs office. Ilisidi, sitting by the fireside in Malguri. Jase, when shadows and earthly sky had sent Jase's mind into chaos.

The beginnings of understanding. The *start* of everything.

The start of everything with the kyo had *truly* involved a seven-year-old boy, a toy car, and a plate of teacakes.

When the goal was to understand, coexistence was possible. Mistakes could be forgiven. Motive . . . surely meant something.

He'd intellectually remembered that. But so many things had come between, so much re-interpretation. Now he had remembered that moment from the *inside*. He had opened that door. Now he could go back there at will and look at the details, remember the sounds, and the texture.

"I remember," he said, and heaved another sigh. Blinked, and made his eyes focus. And his hand felt the glass he held. "If I drink this I fear I shall fall over. My mind needs to settle. One has remembered things one ought not to have forgotten." Which did not make thorough sense. "I remember." Third deep breath. He held out the brandy glass for Jago to take. "I have had enough, Jago-ji."

"Will you go to bed, Bren-ji?" Banichi asked.

"Yes," he said. His body was leaden. He was not sure he could get up. But he made the effort. "Jase. Sorry."

"Rest," Jase said. "You need to be sharp."

Sharp. He stifled a wry chuckle, nodded, and let Jago's hand on his elbow guide him out of the room . . .

13

Everything was ready for the meeting, the guards in place, the kyo proceeding in their slow way toward the appointed meeting room. They were using *Phoenix* and not the station for this second meeting. He could not remember why.

But he saw Prakuyo an Tep, or one among very similar faces who *might* be the kyo they had rescued.

He bowed. He wished to say hello, or what passed for a greeting. It was a simple word.

And he suddenly, absolutely, could not think of it. His mouth wouldn't shape it. Prakuyo an Tep addressed him in ship-speak, but he could not get the meaning from that either.

He stared at all those faces, and suddenly, the venue was kyo, aboard their ship, in dim lighting, amid strange smells, with gravity pulling him into the floor. And Ilisidi was depending on him. She was at risk, and Cajeiri was, and he could not summon a single word.

He could not remember. He simply could . . . not . . . remember.

He waked, heart pounding, in bed, in the dark.

God—had it happened? Was it true?

Had he just lost not only the words, but all the time between?

Or was this the greatest case of test anxiety in history?

God.

He couldn't afford this. If he'd broken down, if he couldn't manage the interface he'd come up here to reestablish, *every-thing* could break down. And they were dealing with people who'd destroyed a space station in a single shot.

He couldn't remember getting here. Didn't know where *here* was. He couldn't remember anything but the kyo ship.

But he wasn't there. Definitively he was *not* aboard the kyo ship. Gravity was normal.

If he was truly in his own bed, in this blind darkness, he would hear fans, which there were, and he would see two small lights, right next to the door, indicators for the door lock. Which there also were.

And the two lights were green, so that staff could come and go. And Jago could.

Jago. Jago had gotten him to bed. He was *not* on *Phoenix*. Nor on the kyo ship. He was on the station. In his bedroom, in his apartment. He wanted to be here, safe, with time left. He desperately wanted to be here, and wanted that disastrous, blank-minded meeting never to have happened.

The two tiny green eyes stared at him, reassuring him it *was* his bedroom in *his* station apartment.

Memory sifted back. He had *seen* Jase last night. That was where things stood. He still had time. A fair amount of time to prepare for the meeting.

Jago had gotten him here. She had sat on the bedside briefly before he went to sleep. She had said sternly, that he needed sleep, which he had agreed was very much the case, though he had been wide awake, in that ship, at the time. And he thought—he didn't know when he had shut his eyes. In the dark, sometime after, he *had* slept.

He didn't, however, feel rested now. He felt wrung out, the nightmare still vivid, heart still beating hard. And the truth behind the nightmare really *was* the truth. He *didn't* have enough shared words, not of kyo, not of Ragi or Mosphei'. The interface with Prakuyo had been a shifting amalgam of all three. They had managed with pointing, with gestures, with diagrams.

And if the kyo they called Prakuyo *wasn't* on the ship, he hadn't at the moment a chance in hell of communicating anything he really needed to tell them.

Bren. Ilisidi. Cajeiri. The first voice message from the ship had said. *Prakuyo an Tep. Speak.*

Prakuyo an Tep. He'd responded. *Bren-paidhi. Come.*

And a final message from the ship: *Prakuyo come.*

So simple. So straightforward . . . if they could trust that transmission. *Was* it the kyo they'd met? The one who had shared teacakes and basked in Cajeiri's enthusiastic attention? Or was Prakuyo an Tep a title? Had Prakuyo passed on what he knew of the languages to another kyo ship and were they using it gain access to Alpha? Why? What if it wasn't even a kyo ship? What if the kyo's enemies had taken that ship, and Prakuyo and—

God. Was *that* the source of the nightmare? If it was a probe from the kyo's enemies, using the kyo's language could set up assumptions they truly didn't want.

His heart began to race again. He sternly reined in that entire line of thought. He had *no* basis for that panicked flight of fancy, and more than enough reason to believe the most likely option, namely that the kyo they knew as Prakuyo was going to come aboard the station once the kyo ship docked, and that he and Prakuyo, who did owe him, were going to pick up where they'd left off, as far as communication was concerned.

But no species traveled lightyears for a chat over tea and cakes. The kyo would be looking at everything, analyzing . . . everything.

What would the kyo perceive of the context they saw here? If they'd come looking for the *we* that was human coexisting with atevi, would they find what they needed, and would they be reassured, or alarmed?

They'd see a station fundamentally the same as Reunion. Same blueprints. Same structure. Same species signature, nothing atevi about it, except that, here, atevi had begun to make changes in the layout of residential space, commercial space, office space. So it was not identical to Reunion—just similar on the outside. They *might* see that atevi influence in their quarters here, but would they recognize it as *different?* Atevi as yet *had* no style of station-building that would say to the kyo—this is different. This is *our* way of building in space.

But they'd *see* primarily atevi folk in the corridors and meeting rooms. *Atevi* were in charge of the interface with the kyo. Dared they let the kyo see the other interface, human with atevi?

The kyo might well assume the station was of atevi design as much as human. Possibly more so: from their viewpoint, it might well appear that atevi had been in command of *Phoenix.* Atevi had negotiated the evacuation. The force that had rescued Prakuyo from Reunion had been atevi, and Prakuyo had seen primarily atevi, once he'd boarded the ship.

But Prakuyo had seen only humans for the six years he spent on Reunion. He might well have accurately understood that that was a human domain.

Humans had built Reunion in an area of space the kyo claimed.

Humans had built another station here, in space that belonged to atevi.

How were the kyo to interpret that history? Did two instances mean a pattern of behavior that only confirmed what the kyo suspected? That humans were expansionist— aggressively so?

They might wonder, was this solar system the origin of humans, and were atevi the power behind human behavior? Or was it the other way around? He had tried to clarify that point in their first meeting aboard the kyo ship, using a kyo pad and pen to draw pictures on a screen. He'd tried to show that the human home world was not the atevi home world, that humans had come to the atevi world and built the station. That the human ship left while the station humans went to the world of the atevi and became part of it. That *association* had occurred here, while the ship went off and built Reunion in kyo space.

But what if they hadn't gotten that from that small scattering of pictures?

He wished he had that drawing, for reassurance, if nothing else, but it was, as far as he knew, lost forever, unless the kyo chose to save it in their files. Save it. Review it . . . and possibly read into it what they or some higher authority *wanted* to see.

There were so many ways for their visitors to draw a wrong conclusion. Clarification required words, and vocabulary was still very much table, chair, floor, food, drink—except for some bad language Prakuyo had picked up on Reunion in ship-speak.

Those, and a handful of uniquely atevi words Prakuyo had latched on to, some of which, like association, he strongly suspected had vastly different connotations for all three species using it. They'd found it easiest to *speak*, such as they could, in Ragi, but that did little to help him understand the kyo. Working in the kyo language was beyond puzzling. It seemed to maintain an insanely flexible dividing line between nouns and verbs.

The kyo *had* to conceptualize some difference between substance and action. It had to be there. There *was* a fundamental difference. Or . . . was he locked in some mental box that happened to be common to humans and atevi, unable to imagine beyond it?

Making sit and chair one word was either incredibly primitive, or reached into concepts that sounded like Jase discussing physics.

Or was it more philosophical than that? Perhaps for the kyo form without function . . . didn't exist. Association? Were humans and atevi *associated* because they performed a unified function?

He couldn't go down that road. Wasn't mentally *ready*. He hadn't nearly enough data.

Human language had had a bad start with the kyo, as it had

with the atevi. There were far too many ambiguities of meaning, too many emotionally charged experiences behind Prakuyo's ship-speak vocabulary. Ragi was neutral—and seemed to
strike some happier chord with Prakuyo. Maybe the sounds
were easier for the kyo mouth to form, maybe it was the way
the grammar fitted together.

Or maybe it was that the words had come first from an atevi
child, who had come armed with a child's picture book and a
happy, feckless way of expecting goodness from people. He
credited Cajeiri with the real breakthrough—perhaps, though it
was dangerous to guess—just the boy's childish innocence had
communicated a peaceful intent. He didn't know.

He simply . . . didn't . . . know.

His heart still pounded. That fear, the memory of that first
encounter was in that dream. Fresh. He could go back to that
dream and try to hammer out an understanding inside it, but he
was, he began to think, truly scared to go back there—not physically scared, the way he'd been that first time, but psychologically terrified. When he dreamed, he dreamed he could not *do*
what three species needed him to do, and he did *not* need a
mental roadblock built on self-doubt. He had worked on the
vocabulary he had. He had run up against concept—a wall that
ought to be permeable, if he could just take for granted kyo
logic was anything like atevi or human logic, and that was a
dangerous step to take, one that might go right off into dangerous error.

They *had* been able to deal in concepts involving tangibles,
like people, station, and getting the Reunioners aboard. They
had arranged a deal. Give us time. We get your fellow out. We
get fuel, we get the people out. We leave.

But reasons? Explanations? Value-sets? Morality?

Perhaps science had to be the key. The laws of physics were
not open to interpretation. Perhaps he needed to put Jase and
his esoteric physics to the fore of this meeting and just step
back and hope. Or should he rely on a nine-year-old who had

met a kyo with a child's curiosity and a young aiji's brash confidence—and bet on emotion and moral sense? He was so used to questioning emotion, to fencing it off and controlling it around atevi—had he a blind spot in that category? Did he trust it too little?

Ilisidi had made no attempt to modify her approach to accommodate a different species. Hell no. She had simply assumed that, being intelligent enough to have starships, they would be intelligent enough to communicate with *her*. And she had confronted them with an *of course* attitude that had made it clear she was attentive and expected answers that would make sense to her. *She* had made a very critical difference, and done it without knowing a word of Prakuyo's language. Prakuyo had made his own interpretation. Prakuyo had concluded she was authority, and was treating him with courtesy, which itself had to be comforting.

Suddenly, his heart stopped pounding. Even skipped a beat.

And who else, he asked himself, do you intend to delegate to solve *this* problem? Gin, Jase, Geigi? Ilisidi? God, he was generating his own panic. Run away from the challenge? His entire *life* fitted him to figure this out. And panicking, when all those people needed him to use his science and get this solved? *That* self-assessment left a very sour taste in his mouth.

Cajeiri, innocence and curiosity, had gotten the figurative door open. Ilisidi, power and curiosity, had shoved it wide. Now *he* had to walk through it, use his own science, and deal. His mistakes, more than the others', might come back to haunt them, involving the only world they had, and a species capable of reaching them, for good or for ill. But in his own lifetime, he had a hope of fixing whatever mistakes he did make.

Walk through a door. Go where he had to. Even if—God help him—it meant going where he didn't want to go. Boarding their ship and maybe not coming back for a very long time—or ever.

It was what the paidhiin did. They'd done it on the planet. It might require—going much farther.

Maybe that had been part of the nightmare, too. He'd been, in that dream, alone with them. He'd been on their ship. There'd been no exit. No way back. Just forward.

And he hadn't been able to summon up a word. Any word. He'd frozen.

He *was* scared—deeply scared. He'd faced life and death situations, made snap decisions that could change the shape of a world, with less fear than he felt now.

This time, he had nothing solid upon which to base—anything. It was all a structure of best guesses. And he'd run out of time to find answers.

He stared into those unblinking, green eyes in the dark, seeing not the lights, but a night terror, the unknown personified. He was good, *damned* good at his job, but this was different. This didn't have the University behind him with centuries of records and a dictionary. This couldn't be solved with Tabini-aiji's authority. Or his bodyguards' firepower.

Bottom line, they were all relying on him for this one. He had to make aggressive guesses about structure, and make mistakes and hope not to insult anyone. If he insulted someone, he had to get past it and fix it.

They'd met without words—but they'd managed. Pings. Flashing lights. Tiny forty-nine by forty-nine pixel black-and-white animations. They'd negotiated a temporary *peace* without words.

And he'd conceived *that* communication on the fly, standing on the ship's bridge, with the kyo ship's guns likely aimed straight at them.

You want your person back. We want the people out. Deal.

And deal it had been. Quick. Efficient.

Adrenaline had been his ally. Quick thinking had arrived at quick response. It was this damned extended waiting and preparation that prompted the night terrors.

But caution was the constant constraint on the paidhi. Observe reaction, get one safe word, the meaning of which seemed plain.

It was the way paidhiin had operated—but with a larger dictionary—for generations.

Until finally, in his tenure, in Tabini's, humans and atevi had thrown convention and caution to the winds and ventured to speak together, freehanding a conversation.

It had only taken them two hundred years.

In point of fact, it had taken him, when he'd first arrived to deal with Tabini—two *days* to make that leap. Two days . . . and one cold moment when he'd been dead certain he'd made a misstep and they were about to start their relationship as adversaries . . .

. . . The man at the desk looked up. Beckoned in the atevi way, with one move of his hand, then pushed his chair back.

Tabini-aiji surprised him with his youth. He was twenty-three with an athletic build and he stood taller than most of a very tall people. Eyes were paler gold than most, unnerving and capable of a cold, cold stare.

Tabini gave a little head-tilt, impatient, as if to say, *Say something, fool. My time is valuable.*

"Bren Cameron, nand' aiji. You requested my presence."

A dark brow lifted. Another tilt of the head, this time in evident surprise.

"You *talk.*"

A conversation had followed. A conversation of few words. But a conversation.

His predecessor, Wilson, had never uttered a sentence in Ragi. Not in forty years of service. Forty years of written communication with everyone he dealt with.

The man, when he retired, had not been altogether sane, in Bren's opinion. But he hadn't so much retired as been fired. Tabini had come into office, a new aiji, a man impatient to get on with the business of his own administration.

Tabini had rejected the next paidhi, Wilson's recommendation. And a second, with teaching experience. And rejected a third, a week later. And a fourth. The State Department, running near the bottom of its short list of qualified candidates, had sent papers on another candidate, much younger, with no publication to his name, one whose graduate thesis was, in Ragi, *A Consideration of the Cultural Impact of Food Preservation Technology in the Aishidi'tat.*

He'd never really had proof Tabini had read that paper. He was *quite* certain that his youth and that vacuous-looking graduation photo had put him at the bottom of the State Department's list—and set him at the top of Tabini's.

One sentence. And another. Two very young men, new to their respective positions, had found each other a challenge. Tabini, who'd likely planned to bully the next paidhi into major concessions such as Wilson had given, had a paidhi who'd explained to him, in limping Ragi, how Wilson's technological concessions could pose a serious threat to the atevi culture, and what they could do to turn those items to assets.

Two young men—who could laugh, rather than take offense, at the inevitable mistakes.

The University hadn't found out about his mortal sin— dealing in the spoken language—until *after* he'd worked his way to reasonable fluency.

The University hadn't been happy. They'd called him back. But Tabini had insisted he had exactly the paidhi he wanted. So the University had given their representative a severe cautionary lecture, first of many, and sent him back.

He knew all the reasons for the cautions. Humans and atevi had gone too far, too fast, too early, when desperate humans had ridden the petal sails down and made contact with atevi in numbers. They'd gotten along right well in that process. The War of the Landing hadn't been fought between atevi and the *first* humans to come down to Earth, oh, no. It had happened well into a period of trust and cooperation. It had happened in too much trust, too *much* cooperation and confidence.

Wrong moves. Wrong assumptions. Culturally *destructive* assumptions that had led two perfectly rational species right over the brink. From happy picnics to full-blown warfare.

Because no one had considered the inescapable biological triggers inside the languages, and what certain assumptions might do.

One could hardly blame subsequent generations for being just a bit cautious. But the fact was, two hundred years later, he'd seen problems growing in their *refusal* to deal more openly with the aishidi'tat.

Truth was, he'd *hoped* for the chance to take the office in a more aggressive direction. He'd just hoped to do it more slowly than he had. He'd had that much sense. But, God, he'd been too confident, shiny new and an absolute novice in atevi politics.

Wilson managed to get onto the Committee on Linguistics, the all-important Committee that regulated the department— the Committee that had once had oversight of *Wilson,* as now it had oversight of the new young man in the office. He was quite certain Wilson was behind the early maneuvers that subjected every submission he made to months of peer review. From the beginning, Wilson had called him reckless. In recent years . . . likely it was just as well Wilson was no longer privy to such information. He'd done the job that *needed* to be done, the job as the atevi understood it to be, and it had been years since that job had involved adding words to the official dictionary.

He'd become a lord of the atevi, in order to efficiently represent Tabini in the way Tabini wanted him to do, lord first of a small coastal estate, and then—in order to have the power he needed for the trip to Reunion—Lord of the Heavens.

That . . . was a bit of responsibility he'd never have anticipated—a title he was embarrassed to claim anywhere near humans.

Unfortunately since the voyage to Reunion, he hadn't sent routine reports to Mospheira, beyond the one massive report he'd sent to the President. He'd just forged ahead with getting

Tabini back in power and getting the shuttles back in service, and God, no, he hadn't Tabini's permission to tell the Mospheiran government about the aishidi'tat's internal problems, let alone let the problem loose in University politics.

On the other hand, thank God, his old ally in the State Department, Shawn Tyers, trumped the Committee on Linguistics these days, being the sitting President in a succession of terms. Likely Shawn was getting hourly communications from the State Department, and the Linguistics Department was likely hammering at the doors of State, wanting to know what was going on, wanting to be in control of the kyo interface, and getting nowhere.

So here he was in the very first paidhi's position—entirely on his own, in the early stages of communication with another, and demonstrably dangerous, species.

Go back to the first rules? Build a dictionary, word by disconnected word—for two hundred years? Develop a list of safe words, taking no chances, until something near catastrophic forced a change?

Or pursue the *personal* contact fate had thrown in their laps and go for broke? Was there more danger in *failing* to make full contact, than in keeping at a careful distance?

They were *not* going to have another War of the Landing on his watch. On that, he was determined.

Perhaps the real answer lay in a middle course. Humans and atevi had the experience of the War of the Landing: they knew the pitfalls.

But might he have, in Prakuyo an Tep, the kyo equivalent of Tabini? Someone eager for solutions . . . someone who could have an *emotional* reaction at a seemingly simple word—*we*—and yet, rather than shut down, figure it out, and manage to use it?

Someone who could take mistakes in stride. That had happened with Prakuyo. More than once, in their short time together. He had dealt with Prakuyo under stress. He had seen Prakuyo's resiliency, his ability to reconsider a situation.

They weren't in the situation humans and atevi had been in. He knew how to spot the pitfalls. They weren't sharing a planet. They had room to be separate. They also had a chance to be something else. He didn't know yet what was wise to be, because humans and atevi had never been here before.

He really had considered, on the voyage home from Reunion, turning all his kyo notes over to the University of Mospheira—and its Department of Linguistics. But, one, the notes contained information that might scare hell out of people. And, two, the University didn't have tight security, and it wouldn't stay contained. He'd meant to work the notes over, deliver *part* of them, but somehow that hadn't happened either, and not just because he'd been just a bit busy with Tabini's reinstatement.

Because there was a third reason, a reason he hadn't even admitted to himself until now. He didn't trust them. Didn't trust the entire department. They'd proceed by a process they'd worked out and used for two hundred years. They'd want to write papers, involve the State Department, and go by the departmental rules of contact, with, God help them, *Wilson* on the committee, telling the Mospheiran legislature how to deal with the kyo when they did arrive.

The politics of it . . . the notion of arriving at a rigid one-to-one correspondence of selected words, the bizarre notion that they could shape another species' concepts by *their* controlling the dictionary, that had muddied the human-atevi interface for two hundred years . . .

Arrogant on his side, perhaps, to think he could ignore two hundred years of that work, but the one thing he couldn't give the University was the experience of sitting across the table from Prakuyo and watching his response. He'd begun to get a *feeling* for the language. He'd gone into a couple of transits aboard ship while *thinking* on kyo grammar, kyo concepts, and he'd become—spooked, much as he hated to admit it. Spooked in an intellectual way, because the logic was there, and then not.

Yet.

Time was, Ragi must have seemed as strange to the first landed. The constant reference to numerology, wading in it, breathing it, must have confused hell out of those first humans who tried to communicate. He'd never been spooked by the numbers. They came easily to him.

He and Tabini had more than once discussed that truly dangerous word *friendship*. Tabini had tasted it at times, worried a little over it, laughed about its craziness, dismissed it from relevance, the same bewildered way his paidhi-aiji fretted over *man'chi* and tried his lame best to imagine how it felt.

Step and step and step. It had worked. Two individuals, wired differently *but aware of it*, had managed not to solve their deepest failures of understanding, but to understand they had them, and to build a bridge across them. He'd had *help* from Tabini's side of the table.

As he'd had help from Prakuyo two years ago.

He needed to pick up, ideally with Prakuyo, where they'd left off.

But on the station. In a sterile box of a room, void of familiar images and obvious situations and common interests, and far across space . . . where did he find the threads?

That had been part and parcel of the nightmare—that he stood in a barren, metal place and faced the kyo with no *words* to speak and nothing to point at, no way to find them.

No way? With his training? With the resources of the ship and an entire world to draw on?

Hell. He was better than that.

Prakuyo had tried. Prakuyo, even under miserable circumstances, had made a start on his own. If the kyo had sent Prakuyo here, then they were not going to start from zero. And if they hadn't sent him—

If they hadn't, well, he could start from what he had.

He had *one* core word in the kyo language: association. From cores—*other* words formed, assembling bits and pieces around them, a modular toolkit, mutating meanings, but likewise *associating* concepts in a relationship that carried history, instilled a way of thinking and directed thoughts down certain paths.

Two languages, unrelated even by species origin.

A boy, a toy car, the dowager, a plate of teacakes, and children's picture books—

And a memory: Cajeiri trying to reproduce a word, making a sound *he* had corrected . . . but Prakuyo had not. Cajeiri had deferred to him, but had Cajeiri been right all along? Atevi hearing was more acute than human. Atevi heard things humans did not. Heard *frequencies* the human ear couldn't. Human and atevi language overlapped, phonetically. The kyo language . . . the kyo's lips had limited mobility. Much of the sound came from deep in their throats. But was he hearing all of it?

He had ideas, God, his head was *flowing* with ideas, but they would take time to become reality. He wanted strong tea, he wanted Jase, and he wanted Geigi, in that order.

He wanted technology to pull up the images he needed at a moment's notice. He wanted technology to manipulate them. He wanted technicians who could record and analyze every sound Prakuyo uttered. And he wanted several trained and utterly trustworthy individuals working on the sound problem, real time, from the moment he entered the conference room and faced Prakuyo.

Then there was Ilisidi's method.

His thoughts spun to a sudden halt.

Ilisidi was the one who'd made the critical breakthrough with *him*, in the early days of his career as paidhi-aiji. He'd already broken rules left and right, communicating with Tabini. But she'd opened her own communications with him—damn near killed him with a cup of tea, then challenged him, pushed him, dragged him into her context and gotten understandings with him because, granted Ilisidi *had* decided to engage with him, she was going to pull him into *her* world, and not the other way around.

She'd done the same with Prakuyo. Well, except the poisoning.

She hadn't remotely attempted to be what she was not. She'd been what she was, acted as she always acted, let the kyo see an ateva who wasn't as outgoing as a child's innocence, or as malleable as a translator trying to live in all possible worlds at once.

The translator could well have given some false clues, being too willing to adapt. Like dealing with quicksand.

Ilisidi had offered Prakuyo the fixed point, the rock that did *not* budge, the one to whom atevi *and* human showed unwavering respect. She was proud, imperious . . . and polite. Her expectations were plain.

Be sensible. Be polite. And expedite a solution. Do *not* waste her time.

She'd met other kyo and they'd understood that, in her, there was a point around which an entire universe revolved. There was a child in her care, and there was her translator, who tried to be all things to all people . . . and gave off constantly shifting signals. Bren Cameron could be the one who didn't mind making guesses, who didn't mind conjecture. He could make the necessary moves, risk mistakes, absorb any blame, backtrack if he had to . . . that was his job.

But she, and her simple expectations, never wavered.

If the kyo had not met and communicated with other species—maybe they'd never met anybody like him, but they might have met her. They might well have produced Ilisidi's equivalent, but six years in confinement on a human station had also produced Prakuyo, who had been willing, eager, even, to explore any means of communication.

Was Prakuyo typical? Or an anomaly? It was difficult to know from the handful of kyo he'd met. Did it matter? The kyo ship had shown patience. Restraint. Ten years of it. That did not imply a species where irrational temper ruled.

Not to risk any mistakes?

On his level, there had to be mistakes. That was his usefulness. Perfection, absolute definitions—weren't how communication between strangers happened. He couldn't be Ilisidi. He couldn't be the child, either. What he could be was the translator. And if the kyo had figured that out, if Prakuyo's experience, even, had given one kyo an interest in communicating with strangers, they had come quite a distance on their own.

He had the keys. Now he needed a mutual context—something they *shared* with the kyo.

Technology. The keys to surviving in space. That was a start. He had no idea what the kyo planet was like, whether they'd even have a context for *tree*. But they had a computer. A pad and pen that could produce a graphic image. Stars. Planets. Physics. Causality.

He could *make* a context. Cajeiri had opened the door with a child's picture book. He *had* images—millions of images—at the touch of a button, and those he didn't have, he could create, the way they had created that graphic of ships and Reunion. They'd nailed down a simple alignment graphic. Then they'd gone to more complex images. Images independent of the method of transmission and reproduction at the other end.

He was *not* in the first paidhi's place, with no experience, no training, and no idea how to start. He *was* two hundred years advanced. He had training and tech at his disposal. He'd already negotiated the Reunioners out of Reunion.

Make the kyo understand the complex answers? Get an agreement with them?

He flung off the coverlet, turned on the lights, headed for his clothes. He wanted breakfast, a light breakfast, enough to energize, not to slow down his brain.

No way? *Hell* if there wasn't.

14

A letter to Tabini was, among other things, days overdue.

Aiji-ma, one regrets to have been slow to report. I have been engaged with a rapidly changing situation and have relied on the Guild and also on the aiji-dowager and Lord Geigi to relay the details, which they have done very well. Problems have been settled. We are now making rapid progress toward a peaceful reception of these visitors.

One is sure you have been informed that Tillington has definitely been replaced. The Presidenta's personal representative has taken over administration of all humans excepting the ship-folk. This person, as you surely know by now, is Gin Kroger, who is well-reputed among humans, including the ship-folk, and who was with us when we last dealt with the kyo. She is very ably managing her office.

Indications are now that the kyo do intend to dock with the station, which is what we hoped to see.

The aiji-dowager, having assisted in the Tillington matter in a major way, is taking the opportunity for rest, pending our encounter with the kyo. The young gentleman has been exemplary in behavior and has acted prudently, assisting from a place of safety, and has wisely delivered his guests to Lord Geigi's hospitality, devoting himself to his great-grandmother's orders.

One must not neglect to mention Lord Geigi, who has worked tirelessly for many days without relief, and spared time to care for the young gentleman's guests.

The kyo have slowed their pace considerably, in a peaceful way, and we are providing direction in diagrams for safe docking of their ship.

I must continue to rely on the Guild and Lord Geigi to convey information to you, aiji-ma, once the demands of the situation become urgent, but I shall not fail to represent your interests as of overriding import, aiji-ma, at all times, and in all resulting agreements, and I shall, on my life, aiji-ma, maintain the safety of the dowager and of your son.

For Shawn, on Mospheira, for public dissemination at Shawn's discretion:

Mr. President, the situation aboard the station has vastly improved in the last number of hours, first with the restoration of the treaty-mandated rotation of command with atevi authority, and now with the arrival of Dr. Kroger. Tensions which might have affected the safety of the station have greatly diminished. The atevi side of the station enthusiastically welcomes Dr. Kroger's advice and cooperation, and I have also heard favorable things from the Captains' Council regarding her decisions. She has my undying gratitude for her support. Mospheiran citizens have remained calm and are to my knowledge equally welcoming Ms. Kroger's experienced management.

The kyo have begun approach and have signaled they are looking for contact with the aiji-dowager, the young heir of the aishidi'tat, and myself as translator. This was the composition of our prior meetings. We have signaled our readiness to meet with them on those terms and the kyo are responding in a positive manner.

As regards the nature of the meetings we may hold with the kyo, speaking for the aiji in Shejidan and the aishidi'tat, we are one world, and while atevi representatives are meeting with the kyo, we shall work in the interests of all the world, Mospheira and its people as well as atevi. We wish to establish a good relationship with these visitors, with whom we hope to renew the cordial and cooperative relationship we established at Reunion. They will now see that our representation of our world as a peaceful neighbor is accurate.

I shall attempt to keep you informed during the progress of the meeting with the kyo, and if I am too closely involved personally to provide that information, I have every confidence that Dr. Kroger, in communication with ship command, will provide you constant updates.

Protection of Mospheiran interests is, in Tabini-aiji's view, inseparable from protection of the aishidi'tat. The aishidi'tat values its treaty obligations as strongly as it does its territorial integrity.

That last was a bold statement. It had become true without Tabini *or* the Mospheiran legislature being aware of it, but in view of the situation with the kyo, it was an essential point. Humans and atevi could *not* afford to quarrel in front of the visitors, and they could not afford to sell each other out in whatever negotiations resulted. Not now. Not ever.

For Toby, at Najida, the third letter:

Brother, so far, so good. Gin Kroger's arrived to take over the human side, and the kyo seem to want to talk to the three they talked to before—which is exactly what we hoped for.

At this point, they're definitely coming in, and we're ready to meet them. The station is quiet, the various administrations are all working with us, and we're getting responses from our visitors that match our best expectations.

I'll keep you posted as I can. Tell Ramaso to advise Najida and the staff at Shejidan that we're all safe and well here. Take care. Hope the weather's behaving better. Do some fishing if you can and don't worry.

Kandana had presented a letter from Tabini as he started his day's work, a letter which had arrived in Central during Geigi's watch, and which had prompted his belated flurry of letter-writing. It said, simply: *Lord Geigi informs us in daily reports. Our grandmother adds her impressions and commends your work. Attend your proper business as you are doing. We find no fault. We understand these foreigners are moving definitively toward the station with intent to talk. We support your mission in all regards.*

For Tabini, it was an unprecedented communication—a letter not asking for information, but simply stating his support and reporting that the dowager, equally uncharacteristically, had praised him. That was the shocking part.

He had read that letter three times, trying to absorb it, seeking alternate interpretations and hidden nuances . . . and finally decided that was truly what the letter said. Ilisidi, despite his irregular schedule and harried attack on problems, which ordinarily would annoy her, had specifically praised him as doing a good job.

That. After an ill-omened nightmare of failure. It was enough to make a sane man veer back into the chaos he'd just climbed out of.

But he had taken his balance. He *knew* what he had to do.

He sent the three letters off to Central, shoved Tabini's letter into the drawer, where he wasn't tempted to read it again, and settled down to do things the scholar's way, tedious, and with multiple-choice answers, somewhat like the University's methods—but not. Not, when it came to risk. Ambiguities might happen. Ambiguities and misunderstandings were themselves instructive—as long as both sides were sensible about them.

He needed nouns, yes. Which in this case were also verbs. A simple, straightforward correspondence such as he'd been trained to make was already out of the picture.

And if his ears weren't an accurate instrument—or if the kyo couldn't communicate accurately without things he couldn't hear, he had to take the initiative in dealing with the problem.

The ship's technicians were a resource. Jase might see to that. He needed as complete an audio analysis as they could make.

The technical part—he'd leave that up to Jase and Geigi.

Nuance. Emphasis. Prakuyo was far more atevi-like, expressionless, when it came to facial cues. Atevi learned to control their expressions from childhood up, a cultural choice. The kyo face appeared to be little more than skin over bone in areas where humans and atevi had complex musculature for expression. Atevi, dealing with strangers, went expressionless by choice and courtesy. Mospheirans and Reunioners were the opposite, faces constantly signaling—demonstrating deference or happiness or anger as their chosen expression, while almost inevitably betraying what they were really feeling by still more subtle muscle action: it was an insanely complex communication.

Perhaps that was yet another key to Prakuyo's preference for dealing with atevi. Calm faces. Ragi did have shifts for number, a confusing lot of shifts and infixes, but particles didn't change the core. If you just listened for the cores, the children's language, you could understand it. If you avoided the infixes, you could still be understood. Speak to Prakuyo in the same truncated way—and sequence the words in the Ragi way—that had gotten them quite far, considering. Mospheiran sentence order wasn't the way Prakuyo seemed to arrange his thoughts. That confused him. Ragi didn't.

He could deal with that. Facts would emerge first. Then they got to the soft tissue of attitudes. That realm of why. That very useful, dreadful word. Why? And its close cousin, Because.

Why, past tense, involved a blown space station and thousands dead. Why, present tense, was hard to explore but likely more useful. Why, future tense, was completely unformed as yet.

And you didn't get to that soft tissue of meaning with a one-to-one dictionary of correspondence, no matter how meticulous your note-taking. Constellations of words and related words led to conceptual clusters—how a chair fit into the constellation of sitting, traveling, or a trip to the accommodation.

It was *not* the University dictionary, Ragi words pinned down like insects on a board, passionately defined in Mosphei', with theories and reputations at stake. The all-powerful Committee had wanted to retain him in Analytics, where he could work on problem meanings, and where he'd probably to this day be sitting at some desk in the State Department basement. Send him across the strait to replace Wilson as paidhi-aiji? Not their plan. Not remotely.

They'd been even less happy when he'd become a guest of the aiji-dowager. They'd tried to remove him from the post, and the State Department, where Shawn Tyers had worked in those days, had broken the news to them that they couldn't. They had a new administration on the continent. They wanted intelligence. Tabini had slowed down food shipments to the island when his return was delayed, planes and ships delayed for repairs, and Tabini wouldn't talk to anyone else.

He hadn't known all that at the time, not remotely. The storm had raged behind doors he couldn't, at the time, have gotten through. And he would not have interpreted Tabini's demand to get him back as Tabini's approval. He'd have thought then that Tabini *wanted* a fool. He equally strongly suspected he'd put his foot wrong with the dowager.

A broken arm hadn't stopped him. The Committee hadn't stopped him. He'd stayed in office. To this day, he had his enemies on the Committee, Wilson now chief among them, but he'd done things, risked things—in a youthful determination he'd matured out of. Oh, he'd so far matured past that brash novice paidhi in the last handful of years—even in the last two. Maybe he could count the kyo ship inbound as *his* fault. The whole fact that Mospheirans were in space and that Tabini had nearly lost his life—could be counted as *his* fault.

But *Phoenix* showing up in the heavens hadn't been his fault. The likelihood that Wilson would have gotten the atevi into space was zero. Humans would have claimed the station, atevi would have continued on the planet, tradition-bound. Humans alone would have dealt with Reunion, or its outcome, with the kyo.

And that might not have gone so well.

Maybe it was blind arrogance to think he'd done step by step what had to be done. But he thought not. Maybe it was foolish arrogance to insist on handling this now with no reference to the University. But he thought not.

He imagined Wilson, now, Wilson's long face and Wilson's expression if Wilson *could* be here now, trying to supersede him. What Wilson would say.

No. Definitively Wilson wouldn't approve what he was doing. The Committee wouldn't, to this hour, approve, even given all the reasons for what he was doing.

But he would create records. A wealth of them, in every format.

He did imagine the reaction of the Committee to having to approach the kyo language *through* Ragi—because that was the language in which he took notes, that was the language Prakuyo preferred dealing with, and that was how they were going to have to deal with the kyo right now, for simplicity's sake, at very least.

That, for Wilson's procedures.

He resigned all sociality for the day, wore his oldest and most comfortable coat, from the apartment's pre-Reunion closet, and settled in his office for what would probably be one of the longest days of his life.

He called Geigi and Jase, explained what he was doing, and what he needed, got from Jase an instant suggestion for an inventory program already in the system, with which to construct his sort of dictionary, and from them both an understanding of the recording and audio analysis needs, and a promise to handle the details.

Done and done.

He brought up the system library and Jase's suggested computer program, which proved not only to have the cross-referencing he needed, but, even better, the ability to analyze and penetrate different systems of organization . . . as long as he worked in ship-speak.

From the library, he began to pull up images, pictures of objects ranging from teacups to stars and planets, pictures of eyes, hands, objects, furniture, and more complicated motion snippets of people—atevi and human—walking, running, showing emotion, things useful in a basic vocabulary. One hoped the inclusion of humans would say something as well, especially the handful that included both . . . those pictures were hard come by, that weren't of him. There were a few of Toby, some of Jase. One of Barb in the market at Najida that had made it into the local papers—the locals had been quite delighted.

If only the Reunioner kids had had cameras when they went . . . and then he realized: security footage of the kids' visit. Vid of them playing with Boji, watching television: he explained what he needed to Banichi and moved on. If such existed anywhere, he'd have it.

It amounted to Cajeiri's picture books, expanded, given motion.

Images of an atevi potter working. Images of the stunning porcelains that resulted. A man, atevi, cooking at a stove. Another over a campfire. A woman, human, holding a bottle, feeding a baby, and after a moment's consideration, the same woman, breast-feeding.

Hundreds of images—some useful for an action, some for an item, or material that could be organized around a concept. Or a core sound like *ai*, that turned up in most words involving power, control . . . responsibility, aishid, aishidi'tat, aiji, and a dozen others . . . the backbone on which many useful words were built.

In Ragi. The oldest, most widespread language of a people biologically keyed to man'chi.

He hoped to find similar core sounds within the kyo language. It was possible that could give him at least some keys to the way the kyo organized the universe.

It was a dictionary of images designed to elicit critical words and organize them around concepts and relationships, organized with the intent to approach abstracts. Specific enough, he hoped, not to go off in unintended directions, flexible enough to reorganize on the fly, should the kyo prove, as likely they would, to organize concepts differently.

And, oh, wouldn't that system comparison function be useful for tracking that?

Feeling left his right foot. He moved it, flexed it, flexed his shoulders—and thought of a sequence that would illustrate parity, and satisfaction. He searched up more pictures.

He began accumulating a subset of specifically scientific images, geological and astronomical images. Volcanos, sunspots, novae . . . and their corresponding mathematical graphs showing energy readouts of the sort a starfaring people would almost certainly comprehend. Simple mathematics using blocks. Geometry. Images of architecture, arches, and right angles. Trigonometry. A child on a slide. An arrow shot into the air. Images with the associated mathematical formulae superimposed.

One never knew what pathway understanding might take.

Ambiguous images: he set into a separate category, which *might* show up kyo interpretation of critical items.

Patterns designed to get words of connection. Words of direction. With. Without. In. On. To.

He sorted, categorized, linked, and cross-linked. Action. Substance. Quality. He began to recall details of their meetings two years ago, questions he had retained that were still questions, nuances of sound. Body language. Questions and more questions.

Dinner, Jago came to say. He didn't break off. He asked that a tray come to his office, with a pot of tea. And dessert. Definitely dessert.

Jago said she would relay that. He was assigning a set of tabs to a sequence of pictures, illustrating a process at that moment, and he murmured yes, and just kept going.

The kyo were definitely coming now, really truly coming . . . so mani said it was time for Irene to go stay in Lord Geigi's household, because at least that way she would be with associates and she would still get information and be taken care of.

Irene understood. Cajeiri had been a little worried she would be upset to be sent away, but Irene had understood entirely, had expected it, once everybody was busy dealing with the kyo. The others might need her, too, because she *was* the best at Ragi, and she would, she said, be all right.

She was a little worried, maybe. Everybody would be. But he promised her that things would turn out all right with the kyo, though she was not stupid, and very well knew that things might not.

But it was a polite promise. And it let them talk about it, and how and when she would go back.

"One does not want parents," she said, which seemed a concern to her. "Parents say 'do this. Do that.' I have no parents. I *have* no man'chi."

For an atevi to say that was upsetting. But he also knew it was not true.

"You have man'chi to me."

"Yes," she said. "Not to Bjorn's father. Not to Bjorn's mother. Not to Artur's father and mother."

She left out Gene's mother. But Gene's mother never asked for anything and never gave orders, and always pretended to be happy despite the circumstance. One well understood why Irene excepted her: she never gave Irene orders. So he understood what Irene was trying to say—that most of the parents tried to tell her what to do, and Irene was not willing to be told.

"You do not have man'chi to the parents," he said. "I say

protect Gene and his mother. Protect Artur. Listen to Lord Geigi and his staff. Report any problem to them."

"Yes," she said. He did not mention Bjorn. But that seemed to have settled one point to her satisfaction.

So he informed mani's bodyguard, at least in the person of Casimi, who was on duty at the doors, and who would surely tell Nawari and Cenedi, who probably already knew that mani was sending Irene back. He directly told the major domo, too, because they had to send over Irene's clothes and all. She intended to put them in a blanket and carry them, but that was hardly the way mani would have a guest leave her hospitality.

And if mani would not have her go down the hall carrying her clothes in a bag, he was equally convinced mani would not have her walk down the hall alone, as if she had been dismissed in disgrace.

"Staff will bring your clothes for you," Cajeiri said, when they had had their lunch alone in the little breakfast room, and added: "And I shall walk with you."

"Is that all right?" she asked, looking worried.

"Of course," he said, which was actually true. He did have standing permission to be in the corridor, on his promise not to go beyond it . . . though that had, admittedly, come before the kyo were so close as they were now, and before things had begun to get truly, truly scary. "Lord Geigi's staff will be expecting you. But I shall be sure they understand everything."

There was a silence then.

"One hopes you will be safe with the kyo."

"I shall be. And, Reni-ji, you will definitely be safe here. Lord Geigi will be sure to tell you how things are going. And you can translate what he says, so the others understand. You will *not* be obliged to listen to Bjorn's parents, or any of the others. In Lord Geigi's household, Lord Geigi is in charge, and *he* will not give you stupid orders. So you listen to staff and Lord Geigi."

"Yes," she said, like Guild on an assignment.

Irene's belongings from the wardrobe case went first, quietly, so as not to disturb Great-grandmother, who was resting in her suite. Mani having strongly suggested that Irene should leave today, it was perfectly understandable that mani would not come out to witness it or offer polite expressions to a person who was his guest by *his* invitation. That sort of attention would make Irene *her* guest, which had serious implications. He was sure mani would not want that.

He had a certain reputation for breaking the rules, though if he had not broken them, he never would have met Irene and the rest, or Prakuyo an Tep, for that matter. So he was not sorry for his rule-breaking. But this time mani had trusted him to manage things, and he certainly did not want to upset mani. They would be entirely proper. Irene was his associate to deal with. She had not come to this apartment alone and she should not be set out alone.

If he went, his aishid would be with them, and they would advise mani's bodyguard when he was leaving, and where they were, line of sight all the way.

So he arranged things, he sent the baggage in good order.

And he could not just drop Irene into the care of Lord Geigi's servants, as if she were a delivery of groceries. No. There should be some demonstration that she now had connections; and he owed a visit, too, to Gene and Artur and Bjorn—at least a short visit, considering he had paid so much special attention to Irene.

So he had his aishid advise Lord Geigi's major domo, who had already understood Irene was returning, to set up everything to work smoothly—all the *proper* way to do things.

Because he was his father's heir now, young aiji. And people knew that. When they *did* show up at Lord Geigi's door, the major d' met them as if they were important visitors, and showed them immediately to the guest quarters.

Everybody was in the sitting room, watching television, or a sort of television—a big screen which could be pulled down, quite a marvelous thing. It happened to be showing a video he remembered, from the Archive, with swords, and horses, all in black and white. It touched memory—oh, such memories.

Then it was gone, turned off. The servants had likely done it.

And everybody looked their way, and after a heartbeat, began to stand up. Artur first, everybody else following. Like a wave.

Everybody except Bjorn's parents. Bjorn had been sitting down. Now he stood up, too, casting a worried look toward his mother and father.

"Nadiin-ji," he said. He was used to waiting for *someone* to choose a chair, but now he was in charge of the moment. He chose his own chair, one with a vacant chair by it, for Irene. He sat down, with everybody watching, and Irene very quietly sat down, and the others, with a glance at Artur, sat down as well.

"Tea," he said to the major d', and servants who had attended them went to the buffet, where the samovar had water hot, as of course it would, in a well-used sitting room.

"So what's happening?" Bjorn's father asked, quite loudly. "What's going on with the kyo?"

Mani certainly would not answer a tone like that. Or tolerate such an assumption of authority. The servants paused in their preparations, shocked.

"Everything's going fine," Irene said.

Bjorn's father scowled and said, "I asked *him*."

That was quite rude. His aishid, armed and at his back, would not understand the question, but they were surely not happy.

Irene said something very sharp to Bjorn's father, then. And Bjorn's father said something angry and loud.

"Nadiin!" Cajeiri said, and sharply, in ship-speak: "Stop!"

That drew looks. He wasn't as loud as Bjorn's father, but his fair imitation of mani's tone was far more effective.

"So he does speak," Bjorn's father said.

"Bjorn," Irene said, and something else involving *manners*, then: "*Talk* to him."

Bjorn did look at his father, but his father made an angry gesture, thrust himself out of the chair, turned, and walked back toward the guest bedrooms. Bjorn's mother, clearly worried, went after him.

Artur's father, and Artur's mother, then Artur stood up. Gene did, and his mother last of all. Cajeiri sat where he was, with his bodyguard at his back.

"I'm sorry," Bjorn said earnestly, and then went after his parents.

There was a moment of heavy silence, so deep that Bjorn's retreating steps sounded very loud. The servants waited. Everybody waited.

"Artur," Irene said softly, and, "Gene," and with a glance her way, Artur and Gene sat down, and the parents did.

"Tea," Cajeiri said again, in the restored quiet, and the servants reprised their preparations.

Then one heard Bjorn's father's voice, loud, and angry, beyond the closed door, and the others looked uneasy. The shouting ceased.

"You are all right," Cajeiri said quietly in Mosphei'. "Kyo will come. Kyo will go. Everybody is safe."

"Tell him," Artur's mother said faintly, "we're glad to be here. We're sorry."

"I understand," he said, in that strange, naked way Mosphei' put it—if there was a polite impersonal, he had never heard it. He hoped he had used a proper form, speaking to adults.

Artur said, in Ragi, "Mr. Andressen is scared. One regrets, Jeri-ji."

Bjorn was trying to manage things quietly, but it was difficult, and his father was not calm: voices still escaped that room.

Bjorn's father had kept Bjorn apart even before Gene and Artur and Irene had gone down to the world. They had, they said, used the station tunnels, and established contact with him early in the year. But after Gene had gotten in trouble with the station aijiin, Bjorn's parents had strictly forbidden Bjorn to see any of them. And when the invitation had come to go down to the planet, they had tried again to contact him, but it was clear Bjorn's father had not wanted Bjorn associated with them in any way, let alone a trip down to the planet.

It was all, they had thought, because Gene had gotten arrested, even if station authorities had let him off, and even if it was an official invitation.

That was what they had thought until they had lived with Andressen-nadi in Lord Geigi's place. Bjorn's father had kept his household better off than most Reunioners, and there were papers Bjorn's father was using that he was somehow not supposed to have, though if they had been left on Reunion, they would have been destroyed.

Was that all the reason Bjorn's father acted as he did? Nand' Bren had strictly warned him not to assume humans reacted the same to problems, but it was clear that Bjorn's father had tried hard to help Bjorn have his tutor, and he had managed better for his family than most Reunioners had been able to do. Now he was sure people were stealing his belongings and possibly the papers, which if he was not supposed to have them, maybe he was afraid station security would take away from him.

It was all confusing. Irene said he was upset about being on the atevi side of the wall, and he asked over and over to go to his job—but his job had never sent asking about him, not that they had heard.

Mani said that he seemed suspicious in his associations, and that he *might* have been important to Braddock, which was not the sort of importance anyone should want right now. He had wanted to say that was not so, but certainly there were things Andressen-nadi had done that made him constantly upset.

The racket died down, at least. His outbursts upset Gene's mother, and made Artur's parents uneasy. Quiet let everyone draw easier breaths, and in that quiet, the servants took the opportunity to serve tea all around. Cajeiri drank a sip for politeness, though he had drunk all the tea he wanted this morning.

Gene and Irene and Artur all did exactly the same, and so did their parents.

He drank a second sip and a third sip. Then he carefully set the cup down on the side table, a signal. Gene and Irene and Artur all did exactly the same—and with a little hesitation (and from Gene's mother, an extra, surely unintentionally infelicitous sip) so did their parents.

He could not possibly be upset with Gene's mother. She had a very nice face. She seemed very shy of everyone. Very appreciative of anything nice.

"Talk to Bjorn," he said in Mosphei', wishing not to have Bjorn upset, or to add to the distress. "Talk to Bjorn's parents."

"Yes," Gene said in Ragi.

"Tell them," he said further, in Ragi, "my father will not see trouble come to them. Tell them the good things you saw on Earth, nadiin-ji. Tell them we shall deal with the kyo and they will all go down to the planet and everything will be all right. Tell them my father is very confident. So is nand' Bren."

"Yes." Heads nodded agreement.

He had to say it. He had to warn them. "Bjorn's father," he said, "cannot stay in this apartment if he disturbs Lord Geigi. Guild has noticed this disturbance. My great-grandmother will hear it. Stop this. Or Bjorn's father must go back to his apartment. Everybody else can stay here. But not Bjorn's father if he upsets this household. Do you understand?" He changed to Mosphei'. "Mr. Andressen is not aiji here. This is Lord Geigi's house."

"Yes," Artur said, the very minimum of an answer. "We stay. We all—" His gesture included everybody in the room. "We thank Lord Geigi. We *thank* him."

Gene nodded. So did Irene. So did all the parents.

So that was the way things were. Association had its difficulties, and association with humans definitely had difficulties.

But in their expressions, his three associates—he felt the connection as strong as it had ever been. Infelicitous four, it might be, and it was including Bjorn that had made the number felicitous, even not being there. But Bjorn would be with them—in the same way as before. Absent. And present.

And he was very glad he had come in with Irene, and that Irene had not had to deal with Bjorn's father in his present state.

"I shall likely not be here again," he said, "until the kyo have left. But whatever needs to be done, Lord Geigi will do. Whatever happens, tell Bjorn I shall not lose him. Tell him too that his father must be quiet. Staff will not tolerate disturbance."

He rose to his feet, and the others did. He bowed slightly, once to his associates and once to their parents, and left.

But at the door, he said to the major domo: "Advise Lord Geigi and Jase-aiji that Andressen-nadi does not give orders regarding Bjorn or any others. Irene-nadi understands Ragi best and she is in my man'chi. She will help talk to the guests, and should Andressen-nadi cause trouble again, advise Lord Geigi that Andressen-nadi will no longer be my guest. Nand' Bren has no time to deal with this. He is busy. So is my great-grandmother. Everybody is busy. Call on my great-grandmother's staff if he will not listen to Irene. Perhaps one could find a small room where he and his household can be quiet for a few hours . . . if this should happen again."

"Yes," the major domo said and with relief. "*Yes*, young aiji."

15

"Did it go well, young gentleman?" mani's major domo asked when Cajeiri arrived by the main door.

It was not possible to lie politely to his elders. But one could just omit the bad parts so as not to upset mani or distract her.

"Reni is doing very well," he said, "and she will help the others. Thank you, nadi."

"There is a package for you, from nand' Bren," the major domo said, "and a letter."

He was surprised at that. And when the major domo brought it from his office and put it in his hands, by its shape and weight, he thought it must be a small, flat sort of book, the sort of thing nand' Bren had sometimes given him when he was bored, or had to be left out of adult business . . . and he immediately hoped that was not the case now, that it was some sort of dismissal from meeting the kyo.

He took it with some misgivings, along with the message cylinder, and, having no office to resort to, he went back to his own little suite, and his bed, to open it.

His aishid followed him, clearly curious.

He opened the letter first. It gave his formal salutation, and nand' Bren's signature, in nand' Bren's beautiful hand.

It said:

I have asked for this machine for you. It is a gift. It contains a dictionary, inspired by your picture books, with the words we have, and the animated images we used when we first met the kyo. We will add more. I ask you take charge of this machine for yourself and your great-grandmother: I have confidence you will quickly learn its tricks.

Your machine will continue to inform itself of new entries as will mine, as one or the other of us adds words or pictures, so they will always contain the same information. It is cleverly designed in this way. Do not put it at risk or expose it to liquids or electricity.

Please review all the images and recall all the words you can. If you should recall words that I have not entered, please advise me immediately. Once we are sure who we are dealing with, I intend to present such devices to our visitors, and hope that we may all find them useful.

You will see they are arranged not in the traditional order, but by similarities you may discover within the words. Should you add words, you will find the option to include them in not just one group, but any which seem to apply.

We expect a good meeting. Please convey my respects to your great-grandmother. I must give her my regrets for dinner this evening, as in evenings before. We anticipate that the kyo will begin docking procedures in sixty-two hours, but this time is subject to change and may be hastened. As I have advised your great-grandmother in a separate letter, I am now working closely with Lord Geigi to set up a meeting-place aboard the station. I estimate that it will be easier and more secure for us all to reside there during the kyo's visit, to save us frequent travel through the lift system.

Jase-aiji is working closely on the technical issues associated with their docking and entry, and he will arrange to have the rooms in a comfortable range of temperature and lighting for our guests. Everybody is doing all they can to have this go well.

Urge your great-grandmother to rest as much as possible, as should we all. We may not have much opportunity for rest once the kyo arrive.

It was a completely grown-up letter. It expected serious

things of him. It told him things as if he were—well, *grown up*. He was very proud.

And it promised something extraordinary, in the flat package.

He opened it. It contained a little computer exactly like Lord Geigi's.

He pushed the blue button and the screen immediately said: *Dictionary.* Below that was a little box with instructions on how to see the next picture and how to add a spoken word to the picture. That instruction was complicated. He saved it for later reading.

Next was a picture of a space station, with the kyo word for it in nand' Bren's voice.

Nand' Bren had a computer. Nand' Bren had had one forever, before anybody on the continent had had one. But he had never suspected nand' Bren could do such clever things as this talking book.

He ran through the pictures. A few had words. Most had none. He understood now. It was a device for catching and holding new words. Once recorded in this—they would be associated with a picture, so they would remember better. He wished they had had such a thing from the very beginning—but then, they had not gone out to Reunion planning to meet the kyo, and he had never seen a device like this until Lord Geigi lent one.

"Look!" he said, and showed his prize to Antaro and Jegari, and Lucasi and Veijico. "Is this not clever? It talks."

Clearly they thought it was a wonderful thing, and they did understand it when he showed them. Operating it was not that hard. He would learn the basics of the device before supper, he swore he would, and he would show it to mani. Of course mani would wave it off and pretend not to be impressed, but only after she had listened and understood it, which she would also do very quickly, and then claim she had no interest in doing it herself.

Now he understood what nand' Bren had been doing, all shut away in his apartment, something he was not clever enough yet to do, but nand' Bren showed it to him and expected him not only to understand, but to add to it.

And he felt—

He finally felt he really could do something, and that what he had done two years ago really *had* been important, not just a clever but useless thing. *Inspired by your picture books . . .* Pictures had been his idea to help Prakuyo learn, right from the start.

He asked staff to let him know when mani might wake. And then he sat and looked at the pictures and tried his best to guess their associations and to see why they were linked together in groups of *little* pictures with lines between them.

He studied until he had the word that mani was up and in the sitting room.

Then he took his gift to mani, who had settled in the sitting room to read. He was all but shivering with the importance of what he had to show—and the fear, not unreasonable, that she would think he really had greatly overestimated himself back then, and now. He had his aishid behind him, able to witness whatever happened—he could rarely escape that. He still had on his next-to-best coat, which he had worn to Lord Geigi's apartment—in the excitement of nand' Bren's gift he had not changed it. That was on his side.

She glanced up, only briefly, and back down to her page. "Your guest is comfortably settled, Great-grandson?"

"Yes, mani."

"One hears that *you* gave orders to Lord Geigi's staff."

He had forgotten that. He had not prepared himself to defend what he had done. He had just thought he had to do it—to prevent a problem, not to make one. He had *settled* his guests, had he not? And *that* was right to do.

"So?" she said. "You seem somewhat anxious, young gentleman. Do you think you did well?"

"Nand' Geigi is very busy and Andressen-nadi is angry and difficult, and Reni-nadi is alone. One hoped to do well, to be sure Andressen-nadi will not try to give orders to her. He has been very forward."

"Ah," mani said, and nodded as if this was a very minor concern, and returned to her book.

"Mani, nand' Bren has sent me a letter. And he has sent me this." He held the little computer in view as she looked up. "This is like Lord Geigi's machine, that showed the maps of the tunnels. This one is for dealing with the kyo, mani."

"And how shall this deal with the kyo?" mani asked.

"It has pictures, mani, like my picture books."

"You were a child then. Shall you bring them a child's picture books now?"

"But these are not a story. Nand' Bren has gathered pictures in groups. He is making *associations* of pictures and kyo words and Ragi! I know exactly what he is doing! He is showing them words that are alike, and he is going to find out what *their words* are, not just the words, but the *associations*, mani, which is really important!"

"Well, well." Mani agreeably took the computer into her own hands, and pressed the button he showed her, and the one going up, and the one going down, and the ones sideways, making the images change. "Well, well, well. And who created this clever machine? Lord Geigi?"

"Nand' Bren has done all this, mani! And he expects me to understand it."

"An unusual gift. So you have some study to do today, do you not?" Mani clicked through the pictures, above, below, and sideways. "Indeed."

"I shall! I am to add words if I remember them! I have been comparing my notebook to the pictures and I have added one word so far!"

She handed it back to him. "We are intrigued. We shall receive the result of it, we are sure. And perhaps a young gentleman will also attend the particular associations *we* shall observe in these visitors and learn something, too."

He failed to understand at first. And then did. *Associations we shall observe.* Mani would have her own set of associations, *not* pictures on a screen, but the sort of things that mani did track, when she was dealing in politics, and allies, and enemies. Pictures were something a computer could hold and show. But what mani would to be watching he doubted any computer could show.

Very likely, he thought, nand' Bren had also planned paths through these pictures that he only partly imagined.

He wanted to know everything. He wanted to be as wise as Great-grandmother and as clever as nand' Bren. But right now he had to find his own way to be useful.

He had talked to Prakuyo once. So had mani. And the little computer meant studying harder than ever he had done for his tutors.

Sheets. Darkness. Sleep. Possibly even *enough* sleep.

The two little green lights were there. Jago had gone, but the spot was still warm, so it had not been that long ago, and Bren stretched out and turned onto his back. He had done all he could do. He had looked at pictures until they cycled spontaneously before his eyes. The kyo ship was coming. They were down to hours now . . . surreal as it seemed. It was becoming more real. The memories of them, their last meeting, had been as remote as Reunion, as foreign as it was possible to be.

Now they loomed close. Strangely—he'd remembered a great deal in static images. Pictures, frozen like the ones in the tablet. Now the pictures in his mind showed a tendency to move. To be snippets of the moments he'd been face-to-face with something all his skill with language hadn't been able to reach . . .

The memory hovered, start and stop. Detail of the one face he knew well. The confusion of others he didn't know as well.

Moments. Trying to restrain Prakuyo, in confined quarters, and realizing later that Prakuyo had restrained himself from an outburst that might have killed him.

Prakuyo's strange sounds that he couldn't duplicate. Nor really understand.

He could lie there just a little longer, thinking. But if he lay there thinking down this track he could only confuse himself. Memories weren't coherent. Too many ship-moves lay between, when dreams and reality merged, when one moved in a half-world of past and present, and tried to work, but managed, occasionally, to write down things that sanity questioned.

If he got up, and he needed to, not to lie here battering at his memory—he might be just a little early for breakfast.

The door opened quietly. A shadow was there against the light. "Bren-ji," Jago said quietly, "Jase-aiji has just called. He says the kyo ship is now confirmed on definite approach to the station mast, following the suggested pattern. They are communicating with ops continually, stating their intended path and progress, but no spoken words, merely lines on the diagram."

"Still good news."

"Good news, Bren-ji," Jago said. "Sleep a little longer. You only wished us to tell you if there was any report at all."

"Thank you, Jago-ji. And rest, all of you! I shall need you. Soon."

So they *were* coming in toward the mast. Final approach. If Prakuyo wanted to talk at this point, staff would tell him and he would jump to it.

But right now, perhaps Prakuyo was reasonable, interested in getting some needed rest and having a clear head. Both of them on the same sleep cycle would be a truly good thing. Though as he remembered the kyo sleep cycle was a degree shorter.

An inconvenient degree shorter.

He had arranged everything, he, and Jase, and Geigi, and Gin. While he worked on the images and the protocol, Geigi's workforce had created a facility ready to house them and receive the kyo in comfort and security—an arrangement that would have taken a government or a University committee weeks if not months to set up. They had now a place to meet on the station and they could with equal ease (but not equal cheer) deal with a shipboard meeting on *Phoenix* or aboard the kyo vessel, whichever the kyo opted to have, on even shorter notice.

But thus far—it looked as if the ship was coming in as requested, using the berth atop the mast, the only place that could accommodate its size.

Credit where it was due. Geigi had set up the station facility and Ogun and Sabin had actually cooperated and conferred together on the logistics of a shipboard meeting, much as the captains preferred not to involve *Phoenix*. The *last* time on a station hadn't gone so well for Prakuyo an Tep. It might be asking a great deal, in asking Prakuyo to enter a place that looked very like Reunion.

But if he were, personally, the kyo in charge, he'd not come all this way and miss the chance to see the inside workings of this place. He'd seen the interior of the kyo ship himself. He was still glad to have seen it, and it had given him valuable insights into the kyo themselves, even if they had not been the details Sabin would have wished him to note.

And hadn't he heard about *that* failure more than once, on the trip home?

He definitely did not want the dowager and Cajeiri to board the kyo ship on this venture, however. They had other options. Having that ship head out of the system with them aboard— that would be a disaster not just to the aishidi'tat.

All that contingency planning, however, was increasingly slipping behind them. Knowing the kyo were going to attach to the mast and not just stand off, he had time to lie abed and collect his thoughts and trust things to the technical folk. And to Jase. Things they hoped would happen were going to happen.

That ship had all its sensing abilities in operation, one could be very sure. Recording. Imaging. Listening. Gathering data of all sorts—as one could be sure the kyo had been doing all along their route. Keeping a close eye on *Phoenix* for any hostile move. But coming into the heart of station operations, the most sensitive areas, the most vital—it became highly unlikely *Phoenix* would be as much concern.

Jase, who had been directly involved with the kyo communications from the start, was in station ops, approving the diagrams that guided them, and techs reading, with an experienced eye, every diagram that came back. He hadn't seen Jase since the operation started, but Jase was doing his job of keeping all parties informed. There were things he wanted to ask, details he'd like know, but he had no wish to trouble Jase with questions at this late stage, and with Jase's mind focused on the technicalities of docking a very large ship to a soft tube with a jury-rigged airlock connection at the kyo end.

Geigi's guests had stayed quiet, so Geigi reported, despite a small emotional outburst with Mr. Andressen. Irene had left the dowager's care, rejoining the others in Geigi's apartment, likely at the dowager's decision. Cajeiri had requested the staff consult her for translation, and further made the point that she would not be taking orders from Mr. Andressen. Nor would anybody else.

That was interesting. Andressen was still posing a problem.

But Geigi reported that all seemed quiet in his household. That was all he needed to know about that. It was all he *wanted* to know.

Regarding the Reunioners still pent in the three old sections, the lid was solid on that cauldron of discontent, too, and Gin was upping the quality, variety, and quantity of food in the meal centers, which had to relieve some stress. Human Central was providing constant coverage of the kyo situation on public displays in those sections, the same as the Mospheiran areas had, with some sort of reassuring, low key commentary. The push on distribution now was going to put pressure on supply later— but later would solve it, was Gin's word on the problem. He didn't know what Gin had in mind, but Gin had taken on the problem. Granted they got through the kyo business alive and granted one of the food production tanks didn't get damaged in the encounter, they would manage.

Tillington, according to Gin's disgusted report, hadn't even tried to deal creatively with the supply problem in the last year.

He'd just shorted the distributions to the Reunioners, kept the Mospheiran population's complaints focused on the Reunioner presence, and focused all attention on Maudit as the somewhat remote solution to the whole issue—refusing to make any permanent adjustment to the Reunioner presence, talking about shortages, keeping the pressure on to remove them.

Gin was gathering evidence, and she'd declared Tillington would not go back to Earth until she'd finished collecting it. She'd fired two of his administrators and confined them to house arrest, for a start, one of them the head of station security; and she'd frozen Tillington's personal assets pending an audit, which might also prove interesting. He burned to know. But wouldn't let himself be distracted.

And all that was happening on the other side of a wall the kyo wouldn't cross and he didn't need to. Thank God.

Tea with the dowager—and the young gentleman—headed the afternoon. A simple trip across the hall—so long delayed—was finally possible. And necessary, in their imminent departure for the residency they would use—and in the kyo's approach, near now, very near.

The servant poured into delicate porcelain cups. Out in the hall, wheels rolled across the tiles, a passing racket, culminating in the opening of the outer door. The dowager, appearing oblivious, took an elegant sip. Bren and Cajeiri did.

The organized disturbance in the household, the moving of carts, all evidence of things in motion—said to him that everything was advancing apace. They had a definite place to be and a time to be there, and the two people who had dealt very well with the kyo in the past were going with him into an isolation area that would give them time to work and a space completely secure from intrusion.

The destination was downstairs—or upstairs, depending on where one conceived the mast to be—into a temporary residency, with a suite they hoped their visitors would find acceptable. There would be a residency for the dowager, and a common meeting space just outside her door, which would make the dowager's presence much less a hardship for her. He had not yet asked the kyo the number that might come aboard. Moving a wall or two to construct those quarters was, Geigi swore, very easy for station workers: arranging doors in the appropriate places, even pressure doors, was the matter of substituting a panel. And they could expand the kyo space considerably.

Furnishings? Furniture to suit their visitors' size? Again, easily done. They could manufacture furniture as ornate as one pleased, use atevi-scale design for the most part. He had handed all that matter off to Geigi, only advising Geigi to make the rooms look like a residence, warm and hospitable, and not like an office, and most certainly not like a prison.

Of course, they had no real idea what the kyo would consider *hospitable*, no idea whether they preferred soft beds or hard, pillows or blocks of wood. On the other hand, Prakuyo had seemed quite happy with the accommodations they'd made for him in the atevi section of the ship two years ago, had been quite taken with pillows in general, and so they assumed atevi-style beds would suffice, given an abundance of small brocade pillows.

The modifications had taken up an entire block of hallway, from one lift stop to the next, and the lift station was included. They had to control that wide expanse for security reasons, Geigi said, and they might as well use the space.

For the atevi side of things, for the dowager's sake, Geigi assured him there was absolutely everything an atevi guest could expect to find—except antiquity—and they had moved a few real items in, fortunate and kabiu. For the dowager's comfort they were moving down her bed, her chairs, her side table, her furniture from the sitting room—her entire breakfast nook— whatever they could do to make the stay easier for her. Geigi had ordered it, with Cenedi to advise and supervise, and the workforce Geigi commanded was massive.

Cajeiri's move, he assumed, had been likewise orchestrated

except that there was, on the table beside the young gentleman, the little tablet. Evidently Cajeiri was claiming personal responsibility for that, and not trusting it to staff.

Bren had left his own transfer details entirely to Geigi and Narani—they knew better than he did what he'd need. There would be meals: Bindanda of *his* staff was to manage cooking—Bindanda, used to cooking for a human, had avoided poisoning Prakuyo before this. Narani and Jeladi were going down. So were Asicho and Kandana. The Guild Observers—they were also to be there, part of the dowager's security, no need to explain the complexity of what they really were: it was their job to report to Geigi and to Tabini-aiji. And any explanation they needed they might get with their own skills, limited to the common room and their own premises—but they had vowed to do nothing that might agitate the kyo.

Jase and his security, currently in ops, seeing that the docking went smoothly and that they had no security breach, would move downstairs to be near the situation, but, granted past history of humans and kyo, were to stay to the background.

Communications, Geigi assured them, was secure, a link to Central, where Gin would be in charge, and a link to the other captains and a direct link to *Phoenix*—to assure there were no misunderstandings and that there would be quick communication if need be. Jase would keep watch over that. There would be arrangements for the kyo to maintain their own link to their ship.

Everything that could be done had been done. Bren took a sip, and two and three, letting his mind settle and the tension in his shoulders ebb.

"We have invited Lord Geigi to dinner every evening since we have arrived," Ilisidi said conversationally, "and on most evenings he has been able to satisfy our curiosity on his own. He has been working to assure our comforts, and his staff has taken excellent care of our Reunioner charges. But we are vexed to hear that the paidhi-aiji has been sleeping and eating very irregularly, and that Jase-aiji has been doing very much the same." Ilisidi's deliberate delivery gave no graceful pause for objection or qualification. "We trust you have not exhausted yourselves, nandi, at the point at which we need you most."

"No, aiji-ma. We are resting at every opportunity."

"We shall weigh a little less there. Are we correct?"

"Yes, just slightly, aiji-ma."

"Well, well, our bones may find it pleasant, though our visitors may find it a bit less agreeable."

"Jase-aiji says that most star-faring individuals learn to adapt quickly. And Prakuyo-nandi did survive six years under those conditions. They will surely not find it difficult."

She gave a little nod. "And Jase-aiji *will* join us, we are informed. He will reside with you. Is this correct?"

"He will, aiji-ma, for advice and information, but not necessarily come within view or notice of the kyo. He will link our security with Gin-nandi, and with the ship, and provide them translation. He will share my apartment, and there is a route he can take to come and go without notice."

"Well. Well. We shall go to this new arrangement. We shall have dinner there tonight. So we trust we shall have gained you for this evening, elusive as you have been. Shall we see Jase-aiji for dinner?"

"I shall make every effort, aiji-ma, unless some emergency prevents it, but Jase, alas, will continue in ops until the ship is safely docked, and likely have a much less elegant supper there."

"Well, well, as it must be. Your own cook is arranging the kitchen tonight, and he has promised us a Najidan dish which I trust will attract your interest."

"One very much longs for it, aiji-ma."

"Then we shall go down." Ilisidi set down her teacup. "We shall begin this adventure. And we shall start it tonight with a proper supper, a dessert, and a glass of spirits all in our lodgings below, paidhi, which we hope you may attend. If you do not sleep well after that, it will be your own fault."

16

It was two levels down, this hallway, a reasonable trip in the lift, a place they could make comfortable for the kyo, with no need of coats or burdens or the security risk of traveling back and forth in the core and the lift system. There was atevi security about the place, tight as they could make it. The staff that would serve was all their own, many of whom Prakuyo, at least, might remember from their last meeting.

They went down, prepared to stay for whatever time it took, and it was Narani who opened the outer door, on a foyer which had the dowager's security already settled in a small, well-equipped room that opened to the side. The door was open at the moment, and the resident Guild and the Observers, who were already ensconced, quietly rose and paid their respects. Jeladi, in charge of the inner door of the foyer, bowed and let them all into a large room. Not quite an atevi place—not traditional in layout or furnishings, but conveniently combining several functions in one. This end was a sitting room, no more brightly lit than the sitting room in ancient Malguri. Beyond, surrounded by hangings that might be drawn back to open the room, a feature of the kyo premises they had seen, was an ample dining table.

It wasn't traditional, but it felt—right. Comfortable in the way Malguri could be comfortable, an environment that might recall the dowager's own home.

"Well," the dowager said, seeing it. "This is inventive. The dining room and sitting room in one. And these doors?"

There were several.

"Aiji-ma," Narani said, having followed them. He indicated the door to the right, nearest the dining area. "Your own premises, with the young gentleman's, and all your staff. Nandi," he added, for Bren, "yours, the second door. At the far end of the central room, beyond the dining room curtains, is a security station, where the Guild Observers reside. Beside that, the kitchen."

Indeed, an aroma of spice said Bindanda was already busy.

"And the kyo apartment?" Ilisidi asked.

Cajeiri's arms tightened on the pad he'd carried down with him and he gazed at the open door, the golden glow that illumined the furnishings beyond. Two years ago, the child would have rushed across that gap. The curiosity was clearly there. But it was not two years ago, and Cajeiri waited, proper and restrained, for his great-grandmother to lead the way.

The place was lit with only a few gold-toned lights, draperies and hangings covered the walls, and there was, centermost, a conference table with seven massive chairs, with multiple modern display screens centermost on the table. Beds were in a separate room beyond, with patterned fabrics and pillows.

Machimi setting was the expression that readily occurred—a surreal place, a constructed place that existed nowhere in the universe except now, here, in the need for atevi to talk to kyo. Geigi had arranged it all, from the few pictures they had of the kyo ship's interior, and from their description of preferred temperatures and humidity. The air was heavy, hot and very humid. Atevi were certainly not inspired to linger, but the tap of Ilisidi's cane asserted itself, strange and definite, as she walked about, looking at details. She remembered, Bren was sure. So did he. It was an image drawn from his sketches, his memory of the kyo's meeting room, aboard the kyo ship, as Geigi reinterpreted it.

"Well," Ilisidi said. "Well. Geigi has managed very handsomely."

"Indeed," Bren said. "Indeed, aiji-ma." The memories came back, details two years had erased, but, more unexpectedly, *words* came. Things present, things discussed, specific moments. Much as he had struggled to keep them alive in the interval, much as a few had come back to him when he was sketching the room he remembered—the heat, the humidity, the ambient of the light of this apartment—brought a welling sense of place and presence. He stood amid draperies and furnishings, in a too-warm room, thinking about a meal they had shared.

And recalling the kyo word for hot, and a dozen other words which had eluded him, from a session with Prakuyo and his shipmates—superiors—subordinates. He had never gotten the relationships among the kyo straight. Or known Prakuyo's rank, or affiliations.

The dowager left, taking Cajeiri with her. Bren lingered a moment, remembering the scent of the kyo. Warm pavement. Heated concrete.

"You are thinking, Bren-ji," Jago said.

"One is remembering," he said. "Geigi has done well. Very well."

Dinner was in the offing. The dowager was settling into the apartment she would occupy with Cajeiri. And there was a small space for the paidhi-aiji to check in with his staff in his own apartment, and change coats.

There was no foyer: there was barely a closet, with two coats, one the lightest he owned, for possible sessions at the kyo's table. There was a sitting room that looked like a transplanted section out of Central—screens, communications, two work stations of the sort one would see in Central. Geigi had given them some of the comforts: Geigi assured him there were sleeping quarters, staff quarters, and three showers, with space for Jase and his two bodyguards if they opted to use it; but as an atevi residence, this apartment had much more the look of a Guild operations center.

Jase would watch and listen from here: he could come and go at need through a door on the far end of Bren's residence and the dowager's, a servants' passage which ran the length of the arrangement, with access to the outer corridor.

The kyo ship appeared on two of the screens here, appearing as steady now as the girder in the frame, a pattern of absolute dark and patches of light so bright it overwhelmed any feature on the hull.

That, too, he remembered: a massive, oblong shape the middle of which spun. It still spun, making the highs and lows of its middle hull flash lazily, constantly changing. Streaks of soot stained its forward edges, collected from this solar system, or the dust between stars. He had seen it this close when *Phoenix* had approached it, in the last of their dealings at Reunion. That came flooding back, too. The same ship? The soot patterning was very little different. One would think the configuration of the ship itself determined that. It looked to be a black-and-white transmission—except one orange streak that might once have been paint, overlain with soot from its travels.

Were the kyo in?

Was that ship moving at all now? Had they gotten the tube attached?

He intended to call Central, compliment Geigi, and contact Jase to find out the state of affairs with the ship.

He got no farther than the end of the console. His pocket com gave off three distinct pulses. He took it out and held it to his ear.

"Bren," he said.

"Jase," came the corresponding answer. *"Where are you right now?"*

"Right now I'm standing in the new apartment, security station, right by the screens. I can see the kyo ship. Where are you?"

"I'm in ops. The kyo are in. Faster and smoother than our best estimate. Docked, tube link established five minutes ago.

We're getting voice contact. I'm putting them through on your line one right now. Stand by."

"Just a second. I'm going to the sitting room console." Algini was with him. Tano and Jago and Banichi were through the far door, in the security sleeping chamber, arranging equipment out of baggage. "Gini-ji," he said. "We have contact."

Algini left to advise the others. He left through the other door, past his bedroom, into the sitting room, to the large console. He dropped into the central chair, com unit in hand, the screen in front of him.

"I'm ready," he said.

"Got that." He heard Jase's voice, saying, of the few kyo words he knew, *"Go, please."* And in the next moment a kyo voice came over the pocket com, deep and gravelly. *"Bren,"* it said, then words he didn't know, and *"ship."*

Heart pounding, he said carefully, in the kyo language: "Bren is here. Is it Prakuyo an Tep?"

There was a small silence. Perhaps, he thought, there was a technical foul-up. Or a consultation. Then another voice, equally gravelly, but a little different.

"Bren. Prakuyo here. Good. Good. Ship dock. We want talk." That came in Prakuyo's broken Ragi. And then, before he could respond, kyo language came, complete with complex booms and resonances: *"Bren . . . Ship . . . Good . . . Dock . . . Talk . . . Good . . . Want . . ."*

For a moment, it was the nightmare. The words froze in his head and he was missing whole strings of them. It was *not* the pattern of communication they'd used in the past. His mind spun, then snapped into focus. Reciprocation. Repetition. He wasn't the *only* one who had been working on the problem of how to communicate.

Following Prakuyo's lead, he said, first in his own, limited kyo, and then in simple, but more fluent Ragi:

"Talk, yes. Please come. The dowager is here. Cajeiri is here. All here. Please come, bring clothes, bring associates, all good.

We have good rooms, beds, tables. Eat, talk, sleep here, all. Safe."

There was a little pause. A little hesitation. God. After all their preparation . . . the kyo might refuse. Might want them to come meet aboard their ship instead.

"Talk Bren, yes. Prakuyo an Tep, yes. Matuanu an Matu, yes. Hakuut an Ti, yes, yes. All good?"

His heart skipped a beat. Felicitous three. Was it deliberate? Possibly Prakuyo himself and two bodyguards? Normal procedure? Or honoring atevi numerology?

"Yes. All very good." He adopted the same dual language, first Ragi, then his best attempt in kyo. "Come aboard. I shall come down to the dock, with Banichi and Jago—we come out to Prakuyo, bring you to rooms here. Guests." And, oh, hadn't that been a tricky concept to establish, with a man who had been a prisoner for six years. "Guest rooms for you, for Matuanu an Matu and Hakuut an Ti. Good." He had clicked *record* when the conversation started. They were catching words as they went, one language against the other, an electronic Rosetta Stone. He repeated everything in limited kyo.

Another transmission came in, in that reciprocal format:

"Talk. Sit. Talk. Good. Prakuyo Matuanu Hakuut come station."

"Yes. Talk."

"Teacakes." Unambiguous and without the kyo counterpart.

"Teacakes!" He broke into a smile. Almost a laugh. "Yes! Many teacakes! Bindanda is here! He will make as many teacakes as you like. Prakuyo, Matuanu, and Hakuut please come to the station. A human there will help you come through the dark. Cold. Cold there. You can breathe air, but cold. Much much cold there, water makes ice. I, Bren, I shall come to meet you."

"Good," Prakuyo an Tep said. Then: *"Prakuyo come now station all good. Matuanu Hakuut come now station. All good. Fortunate three."*

Fortunate three. No coincidence, then. That consideration of atevi custom was a hopeful sign. Very hopeful.

"I shall come now," he said. "I shall come down to meet you, Prakuyo. Yes?"

"Yes," the answer came.

The contact broke. Bren pushed another, lit, button.

"Jase?" Bren asked.

"I'm on."

"Did you hear?"

"I heard. Pretty smart, your Prakuyo. Good move, that both-languages idea."

"He says he's here to talk. He remembers the teacakes. Takes a load off the worry in that sense."

"Decidedly."

"They're ready to come aboard. Are we rigged yet?"

"Conveyor line's rigged. Or will be by the time you get down there. They're working on it right now. Passenger tube seal is clamped and solid. It'll pressurize on need."

That was the safety that put an airlock beyond their airlock, one in station control, which meant the sealed mast docking section *wouldn't* void, comforting thought, should the mate-up to the ship somehow be flawed.

"I think there will be only three of them coming. I tried to explain about the conveyor line and the cold down there. I'll have just Banichi and Jago with me. The mast workers we have to have. They should be careful how they move, what equipment they carry, not even the suspicion of weapons."

"They're briefed," Jase said. *"They're hand-picked ship crew."*

"Good." The logistics still loomed like a mountain. "Can you get a man here to pick us up and get us where we need to be? I'm not betting the whole mission on our navigating the lift system on our own. I think we could do it, I'm sure we could do it, but I don't want to make any mistakes in this."

"Polano will be in your foyer. Ten minutes."

It was happening. He needed a heavier coat, even given the cold suits they used on the transit. They didn't know what the kyo were going to do, whether they expected the deep cold, whether they'd suit up. It was a bare-bones system, no better than it had been since the days they'd built the station. Mostly, these days, it was for shuttle crews, young, strong people used to coming and going on the system, which was cheap, easily adjusted, never improved from the days of construction. Damned sure, once they started moving the Reunioners down, they had to do something about that antiquated system.

Right now they had to get three kyo, whose ship was over-warm to both human and atevi, through it without an incident.

Jago had arrived in the room. Tano had settled, at an adjacent console. "I am going down to the mast," he said to them. "Banichi, and you, Jago-ji, will be with me." Banichi and Jago were the two who knew the kyo, and the kyo knew them.

"Yes," Jago said, and left, quickly, back to the inner hall.

"Tano-ji. Word to Cenedi. Advise the dowager we may have three more for dinner."

There was a cold-suit locker where they exited, Bren, Banichi, Jago, and Polano worked weightless, floating with light tethers, and with breath frosting despite the best heat the area provided. They were not novices. The mast workers, three in number, ship crew, Jase had said—assisted them, and they assisted one another in turn, Bren first, and Polano second.

The gloves made the pocket com difficult. Bren left the right glove off and simply tucked it into his insulated, heated pocket, righting himself so he could see the technicians' console.

Regulations said the workers were to be in constant contact with the ship or shuttle.

In this case—not so easily.

"We shall go out, the three of us with the safety workers," Bren told them, and switched over to ops-com. "Jase-ji, tell them I am coming out on the line to meet them."

"I'll try to relay that," Jase said in ship-speak, audible to them all. "We've done a graphic to illustrate the system. They're stable. The kyo ship is not linked up for water or power. Took a bit to get the personnel tube secure to their lock, but we've tested it. We'll remote the number two inner lock from our side when we're sure the number one is shut and they're all the way through on our side."

There was a delay. Bren put the face shield down to conserve heat, kept hands in his pockets, safe within the lift. Then Polano relayed, "They're through to the tube, sir. Seal is good."

"Understood," Bren said. He had no detailed knowledge of how the system worked, except there were sensors—and failsafes. The kyo were now inside the tube, technically within the station at this point.

Time to go meet them, in a lot of cold black. The worker in charge opened the lift door. Outside was a pressurized section of the mast, but past the lighted lift access apron, and the attachment for the conveyor line, there was utter dark, and a dangerous cold.

The lead worker took a handgrip unit and started out, casually expert. The second safety man, clipping to a safety stanchion on the apron of the lift, guided Bren's grip to the next handle. That immediately clamped onto the line and whisked him out and away into the dark and cold, right behind the lead worker. He felt the vibrations of other entries onto the line, knew without looking that Banichi and Jago, likely Polano and the second safety man were also on the line. The guide in front, several meters distant, passed girders and conduits, the light of his handgrip and Bren's own gliding eerily over the structures, then going to utter black. The line itself, similarly illumined, headed straight toward a distant spot of yellow light.

That was the access tube, the beginning of whatever connection ops had cobbled together. And their progress, hauled along by mechanical means, was just about to meet the party outbound from the ship, at the other end of the line.

More encouraging lights, red, yellow, and green, outside on that yellow expanse began to blink in sequence, indicating the second lock was ready to bring their visitors through.

The traverse on the line moved air against Bren's lower face, thin and fiercely cold. One wouldn't freeze during the transit. But it was the driest cold one ever looked to experience. Mountaintop cold. Thin air. He was anxious to reach that widening yellow spot, where the line anchored.

That yellow spot enveloped them all, having slight shadow in its depth, like the bell of a garden flower. They stopped at the apron within that bell, drifting, breath sparkling frost in the glaring light as one after the other of them arrived and the conveyor links piled up, waiting.

Waiting.

Then the garden flower irised open at its depth, as the last airlock opened. Like figures from a dream, three stout, suited, masked visitors drifted out, propelling themselves along the side-rigging of the tube. The first came unencumbered. The other two, slightly behind, hauled along a sort of sled with what might be baggage. The kyo had indeed suited up, taking no risks with the rigging, the bitter cold, or the air pressure.

"Bren!" a voice said, from speakers on the helmet; tinny, but deep, deep, booms attending.

"Prakuyo?" Bren asked. "Bren here." He held out a hand. Prakuyo caught it. "Come, come, Prakuyo-ji, hold the line— safe. Safe, this. Cold. Cold. Bad air. Hurry."

No bilingual repetition this time. Just a quick greeting. Details could wait for warmth.

"Yes," Prakuyo said, and Bren, with their hindmost guide already going out on the line, simply grabbed Prakuyo's massive gloved hand and set it on the grip.

"Hold! Hold tight!"

Prakuyo held, whisked away as he caught the next, and felt the others on the line, counted the number, and had no idea how the workers were dealing with the sled. Prakuyo, with an effort to look back, looked out through the lighted visor, humanlike but not human, eyes murky dark and wide, looking perhaps to be sure his companions were coming, looking perhaps, too, to recognize his face in the ghostly light, while he tried to recognize the kyo he knew.

"Welcome," Bren said. It was always hard, out here, to get enough air to talk. "Good you come."

"Banichi. Jago."

"They are coming. Hold tight!"

The line swept on, toward the lighted, metallic gray flower that was the open lift. A third worker, from some refuge never far from the lifts, floated at the lift door, clipped and stable, ready to assist them as they arrived. Human as the others. But cold suits muffled them, obscured identity, even species.

They reached that gray metal flower, and the worker in the lead simply let go and let inertia carry him to a safe rebound within the car, where the third worker assisted his stop. No such panache in their arrival: Prakuyo met that assistance, and arrested his momentum. Bren caught the tethered worker's offered grip and let his arm absorb the stress, turned slightly as Prakuyo reached a safe stop, and the worker inside drew him in. He reached his own landing, caught the worker's offered hand, turned as the other two kyo, without the baggage, followed with satisfactory dispatch. That booming sound of theirs came through the thin air as all the kyo reunited inside.

Jago arrived. Banichi did, close behind. Baggage arrived with the hindmost worker, weightless, but not without mass: stopping it without a bump required Banichi's slight intervention. They maneuvered it into Prakuyo's companions' control, as the hindmost worker sealed the lift door, and the companions bobbed a slight gesture as they floated, a sort of bow, or approval, or just relief to have arrived.

"Up, sir?" the worker asked. It was always protocol to get the door shut, the car moving, and heated air flowing in as fast as possible.

"Up," Bren agreed, and with a booming thump, the lift car began to move. The floor caught up with their feet, and the vertical railings immediately became useful for finding one's balance.

"Banichi," Prakuyo said then. "Jago."

"Indeed, nandi," Banichi said, pushing back his cold suit hood to show his own face. He made a little bow, assisted by the acceleration. "One rejoices to see you in good health, Prakuyo-nandi, and your associates. Welcome!"

A boom vibrated the air. Prakuyo made his own bobbing bow, such as his suit allowed, the car having achieved about one gravity in the climb, and in rumbling words punctuated with occasional booms of indeterminate significance, addressed his companions.

Then Prakuyo asked them, "Dowager? Cajeiri?"

Bren pointed up, the direction they were going, and the kyo bobbed and uttered that sound that might be agreement, or excitement, and began to release helmet latches, not without little shudders and bobs. A foreign scent came into the cold, dry air. A wave of escaping heat and moisture. Frost formed on the insides of the helmets, and on the lift doors. And the air thrummed and boomed with that part of kyo expression that neither humans nor atevi were apt to reproduce. There was light enough to see faces, but, Bren thought, it would be a wonder if kyo could tell one human face from another, no more than he could tell which of the three might be Prakuyo, except being the one nearest him. The faces were all middling gray, skin taut and smooth about eyes and flat nose, mottled with spots that iridesced shades of gray-blue and gray-green. Mouths and jaws were surrounded by folds and an angled musculature different from atevi or human—and that offered distinction, one from the other. One *did* remember that pattern about Prakuyo's jaw, the crisscrossing of faint wrinkles and the sweep of the lid at the corners of the eyes.

One remembered. One remembered those nuances, close at

hand. Prakuyo was massive, strong, and while he had grown woefully thin in his imprisonment, his skin hanging in folds when they had known him, now he had recovered his bulk, broadened, grown solid. Larger than his companions. But that slight bluish blotch on the forehead, dotted with freckles, yes, that was indeed Prakuyo. Of all others, that was indeed *their* kyo.

"Banichi," Prakuyo ventured, correctly. "Jago."

"Yes," Banichi said in kyo, with a little nod, and Prakuyo launched into something booming and rapid, perhaps identifying individuals, in a rumbling exchange of which Bren identified only two or three words beyond *human* and *atevi*.

"Human there," Prakuyo asked, then in Ragi. "Who?"

"That is Polano," Bren said in Ragi. "Jase-aiji's aishid, from the ship. Those three are also Jase's people, from the ship. We are safe. Welcome aboard." He rendered that into fragmentary kyo and all three kyo nodded and bobbed.

"Good," Prakuyo said. "Go see dowager?"

"Go see dowager. Good place. Supper soon." That, in kyo only. Bren pointed straight up, and the wrinkles below Prakuyo's mouth moved in what experience remembered as a pleasant expression. Again Prakuyo amplified that with his companions, regarding whose status there was no indication— and possibly no human or atevi correspondence. They had brought the baggage, and handled it, while Prakuyo did not. There was equal animation in the voices and the gestures, no evidence of deference, but all such interpretations were a guess. The words *Bren, Cajeiri,* and *dowager* were, however, definitely part of the discussion.

Another word also stood out: car. And one remembered, as the numbers ticked by in the readout above the door, a toy, a remote-controlled car, that had helped break down the wall of suspicion, two years ago. Cajeiri's treasure, given to a departing Prakuyo.

The lift changed directions, and from their guests, came a

little click and boom of startlement. Another shift of direction, so that a reach for the safety hold was instinctive in all of them. That drew a strangely musical boom from the companions, a sound that they had heard Prakuyo make both in surprise and in amusement. Prakuyo answered it with a series of three lower-pitched sounds.

The car slowed, approaching their destination, and eased to a stop. The door opened and let them out.

"Here," Bren said, and exited first, carefully offering direction for the kyo, providing them ample room and time—their guide was holding the car. They came out cautiously. Massive folk, with limited mobility in their necks, and more so by reason of the suits, they turned to look this way, and turned slightly to look the other way, a curiously graceful movement, on one foot and the other. Then they faced Bren, looking for direction.

Routine dictated they shed the cold suits beside the station lift. Bren and his aishid slipped out of theirs quickly and their workers gathered them up, taking them back into the lift. The kyo made distressed sounds, helmets tucked under their arms, their baggage sled beside them—not, one could guess, trusting enough to shed their suits in the corridor and send them away.

"Come," Bren said in kyo, and with a gesture down the hallway. "Come. There will be food, beds. A room to change clothing." It was, he thought, curious the words they *had* achieved, in a household that dressed for dinner.

He led the way with Jago, and the kyo followed. The smallest of the three unfolded a handle from the carrier base and brought it along, and Banichi and Polano brought up the rear. It was a clear hallway ahead, few doors, no signage, and no long walk at all to reach their destination.

Bren stopped at the residency door, Jago beside him, as it opened. He said, in ship-speak: "Polano, thank you. Well done. Very well done. We'll manage from here. Tell the captain thanks."

"Yes, sir," Polano said, conservatively, not leaning at all on

familiarity in front of visitors. It was not Polano's first encounter with kyo, but he was on formal manners, careful in his
movements, few words, likely relieved to have done his duty
and to be away, doubtless with a memorable event to share
with his partner Kaplan, and with Jase.

They came into the foyer, and straight into the main room,
Narani attending the inner door.

Narani attracted Prakuyo's attention, and Prakuyo glanced
toward him with a gaped expression, as if Prakuyo might say
something, while the other two were more subdued, stalled in
the doorway, rocking a little as Prakuyo stood and remembered.

"Rani-ji," Bren said, "our guest Prakuyo, and these are his
companions, Matuanu and Hakuut, likewise our guests."

"Indeed!" Narani said, and Prakuyo, bobbing and booming:
"Rani-ji! Yes! Good!"

"Nandi." Narani gave a proper bow, holding the door wide.
"We are delighted at your safe arrival. Welcome!"

"Are they here?" The dowager's door had opened. Cajeiri burst
forth, and at that young voice, Prakuyo gestured outward and
clasped his arms about his middle, bowing. "Is Cajeiri? Yes!"

"Nand' Prakuyo." Cajeiri came and gave his own little bow,
and broke into a broad smile. "Cajeiri, yes! And my great-
grandmother is coming."

"Large!" Prakuyo said, measuring a hand span, "Cajeiri large!"

"Indeed." Ilisidi emerged, with Cenedi, took a position beside her great-grandson, hands on her cane. "He has reached a
felicitous nine years. It would be a wonder were he not grown
larger."

Prakuyo paused, parsing her words, perhaps, and then gave
booming approval. "Nine. Felicitous nine years! Yes." Which
led one to wonder how mature kyo reckoned nine years to be.
"Ilisidi dowager." Prakuyo bowed. "We are welcomed! Here see
Matuanu an Matu and Hakuut an Ti. Welcome!"

"They are indeed welcome. We are glad to see you in good
health, nand' Prakuyo. We did not expect your visit so soon, but

you have arrived in good order, we presume, with some matters to discuss. We have arranged a good supper. Bindanda is here to manage the kitchen. You remember Bindanda, perhaps."

"Danda-ji?" Prakuyo repeated, pulling that name out of her uncompromising welcome. "Teacakes!"

"Indeed there shall be," Ilisidi said. "And very shortly there will be supper. Will you join us?"

"Supper," Prakuyo said. "Yes. Yes. Good. Very good." He gave a little bow, and rendered an enthusiastic explanation to his companions, who stood by with the baggage.

"Here," Bren said, motioning to the open door on the far side, "guest room. All good. Prakuyo's."

"Guest room," Prakuyo said, and explained it to his companions with more words, all related to the topic, all enthusiastic, all happy, and possibly involving where to put the luggage.

God, Bren thought, seeing their guests bow and go off to see the guest quarters—it was going so astonishingly well. No hostility, no threats, no demands or conditions. Prakuyo seemed to be in charge, the others backing him up—perhaps even serving as bodyguards, the same as Banichi and Jago had been with him on the ship. Perhaps they were just there as a reciprocation of numbers. They were an assorted lot, Matuanu larger than Prakuyo, and Hakuut not as tall as either.

Prakuyo and his companions entered into their guest room, with booming and thumping and excited voices. They were discussing the furnishings, and perhaps the disposition of luggage.

They were aboard. They were in. Nobody was angry. He felt drained of energy. Relieved. Exhausted. Feverishly anxious to talk with Prakuyo and apprehensive at once.

And they'd only started.

"They *seem* happy," Cajeiri said.

"Seeming is not being," Ilisidi said. "And they will think the same of us, since persons sent so far to speak to us are surely not shallow-minded or feckless."

Cajeiri bit his lip. "*We* shall not be feckless, mani," he said quietly.

"Indeed," Ilisidi said. "One would not countenance it."

Bren cast a look at his aishid, looking for cues. Ilisidi had come only with Cenedi, and Cajeiri had come out without any of his young bodyguards. The Guild Observers were behind closed doors. There were a far greater number of Guild not in view than present in this room, and one wondered if things outside were proceeding as smoothly, regarding the ship.

"Have we heard from Jase-aiji, nadiin-ji?" he asked.

"The kyo ship is holding its position, nandi," Banichi said quietly. Tano and Algini, among those not in sight, were undoubtedly tapped into the information flow, right along with Geigi, right along with Jase, who bridged between this room and ops' opinion of that ship. "They are staying under their own power, maintaining as they were."

Not relaxing their guard, surely. He was not wholly surprised at that. It was much what they had done at Reunion.

"Is Jase coming down?" he asked.

"He will, but he will stay to your suite, nandi, unless requested otherwise."

His suite. Which was connected to information constantly, where Tano and Algini were in touch with Geigi, and with Jase, and Jase was connected to ship-com.

Nobody was relaxing yet.

One wondered if Prakuyo was investigating the communications he had in the guest suite. It would give him, mediated through ops, as good a link to the kyo ship as they had. The display screen beside it was locked on the same view they had had, the exterior of the kyo ship on camera. That, they hoped, would tell Prakuyo what the communications unit connected to.

Or perhaps Prakuyo would decline to experiment, and ask him. He thought, if he were in Prakuyo's place, that would be his choice—not to give those watching a notion he was reckless.

Prakuyo was occasionally demonstrative. But not, he thought, reckless in any sense.

"Tell Jase to tell me if there is contact with the ship," he said.

Record that contact, if it happened?

That was a given. They were recording everything.

17

Dinner, when it arrived, an event quietly announced by staff, brought them out of their quarters, and the kyo likewise ventured forth quietly, now dressed in loose patterned robes, Matuanu's greenish blue and Hakuut's greenish gold, muted shades which agreed with their gray, freckled complexion. Prakuyo's, however, was various shades of off-white, bringing to mind his curiosity, two years ago, about Bren's clothing, which, as paidhi, was shades of white on formal occasions—like their visits to a kyo ship. Was it deliberate? Was he saying, in his own way, *I'm here to hear and be heard?* Or had his interest simply reflected a personal preference or a mark of rank?

They boomed and hummed softly in apparent appreciation of the elaborate table setting, and taking their cue from their hosts, they sat down at the table only after the dowager had been seated, settling in the chairs, which were generously wide even by atevi standards.

Perfect. Bren heaved a great sigh of relief as staff began to serve the drinks—fruit juice, this evening, in addition to the water. The fare was safe for humans, and therefore safe for kyo—Prakuyo having survived it in the past. They had had no means to inquire about the acceptability or the safety of alcohol, but at the sharp flare of nostrils and interest from Prakuyo when staff poured vodka into the dowager's fruit juice—

Prakuyo indicated his own glass.

"Maybe safe, maybe not safe," Bren cautioned.

"Safe," Prakuyo declared, quite definitely, though he smelled it and tasted it carefully when served, then gave a rapid series of soft booms that drew interest from the others.

So it was vodka all around, except Cajeiri's glass. "Moderately for our guests, very moderately," Bren said to staff, none of whom were fools.

The courses were a great success, all round, food, drink—even conversation, limited as it was, in the dual mode, kyo, then Ragi and Ragi, then kyo, expressions which, without the little screen handy at the table, Bren struggled to remember. Yet. There was a little reminiscence of dinner at Reunion, which triggered a lengthy spate of Prakuyo talking to his companions.

And there was discussion, too, involving the centerpiece, two bits of driftwood, arranged artfully with a bit of water-smoothed stone.

"Come away planet?"

"It came from the planet, yes," Bren said in Ragi, then in his best kyo effort. "Wood. The wood comes from trees."

"Wood. Trees," Prakuyo repeated, carefully, and appeared to translate, to nods and bobs from his companions. "Alive? Now dead?"

Bren nodded, and with an upward gesture. "Tall."

"Not food."

Bren nodded. They'd had fruit on the kyo ship, and bread. Grains. Prakuyo had lived on fish and synthetics for six years on Reunion, which had not sufficed for him, though whether quantity or substance was at issue remained a question.

"Does your world have trees, Prakuyo-nandi?" Ilisidi asked, a step into what might be more sensitive territory—but reciprocal. Bren translated it.

From the exchanged looks, there was a little consideration on that point. Then the smallest said something, and Prakuyo nodded.

"Trees," Prakuyo said, and indicated something very wide

rather than tall. He offered a kyo word, which Bren repeated, then, indicating the stone, another word, also repeated. Then . . . with a lift of his water glass, Prakuyo made a gesture, as if holding something in one hand, smoothing it with the palm of the other, and offered two more words, similar, but with an added sound, *ka*. Perhaps stone and wood altered from its original form? By water? A third mimed gesture. This time, he held something in his hand, and seemed to carve it with his dinner knife. Another pair of words, same core, with *ba* attached.

Stone and wood . . . altered by intent? Words altered by suffix, denoting *by nature* and *worked by hand*?

No conclusion. Yet. But an interesting possibility—all from a simple centerpiece.

No atevi art existed without purpose. And no centerpiece landed on this table without careful consideration. Kabiu dictated a dining table should have something at its heart, and the usual flowers were not easily to be had here. Atevi might read meaning into the choice and color and number of blooms . . . but Ilisidi and her major d' had chosen items so basic, so important—

So very basic to the planet.

It was *not* casual, that choice. Ba and ka might be a tricky way of describing materials. Or artwork. But atevi *talked* in presentation pieces and table arrangement. There was more to the statement, in atevi terms. It was about basics, and foundations, the beginning of a relationship.

But it was also, under these circumstances, planetary geology on a plate, for the discerning eye. The action of water and gravity and time on two things very durable. Physics.

More, it was a gesture of openness, that arrangement, revealing aspects of the planet below them. Three species from three worlds sitting together at a table and the object in the middle of it all, a representation of one of the most fundamental aspects of nature—atevi kabiu, at its finest.

And the kyo had taken the bait. Chance had nothing to do

with an atevi arrangement settling kabiu. He had been occupied with his pictures. Ilisidi had laid the traditional opening statement on the table, and asked—Does your world have trees? Do trees find their way to moving water, to weather like this? Is this sedimentary rock, smoothed by ages, recognizable in process?

This is our world.

Do you recognize it?

We find both beauty and symbol in these items.

Do you?

Prakuyo touched his eye, and pointed to the object. Laid a hand on his midriff. "Good," he said.

"Indeed," Ilisidi said, and gave a little nod. "One is gratified."

Triumph. At least in setting a tone, and making a statement— and discovering that, first, kyo recognized natural from manmade in that item, and that they were sensitive to symbology.

That invited questions, at an appropriate time, about those kyo colors, and patterns.

Wide trees? Low-lying woody vegetation? There was surely water in some abundance.

And what ceremony had kyo offered *their* arrival on the kyo ship?

Pure water. Among other things edible. And Prakuyo's water consumption, while a guest aboard the ship, had been considerable.

They preferred dimmer light, cloyingly thick, to a human, air, so it was possible Prakuyo's gesture had described not the width of trees, but the wide expanse of forests—

Bren made a mental note for one of the first images to bring up, when they got down to business.

Prakuyo's skin seemed sensitive, thin, about the face—lack of protection from the sun's ultraviolet rays? Their colors seemed muted, browned to human senses. Might kyo see ranges of color neither humans nor atevi saw? The booming and thumping that was so much a part of their communication had the power to make the very table vibrate. Might they feel those vibrations through, not just ears, but other internal organs that were, so far, not even guessed at? To his recollection, sounds carried better through water, through water-laden air—would they change in greater barometric pressure? He was a linguist, not a physicist.

The arrival of the main course, a pasta with green sauce, met with great approval, and drew its own conversation.

It was sparse, very slow conversation, more eating than talking at most times. Servants came and went. Bren had asked for no more than a taste of the vodka, and ate lightly. As the meal drew to an end, and before the dessert course, Bindanda, as was Ragi custom, put in his appearance and gave a little bow, to receive his due for the meal.

Prakuyo recognized him at once. Perhaps it was Bindanda's size. Geigi himself didn't equal Bindanda's prosperity.

"Is this Danda-ji?" Prakuyo exclaimed, and rose, making a strange little hum.

"Indeed," Bren said, "indeed it is."

"Teacakes!" Prakuyo said. "Good! Good food!"

"Prakuyo-nandi," Bindanda said, bowing, and replied, with satisfaction, "Teacakes there shall be, nandiin, immediately!"

Bindanda vanished, and shortly after, staff brought out a plate, yes, of orangelle teacakes, fresh from the oven.

It was a crowning success. There was more than one plate of teacakes, and not a one left by the time they were through.

"Good," another of the kyo remarked. "Good. Good."

"Excellently done," Ilisidi said, and made a move of her hand, summoning Cenedi, who stood behind her chair. Cenedi handed her her cane, turned her chair from the table, and Ilisidi rose. They all must. The kyo likewise rose.

"We shall sleep now," Ilisidi declared. "We wish our guests a good night."

No brandy. It was not Ilisidi's habit to retire without it. And leave a potentially good conversation? She was the soul of curiosity.

No. It was not weariness. It was a maneuver.

"May I stay, mani?" Cajeiri asked.

"Young people should have their sleep," Ilisidi declared, at which Cajeiri let his own surprise show, but he dutifully bowed to the company and attended his great-grandmother in her retreat.

Their door closed. Bren said, first in Ragi, then in kyo. "We may sit and talk, Prakuyo-ji, if you wish. Sleep or talk?"

"Talk," was Prakuyo's answer.

"Banichi-ji. Jago-ji. Go tell Narani we shall need him."

Silent bows, Guild-style. His aishid left, into his suite, and shut the door, not only to bring Narani, but ready to exchange with Tano and Algini what they had observed, and to hear what they had perceived—a quick analysis of what had happened and where things stood, which could flow by back passages to the Observers, to Jase if he was present, and from Jase to Geigi, to Gin, to Sabin and Ogun.

Advise the kyo formally that they were welcome to contact their ship? Of course. He wanted them to do that. He wanted neither side to grow nervous.

And there could be more teacakes. With tea very slightly laced with brandy. Narani served, with Bindanda—who had shed his kitchen apron and turned up in a servant's modest coat: an elderly man and a middle-aged and portly one, both Guild themselves, keen observers, and quick to take a cue. Banichi and Jago came back to stand watch.

Bren settled at the table in the kyo's outer room, and the kyo sat down, one human and three kyo, a company of eight. Asicho saved the felicity, coming and going by turns, listening, cleaning up.

"These kyo?" Bren asked, unwilling to assign rank, or to use that touchy word *associate*.

"Matuanu an Matu. Hakuut an Ti."

Well, that gained nothing.

"Association?"

Prakuyo waved a hand, boomed softly, said something involving the names in kyo, then in Ragi:. "Matuanu an Matu Banichi. Hakuut an Ti computer."

A bodyguard. And a computer tech?

"Bodyguard. Aishid?"

"Yes. Aishid."

"I understand." Gesture to eye and head. Booming and nodding from the kyo.

Bodyguard. Or something very close. Someone who protected. But weapons and body armor were not in evidence, unless they wore them beneath the robes. Matuanu, largest of the three in girth, had a distinctive double wrinkling at the corners of his mouth that gave him a perpetually amused look. But it was not, one had always to remind oneself, a smile: it was the set of the folds.

Hakuut was the shortest and slightest of the three, with a mouth quite lacking in folds and a shadowing beneath the eyes that might be cosmetic—or natural. It made the eyes very distinct, pale by comparison, and the movement of those eyes was attention-getting, quick and lively. If cosmetics, did it indicate rank? Gender? Personal preference? One had no idea. And were the darting glances apprehension, or just curiosity about everything around him?

Those eyes sparkled when Bindanda, on request, brought in four tablet computers—*that* had been a mild emergency, procurement of two more of those, with Geigi's off-site help, but the devices had arrived before dinner, exactly the same as the others, and instantly loading themselves with all the information the moment they located their assigned group, clever little machines.

Bren turned his on, demonstrating the button, then wished Narani to hand their guests the others. There were styli to hand about—Bren had thought of that item, recalling similar tools on the kyo ship; and the kyo had no question at all how to use them. Hakuut did a mouth-gape and uttered a little set of clicks as a button-push brought the screen up with the same image as Bren's, a world in space.

Programming had dealt with that. Bren had the master code, which brought all the screens into sync, and displayed whatever image he chose.

He called up a picture of a star and touched the star with his stylus. The area glowed. Then he touched the right side of the screen, and from the machine's speakers came, in Ragi, "Star." He lifted his stylus. Touched the left side of the screen. It said the word in kyo. "Pak."

"Star," and lifted his finger. A second touch and his own voice played back, naming the object.

Hakuut's eyes widened. Fingers twitched, the stylus tapped. "Star," his machine said. And if a kyo could show a childlike delight in a toy, that was the body language, even the momentary expression, mouth open, stylus poised. Tap. "Star." Then: "Pak." Tap. Tap again. The machine said, "Pak."

The others figured it. "Excellent!" Prakuyo proclaimed it. "Good!"

It took a little sorting out, especially the demonstration of how to add a word in either language. That evoked a great deal of chatter from Hakuut to the others.

Then, from Hakuut, a gesture to the units and a question involving, apparently, the ceiling and walls—a question, Bren surmised, as to whether the devices were linked only to each other or linked through another unit.

So there, first off, was a question of trust.

Should he admit what any person used to such systems might suspect as a matter of course: that they were under observation, they were being recorded?

In fact they were not only being recorded, every individual word was being computer-captured and linked to context—

because nobody since the first human settlement on the planet had had to deal with a completely strange language. Ragi at least was within human ability to pronounce, but neither human nor atevi could figure the booms and thumps that ranged into the bottom range of hearing. Yes, the devices all linked to a master system.

Tell them that Tano—whose specialty was demolitions, about as far from linguistics as one could get—was in the sitting room of the paidhi's apartment making the best real-time analysis he could manage? Tano was following the conversations, looking at the situational use and helping the computer build a sort of dictionary, flagging repetitions in other contexts, and, if Tano thought of one, even assigning a best-guess definition.

It certainly wasn't Tano's field of Guild expertise—but Jago, who was their best at languages, was part of the security team Prakuyo knew, and Jago and Banichi needed to be present with him. Tano and Algini, whom the kyo did not know, and who had more expertise with computers, were behind the scenes, taking notes, making decisions, communicating offsite. Waveform analysis was also part of that record, and *Geigi* was involved with that, with techs who again weren't going to get regular shifts or sleep. Bren ached to get a look at the record, whether the sounds were individual, freeform, or whether they were regular, specific and precise. He wanted *hours* to sit and go over that record.

He didn't have hours. He had to steer the conversation that provided the data into areas they wanted to talk about, and he had to make the decision to tell Hakuut the truth or withhold it.

"More computer," he said in kyo, with an encompassing wave at the surrounds, as Hakuut had done. "We want to hear." He tapped his ear. "Humans, atevi do not hear all kyo sound. The atevi ear is better. But not hear. Machine hears."

A little animated kyo discussion followed that, rife with those frustrating booms and thumps and hums that neither human nor atevi throats could duplicate. Back at Reunion, when Prakuyo had expressed distress on one occasion, tea had quivered in a cup. The sound when Prakuyo was really agitated, as he had been in the struggle to rescue him, made itself *felt*, quite scarily so. Waveform analysis could reveal what they could not hear. But it didn't tell them what it meant. It didn't tell kyo, either, what it meant when a human tensed a small muscle near the mouth.

The kyo were discussing something, maybe the monitoring, maybe the limitations of human hearing—there was no knowing. But he didn't intend to have the conversation spiraling off into speculation neither side could answer.

He keyed the next word, deliberate distraction. *Solar system.* A generic star system. A touch on each object generated not just his voice and the word, but the path of the planet or moon around the star, the moons taking that distinctive sine wave pattern of a body caught in a moving gravitational well.

Hakuut was with him immediately, and repeated the words, then, with screen taps, put in the kyo words for planet, and for moon, orbit and year. Lifted the stylus and touched again, obviously delighted to hear it play back, first the kyo word, then, a third touch, the atevi word again, going on to make some observation that contained the words *atevi solar system* and *planet.*

Prakuyo made a thump, somewhere in his chest. Hakuut glanced at him, then closed his mouth and was silent.

Was that a caution, from Prakuyo? A warning not to push too far, a little wish not to go into whatever that statement had been?

Prakuyo made a triple boom, then took over. Using his own screen, Prakuyo repeated the words quietly, slowly, in a way now, Bren noted, that carried far less of the resonance of normal kyo speech.

Curious. Was it to accommodate him, when he had said he didn't hear everything?

Was it some simplification, the same way Ragi—which leaned heavily on numbers, with complex substitutions to make an infelicity felicitous—had what they called the children's language, which used far simpler forms and notably lacked those particles?

Hakuut and Matuanu immediately followed suit, and when they next spoke, their speech was higher, more in the front of the mouth, lacking those deep sounds.

Baby talk, God help him. It was a little embarrassing—and possibly psychologically affecting how they heard him. But when he repeated those words in that simplified form, he drew hums and booms of approval.

Prakuyo was, all things considered, no fool. If there was a way, Prakuyo tended to find it, from survival—to dealing with foreigners.

Bren called another graphic, assembled photos with no size reference: the atevi solar system, the Earth, and Alpha Station, a tiny *Phoenix* orbiting nearby, and the kyo ship a white shape docked at the mast.

"Here," Bren said, and pointed to the Earth. "Atevi planet," he said, and touching the planet, he said, "Earth. My name is Bren. The planet's name is Earth."

The kyo carefully repeated the word, touching the image for a playback until they agreed each had said it correctly.

He touched the station in the image.

"Alpha Station," he recorded, and: "Ship. The ship's name is *Phoenix*. Kyo ship. The kyo ship's name is . . ."

"Hraksuhi ha Ahko."

That took some work. He said it twice before Prakuyo said, "Yes." And had no clue whether it was a poetic name or some other designation.

Bren went on, planet to planet, giving atevi names.

Then, up close with the Earth and Sun. Orbit of the planet. Year. Rotation of the planet. Day. Hour. Minutes. Seconds. They had *time* in their collective knowledge.

"Kyo planet?" he asked then, casually, and Hakuut said something that was half a thump.

A rapid, soft sound from Prakuyo, one Bren didn't recall hearing before. Hakuut's skin pattern flared, spots coming into view and fading.

Reciprocity, offering information, then asking it in return. It might be a pattern. It might be an ethic. He might have burdened them, offering information, then asking a return.

Pushing too far too fast. Ramirez had done that.

Then Prakuyo said, "Kyo planet name is Tuan."

It was, however, a good time to state principle.

Tuan could mean forbidden. Could mean almost anything. He ventured to confirm what it was.

"Tuan. Earth. Two planets. Earth is atevi planet."

"Tuan is kyo planet. Atevi planet is Earth." Then. "Earth is atevi and human planet?"

Oh, that was a sharp question. And not an easy one to explain. They'd traveled that territory before—back at Reunion, and never quite explained it to Prakuyo's satisfaction. Now they were orbiting the reality of that question. They were on a station where that question mattered.

And he'd prepared a graphic.

"Earth is atevi planet." He tapped the screen. There was so much to tell—from the human viewpoint nearly inexplicable. How did you possibly explain you'd misplaced your whole solar system?

Explaining the accident to the ship—was impossible.

Explaining the atevi perspective was far easier.

He showed an atevi country cottage. Children playing.

Showed a night sky, and pointed to a bright star. "Star comes. Atevi see it. Atevi look with telescopes." He showed that picture. "They see Alpha. Many years."

Discussion. "Human make Alpha Station?" Prakuyo asked.

"Yes. *Phoenix* came to the Earth of the atevi. They built Alpha. Many years. Humans on Alpha see the Earth, want go to Earth, make association with the atevi. Phoenix says no. Phoenix not want association. Phoenix goes. Humans on Alpha come down to the Earth of the atevi." Picture of a parachute. "Humans come down to the atevi. Ask help."

"Help."

"Food. Houses."

Photo of same. Two people. Children, playing in front of the house.

Photo of the world. And indication of a point on it. "This is an island. Water all around. Island. This big island is Mospheira. Atevi give this island to Alpha humans. All happy. Alpha humans are now Mospheiran humans. Mospheiran humans give atevi machines. Atevi give Mospheirans food. All safe, all good."

Discussion, then, a fairly lively one, in which he caught the words *station* and *planet, atevi* and *human.*

"More," he said, and changed the image to *Phoenix.*

That brought silence. Sharp attention.

"*Phoenix*, two hundred years, makes number two station. Reunion. Mospheirans do not see Reunion. Two hundred years, humans on atevi planet do not see, do not hear *Phoenix.* One year *Phoenix* comes to Alpha. *Phoenix* says not good at Reunion. Kyo are upset. Bad. Bad upset. Please come help Reunion humans come to Alpha. Atevi say—yes. We go. *Atevi* help Reunioners come to Alpha. Atevi send dowager, Cajeiri, Bren on *Phoenix.*"

He left it there. Going much further led to risky places. And no use trying to explain the warring factions, either on the station or on the Earth.

Silence persisted a moment. He waited. Nobody stirred.

"Reunion," Prakuyo said then. "*Phoenix* go Reunion. Come. Go. Come. Many years."

What was that human ship up to? Why this going and coming? Really good question, that one.

"*Phoenix* goes from Reunion, wants to see a star and planets. Kyo come. *Phoenix* upset. Big upset. *Phoenix* goes quick."

They had not yet discovered a word for mistake. Or sorry. Or bad move.

Tea quivered in the cup. The table might be vibrating ever so slightly. Human ears didn't hear it. Waveforms would surely show it. There was such a feeling of danger. Of apprehension. Like a thunderstorm in the distance.

In deep silence Narani came over and substituted clean cups. Bindanda quietly poured tea. They might have heard it. Human ears could not.

"Atevi and Mospheirans," Bren said, "want kyo all happy. *Phoenix* does not go to kyo space."

Audible thump. The cups quivered.

"Bren say ship not go. *Ship* say?"

Does the ship take your orders? Another really good question. And one with a complicated answer.

"The dowager says ship not go. *Mospheirans* are not happy to hear *Phoenix* upset the kyo."

Two times Prakuyo struggled to say something, ending in a triple thump deep in his throat and a slight shake of the head. "Not good," Prakuyo said. "Not good the ship comes to kyo place."

"Good the kyo come to Alpha," Bren said quietly, maintaining calm. "Good Bren and Prakuyo and dowager talk."

Emotion showed in the booms and thumps. What it showed, there was no knowing. Not-good covered so damned much territory. Good. Not good. Black. White. Shades of gray were the very devil to manage when one started with *table, chair, food.* Abstracts were like so many grenades, apt to go to wrong places and blow up on them. Alien minds, alien cultures, alien ethics— all, all unpredictable in combination. Substances that became actions. Actions that had substance.

Low booms came from Prakuyo, slow and somber.

"Bren. You. Bren. Atevi human."

"Yes. I, Bren. Atevi human."

"Not ship human. Not Reunion human."

"No. Mospheiran human."

"Polano—" Prakuyo said the name very carefully, as he

would a word he was trying to get right, and Bren nodded. "Po-lano ship-human. Jase-aiji ship-human."

"Yes."

A rumbling discussion with his associates, then Hakuut colored brightly and said, in careful Ragi:

"Kyo-we see Bren, see dowager, see Cajeiri, see Polano, see . . ." A nervous tension, a glance at Prakuyo. " . . . Much atevi." Holding his hands wide. "Atevi and atevi and atevi. Much atevi? Yes?"

"Many atevi. Yes."

"Good!" Hakuut's voice gained confidence. "Atevi food. Atevi bed. Kyo-we want go see all the station human. Want see the *many* station human. Many *ship*-human. Yes?"

Hakuut was quick. And armed with vocabulary. Did the subordinate ask the pointed question, giving Prakuyo the chance to disown that question? Possibly. Prakuyo hadn't disowned it yet.

Did he accept the question, from the one who seemed junior-most?

Ilisidi certainly might not. *He* was, however, just the translator.

"Here. They are all here." He brought up a picture of Alpha, touched one side . . . it lit up. "This is atevi side of station." He touched the other. "This is human side: they are Mospheiran."

"Mospheiran." There was no luck with the m sound in initial position. It came out an h. So did the ph.

"Mospheirans do not speak Ragi. Atevi do not speak Mospheiran. Associated—" He pressed his hands together, then opened them wide. "Not one."

God, he hoped they got that. But Hakuut blinked, then spoke rapidly to Prakuyo, who hummed.

Then Prakuyo said: "Jase-aiji is in Bren room. Yes?"

God. Subsonics. What did they have? Radar? Could they hear the voices? The movements behind two walls?

Jase had been in ops. Jase had *talked* to the kyo ship. Prakuyo had identified that presence, right along with his.

"I shall call him," he said matter-of-factly, and took out his pocket com, with no reference to the listening that was already going on, and the likelihood that Jase already knew his name had been invoked. "Jase-ji? Prakuyo heard your voice. He'd like to see you. Will you come join us?"

"*No problem,*" Jase answered smoothly, and Bren translated it: "Jase-aiji is happy to come."

How much else might they have heard? He had no idea. Guild could drop into their own modes of expression.

But, God, there were the Observers, as well as those more accustomed to strangers. One only hoped they were circumspect.

A door opened in the larger room. Steps crossed the tiles, and the carpet. Even human ears could follow that set of sounds. Jase, in ship's uniform, arrived in the doorway of the kyo sitting room, gave a little bow, atevi-style, and offered a pleasant face.

"Prakuyo-nandi!" A bow and then, in kyo. "Good see Prakuyo. Hakuut. Matuanu. Good see."

The two kyo rose and bowed and bobbed, Prakuyo acknowledged the arrival with a lift of his hand. "Jase-aiji good see. Sit, yes."

Jase, with a glance at Bren, slipped into the chair next to him. There was, naturally, the solemn quiet of tea service, a quiet sip or two, time to factor Jase's presence into the situation and give Jase a moment to settle.

Jase had kept ops chatter confined to charts and diagrams, Jase had assured him. Hadn't tried verbal communication, except small words like *go*, and *yes*. No freehanding of conversation.

Had he identified himself to them? Possibly, so routine a matter Jase might not have registered it.

But how much detail of a voice *did* kyo pick up—granted sound might be a far, far more important sensory gateway for them than it was for humans or atevi?

They'd not gotten *nearly* as much booming and thumping in

their meetings with the kyo at Reunion. Had that been profoundly restrained—*not* to give way to emotion in the negotiations?

Prakuyo had had less restraint—personally. They had remarked that at the time.

Prakuyo and the other two showed no such restraint now, among themselves. A group of kyo *all* emoting, he suspected, could more than rattle a teacup. *All* upset at once was something he didn't want to see.

"Good Jase-aiji come," Prakuyo said. "Kyo-we want see Reunioner. Want see Mospheiran. Want see atevi. Want see station."

Jase drew in a breath, made a face, and kyo eyes flicked his way, wondering, possibly, what that twitch could possibly mean.

Bren knew. "Security nightmare," Jase said.

"They want to see the association," Bren said in ship-speak. "They want to see— Cooperation." The image of kyo in the broad main corridors with random traffic, God, no. With the general apprehension, the recent brush with a Reunioner-Mospheiran quarrel breaking into riot. No. Quiet areas. Where there were humans. "We can take them to Central," he said. "Let them witness a handoff. Take them to human Central, then over to atevi Central at the handoff. Gin. Geigi. Their staff is steady—we've had proof of that."

"To do that, we have to take them through the crossover," Jase said.

A public area. Random persons. Security could make it a little less random.

"Can we fix that?"

"I can do it," Jase said. "Shall I?"

"Yes." He shifted to Ragi and said to Prakuyo. "Yes. Jase is going to talk to the station. This night we sleep. Tomorrow we go to see the station."

He *hoped* Prakuyo would take the delay and not interpret it as a setup, which it somewhat was. He *wanted* to close down the session and get some rest—the adrenaline was running out. He *wanted* to sleep. Finally. Things were working. The situation hadn't blown up. He *wanted* to sleep.

"More words," Prakuyo said. "Go tomorrow. More words now. Talk. Listen."

God. At least the word for the visit upstairs was tomorrow, one Prakuyo had remembered on his own.

They were set. It was working. The kyo were working on their own charge of excitement, everything new, and quite possibly *they'd* gotten regular sleep on the trip in.

He'd last. Staff would.

18

Narani, Bindanda, Banichi and Jago all stayed staunchly on duty, with minor absences . . . sitting down for a while, one hoped.

Bren, meanwhile, worked through more associated picture groups, on tea-fired nerves, and with a very different perspective, now, on what he'd once naively thought to refrain from saying, and what perceptions had, like the tapestry of associated words, knit itself into inescapable association.

Hide their level of technology? No. It wasn't possible.

Everything the Earth of the atevi owned was oh, very clearly laid out. From their orbital vantage, simple optics was all they'd need to read the street signs in Port Jackson. Right below the kyo ship were seas and mountains, grasslands and forest, cities and towns, and *not* that extensive a technology. Planes flew . . . trains moved, particularly on the continent. Cities were few. Townships were far more frequent. It might not be as evident to starfarers like Jase, in his steel-and-composites world, drinking energy in monstrous quantities, breaking materials into elements and making them something else—but to people more familiar with the economy of earth and fields, water and wind? Achingly evident what level of population, what utilization of resources, built what level of technology—and the technology that made the table they were using was not the same that had made that bit of driftwood on the dining table.

It was not the foundations of a star-hopping civilization,

down there. The advanced technology had come in from the heavens, with humans, and his own account to them had said as much. Several of the trains they might spot down there were steam engines. The world had two real spaceports and two airports whose landing strips could accommodate a shuttle. He had so foolishly imagined, from the ground, trying to pretend otherwise—but from this perspective there were no secrets at all, no way to pretend there were other ships than *Phoenix*. There was one stalled in building—the story of that was equally complicated, and itself tangled in the mess at Reunion.

There were Gin's robot miners. There were two shuttles aloft, more on the ground. The mast itself could accommodate one more shuttle, with a starship in dock, no more than that. God, even getting into the station—on the conveyor line system that had never improved since construction days—must have struck them as dangerously primitive.

They were fooling no one. What they posed to the kyo was not a threat—so much as a mystery. What existed at Alpha was a creation from outside. What existed on the planet came from the earth itself.

Could the kyo possibly see a threat in a steam locomotive? Could they see one in a satellite system that was only this last year beginning to offer weather predictions on the Southern Ocean?

It was not the same technology. It was as hybrid as their civilization.

And when he thought of it not from the planet's surface looking up, how did his explanation of *Phoenix* make sense to them—a ship building yet one more station, out in the middle of nowhere, and that one ship using all the resource that station could gather over a matter of years—to go out—to do what? Look for a home they'd lost, when an accident had thrown them far, far off their intended course? How could he explain that, with their limited vocabulary?

Well, steam trains and scattered airports and all, they were all laid out below, the result of that one ship and desperate colonists quitting the station and heading for the green, good world below, the lifebearing star-system that also had, close by, the abundance of iron and ice the ship had needed.

Phoenix had built a station they fully intended to leave. And they'd done it again at Reunion. How did he make that make comfortable sense to the next solar system they'd set their sights on? It didn't make comfortable sense to him. Why? If the goal was to search for human space, why not just refuel and keep moving? The question still nagged him. Had Ramirez truly planned to abandon Reunion—to build—what? A *Phoenix* captain's world *was* the ship, and stations served it. Was it still a mission, in Ramirez' mind?

It hadn't been an issue to trouble Mospheirans and atevi—until Ramirez went where he shouldn't have.

A closer look, Gin had said. There were things you wouldn't know, if you didn't look close up.

Was *that* how Ramirez had made his mistake?

He couldn't ask. He couldn't get into that issue. Not yet.

He had pictures. That was what he had to work with. And time. As much as he could get, while the kyo were interested in listening.

They had touched on authority. And who had it.

He called up a picture of Tabini-aiji. Shawn Tyers. "Number one atevi. Number one Mospheiran human. Tabini-aiji is aiji on the continent. Shawn Tyers is aiji on Mospheira." He showed the vast expanse of the continent. And, again, the island that was Mospheira.

"Small," Hakuut observed.

It had always been big enough—big enough to be the whole world when he was Cajeiri's age. But they were looking down from the heavens, seeing the proportion of it—atevi to human.

"Small, yes," he said. "City here is Port Jackson. Airport

here. Big mountain is Mount Adams. Atevi lived on Mospheira. Then humans come down. Atevi aiji give Mospheira to humans. All humans here. All atevi—on the mainland."

"Humans come to Earth of the atevi—want—?"

Second time for that question. "Food. Want to be safe. Want children."

That provoked a discussion, which concluded in:

"Atevi planet."

"Yes." He showed a picture of a mecheita rider, one of the Taibeni, a living exemplar of the old culture . . . part of the forested landscape. "Atevi planet."

The picture—they found astonishing, though whether the ateva, the mecheita, or the trees, or just the act of riding triggered that astonishment was unclear. He had a video clip showing the rider mounting and the mecheita running—that astonished them. A picture of the dowager's home, Malguri, on its hill. The stone building intrigued them, and they seemed to find something comparable to discuss.

They worked out build, building, and house. Man. Woman. Mother. Father. Baby.

Train. Boat.

That was a photo of his own, Barb and Toby, on the *Brighter Days*, on a sunny day. The bay sparkling behind them. Both were smiling. Wind was blowing Barb's hair.

"Man. Woman," Prakuyo said.

Wise to turn it personal? Maybe it was . . . for the sense of trust they wanted to build.

"Man is Toby. Woman is Barb. Toby is my brother. Toby's mother is Bren's mother. Toby is Bren's brother."

"Brother," Prakuyo repeated, and there was a little nodding, a little soft booming, a little discussion. "Bren brother. Toby."

"Barb?" Prakuyo asked then.

"Barb is Toby's associate."

More speculative discussion.

"Baby?" Hakuut asked.

He caught himself short of a laugh. "No baby."

Kyo faces showed a little freckling, Hakuut more than the others.

"Cajeiri mother?" Prakuyo asked. "Aiji-dowager?"

"No. Cajeiri's mother is Damiri. Cajeiri's father is Tabini-aiji."

A ripple of hums and thumps. "Cajeiri father number one atevi."

"Number one atevi, yes."

"Dowager?"

"The dowager is Tabini's father's mother."

That triggered a small and lively discussion, thumps and booms.

"Aiji number one atevi."

"Yes."

Another small discussion, then Prakuyo said,

"Cajeiri father number one atevi. Bren, Cajeiri, dowager go on *Phoenix*. Go Reunion. Go Reunion. Go Reunion." Prakuyo opened his hand. *"Hed."*

Hed. Was that *why*? Maybe it was *give me a sensible answer this time.*

There was *one* point to hammer home. *"Tabini-aiji* hears kyo upset. Shawn-aiji hears. Tabini-aiji and Shawn-aiji say ship go quick make Reunion stop. Tabini-aiji say dowager, Cajeiri, Bren go see. Bring all Reunion human to Alpha, shut off Reunion, no more upset the kyo."

If that wasn't oversimplified enough, he didn't know what could cap it. But knowing they didn't understand the entire reason was better than concluding they did.

"Ship-aijiin." *That* was a challenge to his statement. *Who* was in control?

"Ship-aijiin," Jase said, trying to intervene, and without the words. "Bren, can we say *dead?*"

Important point, and they were stuck for a word in that direction. Bren took another. "Sabin-aiji take ship. Sabin-aiji hears Tabini-aiji, Shawn-aiji. Sabin-aiji, Jase-aiji come take ship, stop Reunioners. No more make station. No more go in kyo space."

He and Jase had had their short, private exchange. Now the kyo had their own consultation, with accompanying heavy thumps and hums. God, it was dangerous. A cultural assumption could go right off the edge.

"Many station," Prakuyo said.

"One station. Alpha. No more station. One ship. One station."

There was quiet, then, a lengthy quiet. They'd arrived at an assertion, perhaps, that the kyo didn't trust or couldn't figure.

For evidence there was the planet below them, with more trains than airplanes, a scant handful of shuttles, three runways, and one starship.

Matuanu said something, no word of which was understandable. Prakuyo listened, bobbed slightly, whether assent or just acknowledgment was unclear.

Prakuyo seemed to be the one in charge, not necessarily as quick with words as Hakuut, or maybe just a shade more cautious than Hakuut.

Prakuyo was also smart. Very smart. He'd picked up on that from the start of their association. And had Prakuyo, with so sharp a recall, been locked up for six years, learning nothing of the language? He didn't think so. Reunioners had avoided contact with him. He'd had very little interaction with anybody. But over six years—Prakuyo had had time to gather vocabulary.

Now Prakuyo had a tablet with keys to the Ragi language instead, a Rosetta Stone, and he sincerely, sincerely hoped, given his necessary claim that Tabini had some power of restraint over the starship, that had not been a monumental mistake.

Explain now that he wanted the tablets back? That wouldn't translate well.

Matuanu had rarely spoken directly to him. Now out of long, long silence. Matuanu, security, said, "Ship go kyo star not good."

Security? Or *military?*

Humans knew that word. Atevi had borrowed it from Mospheirans.

"Ship going to the kyo star is *not* good," he said. "Atevi and Mospheirans say ship not go. Bad upset kyo. No more upset kyo."

Reunion's images were vivid, the ruined station. The miserable, starved figure Prakuyo had become. The memories Prakuyo had—the memories the Reunioners themselves had of that place—were all one nightmare.

"Reunion stop," he said. "No more Reunion. No more human ship go in kyo space. No more atevi ship go in kyo space. Yes?"

"Yes," Prakuyo said, and there was, for the first time since the question of *Phoenix* had come up, a low, restrained booming—a signal, one began to believe, of a kyo in a better mood.

With that, they had come to at least a positive resolution—some sort of good outcome. From here it could go on for hours—or go downhill, with everybody increasingly tired, increasingly apt to miss points.

"Sleep now," Bren said. "Bren sleep. All sleep."

"Yes," Prakuyo said, in what was probably a very close approximation of the same conclusion: they'd all had a tension-filled day. They'd had supper, talked, fairly successfully.

Time to go behind closed doors, with a chance to communicate with each other and analyze the situation and *then* to sleep, and try again in the morning.

"Safe here," he said, got up, bowed, as the kyo did. He went to the sideboard, where the display was in off mode. He flipped it on, instant view of the kyo ship. "Talk kyo ship, yes. No problem. Push this button." Central was set to take such a call and send it right through. "Good you talk to kyo ship. You sleep safe. You need, come Bren's door."

"Good, good, good," Prakuyo said. "Thank."

"Thank you, indeed, nandi."

The devices he had passed out were still on the table, in the kyo's possession now, for good or for ill. Rosetta Stone. And fishing net.

Everything they input went to all units. The kyo weren't fools. They surely observed that.

So would they themselves put fish into the net?

He hoped they would. It would augur well if they did.

He had a nagging fear about what he had done. An association, the kyo had said back at Reunion, could not be broken.

Nor could words once given be taken back. He could have posed the aishidi'tat a lasting, wide-reaching problem. Involved them in a war in which they had absolutely no stake—except what he established here.

On the other hand—the kyo had never met anybody but themselves—and their enemy—until they made contact at Reunion. Two hundred years ago, humans and atevi had stopped killing one another, because there had been paidhiin. Paidhiin were their hope now. *Prakuyo* was their hope, because Prakuyo, at least, had come to talk and while they were talking, bad things were less apt to happen.

There were danger points beyond the ability to talk to each other. There were cultural questions, instincts they could fall afoul of—

But species smart enough to develop a stardrive—had to have found some basic sense of reason. Smashing systems one didn't understand was a strategy that kept barbarians from greater things. A better plan, by far, to investigate from the inside. And learn.

The kyo certainly had positive qualities.

Ten years sitting and watching Reunion after their initial strike. Curiosity.

Not immediately blasting their way in after Prakuyo themselves. Restraint and curiosity.

Purpose overriding passion, if passion existed in them.

Exactly what *had* Prakuyo wanted, approaching Reunion?

What had Prakuyo expected—when Prakuyo's folk had blasted hell out of the station four years prior?

Behaviors didn't make sense. But then—his own aishid had been completely appalled, when he had moved to join them under fire. They'd been angry at him. Furiously angry.

He left with Jase, with Narani and Bindanda, with Banichi and Jago. They crossed the main room, quiet and deserted now, all doors shut but the one they had just left. Their own door opened, expecting them: the monitoring had signaled their approach.

They entered the front room, with its security station apparatus. Banichi and Jago shed jackets and weapons. Tano sat at the middle console monitoring—whatever went on, Kandana and Jeladi and Asicho seeing to Banichi, Algini watching all of it—they were all there, and one suspected Cenedi and the Guild Observers at the very least were there electronically. He gave the Guild sign for quiet, and his own signal for writing, and said, in an entirely normal voice, "It went very well, nadiin-ji. One does not believe it could have gone better."

Banichi handed him a very small piece of paper, of the sort the Guild used, stuff that would not be paper if water or fire hit it.

He wrote, *Their hearing or their equipment heard Jase arrive*, and handed it to Banichi, who read it, nodded and passed it on, while he asked Tano, "Did it work, Tano-ji?"

"We found some seeming relationships," Tano said, while the note passed. "Then the meeting became much quieter."

"At a certain point I said we didn't hear everything in the sounds, and they changed their mode of speech . . . somewhat like the children's language, one suspects. Send word to the dowager and the young gentleman that everything went as well as we could hope. You did follow what we said."

Silent agreement all around.

"The teacakes were a great success, Danda-ji. Did Jase explain? We shall visit Central handoff tomorrow, to let our guests see something of the human establishment and our Central in operation. They have requested it. Jase will deal with the technicalities." He ached to get his hands on whatever sorting Tano had done. "I think I may take a very small brandy—any of you may join us, after so much effort today. I think we have earned it, and our guests I suspect are as tired as we are. Did Geigi's analysis turn up anything unexpected?"

"The sounds are complex," Tano said, and keyed up a waveform on his screen. It was, indeed. "We could reproduce them mechanically. But they are varied. We have some from Reunion. These have more variety, some quite elaborate. Sorting one source from another is difficult. They often set up resonances."

Prakuyo's mood, until he had rejoined his own people, had been restrained, excepting a few moments. So had the kyo on their ship—compared to now.

An appearance of cheerfulness, for their benefit? Nervousness on their side?

No knowing.

The note had finished its rounds, and vanished, from Narani's hand, into a forsaken cup of tea.

"At least," he said, "We have a beginning. A good beginning. Arrange things on the dowager's schedule—our day can begin when she wishes it to begin. Banichi." He held out his hand, wanting another of those small, disposable papers. He wrote in Ragi, *Prakuyo remembers words very accurately. He has trouble pronouncing ship-speak, but in six years he may have learned far more than he has wanted us to know. He is making us work for it. But I am suspicious he knows more ship-speak and more Ragi than he admits—and more than he can pronounce and their hearing may be unexpectedly acute. Be very careful what you say, at all times.*

Cajeiri waked—in a strange place—with someone moving in the room.

He was quickly wide awake. He was in his room inside mani's protection, with his own bodyguard, and that somebody
was moving in the room—he was sure it was one of his own
aishid—meant something was going on in the middle of the
night. "Who?" he asked, whispering so as not to rouse the rest
of his aishid—likely as it already was they were awake, too.

"Antaro," the whispered answer came back. "Nothing is
wrong, nandi. Nand' Bren is back in his suite. I have just come
in from a briefing."

He pushed himself upright. "Tell me."

Antaro came near and sat down on the side of his bed, and
now the rest of his aishid was stirring, shadows lit by one tiny
spark of light by the door switch. They gathered, likely aware
that Antaro had left and aware that Antaro was back.

"Nand' Bren is back in his apartment," Antaro said, whispering, "and Jago came through the servant passage to report.
Everything is going well, but we should be careful what we say,
because our visitors may have very good hearing or brought
equipment in or both. Cenedi thinks if they have equipment,
they may be picking up things from up in the station. Mani is
asleep. Cenedi will tell her in the morning."

He whispered: "Did nand' Bren learn anything new?"

"Nand' Bren and Jase-aiji were both in the session. The kyo
knew Jase-aiji was there. Nand' Jase worked ops with the ship as
it came in and they may have assumed he was there; but nand'
Bren says they asked for him only after he had come in from upstairs, so nand' Bren says assume they do hear, and he thinks our
visitors know more ship-speak and more Ragi than they admit.
Senior Guild agrees. But it did go very well. They worked a lot
with the electric dictionary, and they talked about Reunion.
Nand' Bren told them that we have no intention of rebuilding
Reunion or going into their space. They all agreed on that."

He would like to see the kyo world. At least pictures of it. It
was a sad thought to hear he never might. But he understood all
the reasons, understood them all the way back to the reasons

humans and atevi had had trouble meaning the same thing, to this day.

"Nand' Bren has gone to bed," Antaro said further, "and nand' Jase has sent a signal advising the ship-folk that things are going well and to be patient. We do not want to use the lift to come and go. It makes noise all the time, but stopping here, it makes a distinctive noise, and if sounds are informing our guests, we should be careful of unexplained coming and going."

"So will we see them at breakfast, Taro-ji?"

"We are told nand' Bren will sleep late if he can, and he is requesting your great-grandmother and the Guild Observers all delay breakfast two hours. This will give him time to study before breakfast, and it will give staff time to begin arrangements. Our guests are asking to see the station working, and to see Mospheiran humans. So they are going to go up to see Central do the handoff."

That was something *he* wanted to see. "Shall we all go?"

"One has not heard."

"Tell them I wish to go."

"It may make the size of the company unwieldy," Lucasi whispered, from the side. "One does not know this. But it may be a consideration."

An *adult* consideration. A *sensible* consideration. Those had not become his favorite words in this last year.

"There is nothing more I know, Jeri-ji," Antaro said.

He had waked up now. Entirely. But it was unfair and even dangerous to keep his bodyguard up so late *they* were suffering from lack of sleep. Things were not safe. They were never safe with that ship sitting out there.

"Everyone should go to bed, then," he said. "Thank you, nadiin-ji. We shall hope, at least."

"Nandi," they whispered, one and all, and went back to their own rooms, that opened onto his.

It was quiet then. And he was wide awake, remembering, and feeling a little chill in the air.

He had wanted to go into that room with nand' Bren. He had wanted to talk to Prakuyo. He had felt shut out, disregarded, and he had just waited for mani to tell him he was wrong for what he was probably thinking.

But maybe mani had felt a little the same, and without being upset—nothing upset mani—understood his disappointment. He and mani by themselves had gotten Prakuyo to calm down and even be happy, that first time, on *Phoenix*. It was mani who, even if she never used a word of Prakuyo's language, had said the right things the right way and made him understand he was offered hospitality, not being locked up.

This time Prakuyo had come with others they did *not* understand and had never met before, so things were different, and now was not then. He understood why nand' Bren had sharply restricted the conversation and talked with them alone.

But Jase had come in, Guild said. Could not he?

Maybe nand' Bren thought he would still deal in toy cars and picture books, when things were more serious than that.

He was not that boy with the toy cars anymore. He was not that boy who had run the ship-tunnels anymore. He was the boy his father had made his official heir. He was young aiji.

But one noted mani had not simply stamped her dreadful cane and walked into that room with nand' Bren either. She could have. Mani had not done that, because, for one thing, mani, with someone at hand to act *for* her, did not need to act, and *did* not act. She had been aiji of the aishidi'tat once. She had held Father's power, and she never acted personally if she had a subordinate to send. That was what it was to be aiji.

That was what he would be. Someday. There were probably times his father wanted to be involved in something, and held back because it was something a subordinate could do, should do, and if that subordinate failed, he would send another. And another. Even if they got killed.

And it meant sitting and waiting for somebody to send word and deciding at a distance whether that was good enough.

It meant staying in Central with mani, only *listening* while other people went into the station tunnels to rescue his associates.

It was not just because he was nine years old.

It was because he was "young aiji."

That was what he had to be. He could inform himself on what was going on everywhere. But touch it, until it was quieter?

No.

That upset him. But it was what aijiin had to do.

Aijiin were supposed to get information. His aishid was fairly good at getting it. They had. But it was not *all* he wanted to know.

Things *were* quiet right now, he thought, if everybody had gone to bed. He hoped they had been able to decide that nobody should shoot at each other, and he hoped the kyo had not guessed there was not much they could do if the kyo did shoot.

There had at least been no word about the kyo ship moving or doing anything. He was very sure *Phoenix* and the ship-aijiin were watching it, and knew exactly what to watch for, except there being not much they could do about that, either.

The ship-aijiin, he decided, were probably in the same situation he and mani were—they had to let their subordinates do what they could do, and wait. Jase-aiji had been down here. He would definitely be talking to Sabin-aiji, who had seen the kyo ship before, and dealt with it.

Ogun-aiji would be waiting. And Lord Geigi and Gin-nandi would both be waiting, all the aijiin of everything—just waiting for reports out of that room.

Probably there were kyo on that ship waiting for Prakuyo to report to them, too.

Nand' Bren said it was hard to understand the kyo, but maybe that was one thing they all had in common. The paidhiin got to go in and find things out, and figure things out.

Prakuyo was somebody important. But since he came, himself, he was probably not the most important.

Prakuyo had changed, which was good. He had been very thin. Now he looked a lot more like the others. He was rounder than Geigi or Bindanda. And one could not think that he had come all this way for teacakes, or conversation. Neither would anybody else. He *really* hoped they would not say anything about taking any Reunioners away with them: he would give them Braddock, but certainly nobody else.

And when nand' Bren had not included him in that late session with Prakuyo and the others, he had had, in that very moment, a feeling that it was very adult business afoot, that had to be done right, and without any stupid mistakes.

But when aijiin were in conflict—and subordinates went in—it made a difference how good those subordinates were.

The Mospheiran paidhiin had been doing it for a long, long time, and nand' Bren was the best there had ever been. He was sure of that. Nand' Bren was the very best.

And nand' Bren had not left him totally without information: nand' Bren had seen to it he had the little screen, and told him it would always keep up to date with whatever people put in.

And now the kyo had them. He had had that from Antaro's reports.

His tablet was on the little table, right beside the bed. He had not turned it on since before supper. He thought now the light might wake his aishid.

But not if he got under the covers with it. So he reached out an arm, took it, threw the covers over his head so he could see it, and pushed the button to turn it on.

It was not the image he had left on it. It was an image of steps on a stairway. Then people, humans, going up such steps.

A ladder. An atevi worker climbing it.

A mountain. Humans climbing the snowy part, in heavy coats.

It was making changes without his doing anything, and his aishid said nand' Bren was asleep.

He touched the Ragi side of the screen and it said aloud, in nand' Bren's voice, *mountain. Climb the mountain.*

He felt a chill. He touched the kyo side of the screen. It said, *Hsuna. Hsuna nak.*

Not in nand' Bren's voice.

He heard a stir in the room. He came out from under the covers, hair all in disarray. The sound had waked everybody.

"Nandi?" Jegari asked.

"The little screen," he said. "One of the kyo is putting words in." The image kept changing. "Every time it changes, one of them is adding words."

His aishid gathered to see, eyes shining gold in the light from the little screen.

"It seems a good thing," Veijico said. "Is it not, nandi?"

Could his aishid ask *him* such a question? He had no idea. He had absolutely no idea whether he should speak, or whether his voice might go to the other machine.

Surely not. It had no way to hear him. Had it? He had not tried to change the screen. Whoever was awake surely would not know they were all sitting here watching.

Was it Prakuyo? He thought not. He thought rather that voice belonged to the smallest of them. Hakuut.

That was spooky. It was really spooky.

19

No breakfast as yet—but there was hot tea.

And two messages had arrived in Bren's message bowl last night, through the servant passage. Kandana, on night watch, had read both, had advised staff, who had decided not to wake him, and Bindanda delivered them with the pre-breakfast tea, the first a message with no seal, no cylinder, on the Guild's impermanent paper.

It came from Antaro, of Cajeiri's bodyguard, and said: *New words are appearing in the device in the middle of the night.*

The second message came from Cenedi.

For the paidhi when he wakes.

That was interesting. He had not touched the device. He had debriefed with Jase and his aishid and gone straight to bed. It was beside him, atop his physical notebook—he took his best preliminary notes on paper, a habit a voyage to another star and back had not broken, and that battered notebook had seen some travel.

But had the fishing net indeed caught words last night?

He turned the device on, sipped tea, and ran through the early section.

Hakuut, he thought, by the timbre of the voice.

The lad—he mentally thought of Hakuut that way, fresh-faced, smaller, less in rank—the lad had worked hard at it: picture after picture. He skipped ahead and looked at those sequences designed to get at abstracts.

Filled in.

God, had the fellow gotten any sleep?

There had to be some clues in there, some places where he hadn't been able to puzzle out the desired path, where it came to abstracts.

But it was everything he had hoped to do in days. There. On every device this morning. Hakuut had handed them a starting-point . . . actually . . . actually—he checked a group of images that he had set up to establish words like same and different, like and unlike. Filled in. He checked one and another of the concept sections. Filled in.

God. A gift.

He poured himself another cup of strong tea and started through it, with an application that exceeded any he'd poured into University graduate finals. He hadn't had to absorb vocabulary this fast, this crazily, since that ages-ago night when he'd firmly believed the Linguistics certification board was going to try to set him back a year, purely on age requirements.

Three in the morning, he'd hit a wall and plowed through it. Three in the morning, and a strange sense of *how* the various numerologies worked in the word cores, and *how* the logic of the shift revolved simply around convenience and ease of pronunciation, not in some arcane set of word classes that human study had created to explain it. It had been, was still, just that simple—once one had done enough of a type. One *could* find a logic buried in a class of things.

And here was a string of identified abstracts, people, processes, acts, connectors, modifiers, done up in seals and ribbons, as atevi would say.

Seals. As in—locked down.

And in the thought that just perhaps Hakuut, who had drawn a sharp caution from Prakuyo during the session, might have done something else the other two might not approve—and because changing one device's content changed them all—he got up from his desk, took the device to the counter where he could make a computer connection, and backed up the state of the device as it was at this exact moment.

Seals and ribbons. His fishing net had hauled up a school of fish. Multiple schools of fish. Enough fish from an alien sea that he might be able to figure out their linguistic ecology.

If he had a month or so to do it.

He didn't have that. He had three hours until he had to show up for breakfast.

If he dared, he'd report himself sick and confined to bed.

But he had made that resolution, which he still thought was the only safe course, to be truthful and forthcoming with their visitors.

He could walk out and say—pardon me, honored guests, but I have been handed a gift which it will require weeks to appreciate, so meanwhile shall we put a hold on everything and simply live here together and enjoy all the food you can eat?

Well, he could not quite say it, or propose it that fluently. That was the problem, was it not?

He had three hours. He had shaved, showered, he had put on shirt and trousers. It would not be the first time his staff had finished dressing him while he read some critical paper.

Ilisidi was in good spirits at breakfast, her ordinary self, not troubling to speak a word of kyo, but definitely in good humor, at one end of the table. Cajeiri's place was on her right, beside Jase, across from Bren—the kyo having the whole other end of the table. Cajeiri had arrived just a little off from his usual excitement, with a serious look in Bren's direction as they sat down.

Bren said, conversationally, "A good night of very peaceful sleep, young gentleman."

Cajeiri was no stranger to double meanings. "Yes, nand' paidhi."

"Good sleep, yes," Prakuyo added cheerfully, as the servants began to serve. "Very good sleep. You sleep good?"

"Indeed," Ilisidi said. "And today we understand we shall visit Central. Very good."

There were nods and thumps and a gentle booming.

"Today," Bren said, just as cheerfully, in kyo, "we see more words in the device. Good help, Prakuyo. Thank you."

"Good, yes," Prakuyo said, and followed it with something to the effect that Hakuut had done the addition.

"Hakuut says the words, yes, I hear Hakuut's voice."

A nod, a little thump. "Excellent, nand' Bren."

"What is this we are saying, nand' paidhi?" Ilisidi asked, re-asserting herself. "Kindly inform us."

"Hakuut worked late, and generously amplified our store of words last night, aiji-ma, so we can make much faster progress on structure. I think your great-grandson has been doing the same as I have, this morning: studying. I could only wish I had more hours. But this will be a great asset."

"Well, well, perhaps my great-grandson can spend a little time with our guests today before the excursion."

Turn Cajeiri loose on his own with Prakuyo and perhaps steal a little more time with the new vocabulary? Jase had written reports ready to pass to various people who needed them—explaining, for one thing, the sensitivity of kyo hearing and why they were *not* using coded com. He might pass them while they were escorting the kyo upstairs, but it seemed fairly urgent to get those reports where they needed to be before kyo appeared in their midst.

He saw, on the other hand, Cajeiri's face, not showing the childish delight at that recommendation one might expect. Rather it was a sober look, a little concern. Perhaps it had not been Cajeiri's aishid's judgment alone that had sent word to the dowager's security in the middle of the night. Cajeiri would very likely have been the one to spot the activity—and sensibly notify those who needed to know and pass the message.

"Indeed, the young gentleman has looked forward to this meeting," he said, with his own sober reservations, and not without the thought that the dowager herself *wanted* her great-grandson to have a try at communication. "Perhaps he might indeed enjoy a little time after breakfast. —Prakuyo-nandi." A switch to kyo. "Cajeiri wants much to talk to Prakuyo and guests after breakfast. Yes?"

"Yes," Prakuyo said. "Yes, good talk to Cajeiri."

"Good, yes," Cajeiri said. "Good you come, nand' Prakuyo."

"Very good," Prakuyo said. *Very* was the guess, based on context and its similarity to *much*. "Very good, nand' Cajeiri. Does the dowager wish to talk?"

Context was starting to fill in, the structure, words inflecting in relation to each other, the advanced forms. One could not duplicate it yet. But one could guess.

"Mani, he asks—"

"We shall listen," Ilisidi said.

That was how he had found them once at Reunion, Bren recalled. He had been beyond worried about how things had been going, and he had come back to find Ilisidi and her great-grandson entertaining Prakuyo, having communicated in their own unique way.

Admit she had understood one word of kyo? No. Answer the question as if she had not needed to hear it? Quite smoothly.

One memory resurrected, a very good one, where Prakuyo was concerned, the moment Prakuyo had known he was free, and Prakuyo had become quite cheerful, talking to his fellows in quiet tones.

Dishes had arrived, quietly, dishes that, served up, evoked that cheerful booming and thumping that had not been in evidence in last night's long session. Bindanda had kept his own little notebook at Reunion, he had admitted it—being Guild, very likely had memorialized in Guild records the very recipes he had observed Prakuyo to enjoy.

And they flowed from the kitchen in quantity now, a good start to a very critical day.

"*Everything,*" Jase called to say, in Ragi, "*is being arranged. Handoff will be at our convenience, and we have suggested*

1430, ship-reckoning, as a good time. Does that work? It's all for you. We can move it."

"We can meet that," Bren said, and settled back to work at the dining table, concentrating on rapid memorization. The devices had an optional disconnect from updates, which was useful right now, keeping the screen from jumping about as the group in the sitting area looked up and added words.

He *could* have gone to his suite and shut the door. He *could* have separated himself from the gathering in the sitting area— which occasionally erupted in thumps and booms, and now and again in soft exclamations from Cajeiri.

But it was good to hear. It was good to know things were on track and people were agreeing and words were arriving. The curtains were drawn back, and he had a view of the group at the table and they had a view of him, while the good-natured exchanges around that table constantly reassured him he was not, at the moment, necessary to the conversation.

Ilisidi presided over that gathering, though her comments were few. Prakuyo and Cajeiri and Hakuut had the liveliest exchanges, with occasional low-voice words from Matuanu. "Add it to the device!" Cajeiri would say, and Hakuut would say, "One has done it!"

One *could* worry about a little too much revelation going on over there, a little too much information slipping out on what met them on their return from Reunion—an account of the aishidi'tat's problems was not an auspicious topic, *unless* it paid for similar information from Prakuyo on what had become of Reunion, or what Prakuyo had done in the interval. That was a question he longed to ask, but asking it led to places he was not sure they should go at this stage, with this limited vocabulary, and by no means did he want to open topics that might lead into a tangle of more topics.

There were words *he* wanted. He ached to get up, go over there, steer the conversation in certain directions at certain opportune moments to get what he wanted, but he concentrated on structure; that was his immediate and fairly urgent need: the little words, the connectors, the directionals, the actions in time, what one wanted to do versus what actually happened . . .

So, so many deadly shades of doing and being . . .

He had found in the discussion, however, a significant equivalency of pronouns, or at least a handful of them. Ragi had *he, associate of mine; he, associate of the second, third, fourth, fifth degree of associations; he, without association to anyone I know,* and *he, my enemy* before one even got to *he, the associate of my enemy* and so on. And that was just one pronoun. But it was at least structurally predictable.

Mosphei' and ship-speak handled those situations mostly with tonality, body language, and facial expressions, precisely where atevi might go stone-faced.

Kyo—had some sort of *we, you,* and *they,* and *we* moderated by particles into a *we including you,* and *we not including you, we including others and you, we including others but not you,* and *we as distinct from others.* Particles starting with *you* similarly designated an outside party. Or not. There *was* a word for *I,* but it seemed far rarer than we. There was a *he,* several versions of *he,* but whether there was also a distinct *she* or an *it* he had not yet discovered.

We. That word Prakuyo had rejected early on. *We* had induced real upset, back at Reunion, when they had all been strangers. Emotional context, there. Possibly it had been, in that moment, just *keep your distance.*

Prakuyo's current association right now sat evident before him: Matuanu, who rarely spoke, and Hakuut, who occasionally spoke too much.

Mirror, he wondered, himself, the dowager, the young gentleman? No, Prakuyo had identified Matuanu as a bodyguard and Hakuut as a computer tech.

That left the question what was Prakuyo? They still had no sure notion.

All the expressive booms and thumps that the teams on- and

off-site were recording and breaking down remained just as inaccessible today as yesterday, an impenetrable system that might turn meanings in a subtle way, or turn an utterance absolutely upside down. They thought now they could identify happy sounds and he knew one—a deep penetrating hum—that was distinctly unhappy. They might be able to teach the kyo what human expressions meant. But emotion itself might be a difficulty. Kyo did seem very emotive. Atevi weren't. It might be a cultural answer to a problem—but society depended on it. Mospheirans vented emotion, but the kyo might be making noise to conceal it, rather than express it.

Could kyo deceive and lie, with those thumps and booms, or were they to some degree involuntary? They had controlled them—considerably—but not eliminated them.

There were likely already mistranslations or almost-translations in the vocabulary they had from the kyo, assumptions equally foundational and profound, but nobody knew enough yet, on either side, to be able to sort those out. Neither side in that sitting area had yet a clue what the triggers were.

But the good-humored exchanges, the occasional bursts of surprise and amusement—those seemed genuine, at least a foundation of good intent, lowering tensions—and raising expectations for fair dealing.

Should one be surprised that the aiji-dowager, who had no patience with people wanting favors they would not outright name and far less with people persisting in trivial discussion, was sitting there, part of the interactions, smiling and seeming amused while Cajeiri and Hakuut settled on a definition of fast and slow.

Oh, one should not in the least be surprised. She was expert at such meetings. And dealing with a power that could blow the station to hell kept her, oh, very alert, and one had an uncomfortable suspicion—entertained. Not a flinch, not a twitch, not a frown. She was the soul of willing hospitality.

She was logging every transaction, every minuscule reaction in her own system of reckoning.

Cajeiri, too, had been extremely careful of his answers and his questions.

Until Prakuyo asked, "You have associates same nine years?"

Bren, momentarily deep in possessive pronouns, heard it and took in a breath. And faster than he could think of a distraction, Cajeiri said, frankly, properly:

"Yes."

"On the planet? Station?"

Cajeiri hesitated. Hesitation on a yes-no answer was not a search for vocabulary. It involved truth. And credibility.

"Reunioners," Cajeiri said on his own, and a half-heartbeat before Bren. "Reunioners come on ship. We talk. Associates."

Bren never looked up from his study. Intervening too emphatically would indicate anxiety on the point. He listened, trying to hope the boy could handle it.

"Reunioners here on station?"

"Yes, nandi. All here."

God, Bren thought, wondering if a proposal for tea, and a general session, could derail the conversation at this point.

But Cajeiri added, quick as a breath. "I go on the ship two years, go down to planet—I see my mother and my father—and new baby comes. I have *baby* associate. Small. On the planet."

That produced a ripple of sounds from the kyo.

"The young gentleman has a new sister," Ilisidi said, as if she had understood it all, and: "One is curious. Did Prakuyo also go home after we met, or has he come here from Reunion?"

A boom and thump.

One might not understand every sound kyo made, but Prakuyo had reacted to that question and shut it down.

"Do you come here from Reunion?" Cajeiri asked.

Prakuyo had his own heartbeat of silence. Then his own diversion: "Reunioner associates on station, young aiji. Yes?"

"Yes. On station."

"Come see talk eat teacakes."

"Mani?" Cajeiri said soberly, probably realizing how deep

the waters had gotten. "One believes he is asking whether my guests may come here."

Attack and counter. Prakuyo had dodged Ilisidi's question—with a countershot.

He should have intervened before now, Bren thought. Intervening now—God knew it was a shade too late.

"Nand' dowager," Bren said, pushing back from the table, "nandiin." He walked over to the sitting area, gave a little bow to Ilisidi, and quietly took a chair. "Prakuyo-ji," he said, "I have heard. Kyo upset the Reunioners. Children upset. Mothers and fathers upset."

"Fix," Prakuyo said. "Want fix."

Was that a proposal—in the direction of peace? Or was it a maneuver?

That proposal wanted the kids' involvement—and meeting with their own lifelong nightmare.

"Aiji-ma," he said, prepared to translate.

Ilisidi lifted her hand. "My great-grandson's guests have ridden mecheiti. A peaceful meeting with foreigners will not discomfit them."

That—was probably true. And the dowager had absorbed much more kyo than one had possibly thought.

Cajeiri looked at his grandmother. "*Reni* would come."

"I think Gene and Artur would not let Reni come alone," Bren said quietly. He *should*, he thought, be appalled. He should feel shame and guilt, and he did. But the dowager had conjured an image: mecheiti outside the bus windows—intruders in the house at night.

The kids *had* done what the dowager reminded him. They had seen things he was sure they hadn't told their parents.

He could evade an explanation. But they had, at least, to advise the parents on this one, or forever lose the parents' trust in him and every other authority involved. He had to explain how it was necessary. Critical.

"I shall ask Jase-aiji talk to the mothers and fathers," Bren said to Prakuyo with a little bow.

"Say mothers children safe," Prakuyo said. "No upset."

"Tell them we request it," Ilisidi said firmly.

These—were the youngsters apt to be advising her grandson on things human, if they all lived that long. And the risk was not the kyo in this room, or a youngster panicking. It was that ship out there, against which they and the planet below had no effective defense.

"I shall advise them, aiji-ma," he said, "that this is what they have to do."

Follow the dowager's orders blindly, because they were hers? No. Follow them because the dowager was going to protect the planet, protect the aishidi'tat, protect her great-grandson, and protect those kids her great-grandson valued, for reasons *she* saw. She had spent the last hour and more taking in an impression of the kyo, reading what signals she could gather, and she was no fool, nor one to be pushed. *She* had an agenda. *She* had added the numbers and met Prakuyo dodge for dodge. And she expected kids who were someday going to stand beside her great-grandson to come down here and do it now.

"Aiji-ma." He got up and went far aside, still remembering kyo hearing, and used the pocket com. "Jase. Jase. It's Bren. We need you."

"Jase here," the answer came back.

"We have a request from Prakuyo and from the aiji-dowager. Prakuyo wants to meet the young gentlemen's three associates. We need to arrange that without alarming the parents. If the parents *want* to come down here, not to be in sight, but to be near, to know what's happening—they can use the inner hall and observe from my sitting room. My staff knows a little ship-speak. The parents can have tea and hospitality and I absolutely guarantee no harm is going to come to those children. The dowager will be supervising, and she will absolutely protect those children from any harm, mental or physical. Can you talk them into it, get them down here?"

A moment of silence.

"Jase?"

"I'll do it," Jase said, himself from a culture that had never had an ability to exempt children from risk. *"They were at Tirnamardi. There was no time they panicked."*

"I don't think I'd bring Tirnamardi up to the parents just now," Bren said. "Just tell them they're under the aiji-dowager's protection, and they're being asked to attend the young gentleman in a state function, if you will. They *will not* be hurt."

"Got it," Jase said. A briefer pause. *"Give me half an hour."*

Study went by the board, given the turn things had taken. Bren settled next to the dowager in the sitting area, listening as Hakuut and Cajeiri pursued their own definitions of relations and associations—shades of the same word in kyo. His mind wanted to dive aside after the entire concept . . . but the here and now demanded absolute attention, absolute readiness to steer conversation away from anything that might bring another, more problematic request from the kyo.

He dreaded any call from Jase in the interval. Half an hour, Jase had said. And if the parents refused, they had to gain the youngsters' cooperation all the same—or bring the kyo up there. And if the youngsters themselves finally reached the limit of strangeness they were willing to tolerate . . .

But the longer he didn't get that call, the more hopeful he became.

Cajeiri was describing his associates at the moment, in Ragi, perfectly composed and pleasant, rattling on about how he had met them on the ship—one grew just a little anxious when he reached the part about them reaching the station and needing to race down to the planet, but Cajeiri very smoothly said that he had told his associates that they would come down and see him.

Which they had done. With that, Cajeiri leaped over all the

untidiness of conspiracy and murder—untidiness which had not taken a holiday when the three Reunioner youngsters had come down to visit.

Steady lad.

All of them had been steady.

There'd been no word what the Andressen boy had decided to do, or what that situation was. One regretted now having dismissed all that set of decisions from his slate. He should have told Jase—

No. No way in hell would Jase bring Bjorn's father down with the others. Artur's parents, and Gene's mother—all they had to be was, please God, *quiet.*

Cenedi, in attendance on Ilisidi, said quietly, "The young people are on their way, aiji-ma. They are going to the lift."

"Well," Ilisidi said. "We shall have a variety of teacakes, shall we not?"

The kitchen, in their mingled household, was in the hands of the paidhi-aiji's staff. And at Bren's simple glance, Banichi nodded and made a call. Teacakes were on order. Water, in the samovar, was constantly hot.

There was a little booming and thumping amid the arrangements, a little exchange of words, including the word *Reunion,* and *ship,* perhaps a discussion of everybody's impression of what Cajeiri had just said.

Narani was in charge in the apartment, Bren said to himself, with a very competent staff. If parents came down, and one thought they well might, Narani and Tano and Algini could show the parents exactly what was going on in their monitoring, and reassure them constantly that the youngsters were safe. He refused to worry on their account. What mattered was the youngsters' nerve, the youngsters' comfort.

Kandana slipped out of the apartment and headed to the foyer doors without a word. That indicated their visitors were on the way, and a moment later all three kyo twitched a glance toward the right wall.

The lift was stopping, Bren thought. He didn't hear it. Banichi and Jago hadn't reacted, perhaps because it was expected, perhaps because they hadn't heard it either.

"One believes they are here," he remarked, and saw the kyo glance expectantly toward the door.

If the parents *had* come down their voices *would* be heard, Bren thought.

The outer doors opened. Kandana was in the foyer. So would several of the dowager's bodyguard be in that foyer, perhaps with the Guild Observers.

"Our kyo guests should know," Bren said, "that it is the custom of atevi houses to have a hallway for servants to move about. We have invited the mothers and fathers of the children to come down, but they will come in by that hallway, to be near."

There was a little discussion on that matter—but the foyer door opened, and Cajeiri got up. Bren did. So did the kyo—to the sight of Irene and Gene and Artur arriving from the foyer, all three in atevi dress, advancing bravely and making their proper bows.

"Nadiin-ji," Cajeiri greeted them, and went to them, escorting them to the kyo and presenting them. "This is Prakuyo an Tep, about whom I have told you. These are his associates, Matuanu an Matu and Hakuut an Ti. These three are my associates, nandiin. This is Irene, this is Gene, and this is Artur."

There were bows on both sides, a little bobbing and booming, at which the youngster's eyes grew very wide. Gene had Irene's hand, held it fast.

"Please come," Cajeiri said, steering them to the left, toward his own chair, and Kandana and Cajeiri's young bodyguard quietly moved chairs in, and little tables, so that they all could sit down.

Bows to the dowager, a nod returned. The youngsters all settled on the edge of very large chairs, eyeing the kyo anxiously, as the kyo, bobbing and muttering, settled down.

"Good, good," Prakuyo said in Ragi, and Irene said, in a voice a little high and thin, "Thank you, nandi."

That drew a few booms in reply, bobs and nods, a gape-grin from Hakuut, and a nod.

"Thank you," Gene and Artur both said, and from Artur, a blurted: "One is honored."

Bren drew in a long, quiet breath and let it go as slowly. Ilisidi never faltered.

Kandana and the dowager's staff, meanwhile, with all the aplomb of service in any great house, set about arranging tea, filling pots, setting out cups, all the bustle and clatter so familiar to atevi households, and in that little moment of necessary movement, tea went into cups, on the little tables between the chairs.

The dowager took two sips. They all took two sips, children and kyo alike, as did Bren. Ilisidi set her cup down. Bren set his cup down. Children and kyo set their cups down.

"Reunioners," Prakuyo said. "Good you come. Good."

"Thank you," Irene said in the ensuing heavy silence, and in kyo: *"Thank you."*

Prakuyo muttered something in which Reunion figured, a place and a time which didn't in any wise constitute pleasant memory. But he said to Irene, quietly, in Ragi, "Good. Good hear say." Hakuut's quick eyes swept the three. "All speak?" Hakuut asked, and Gene held up fingers measuring a little distance.

"Little," Gene said, and that provoked a little thumping and booming and discussion among the kyo.

The whole household had stopped, servants and bodyguards standing like statues. Ilisidi lifted her hand in a circular gesture and motion started. Servants moved among them again, living barrier, not accidental timing, no. The servants offered teacakes and sandwiches, which none of the youngsters took. The dowager thoughtfully chose one of each, and let them lie. Bren took a cake and did the same.

Prakuyo said, again, after a pause for two sips of tea, and not a bite of food, "Reunioners all talk Ragi?"

"On the ship," Cajeiri said in kyo. "We talk. They talk ship-speak, I talk Ragi. And kyo."

"Good," Prakuyo said again, and had a sip of tea, as Ilisidi did. The kyo all drank tea. Cajeiri did. Irene sipped her own, and Gene and Artur took up their cups carefully.

So did Bren. A little quiet space, tea, and wary looks. "Their mothers and fathers are watching us," Bren said in Ragi. "The mothers and fathers do not understand Ragi or kyo. But they want peace." Deliberate new word, one, with its opposite, that they'd tried back at Reunion—and gotten no satisfaction on.

"Peace," Prakuyo repeated, remembering. "No war."

"Peace. Peace—" He shifted to kyo, "No war, no enemy, no upset." He didn't use the word association to describe it—that hadn't gone over well back at Reunion. "Peace means all good. All happy. No more upset. Peace. Atevi and humans want peace."

"Peace," Prakuyo said, and a kyo word, the root of which looked to lie in *quiet.* Matuanu and Hakuut rumbled and hummed.

"Peace," Hakuut said.

Prakuyo said a word, then: "Opposite peace. Fire. Burn. Wreckage."

"War," Bren said in Ragi, and in kyo, the word they had used for war back at Reunion.

"Big war," Prakuyo said. "Many years war."

Vocabulary failed. "No word," Bren said after a moment. "No Ragi word."

"No Ragi word," Prakuyo repeated. "Ship-speak word? All gone. All wreckage. All wreckage."

"Annihilation," Bren said reluctantly.

"Big word," Prakuyo said.

"*Bad* word. Atevi don't make annihilation. Mospheirans don't make annihilation. Want peace. Want all people safe. No annihilation."

A ripple of soft booms, a series of nods, as if that question had been understood.

"We talk to the children," Prakuyo said, changing the subject, possibly because of the children's presence, possibly because he simply wasn't ready to address that issue at all. And in Ragi, with a look that included all of them before settling on Irene: "Children all go down to Earth?"

"We went," Irene said in Ragi, "to visit the young gentleman. It was his birthday."

"Birthday," Prakuyo repeated.

Birthday wasn't in the vocabulary either. "The day the young gentleman is new baby," Bren said. "Nine years now."

That produced a noisy stir of interest. Surprise. "Say," Prakuyo said.

"Birthday."

"Birthday." Kyo mouths had trouble with that one. "Birthday!" Prakuyo seemed to find significance in the idea. "Good. Birthday. Come down Earth on birthday. Nine years. Felicitous nine."

"Yes, nand' Prakuyo," Cajeiri said. "Birthday. Party."

"Party?" Another difficult word for a kyo mouth.

"Many guests. Many teacakes. Good food. Happy day."

"Party!" Hakuut said, with a flutter of booms. "Teacakes!"

Youngsters, Bren thought, with a feeling of things spiraling outside all careful boundaries, the *safe* words. Children didn't think in terms of *safe*. They shared what was *important*. In a list of words of cosmic significance, he wouldn't have thought of *birthday*. Let alone *party*. He wouldn't have mentioned something that *might* have significance to the kyo and *might* go off in an extravagant and unanticipated direction.

But the youngsters scored points for credibility, where credibility was life and death, where the kyo's second word for war had a moment ago loomed dark and absolute.

The kyo discussed among themselves for a moment, with a number of quiet sounds there was no interpreting. The tone was not threatening, more that, of all things, they had collectively discovered something oddly congruent in their cultures.

They might, with thought, find something significant in Reunioner children celebrating an atevi child's birthday. And not just any birthday . . . the ninth. And not just any atevi child: the child of the number one ateva, who governed the aishidi'tat. If Prakuyo had come looking for evidence of that elusive *association* between human and atevi, did he see it in this?

Prakuyo asked the youngsters gentle questions, how old they were, how long they had been on Reunion—not as innocent as the youngsters might think, those questions. He knew what Prakuyo was fishing for. Prakuyo probably knew he knew. Possibly Cajeiri had that one figured out, and he was absolutely sure the dowager did. Cross-checking. Testing. Being sure the stories matched.

The youngsters relaxed in questions they knew how to answer, the sort of performance even younger children knew how to give—and their faces began to echo their emotions. Bren was tempted to say something. He was about to issue a caution.

And Gene laughed. Nerves. Surprise. Prakuyo had asked in Ragi if he and Irene were connected, but it sounded like the word *married.* And the kid, being rattled—laughed and said no, they were not married.

Silence from the kyo. Absolute, dead silence.

Hakuut asked: "Sound?"

How to answer that one? How did one explain—laughter?

"Good sound," Bren said. "Laugh. Laugh is opposite of upset."

"Laugh." It came out softened, strange. "Laugh is good. Laugh is . . ."

Triple boom.

"Laugh," Prakuyo said.

Then a sudden, scary boom, from some chest-deep source neither human nor atevi biology managed. "Angry."

"Angry," Cajeiri said then, and made an angry face, and struck his palm with his fist.

Then: "Happy." Broad smile, open hands, in an exaggerated way one almost never saw atevi behave except at home.

"Happy," Hakuut said. "Good." Triple flutter. The youngsters' faces were clearly relieved, freed of atevi restraint despite the circumstances. The kyo boomed and thumped.

Emotions on a platter. Dare one trust congruency?

Back in his apartment, with the parents, the instruments, the analysis bouncing to both Centrals and ship-com, technicians had just gotten a solid piece to work with, if they were not deafened.

Prakuyo interrupted the exchange. Hakuut's speckle pattern instantly became visible. Hakuut gave a quiet thump, looked down and hooked the fingers of one hand into the other, silent.

Hard not to assume, but in many ways Hakuut seemed as outgoing—and was perhaps, in his own way, as bright and complex—as Cajeiri.

The youngsters likewise went solemn and quiet, a little worried at the lapse.

"And what is this?" Ilisidi said with a flourish of her hand. "Are we afraid? We think not. Prakuyo-nandi, we grow impatient. Do we speak of *fixing* problems? Of war. And peace? Tell us. Are these children safe? Do we hurt children? We think not!"

"Not hurt," Prakuyo said. "Not hurt. More Reunioners sit in Bren's place. Bring!"

No question the kyo heard them. Bren said again, quietly. "Mothers and fathers of the children, Prakuyo-nandi. They want to be near their children."

A soft string of booms. "Mothers and fathers come sit now. Eat teacakes. All be safe."

So much for their controlled situation. Prakuyo was challenging him—or thought they were in some game of catch-me-if-you-can.

Prakuyo knew, however, that *he* knew that Prakuyo could hear what went on in that space, and, knowing that Prakuyo knew, he *had* put the parents there.

Well, as for teacakes . . . he had personally had a surfeit of teacakes—and at some unpredictable moment the kyo were going to have eaten as many as they could tolerate, too. But for right now, for a full disclosure—to *ask* for a disclosure from the other side—hell, walls down. All walls down. Bring out the staff. Everybody. Staff, Guild. Everybody.

And try for reciprocity.

"Aiji-ma," Bren said quietly, "he wishes to talk to the parents. I think we should also introduce staff. All staff."

"These are sensible folk," Ilisidi said. "They know. We know. They know we know. Let us save some time and know each other."

The order brought a number of people out—Jase, with Artur's parents, and Gene's mother; Tano and Algini, who had never yet put in an appearance with the kyo, Narani, and domestic staff from the dowager's apartment as well; Nawari, and others of the dowager's security; one-armed Ruheso, and the other three Guild Observers. Artur went to Bren's apartment door to bring his parents in, and Gene took Irene by the arm and went over to meet his mother as she came out, right before Asicho and Jeladi.

All in all, it was a room-filling collection of atevi and humans—ship-human, Reunioners, and, if one counted the paidhi-aiji, Mospheiran.

And a sizable number of introductions, and explanations. The kyo had asked. The kyo had them all to meet, a number of atevi in Guild black; Jase; a number of serving staff. It was orderly—preponderantly atevi—and the youngsters kept close to their parents. Artur brought his mother and father to give polite little bows to Ilisidi and Cajeiri. Gene and Irene followed their example, with Gene's mother, all very smoothly managed, court manners, the parents very bravely taking the cues they were given.

The dowager nodded, satisfied, sitting in place. Cajeiri eased out of his seat to stand quietly, anxiously by. Bren positioned himself to manage the parents in that meeting, and said, in ship-speak, "These are Prakuyo-nandi, Matuanu an Matu, and Hakuut an Tri. Honored guests, this is Artur's father, Artur's mother."

There were bows, small, restrained booms. The kyo were on formal manners.

"Gene's mother," Bren said, then, in no order, only nearness to him. Gene *had* no father, and how and when that had happened, whether it was choice, or some connection to the massive loss of life in the kyo attack—had never been a matter on which Bren had questioned the boy. The question occurred to him in that split-second, as Gene's mother, this diminutive woman said in ship-speak, with tears running down her face, "My son says you had a bad time at Reunion. So did we. Can we just have peace?"

Thump. A vibration that made itself felt in the bones, a second from Matuanu, and Guild all about instantly, dangerously on alert.

Kids. Parents. Kyo. And a history.

"Peace," Prakuyo said in ship-speak. "Kyo want. Peace."

"Then," Gene's mother said, and held out her hand, "we're glad you're here."

"Gene's mother," Bren translated, "says welcome. Good you come."

"Welcome, Gene's mother," Prakuyo said, and reached out a massive hand and touched hers, only touched.

Gene slipped an arm about his mother, leaned close, and said something which kyo and atevi might have heard. Bren couldn't, though the room was quiet.

Bang. The dowager's staff. "Staff will serve. We shall sit. Back to duty."

God. Matuanu and Hakuut had twitched to that as if it were a gunshot. Prakuyo hadn't. The parents and kids definitely had.

Bren drew in a breath, gestured toward the chairs. "Everyone sit down," he said in ship-speak. "Captain Graham, where are we on the Central matter?"

"Forty-three minutes," Jase said, taking his own cue. "I'll assume the arrangement stands?"

"Yes," Bren said. There were times, in crisis, when his nerves became astonishingly steady. They had been steady, for several critical moments now, cold, analytical, resolving that his tolerance for kyo demands had gotten them to a situation all common sense should have avoided, and the only way out was to deal with it as it came. Yes, he could have handled an incident. He could have excused it, and talked their way past it, because the issues were too critical, what was at stake was too important. Thousands dead at Reunion, families shattered, all those things—Prakuyo confined six years as a hostage with no negotiations in progress—they'd gotten past that. The past ultimately might have to be discussed. But coldly. Remotely. With a desired outcome in mind.

Gene Parker's mother had laid it on the table. Your wounds. Mine. Peace.

Impartiality shot to hell.

Forty-three minutes till they had to break this up and get rattled parents and three incredibly stable kids upstairs, and escort the kyo up to tour the nerve centers of the station.

Prakuyo hadn't asked about Gene's father. Or the fact that pale-skinned Gene and dark Irene didn't look to be out of the same parentage. The kyo had hit Reunion that first time . . .

And pulled back. For four years, before Prakuyo had approached the station in a small, vulnerable craft.

Mistakes. All around.

Forty-three minutes to get the emotion dialed down and remind everybody that a repeat of what had happened at Reunion was unthinkable. He didn't have that many diplomatic tools, no understanding of what value kyo put on life or individuals . . .

Learn what they could. Keep the kyo from shooting at them. Get the kyo to see them as individuals. Get the kyo to form some sort of emotional contact points, some common ground that might at least make knowledge itself a fair trade. If they became people in the kyo's reckoning, whatever people meant to the kyo . . . if the kyo no more than concluded they might offer some benefit to the kyo . . . the less likely it became that the kyo would slide them and their whole existence into the liability column. The kyo admitted they already had a war, which they suggested now was not just a conflict, but a war of annihilation. They were jealous of their territory, but taking on a second enemy, even one unarmed and virtually helpless against the kyo—he had to hope the kyo weren't bent on creating a protective desolation around them, and he had to take every chance, *any* chance, to make the kyo see future relations as peaceful.

He'd been, three and four times today, pushed into giving the kyo everything they asked for, the chance to see humans and atevi, then see the Reunioners, talk with them, meet with the parents . . . and they'd come way too close that last time to an unfortunate reaction.

They had the Central visit to get through. Get all the kids and the parents back upstairs, tour the kyo through Central as they'd promised, and then start pressing for reciprocation . . . for kyo revelations, leading ultimately to some basic truths from them before he handed them any other gifts.

There was yet more tea . . . they had to bring in yet another tea service, from staff. There were little sandwiches, for which none of them had great appetite. There were enough chairs, pressed into service from the conference room.

There was a little talk, the kids sitting close to their parents, Irene staying close by Gene and his mother, and all of them saying very little since Anna Parker's declaration.

"Reunioners go to planet?" Prakuyo asked at one point. "Go now?"

"Year," Bren said, dodging around their lack of shuttles, their general inability to manage the logistics, which the kyo could see. "Make houses." As if that were the only delay. The kyo could see for themselves that there was a lack of docking space. A lack of shuttles. One ship, construction long delayed. A new but probably relatively primitive communications network, to their observation.

"Humans make other station?" Prakuyo asked—challenging the facts as given.

Time to draw a little harder line. "How many stations kyo have?"

A flurry of little booms.

And no answer.

You know, Bren thought. *We've told you what we have. You see what we have here, but you're not entirely sure. We could be a colony, still primitive. There could be more to us, couldn't there . . . in that direction at our backs, where you can't see what is, just what things were, a long time ago?*

Let's see now if you tell me something substantial about yourselves.

"Nandi," Jago said, "the time."

It was indeed time. They had fifteen minutes left. And he'd timed the blunt refusal of Prakuyo's request knowing they were reaching that limit . . . with something else Prakuyo wanted.

"Our human guests should go back upstairs," Bren said in ship-speak. "We have a schedule to keep." And in Ragi: "Tano-ji, will you and Algini escort them up, and join us in atevi Central?"

"Nandi," was the answer, and their guests, in some uncertainty, stood up, and bowed nicely, and clustered together, awaiting direction, which Tano and Algini moved to provide.

"Nandiin," Irene said, with a proper little bow, and to the kyo, "Nandiin."

"Good," Prakuyo said. "Thank you come."

"Thank you," Irene said in kyo, not badly done, Bren thought. Anna Parker, too, managed, "Thank you," in kyo.

That . . . was not badly done, Bren thought, standing, watching every move, every twitch of body language.

"Thank you," Artur said in kyo, and Gene likewise.

There could be worse outcomes. The only tense moment, diplomatically speaking, in the last hour, had been his own answer to Prakuyo, and Prakuyo hadn't raised an eyebrow—figuratively speaking. Hadn't shown any spots. Hakuut had lost a few. But Hakuut's freckles had come back quickly. Hakuut stood, now, a little restive, bobbing a little as the children and their parents exited to the foyer, with Tano and Algini. Hakuut was the lively one. Matuanu had never twitched at his refusal. He'd just given a long, low rumble that might be words.

"Go to Central now," Bren said, once the kids and parents had cleared the foyer. "Time to go."

"Prakuyo go to Central," Prakuyo said. "Matuanu and Hakuut stay here."

Leave two behind?

Why?

Leave *their* establishment to be gone through—with all its equipment?

They could lock the door to *his* apartment. That said something, too.

Was Prakuyo challenging him again? Was that the game?

Or was it leaving Hakuut's curiosity and Matuanu's dour presence alone in this place, to run a little search, or deliver an extensive report to that ship out there.

It put Guild and household staff in charge of saying no if someone wanted to go where they ought not, which set up a potential difficulty. Ilisidi might manage the situation, fragile as she was. The kyo respected her as one of the original three.

Jase could stay. But the one of them who *could* hold his own in language, and who had at least the cachet of the original three . . . was nine years old.

Cajeiri *and* the dowager, with Ilisidi in her quarters, Cenedi in charge—*her* guard, and the Guild Observers—that arrangement upped the stakes if the kyo intended to investigate the premises. Or challenge the staff.

He signaled Jago, said in Ragi, not remotely making an effort to be quiet, not knowing the limits of the kyo eavesdropping, "The walking involved will be strenuous for the dowager. Since our guests wish to stay, she could well be here, and it would satisfy the numbers if the young gentleman were to remain with her." The hell it satisfied the numbers. Two and two were the worst numerology—which only worked if he and Jase and Prakuyo were, though absent, part of the arrangement. "I think I am quite resolved on this."

Jago was never slow to take a hint, especially when it came with a deliberate move of the eyes toward the situation in the sitting area.

"Shall I suggest this to the dowager?"

"Suggest it to Cenedi, indeed." One sincerely hoped that by his upping the stakes, and countering the two kyo remaining with Cajeiri *and* Ilisidi, would make Matuanu, in particular, inclined not to act without Prakuyo assessing the situation.

Jago went off to speak to Cenedi, who would read the numbers very much the same way, and relay them to Ilisidi, who was *not* in the habit of taking her instructions from the paidhi-aiji.

But neither was the aiji-dowager in the least slow to take a cue and to find it convenient on her own grounds.

So he was not surprised when the dowager declared she had had quite enough of hiking about the corridors and riding in lifts.

"My great-grandson may do as he pleases, but should any question arise among our guests, having *someone* here able to translate would be a convenience. He can surely find some activity of benefit here, where he is of use. He has spent quite enough time in Central, surely, to satisfy his curiosity. And he and Hakuut-nandi seem to have an accord."

Cajeiri had stood up when his great-grandmother had begun to make a statement, and when Ilisidi had gotten to the part about having *someone* to translate, an experienced eye could see the shift between young boy about to protest, and wise young lad realizing he was being handed a solemn, important order.

"Yes, mani," he said with a little bow, and, clever lad: "Cajeiri sit talk to Hakuut and Matuanu."

If there had been *any* plan to leave those two to explore the place—which, with senior Guild and Guild Observers in residence, would have been resisted—they had headed that off.

And if Prakuyo's hope was simply to have a chance to talk to him off the record that the kyo were likely *sure* they were making, they had just arranged that, too, give or take the dowager's presence, and Cajeiri's.

20

Something was going on, Cajeiri was well sure. The one kyo he was most sure of was up to something, or checking what was fact, or just trying to see what the rest of the station looked like, being very like the place he had been a prisoner for years.

It was a little scary to be left to protect mani, but they certainly had enough Guild in the premises to deal with any threat, except from the ship out there.

Was mani scared? If mani was ever alarmed, he was not sure *scared* was the word to describe it, because mani could be dangerous, and he was sure nand' Bren did not want any alarms at all in his absence.

Nand' Bren had left him to deal with the kyo, and mani would watch, unless she had to do something, so it was up to him to make sure that did not happen.

So how did he keep everybody out of mischief?

He had a game set. He had brought it because he had never trusted he would be included in everything. He had made plans not to be bored.

Now, in the most important thing he had ever been trusted with, he thought of that, which atevi had gotten from humans two hundred years ago and changed to suit themselves.

"Shall we have my game set?" he asked mani.

"An excellent notion, if our guests find interest in it."

"Jico-ji," he asked Veijico, who asked staff, and they had it from his room very quickly.

He set out the checkered board. He held up the aiji, and identified it, and the opposing one, and showed their moves. He held up the aiji-consort, and identified her, and showed her moves. In similar fashion he held up the aiji-dowager, and likewise the advisor, and the aiji's fortress.

Then the clan lords, all alike, within the association.

He and mani showed the capture—of course he put a clan lord in jeopardy of mani's advisor. That piece went to the side.

Then they reset the game, and mani suggested he play against Hakuut, mani advising him, and Matuanu advising Hakuut.

He began thinking just then that it showed exactly how they were, except if they substituted the heir apparent for the aiji-consort. And mani was a very, very good player.

Hakuut, however, was quick, and so was Matuanu.

"War," Hakuut said. "It is war."

Maybe it was *not* such a good idea, this game.

Mani never played to lose.

He had made dangerous moves. He had involved his guests. He had said things too fast, and Prakuyo, being smart, had asked about them, until it had gotten very scary in that meeting. He had tried to be clever now, and he had set up a war on a tabletop.

He did not believe in omens. Mani called them stupid. But some people thought they showed the numbers of the universe, the true numbers, that would turn up again and again, no matter what, and if you saw a bad omen it was a warning.

But some people said you could turn a bad omen to a good one if you were clever, and, baji-naji, by fortune and chance, the flex in the universe would let it be true.

Where did he find good, now that he had set war down between them?

Could there be good in it? Did mani even consider the omen?

Probably she really had. Mani was learning something. Mani learned from everything. That was what made her dangerous.

*　　*　　*

Passing through the crossover point—was a worry. Jase, Gin, and Geigi, however, had it quietly managed—an uncommon presence of security, ship-folk, atevi, and Mospheiran, keeping the area of the lifts quiet and virtually deserted—with the traffic of clericals and warehouse and supply personnel going on beyond the glass, and fingers on the buttons, in Central, to make *sure* random lift cars didn't arrive while they were in that critical area. Prakuyo paused in front of the lift, looking about at the security, which he might not recognize as such—only two carried sidearms.

Then, apparently satisfied, he accompanied Bren and his aishid and Jase into the Mospheiran-side lift system, and took an assured grip on the safety rail, having learned the ways of the zigzagging lift.

"See Mospheiran Central now," Bren said, to which Prakuyo said, "Yes. Good."

The behavior of humans and atevi, confronted with the completely unknown in the same room with them, was a worry. But of all sets of humans and atevi available, outside the ones appointed to deal with the kyo, the ones working in Central and in ops were surely the steadiest in meeting the unexpected and the least apt to do anything to startle the kyo.

Gin and Geigi would have prepared their staffs, Bren had no doubt, and experience of both gave him faith in both staffs. For Central as a whole, it was yet one more change in the handoff schedule, just one more rescheduling and one last trial of their nerves, one could only hope—and after this, Bren hoped they could work toward a regular, sensible rotation, even before the kyo ship left. The Mospheiran staff had been set at watch and watch when Tillington had ordered the Reunioner sections shut. Then Geigi, getting control back, had held *his* staff on watch and watch until he could hand off to Gin on her arrival; and the latest drain on energies, the kyo ship's arrival, had meant odd schedules for ops, generally requiring atevi staff to be on duty nonstop. The schedule had been a patchwork for weeks, and was sometimes a question of whether they had con-

sistently clear-headed people sitting at the boards, on whichever side of the operation.

This was the day, the hour, they wanted steady nerves. The
appearance of the kyo was intimidating enough, but the subsonics were something none of the techs would have experienced,
and they were frightening, close up, maybe damaging if a rattled
kyo really cut loose. One could imagine, Bren thought, the relationship between Prakuyo and the humans who had held him
for six years. Prakuyo had suffered neglect. *Nobody* had been in
that immediate hallway. And that story might have two sides.

Prakuyo uttered small sounds, all to himself, watching the
numbers tick past. Anxious. On edge. One had to account, too,
what Prakuyo might feel, moving within the station halls—
sparse, bare of ornament, scant even of signage, and very much
like the corridors of Reunion: same architecture, same materials, same dimensions. It was nothing like the kyo ship.

A long time, in that barren cell. In that barren hallway.

Had Prakuyo opted not to bring his companions on this
venture—because he was not emotionally prepared to deal with
company in the experience? The *kyo* were emotional—Hakuut
more than Prakuyo, and *young* still was the impression one
had. But Prakuyo was far from at his ease.

Dry air, for a kyo. Brilliant light. Prakuyo blinked rapidly as
they walked down the hall from the lift and entered the starkly
lit Central—no shadows there: all bright as planetary noon.
Prakuyo gave a controlled, quiet thump, and drew every eye in
the room, techs turning heads, swinging chairs just slightly.
Gin waited in the center of the arc—Gin, in Mospheiran business wear, a brown suit and a bright gray blouse.

She gave a little bow. "Prakuyo-ji," she said, which was what
they had called him on the ship, and Prakuyo gave a moderate
little boom, a little mouth-gape, which could be pleasure, or
just relief.

"Gin." It came out *Kin*, or something close to it. Prakuyo
returned the bow, and looked about him. "Gin. Good see."

"Good to see you," Gin said cheerfully. "Very good. My staff—"

Jase stood there. Bren stood there with his aishid, all familiar enough to the crew in Mospheiran Central, while Gin solemnly, as if all the names would be remembered, introduced Prakuyo to the chief of the shift, Okana, to the communications chief, the utilities division . . . every section, very matter-of-factly, and introduced Prakuyo to them, told Prakuyo what hours they worked, and how they were holding just a little overtime to be able to demonstrate how they routinely switched control to Lord Geigi and the atevi side of the station.

"First," she said in ship-speak, "the chief calls the atevi chief and we both agree we're ready."

Bren translated that into Ragi: "Gin will ask this man call the atevi Central and say they are ready."

"Go," Gin said, and the chief tech pushed a button on the console. Three flashes came back.

"The atevi chief says ready," Gin said. "Utilities goes first. Communications goes last. Works best that way."

There was a low buzz of technician talking to technician, confirming, screens coming up with green display, buttons blinking red, then going green, starting with the utilities console, where screens one by one went out, and boards shut down.

"Shall we just do as ordinary?" Chief Tech Okana asked.

"That will be fine. Don't linger in the hall. Go home. If anybody asks you, say it's all fine. Talks are going well. You're doing your part, and well done. Night, people. Good night. Go home. Have a drink there. Not in the bars."

"Two," someone said, and there was a little nervous laughter.

"Happy sound," Bren said in kyo. "Gin says go drink alcohol."

Low ripple of booms. "Good. Prakuyo like drink."

Had Prakuyo just made a joke? He ventured a soft, single laugh of his own. "Yes."

The shutdown completed with fair dispatch, leaving dark

screens, dark boards, and people filed out quietly, talking among themselves only when they reached the hall.

Lights dimmed to something comfortable for kyo. Gin walked over, gave a little nod. "Respects from the President to our visitors."

Bren translated that. Prakuyo gave a little boom and a nod. "Good to Mospheira Presidenta. Good to Gin-nandi."

"Thank you, sir," Gin said, and left, down the hall, solo. Mospheiran security remained at the doors. Bren made a gesture toward the same door, and, with his bodyguard and Jase, escorted Prakuyo out past the security guards, and on down the deserted hallway to the lift.

The game progressed. Hakuut reached, began to knock over a clan lord.

Thump, from Matuanu. Hakuut's hand hovered. Cajeiri sat expressionless, giving no clues. *He* saw what mani had set up, directing him. Now Hakuut saw it.

"Good," Hakuut said with a slow series of booms, and declined to take the clan lord.

The situation at atevi Central was the same . . . but this time the individual who met them was plump as Bindanda, almost as prosperous as Prakuyo himself, and dressed in court splendor for the occasion.

"Welcome," Lord Geigi said, and technicians all about made a small turn of chairs, a little nod of courtesy. "Welcome, nand' Prakuyo! Nand' paidhi! A felicitous meeting!"

"Nandi," Prakuyo said, with a little bow, and he seemed happier in the meeting, perhaps with more comfort knowing what to expect, more comfort in the greater proportions of the room and slightly less light, less sense of threat from an atevi environment.

"Has our guest heard the function of the boards from Gin-nandi? I shall spare him, if so. But you see we have received the handoff from human Central. The three blinking lights indicate ongoing problems they wish us to continue to monitor, and the steady lights mean no difficulty."

Bren paraphrased that as best he could, pointing to the three lights as "Human Central ask atevi Central fix three bad things please. Others are all good."

"Reunioner in Mospheiran Central?" Prakuyo asked, in the relative safety of this place.

"No," he said in ship-speak. "This station belongs to Mospheira and atevi. Reunioners will go down to the planet." And in kyo: "All Mospheiran in Mospheiran Central. Reunioners all go down to planet. Learn Mospheiran."

A nod. A little rocking, whether or not Prakuyo understood or believed it.

Geigi, meanwhile, introduced his staff, named clans, named associations, to which Prakuyo also nodded fairly enthusiastically—perhaps that *associations* made some sort of kyo connection.

"Atevi have Central twelve hours," Bren said, "then give to humans. Twelve hours humans give back."

Nod of understanding.

"All good," Prakuyo said.

"We go back to Hakuut and Matuanu now? Yes?"

Prakuyo nodded, bowed generally to Lord Geigi and the techs, and Lord Geigi showed them to the door, to the hallway. They walked toward the lift station that had brought them, with one more transit of the crossover yet to go. Jase talked on com, advising security to watch the area of the lifts.

Everything was going smoothly with the kyo downstairs, Bren was quite sure. The place was under close watch. Any cross word, any problem would have reached his aishid, and they had a signal prearranged which would have told him.

Things were going as well as they could have possibly hoped. Prakuyo had seen what he had wished to see, nobody had panicked, they had been able to answer all the questions, and there had been no report of problems from the dowager's vicinity.

*　　*　　*

They had reached a lengthy problem. Cajeiri looked at the board, and thought, and thought he knew what mani was doing, but he was not sure.

Mani seemed to put the second advisor in difficulty.

And after a number of moments of silence, there came a soft booming from Matuanu.

Was it laughter, Cajeiri wondered.

And the more he looked at the situation, the more he saw there was a dilemma ahead.

"Good," Matuanu said. "See."

He directed Hakuut to make a move. Hakuut set down the piece.

Instantly mani ordered the consort moved.

Matuanu instantly directed the countermove.

The dowager immediately directed the aiji moved from the sideline.

Slow hiss. And then a triple boom. A nod from Matuanu.

Stalemate. There were no moves from here. A lightning-fast, reckless game—and a rapid, ruthless end.

And no one won.

He had worked long and hard, and *he* had gotten mani to stalemate twice this last year, but he was never sure it was by his skill. He suspected it was mani's.

He suspected it right now.

"Perhaps our guests would like to have the set," mani said, "if they enjoy it."

Cajeiri gathered up the pieces and quickly put them in their case, in the traditional array. He folded the lid shut, got up, and offered the set to Matuanu, with a little bow.

Hakuut took it in both hands, likewise with a bow, and gave it to Matuanu, who took possession of it, stroking the leather case.

"Thank the aiji-dowager," Matuanu said, and Hakuut made a much deeper bow.

"Thank you," Hakuut said. "Thank you, aiji-dowager. Good."

Play sharpened instincts, kept suspicion quick and deep and focused on a small reality, a single narrow set of pieces, and all their capabilities.

Matuanu is aiji, he thought: aiji, aiji-dowager, or aiji-consort. Hakuut is clan lord, certainly not the fortress.

What is Prakuyo, he wondered. Is he aiji—or advisor?

The lift settled and thumped into its place, back at their beginnings, undamaged, undismayed, and, Bren hoped, relieved of some suspicions. But in front of the foyer door with that door open to receive them—

Prakuyo stopped.

"Talk," Prakuyo said. "Talk to Bren."

Nothing about Jase. Bren took in a breath. Jase said, quietly, "I'll go on inside."

Jase did that. Jeladi, inside, shut the door, leaving Bren, his aishid, and Prakuyo alone in the corridor.

"Talk," Bren said.

"Prakuyo come station. Come human station. Come atevi station. Bren come ship."

Second slow, deep breath. Fair. He couldn't say it wasn't.

"Yes," he said.

"Nandi," Banichi said. "The aiji will not let you go without your aishid. The paidhi-aiji, nandi, does not go anywhere without his aishid."

God. It was what he had dreaded, what he assuredly didn't want, and effectively—he had to.

He could not have Ilisidi or Cajeiri with him—that was utterly out of the question. But Prakuyo hadn't asked that.

Bring his bodyguard?

Bring the four people he cherished most—into a situation that might, conceivably—be a question of no return?

Man'chi—had to be his thinking. Leave them? It was too great a betrayal—nothing about leaving them could be for their own good. He couldn't do that to them.

"Bren. Come."

"If I come—I have to ask the aiji-dowager. If I come—my aishid comes. They come with me."

"Yes," Prakuyo said, pulling the last prop from under any argument. For persuading the kyo to peace—would he? He had to.

Would they go with him? That, too. They had to.

"Aiji-ma." The dowager and Cajeiri sat with Matuanu and Hakuut, still. The tablets were in evidence, on the table in the midst. Bren bowed, keeping his face pleasant. "We had a productive excursion and Prakuyo has seen atevi and humans working in parallel and in harmony. Prakuyo now has asked a reciprocal visit. He wishes the paidhi-aiji to visit the kyo ship, and one believes the pattern of reciprocity . . . as he has visited alone in the upper station . . ."

Ilisidi cut him off, hand lifted from the chair arm, and for a moment, just a moment, a flicker of chilling coldness, before her expression turned as casually gentle as if she were dealing with household staff. "Well," she said, smiling, "well. We shall continue to afford all possible hospitality to Matuanu and Hakuut, while the paidhi-aiji tours the ship. How long do we estimate this to be?"

He was, he realized, too entirely rattled to render that in any reasonable fluency. He bit his lip, hauled his wits back into order, and saw Cajeiri's face, likewise, absent any enthusiasm, any questions, any request to go along. No, Cajeiri understood the situation.

Prakuyo, likewise, had spoken to his fellows, very quietly.

Tano and Algini had left him to go advise Jase, to advise the staff, and to pack.

Take their sidearms? Guild did not give those up without an order. But there were alternatives, not as visible.

"The aiji-dowager," Bren said in kyo, "sends the paidhi-aiji to see the kyo ship. The aiji-dowager and the young gentleman ask Matuanu and Hakuut sit, eat, talk this place."

There was rapid discussion, a great deal of thumping and booming—no threat, but an underlying impression of disquiet with the idea.

"All come," Prakuyo said, then.

"No. Prakuyo one, go station. Now Bren-paidhi one, go ship. Aiji-dowager has many, many years. Young gentleman is child, not many years. Dark, cold not good. Bren-paidhi go. Bren-paidhi aishid go. Go on ship, sit, talk,' good."

Prakuyo looked at him, he looked at Prakuyo, Matuanu had something to say about it, about as much as he had ever heard Matuanu say and not a word of it understandable except human and atevi. Hakuut had a comment, something about stay or stop.

"Bren-paidhi come ship," Prakuyo said then, which, if one was any judge, didn't entirely please the other two.

"Bren-paidhi come ship. Aishid come ship."

"Yes," Prakuyo said.

So they had a deal.

Change of clothes, heavier coat, lighter coat: the kyo tended to keep things warm. Shaving kit, toiletries, the sort of thing that could support a day trip, maybe an overnight trip, if there *was* negotiation. One didn't want to show up with evident provision for a long trip, God, no. If nothing else, absence of such provision might give him the excuse to send one of his aishid back to report the situation.

But a long trip was what he most feared. What he feared for himself. What he feared for his aishid.

Jase had found out, too.

"I could go," Jase said very quietly, meeting him in the front room, amid all the equipment.

"No."

"You're essential. I'm one of four."

Bren shook his head. "No. I can deal with this. But thanks, Jase."

"You've got a brother . . . you have obligations."

"I have several brothers. You're one."

"Bren,—"

"You are. My younger brother. So I take care of you. And I go. Take care of Toby, take care of everything, if things don't go well. Get the dowager and the heir to safety. Take her advice. Protect Tabini if you can. That's all I know."

Jase didn't say a thing, just stood there, while Narani and Jeladi arranged the lightweight coat, made sure their lord was as presentable as a trip in a cold suit could allow.

"See you," Bren said lightly. "Soon, with an agreement. At least maybe more information. *We* brought Prakuyo back safely. We have a history of that with them. Maybe he'll reciprocate. That *is* the pattern we hope we've set up."

Prakuyo exited the apartment fully suited up, protection against what was, for him, the unbearable cold of the core. The rest of them would put on cold suits on the way down. Polano met them at the lift. Ship security had taken complete control of the core berth that ordinarily belonged to *Phoenix*. It might be the kyo ship attached out there at the moment, but *Phoenix* crew guarded the access, and it was, Jase had said, ship personnel that were there to work safety, so they would be, until the very last moment, within ship territory and within reach of intervention, if they suddenly didn't like the tone of things.

But what could they do? Bren asked himself. The kyo were hardly likely to attack the paidhi-aiji while he was outside the kyo ship, especially with their own representative beside him, and once within— At what point, except gunfire coming in their direction, or kyo interference with his bodyguard—or even then—could the paidhi-aiji refuse a venture that aimed at the very heart of his job, a venture that stood the primary chance of solving the situation before it escalated to what had happened at Reunion?

He couldn't refuse, no matter what met them on the kyo side

of the airlock. Whatever lay behind this invitation, he *had* to find a way to deal with it. That was the nightmare, all the way down, while they prepared, with the little baggage they did carry, to go out on the lines.

The front safety man went. Prakuyo followed directly, a vanishing spark in the dark.

They were alone, without the possibility of the kyo overhearing, for the first time since Prakuyo had set foot among them.

"One has not had the opportunity to consult," he said. "One has no idea how long this venture might be or even where it might take us."

"We are here," Banichi said. "Man'chi holds, Bren-ji, and in this, the Guild does not advise. We shall protect you."

So long as any of them had breath. He knew that. It was on him not to bring things to conflict—wherever it required him going. Whether he was back and safe in three hours. Six years. Or never.

He was out here. He was about to grab that line. And then he was going to do—what? A reciprocal tour of the kyo premises? That might be all it was.

He somehow didn't think so. Prakuyo had pointedly avoided certain questions. Prakuyo was, whatever else, canny, capable of trickery, and motivated by something other than nostalgia for past favors.

He took a deep breath of dry, freezing air.

"We shall go," he said, and Banichi and Jago went out on the lines, to be first in, whatever awaited them in the kyo ship's airlock. Bren launched himself, with Polano's small assist, and felt Tano and Algini hit the line behind him.

Passage through the dark and biting cold toward a distant point of light.

It assumed a surreal character. Fear? Oh, abundant. Trust? Only in the four around him. They had done something as scary as this—himself, the dowager, and Cajeiri together—but then the stakes had been *Phoenix* and five thousand refugees.

Now it was *Phoenix*, five thousand refugees, Alpha Station, and the planet atevi and humans lived on, and it was cold as hell.

The entry tube gaped like a yellow flower bell, receiving them into its safe confinement, and the safety man saw them in, where they had to let go of the traveling line. Banichi and Jago secured handholds inside the tube and took hold of his arms, steadying him as Tano and Algini came in behind him. There was no immediate sight of Prakuyo.

All right? the safety man queried them with a gesture.

All right, he answered with the same signal, and the safety man made a gesture toward the curve ahead, which was lighted, and where Prakuyo was not.

That way. That was where Prakuyo had gone. Without them. He tried to ignore the alarms that disappearance raised.

The safety man showed them two buttons on the turnaround stanchion for the line. One stopped it. One started it . . . by implication, if they needed to come back.

Bren signaled understanding. So did Banichi, for the rest of them. And the safety man punched the green button, took the available handgrip, and left them, returning to the station lift, dwindling into dark, one star moving away.

Bren turned toward the interior of the tube, carefully, because rebound here was dangerous; but Banichi established a gentle hold on him, and with mutual help, they made fast progress along the hand rigging, into the lock.

No Prakuyo. The lock cycled, agreed that the tube was pressurized, green-lighted the opposing door, and opened it on a similar stretch of corridor, a long, twisting passage.

With no Prakuyo.

"We go," Bren said, fighting for breath, shivering in a longer than usual exposure to core conditions.

But now it was not the core. They were technically outside the station, making their way along a long, temporarily pressurized tube to a kyo airlock for a ship that rode above them.

That airlock, far ahead, opened as they rounded a slight curve, revealing a small shadow within a misty cloud of escaping air—a shadow one hoped was Prakuyo.

The parka wasn't adequate for the cold out here. Prakuyo's suit was by far the better idea—especially, he suddenly realized, for the heat-loving kyo. Which made one wonder, was Prakuyo's disappearance that simple? Had he rushed ahead simply to escape the cold?

"Freezing," he managed to say, and his aishid took the cue and carried him along faster than his chilled muscles could manage.

The small figure became, indeed, Prakuyo waiting for them, beckoning them in.

The lock thumped shut. Warm, moist air blasted into the lock, and the inner door opened.

This part he remembered. They entered into a smaller chamber, the lock closed behind them, and the chamber began to move, much like the core lift, in a way that caught them up with the ship's internal parts. Feet found the floor, numb as they were. Prakuyo released his helmet, drew in a breath of the warm, moist air.

"Good, good," Prakuyo said, unsealing his suit: "Safe."

The parkas were cold enough to freeze the moisture, a shining skin that crinkled and shed ice crystals with movement, with no warmth to offer comparable to the air. Bren began to shed his, with Jago's assistance, while his aishid shed their own. There was no sign of others in this kyo version of the station's lift, just a row of large storage containers. Prakuyo touched a plate on one of those containers, and the top slid back, affording a place to put the chilled cold suits. Another touch, this time to the wall, and a door slid back on a more upright closet for Prakuyo's helmet and Prakuyo's suit, which fairly well stuck to the surface inside.

A third touch, to the opposite wall, and another door opened on a dim, brown metal corridor. They followed Prakuyo out and down that corridor on removable grating that showed conduits and pipes below their feet, likely to do with the airlock. Weight a little greater than Alpha, though not as different as he remembered. Heavy, damp air that challenged his lungs, and twilight lighting. Detail was shadowed in that dim light, but Banichi and the others doubtless saw better than he did, heard more than he did.

The curious thing, after living with three kyo for a day—was the silence. There were machine sounds, low hum of fans, something starting up, but no sound of life other than their own steps on the grating.

Another doorway. The grating gave way to brown tilework, and the bare walls to hanging drapery. This—he remembered. His aishid would remember—not the same ship, he thought: *not* the same ship, or they had changed the drapery. Greens, browns, here. Angular geometric designs and occasionally a drapery of curving lines. Aesthetics? He wondered. Or . . . on a sudden thought as he began to see repetition of design . . . writing? Signs?

"Come," Prakuyo said, pausing a moment, and opened another door, this one on a downward spiraling ramp. Though attached to the station, the ship stood active, maintaining walkability in all its levels—not so large a ship as Phoenix. Its curves were more extreme.

The ramp led into a level below the airlock, a darker, slightly cooler, dryer place, another hallway, but barren. And a chair where another kyo sat. That one extended legs and rose, with a little flutter of booms.

"Stay," Prakuyo said, and that person gave a little bob and sank back again, crosslegged, in the curious bowl-like seat.

"Bren," Prakuyo said, and paused. "Not aishid. Safe. You come."

Safe? And asking his aishid to stand back? Not reassuring.

But Prakuyo advanced only a little distance, then stopped near a recessed area in the wall.

"Wait, nadiin-ji," he said to his aishid, and joined Prakuyo.

In that slight recess beside Prakuyo was a clear door with ventilation slits, and beyond, a huddled gray shape on a bowl-shaped bench.

He was looking into a cell.

"Up," Prakuyo said sharply, from where they stood, and the dim shape moved, turned a shoulder, achieved ragged hair and a glimpse of glaring dark eyes in a bearded, shaggy human face.

Reunioner, Bren thought. Some survivor who hadn't come to the exit, who hadn't been willing to be evacuated.

Who might, all this time, have been questioned by the kyo and might have told them God knew what . . . granted they had gotten past the language barrier. He'd always suspected Prakuyo understood more ship-speak than he had admitted to. Could Prakuyo have questioned this man, gotten information that made him doubt the truth of what they'd told him? Perhaps that accounted for the hint of distrust that lay beneath his affability.

Or was the problem that they'd gotten *nothing* out of this man?

Was *this* the purpose of the kyo's visit? That *he* should lend his skill to—whatever they wanted with this man? Who on Reunion could be worth so much effort, to bring him all this distance?

"Who are you?" Bren asked in ship-speak, the safest, most obvious question. And: "Are you all right?"

The man got up—he was dressed kyo-style, in thin robes. Hair and beard, a great deal of both, were matted and snarled. But the stare . . .

The stare was that of a man seeing a ghost. A step forward in the dim light. And another. A hand lifted . . . and those staring eyes looked past him, widened—

The man recoiled against the back wall so fast his aishid reacted, weapons out. Prakuyo flung out an arm between them and the door, forbidding, and Guild weapons went to safe position.

"We are safe," Bren said in Ragi, on a half breath. And in kyo: "Prakuyo-nandi. Safe. Safe." His heart was pounding. The man in the cell sat tucked up in the bowl-like bench at the back of the cell, staring at them from under that matted mane . . . could one grow that much hair in two years?

"Who are you?" Bren asked again, in ship-speak.

No response. Maybe it was his bodyguard, armed and quick on the trigger, that alarmed the man. "Nadiin-ji," he said quietly, "stand back somewhat. I am in no danger. This man is a prisoner and unarmed. The door may be transparent, but it is not slight."

"Nandi," Banichi said, and drew everybody back a little. Their dark skin and black clothing faded into the shadows of the dim hallway, but golden eyes flickered as they caught a little reflection—the light came at that sort of angle, and that sight would not reassure the man.

"More light?" Bren asked and Prakuyo waved a hand over a nearby wall control. The ambient brightened. The man in the cell tucked up, pulling knees to chest, squinting as if his eyes were unaccustomed to bright light.

"Safe," Bren said in kyo. "Come. Come to the door."

Not a move. Not a twitch.

He said, then in ship-speak. "You're safe. Come. Get up. Come here and talk to me."

The look stayed much the same. There was no clue as to whether the shaggy prisoner understood kyo or ship-speak. One began to fear the man might not be altogether sane.

"What's your name?" he asked again in ship-speak, sharply this time, and got a response at last.

"Who the hell are you?" The voice came out strained, little more than a whisper. But coherent. "Are you even real? God . . . am I that far gone?"

At least he *could* talk. Arms stayed around knees. Features, expression, were all obscured by dark, tangled hair.

"I'm quite real. They brought me here to talk to you." That much had to be obvious. "Will you talk?"

Eyes flickered, from him to Prakuyo to his aishid, then:

"What *are* you?"

"A negotiator. A translator. I can do neither if you don't talk to me. Can we try again? What's your name?"

"Guy."

"Guy."

A nod. Slight, within the mop of hair.

"Is that all of it?"

"Guy Cullen. *Who* are you? *What* are you?"

"My name is Bren Cameron." And bearing in mind Prakuyo *was* beside him, and knew a little ship-speak, caution was in order, what he said about himself, what he said about his relation to this man. "I'm a representative for the atevi."

"Atevi."

"Behind me."

Blink. Twice. As if the name meant nothing to him. A Reunioner—maybe a panicked holdout from the evacuation—wouldn't know atevi. Wouldn't know any of the things that had happened.

"You stayed on Reunion."

"Don't know Reunion."

That was a poser. *"Phoenix,* then?"

Second shake of the head.

Ship and station names meant nothing to the man, and his speech was off, some syllables hardly voiced. It could be injury. It could be a speech impediment, or maybe an artifact of disuse. Maybe the man wasn't understanding *him* that well; or maybe the man was just holding back information.

"Where *do* you come from, Mr. Cullen?"

"*Negotiate* me out of here. Get me out and I'll tell you."

So. Holding back.

He lifted an eyebrow. Controlled expression. Suspicions occurred to him—a kyo setup to get a reaction. A tame prisoner, working with them. There was a word for that, a word with origins lost in some obscure past, something he'd been accused of more than once in his career: Stockholm syndrome.

Was this man some ages-old offshoot of a *Phoenix* base predating Reunion, perhaps, pretending ignorance? Second or even third generation prisoner, playing a part for—what? Freedom?

The prisoner's initial reaction to seeing him had been intense, instant as reflex: a damned good act—or honest shock. Maybe it had been his aishid that provoked that reaction. But amid so much that was alien—the focus had been on *him*.

Regroup. Give him the benefit of the doubt, for starters. "I understand. You don't want to betray places. You don't want to endanger those you care about. But I can't get you out if I don't know why you're in. So let's start with something the kyo already know, but I don't. How did you come aboard this ship?"

"Loaded on with all the other cargo."

"When? How long ago?"

"Hell if I know. Year? Two? Quit caring a long time ago."

"Where?"

"Hell if I know."

"You were somewhere before that."

"Another cell. Another ship."

"And before that?"

"I don't *know*. I don't remember. And even if I did, why would I tell somebody standing on *that* side of this door— dressed like that. Where's *that* from?"

Things were not right, not right, not right. It was a puzzle Prakuyo had set him, a puzzle with sinister overtones, and he was miserably failing it, with his own credibility at stake. He was set this puzzle, he was expected to solve it, and his success or failure would affect a great deal more than this man's outcome, or his own.

"Mr. Cullen, I'm in the employ of the atevi government; the

clothing comes with the job. The kyo asked me to come here. The kyo evidently wanted me to see you. You want to be a puzzle. That's fine. But if you sincerely want my help, you'd do well to stop cowering over there and come up to the door and talk to me."

Another sullen glare. "I'm not telling you a damned thing."

Had *Phoenix* left a crew at the Gamma fuel station when they'd abandoned Reunion? Crew the kyo had gathered up from the fueling site and held for over a decade?

"Mr. Cullen. I don't know how much time I'll have with you. I don't know how you got here or what you did to get yourself locked up. Species being species, I'd like to help you, but you're not giving me any means to do that."

Cullen made a tighter knot of himself. Head bowed against his knees. "Just go. Get out of here!"

"You were transferred from another ship. I take it this was a kyo ship?"

A tense pause, then a sharp nod.

"And before that?"

"My own ship."

"Your ship. Not *Phoenix*. A mining craft, maybe?"

Cullen glared up at him under that shadowed mop of hair. "No damn miner. A *starship*. A ship *fighting* these bone-faced bastards."

The floor just dropped out from under all reason. He hoped a career practicing atevi impassivity kept shock from being evident, but it felt as if all the blood had drained from his brain, his face, his hands. He folded his arms and tried to take in a reasonable breath.

"Where, Mr. Cullen? Where do you fight them?"

"Wherever we meet them."

"How long have you been at war?"

"Eighty, ninety years, about that. What rock have you been living under?"

Ninety years? *Ninety?*

Everything, *everything* began to make terrifying sense. He was standing still, trying to give no clue what he was thinking, but shaken to the core, and telling himself it had to be a trick, a trap, something other than a vast, star-spanning circle. *Coincidence* couldn't stretch that far . . . that they had just met what *Phoenix* had been hunting for centuries.

Phoenix's own point of origin. Human space. A location lost from *Phoenix* records hundreds of years ago, when some trick of space and starship physics had thrown them off their course and into the radiation hell that had cost the ship so dearly.

Cullen had nothing to do with Braddock or *Phoenix* or Reunion . . . other than a distant common ancestor.

This was the Enemy. The kyo's mysterious enemy.

Instantly pieces began falling—*crashing*—into place.

Reunion. *Phoenix.* The enemy. Similar ships. Similar architecture—similar—what had Gin called it? Electromagnetic signatures?

God . . . no wonder the kyo had attacked *Phoenix*'s base.

A part of him wished he had a recording of Cullen to analyze, because the degree of change between Cullen's speech and his itself offered clues, a clock set on the time of separation, from the point of common origin, but figuring it out would only, he was quite sure, confirm what his gut already knew.

"Your ship, I take it, was lost."

"Lost? *Lost?* They blew it to hell!" Cullen flung himself to his feet, came the handful of steps to the transparent door, rested a fist on it, leaned against it. "You said you wanted to help. *Can* you get me out of here?"

No. Promise nothing. Be careful. If he's theirs—it's one thing. If he's not—it's much, much worse.

"You're a prisoner of war. I have no way to do that. However, I can at least try to better your situation, Mr. Cullen. Can you talk to them?"

Blink. "Talk to them?"

"Can you talk to them? *Have* you talked to them?"

"No." Shake of the head. "No."

"I can."

"You can make sense of that—" A helpless wave of the hand. "How?"

"It's what I do, Mr. Cullen. I mentioned—I'm a translator. And a negotiator."

"How did *you* get here?"

"I was invited. —Bottom line, Mr. Cullen, the atevi I represent have absolutely no interest in your war with the kyo, but I *do* have a concern for your situation, and I'm sure the kyo suspected I *would* have. I'm here on their sufferance, and they might well decide to end this interview at any moment. Answer my questions. Give me some indication what I'm dealing with. *Why* are you at war, Mr. Cullen? What's the issue?"

"Ask them. We don't know."

One could probably ask the kyo to exactly the same effect. But it wasn't on him to judge. And it didn't, in the long run, matter.

"When you encountered the kyo, Mr. Cullen, where were you? What was your ship doing?"

"Their territory," Cullen said. "We were scouting."

Scouting, with instruments at least as good as *Phoenix* had— didn't mean going there before looking around. It meant going there *after* looking around, with the notion there was something there that needed a closer look. A contemporaneous look.

If some ship had deliberately encroached into atevi and Mospheiran territory and refused contact, atevi and Mospheirans alike would agree it was an ominous move, which argued that three species understood it was a wrong move. *Phoenix* had come into a kyo-held system exactly that way. Ramirez had *known* a viable planet existed where he was going—

But had he *known* a technological species was there? Was it that looking into the past problem?

He'd run, instantly, upon being discovered—a move which might have saved the ship, but which had doomed Reunion.

The kyo had apparently known about Reunion for years. Tolerated it—or watched it, to see what it would do.

Until *Phoenix* went somewhere it shouldn't.

Did that mean Reunion had been outside what the kyo considered their space? That it wasn't until the ship connected to Reunion had actually invaded kyo territory that Reunion had ticked over from anomaly to active threat?

One had to ask . . . where was that system *Phoenix* had penetrated, relative to Cullen's part of the universe? Where was Reunion in that configuration?

As for coincidence—common belief held that *Phoenix* had spent centuries searching for their own origin point: and trying to find the right direction. They'd found nothing. The search centuries ago had led *Phoenix* first to atevi space, lately to kyo space, but not to human space.

In one sense, it was strange to think of a linearity in three dimensional space, but stars, so Jase had explained to him, clustered in groups, and those groups in turn lay in lines like pearls on a spiraling string as they raced around the center of the galaxy. It might be an overly simplistic view of the universe . . . but had *Phoenix*, all along, been searching in the right direction?

Did that long-sought human space lie just beyond kyo territory? Possibly the next pearl on the string? And had Ramirez, contrary to that common belief, always known it? *Phoenix* senior captains had a history of keeping secrets. Had the program been to build a chain of stations and colonies stretching back and back to human space? To complete the ship's original mission of extending human territory, if somewhat in reverse?

For the ship-folk, the universe *was* the ship. The ship needed fuel and it needed a goal. The ship might not really care how many generations it took to get to a goal. Or a world. It seeded humanity—down a string of pearls.

The thoughts came like lightning, in an instant, lighting up a whole well-known landscape of old questions—and new paths developed branches he couldn't access, not here, not now.

"I've said something," Cullen said, grown quiet, fist still against the glass. "What have I said?"

"Nothing. And a lot."

If he was right . . . if the location of human space had been known to Ramirez . . . it was possible that information had died with him. It was also possible it was still locked in ship's records. There were ways that the seniormost *Phoenix* captain could isolate portions of the log, time-lock them, put them off-limits to the three junior to him. If it was lost—it was one thing. If it was locked—it might open up again.

To Ogun.

"You're thinking about something," Cullen said. "I *have* said something."

"Something, yes."

And if Ogun knew . . . maybe he had a very good reason to have kept quiet, to have resisted the return to Reunion. Maybe Ogun had it figured. Maybe Ogun realized that if *Phoenix* humans, colonists and ship-folk alike, learned that human space was remotely within reach . . . politics would take over and all hell would break loose. If Mospheirans knew—some would be all for contact, and others, deeply committed to their own way of life, would be passionately opposed to it. Some Reunioners would find a rallying point, a future that didn't depend on the charity of Mospheirans. The ship-folk . . . would find focus, and mission.

And they'd drag the atevi right into it.

All based on the ship reuniting with humans who were currently at war—with a species that had turned a station to slag in a single blast.

And if that was the case, if Ogun had deliberately kept that location secret . . . Bren discovered himself in total agreement.

If this man's existence—even if *word* of this man's existence—reached Alpha Station, at the other end of that access tube, the stability of everything he knew, the lives and safety of every person on that station and the planet below, were set at risk.

He had never, never in his life, thought the terrible thought he had now—that if this one voice were silenced—if he had to make the Guild's kind of choices, not for evil, not for ambition—he could let generations of ordinary shopkeepers and craftsmen go on about their lives, have their children, grow up and grow old in peace.

He could do it. He *would* do it. He could not let some stubborn human notion of returning to a home they didn't remotely understand plunge them all into war. Neither Mospheirans nor ship-folk were the people who'd left human space. They were something else.

They were one thing. And Cullen was another, a being far more dangerous to their existence than the kyo had ever been.

Keep him secret? Yes. Killing him—no. He didn't want Cullen to die. He didn't want Cullen to suffer, or to live in this cage for the rest of his life.

The kyo controlled that. The kyo had brought Cullen all this way—

To do what?

To see whether they were the same people as Cullen? To see whether he would react in strong identification with Cullen?

Or—disturbing thought that settled like lead in his stomach—was it just to see if he could get military intelligence out of Cullen, which added up to killing more people.

"How long have you been with the kyo?" he asked Cullen. "Do you have any sense how long you've been here?"

"Don't know. I used to judge time. I lost all track. Ships moved. Sometimes it was better. Sometimes it was worse. Years. Years and years."

Diminishing the value of any military information. The hair, the general condition, said that was likely the case.

Was it possible, just possible, he was a rare survivor? Perhaps the only human prisoner they'd managed to keep alive? Was it possible Prakuyo had brought Cullen here to show him, Bren, to convince him to *represent* the kyo, dealing with humans?

The nightmare outcome, of the ship just leaving dock with him, to go do a job that could take a lifetime, resurrected itself with a vengeance.

People were dying out there . . . wherever *there* was. Humans and probably kyo.

But *he* wasn't Cullen's sort of human. He was from a little island whose whole history had become part and parcel with atevi, in a way that worked—in a way that *he* made work, in this generation. He had a job here. Obligations. Without him— things here could still go so very wrong, for people he owed, deeply.

He *wasn't* Cullen's sort of human.

But Cullen was.

Cullen was.

Possibilities existed. But back off, he told himself. Get an emotional distance. Lay the groundwork, discover the man . . . then decide.

"Let me see what I can do to help your situation," he said. "First things first. Would you like a shave and a haircut? I very much doubt the kyo have a razor, but I packed for overnight."

"You said first things. What's second?"

"Communication. Communication between you and the kyo."

Wary look. A little drawing back. "I don't know anything. Not a damned thing."

"I sincerely believe that's not why they've held on to you, Mr. Cullen. I doubt after the passage of years that you know anything they'd be interested in, that optics couldn't figure out. I do think you've been a puzzle to them. And that's a bit of a wedge, Mr. Cullen. Maybe you can do more than survive. Maybe you can do some good for the wider situation."

"I don't know anything about *any* situation. I just want out of here. I'm nobody, do you understand? I've got nothing for them."

"I don't know what you're capable of—yet—but I think a

man who's held up through what you've been through is something more than nobody. I can't change everything. I can't undo what's happened. But I can give you a way forward from here."

Cullen stood, silent, at about arm's length.

"Well, Mr. Cullen? Will you listen to me?"

A shaggy-headed nod. Arms folded, as if the overheated air had an edge of chill.

"That's good, Mr. Cullen. Very good. I'm going to leave now. I'm going to see about that razor." Prakuyo sat in a very dim room some distance up the hall, in a bowl-chair among other chairs, with an extendable platform at his elbow. There was a lighted screen on that platform, of a sort not unlike their tablets. There were a number of chairs, and a low table. Several objects sat on that table. One was an incense burner, the representation of a kyo sort of mythic being, vented, here and there. Another was a wand of unknown use. And a small closed pot. The incense burner was not lit, but it exuded a smell that hovered not unpleasantly between spice and burning wood.

"Want talk," Bren said, standing in that small room, with Prakuyo alone, seated, and Banichi and Jago behind him. Tano and Algini remained outside, watching the hall. "This man . . . is the war. This is the kyo's enemy. Yes?"

Soft boom, loud enough, given the enclosed space. In the dim light, with the light coming up from the little screen, the details of Prakuyo's face became different, severe, like a model of a kyo by lamplight. "Enemy. Yes."

God. Where did he go from here? Where did he start?

"Prakuyo hear talk?"

"Yes," Prakuyo said. "Want know."

"The man's name is Cullen."

"Cullen." It came out *kh'-yen*.

"Bren ask Cullen where Cullen ship is. Cullen says kyo fight Cullen's ship."

"Yes."

"One human? Not more?"

"One," Prakuyo said. Prakuyo shifted in his chair, and leaned back, expectant of information.

"Want open Cullen's door. Talk to Cullen. Fix Cullen's— face." He made a gesture to his own clean-shaven face. His hair. "Cullen says yes."

"Tea," Prakuyo said. "Bren, aishid tea. Prakuyo go up, talk to associates. Tea. Here."

Prakuyo was going up to talk to his associates and he, and his aishid, were graciously offered tea, and a chance to reflect. Atevi custom, excepting their host leaving. Time to reflect, time to talk together, all built into the gesture. Think about it. Talk about it. Discuss the situation.

And it would be no more private than any kyo conversation had been in the hospitality they had offered Prakuyo.

One was absolutely sure of that.

Cajeiri touched the mark on the screen that triggered a random image of some already established word. Flowers appeared. Trees. A garden.

"Kaksu," he said, maintaining the appearance of study, even as he strove to hear Cenedi's latest report to mani.

The garden image flashed red along the border. He tried again.

"Kak aksu."

The light went green.

"Garden," Hakuut said, though it sounded more like Kar-gen. But the clever device had learned Hakuut's mouth's limitations, as it had learned the limitations of his, and flashed green.

The place seemed scarily quiet. Matuanu sat, just sat, doing nothing, watching everything. Nand' Bren's door was shut. Jase was somewhere Cajeiri had no idea. Mani's door was shut. Cenedi and mani had been talking.

Hakuut was willing to sit down and talk—to keep busy. But Hakuut was listening to things that went on, trying to find out things. So was Matuanu, Cajeiri was sure.

But nobody's hearing could reach to the ship out there. Everybody was waiting for somebody to call. That was all.

And nobody was going to be happy until somebody did.

Personnel appeared, bringing a pot of something like tea, and cups, and set it on the table, then departed, with bobs and bows. The light stayed dim. The incense smell obscured the scent of the tea. The chairs were deep for atevi frames, entirely uncomfortable for a human. He had met kyo-designed chairs before, and found a way to sit on the padded rim, feet on the floor.

Tano had come in. Algini had come. They all sat, in chairs about the small table.

Jago quirked a brow, with a shift of the eyes toward the tea service.

Shall we trust it? was the obvious question. "We may serve it ourselves," Bren said, and added pointedly, "One wonders how the aiji-dowager and the young gentleman are faring at the moment. One hopes Prakuyo will be in contact with his own associates to reassure himself. One trusts he knows he can do that."

Tano moved to the pot, poured five cups, and served them.

Bren took a cup of tea, which smelled vaguely like fruit. There was absolutely no percentage in the kyo poisoning them at least for atevi or human logic there was no percentage. As for accidental poisoning, he was relatively sure they had sampled this tea once and twice, on the kyo ship two years ago, without adverse reaction. He tasted it, waited a minute to see whether there was any slight tingle, a burning, or a sweetness that exceeded a fruitlike flavor, before he ventured a sip.

His aishid observed similar caution, except Algini, who merely made a ritual pretense of drinking. That was the rule. There was never a time, under a foreign roof, that all of them made the same commitment.

Bren set his cup down. The others did.

"His name is Cullen," he said in Ragi, and gave a little

upward shift of the eyes, as good as saying—they're listening. But of course they were. He felt the tension in his bodyguard, unabated in the whole venture—not extreme, but wary of every sound, wary of presence, wary of the lack of it.

And he chose his words, even in Ragi, to avoid ambiguity that might cause mistranslation to those listeners . . . and to plead their own case to an upstairs audience.

"This man is not from Reunion, not from *Phoenix*, not from Mospheira. He speaks a language I can understand, though time and separation changes a language, and I estimate from these changes that several hundred years lie between his language and ours. One suspects, to one's great distress, nadiin-ji, that Cullen comes from a human world somewhere beyond the territory kyo claim. One further suspects that the ancestors of the humans in that far region are the humans who built *Phoenix* and sent it out hundreds of years ago. These Cullen-humans' ships, their stations, likely come of a similar tradition of architecture with *Phoenix* and Reunion. They may strongly resemble each other, to kyo observation, even after all these centuries."

"Hence the attack on Reunion," Banichi said.

"Indeed. Hence *everything*, nadiin-ji. As the *Phoenix* records have it, *Phoenix*, being lost and off course, traveled to the Earth of the atevi, searching for a green world, food, and fuel. But a world with inhabitants was not a world they could claim. Hence *Phoenix* left the Earth of the atevi—preserving Alpha Station as a base. They kept going, looking for the home they had lost, looking for those other humans, to restore contact—trade, association—with those who had sent them out in the first place. One suspects, given Cullen's presence, that some key records were *not* destroyed, that someone within *Phoenix*, likely senior ship-aijiin, knew at least in which direction human home space lay. They looked in that direction and saw at great distance a star and a world that might serve for their colony, perhaps more than one such star and more than one such world.

They built Reunion as a point halfway between Alpha and another destination, a station with no green world to tempt its people to settle. It was only to provide fuel and services for the ship, perhaps to provide people, over time. All this is what I guess. What I know is only that Reunion was built in the direction of human space and that between Reunion and human space is kyo territory."

"The ship-folk did not know about the kyo?" Banichi said.

"That remains a question. It seems doubtful the people who built *Phoenix* were aware of the kyo. Cullen says the war began about a century ago. He doesn't know why. Possibly it was over territory. Possibly because some human ship did precisely what Ramirez did. One simply does not know. Whatever happened, happened long after *Phoenix* arrived at the Earth of the atevi.

"It's even possible that, by backtracking along its original course—*Phoenix* found the star that should have been its destination centuries ago. It would be ironic if that were the case—that it should work so hard to recover its course, only to find a kyo star and fall into a war that they themselves might have triggered centuries earlier. Mind, this is only my speculation—but the people of *Phoenix* had no idea that the kyo existed.

"Did Ramirez know? It seems likely: spacefaring technology leaves many traces. On the other hand, perhaps this star system Ramirez had chosen has no inhabitants, but simply lies within territory the kyo consider to be theirs. Perhaps it has a kyo presence at some times, but not others. Gin-nandi reminded me that optics and other detection devices the ship-folk use are limited more by time than they are by distance. If we could see Reunion now—even if it no longer exists—we would see it as it was many years ago."

"One has heard," Banichi said, "but it makes no sense."

"Yet—we would. So Gin says. So perhaps what Ramirez saw from a distance was not the state of affairs when he arrived. Something surely surprised him. We know that Ramirez-aiji ordered children born, Jase-aiji and Yolanda-nadi, and that he ordered them to learn several languages of the Earth of humans, but never told Jase or Yolanda why. Did Ramirez-aiji intend them to be paidhiin to the kyo—or did he hope to meet humans? He is dead, and we may never know. He met a kyo ship. He recognized it as not human. And he ran. For whatever reason, he ran, and in running, so I believe, triggered the entire chain of events.

"The kyo saw *Phoenix* as similar to the ships they were fighting, and perhaps they had observed it more than once. Perhaps they had been watching Reunion develop on their flank, so to speak, at a great remove from other humans, and thought perhaps there was a wider human presence than they had suspected, all but enveloping them. They observed it. Perhaps they had seen the Earth of the atevi at very great distance, and wondered whose it was . . . but because they were looking into time—we remained a mystery.

"Ramirez-aiji apparently never tried to use his two translators, who were still very young. He fled, hoping to divert pursuit. But at this point, the kyo acted to remove Reunion, believing it was their enemy. They acted, and then realized they had not struck a military base.

"Prakuyo's ship waited, at that point, simply waited to find out what this place was, and what would come in as a consequence of what had just happened.

"Ramirez-aiji had taken an evasive course. When he did bring *Phoenix* back, the kyo were watching, doing nothing.

"But *Phoenix* fled again. No other ships came. There was no other reaction for years. The kyo might guess where *Phoenix* had gone, to that other Earth they had seen . . . but everything the kyo believed about *Phoenix* confused them.

"They watched Reunioners rebuild. They did not know what these people were, or whether they were in fact the same as their enemies, or whether the similarity of *Phoenix* to their enemies' ships had led them to attack completely innocent foreigners.

"All this is my surmise. Prakuyo made an attempt to contact them, or at least to have a closer look. The station found the means to destroy an unarmed shuttle and take one survivor prisoner.

"Prakuyo's ship resumed its watch over the station, perhaps having some means of communication with higher authority, or not. The kyo observed at least that no one came to rescue these people—but if I am right in my conjecture, between the direction of their appearance and the unpredicted behavior of *Phoenix* and Reunion, they feared they had indeed struck a completely uninvolved people, and might potentially have widened their war in a disastrous way.

"We appeared with *Phoenix* and we accepted contact. They tested us, and we agreed to attempt the recovery of Prakuyo, whom they assumed to be dead. I believe they recognized *Phoenix*, and they were trying to figure who we were, and what we were, and whether we were allied to their enemy, with implicit consequence for their war. *We* offered to remove Reunion. That was a reassuring move for them.

"But with the return of Prakuyo, new questions must have come up, thanks to Cullen. Prakuyo had learned something of the language Reunioners and the ship-folk use—enough, perhaps, to suspect that *Cullen's* language is related to the language on Reunion and on *Phoenix*—and because he could see that humans have atevi for allies—Prakuyo had to wonder what our alignment may be.

"So there remain very serious questions that the kyo cannot answer.

"I think they have come here to answer those questions. And I tell you, my associates, my household, I am as afraid of this man Cullen as the kyo themselves may be fearful of him, because Cullen *is* one of the humans the kyo are at war with, he *is* from the place *Phoenix* was seeking, and if Mospheirans and ship-folk find it out—Mospheira and the Reunioners and the ship-folk will all be in turmoil. Perhaps a few—only a *few* will want to rush off to join Cullen's kind. The wiser and more cautious ones will know that Cullen's people pose a threat—to their way of life, certainly, and possibly to their lives, considering this war. We know *nothing* of Cullen's government, nothing of his way of life, and nothing of his leaders' character.

"Cullen's existence is an even greater problem for atevi, who have nothing to do with this human war. I will tell you, nadiin-ji, that my own man'chi is deeply, definitively, to Tabini-aiji. I am deeply distressed to see this man's situation, but I am more deeply distressed at this war in which atevi and Mospheirans alike have nothing to gain and everything to lose."

He finished. He had poured out everything, all the while parsing it in two languages and keeping much of the word choice to words Prakuyo knew. There was prolonged silence after, faces who were family to him, all, all profoundly troubled, all—knowing him—perfectly capable of understanding what he had just done.

It was Banichi who asked the question . . . with all the implications regarding Guild action.

"What do you urge, nandi?"

"I do not wish Cullen any harm. I shall seek Prakuyo's permission, and Prakuyo's advice, if he will give it. I am going to try to find out something about Cullen without telling Cullen anything about us, because should he ever go back to his own people, I have no wish to have him tell other humans *we* exist. I have been very careful to tell him only that I am an atevi representative, I have said nothing at all to explain the existence of other humans, nor have I stated that this ship is in dock at a station. I have let him assume, if he will, that this is a meeting in deep space and that I am from some unknown source, working only with the atevi.

"One does not know how much authority Prakuyo has on this ship, but I shall attempt to reach an understanding with him. I seek no association with Cullen. I shall do as much as I can for Cullen's comfort." He drew a deep, desperate breath.

"Nadiin-ji, I am taking a decision on myself that is far, far beyond any authority I hold, and that pains me greatly. But there is no other course."

"Tabini-aiji appointed you to decide such things, nandi," Banichi said, "when he appointed you Lord of the Heavens."

That meaningless title.

That suddenly utterly relevant authority, to bind things in the heavens with the authority of the aiji who sat in Shejidan. There was no way in the world Tabini could have foreseen the current circumstance.

But Tabini had known there were things in the heavens no one on Earth could predict or judge. In creating that title, in ordering the paidhi-aiji to go up and figure those things out— Tabini had given him personally the authority to make a binding decision, should it become necessary.

Indeed, he had met that necessity.

"Certain few will need to know what we know," he said. "But even those, not immediately. Not until this ship clears dock and takes Cullen with it, beyond any likelihood of return. Nothing must prevent that. And *Phoenix* could raise an objection, if they knew."

"Yes," Jago said, and the rest said, "Yes."

21

It was not strange that Prakuyo turned up at the door of the little room again, not strange that he came with two aides and ordered a new pot of tea. The little room had enough chairs, but Banichi and the rest distributed themselves as the Guild usually did, two outside the room, guarding the door, two inside, to hear the conversation. Prakuyo's aides also stood.

They shared tea, he and Prakuyo, one, two, three sips. Then Prakuyo set down his cup, leaned forward, picked up the wand, the tip of which began to glow, and lit the incense. Smoke curled up, threatening to bring woodsmoke and spice nearly to painful levels in that small place, but if it soothed Prakuyo, that was to the good.

"You talked to your aishid," Prakuyo said. Then he drew over the lighted tablet that had remained on its stand, waved his hand over it, touched, and a recording began—every word they had just spoken.

One refused to be at all shocked. "Yes," Bren said.

"Say all in ship."

"Say it in ship-speak?" Bren asked.

"Yes. Say."

Prakuyo played the start of it. Bren translated.

Then the next bit.

Rosetta Stone, Bren thought. Definitely. He was making a record that might come back to haunt them. Or that might make a solution possible. He translated it, almost line by line, with no hesitation, and the occasional expanded explanation of a word.

"You want kyo go away take Cullen," Prakuyo said at the end. "You want dowager, Cajeiri not hear Cullen."

"Cullen is not Mospheiran. Not Reunioner," Bren said. "You take." It was maddening that he lacked the words to explain. He tried to think of any combination that would make sense, beyond a cold rejection of a strange human. Cullen set free—going back to tell his people he had met a strange human somewhere in kyo space—was no good outcome either. "Not good Cullen tell Cullen's humans. Not good Cullen tell Mospheiran humans and ship-folk. Not good."

Several deep thumps. "Ship," Prakuyo said. The word *speak* was nearly incomprehensible as he pronounced it. "Say in ship."

"Mospheirans and ship-folk don't know Cullen's humans," he said, "but if Mospheirans and ship-folk knew more humans were far across kyo space, some would try to go, and this is not good. Not now. Not in this war. Many years from now, in long peace, yes, good, if the kyo say yes. But now it's not good, not safe. Not good for Mospheirans to talk to Cullen. Not good for Cullen to tell these far away humans where Mospheirans are."

"War," Prakuyo said.

"War. Upset. Danger. Mospheirans will take the Reunioners onto the planet, and all will be happy."

A deep rumbling. "Atevi give humans place."

"Yes. But not *all* humans. Not Cullen humans. Many, many, many humans. Too many."

"Understand. Kyo don't want many humans."

"Yes. Atevi don't want. Kyo don't want. Mospheirans don't want. Not good human ship come through kyo place."

Thump. "Yes."

"Yes," Bren said. "Yes. Kyo place. No humans. No atevi. Peace."

"Good," Prakuyo said.

"I want to *talk* to Cullen. I want to make Cullen happy on kyo ship."

"No." A triple thump. "Hurt."

"I don't hurt Cullen."

"Cullen hurt Bren," Prakuyo said. "Not good, not good."

"My aishid," Bren said. "Strong."

"Danger," Prakuyo said. "Big danger."

"I have to try, Prakuyo-ji. Please. I want to try."

Prakuyo gave a ripple of low thumps. "Careful," he said. He reached within his robes and offered a plastic card. "Door," he said. "One door. Careful. Bren say 'Prakuyo,' Prakuyo hear, Prakuyo come."

Prakuyo left them, but there was no question they were monitored, visually as well as by audio.

They delved into the baggage that had sat in the corridor since their first meeting with Cullen, and extracted Bren's personal kit.

"You will not do this yourself, Bren-ji," Banichi said.

Banichi rarely put his foot down. And it might help to have a human observing a human face for warnings of intention, and to be in Cullen's constant view, for reassurance.

"I shall manage," Tano said. Tano was, in fact, extremely quick on his feet, and deft of touch.

"Yes," Bren said. And added: "I think we should apply the scissors sparingly. It would improve the kyo's view of Cullen-nadi if he looked much more like us and much less like a Re-unioner."

"Can a comb manage it?" Jago wondered.

"We shall try," Bren said, and with his aishid moved the little distance down the corridor. There was no one but themselves . . . and Cullen, in his cell. Of sound, there was only the universal ambient of the ship's operations, the air in the ducts, and their footsteps. It was quiet, as quiet as ever it was, on a ship.

"Mr. Cullen," Bren said.

Cullen was sitting back at the end of his cell, in the bowl-bed, the only furnishing but the sanitary arrangement and water source in the other corner. He slowly got up and came toward them, but not all the way to the clear barrier—wary now, in a much closer atevi presence.

Bren came close to the barrier. "Mr. Cullen. I said I'd try to improve your situation. I've talked to the kyo. I've assured them you're not violent, and that I'm in no danger. I'd like to introduce you to my aishid, my bodyguard. This is Banichi, Jago, Tano, Algini. They don't speak your language for the most part, but I do speak theirs. And eventually I'd like to introduce you, properly, to one of the kyo, who I think would like to talk to you, sensibly and quietly—he isn't fluent, but he's quite patient, a very reasonable fellow. And I think if we could get you cleaned up a bit, we could go a long way toward helping your situation."

Silence. Just silence.

"If you want us to leave, Mr. Cullen, my aishid and I will go away and you'll not likely see us again. I can help you. I'd like to see you make a better impression on the kyo. If you tell us to leave you alone, we will, and I'll tell the kyo in charge that we can't work with you and you just want to stay to yourself. Which they may allow. But that's not the future I'd hope for you."

"What is?" Cullen asked.

"A comb, for a start. A shave, if you'll accept it. Tano is willing to do that for you, while I sit with you, and he has a very gentle touch. A shave, a trim, at least, maybe a bath. It's well, between species, to bathe. A lot."

Three flat blinks.

"Maybe," Cullen said.

"I'm afraid it has to be yes or no." He had the comb in hand. He put the end of it through one of the ventilation slits. "Here, for a start. Combs have to be in short supply on a kyo ship."

Cullen took it, considered it, then started working at the mass, slowly, bit by bit. It looked a hopeless task. But he stood there, trying.

"So," Bren said quietly, while Cullen worked at the tangle. "Cullen. *Why* are you at war with the kyo?"

Silence. Silence went on for maybe a minute, while Cullen worked with the tangles. Finger-combing had lost ground a long, long time ago, maybe in a time of illness. Or depression.

"Do you even know?" Bren asked.

"They hit us, we hit them."

"Where do you come from?"

Silence. Then: "Place called Arden."

Arden. A name that meant nothing to him. Planet? Station? It's possible the answer could be found in *Phoenix*'s records, though Jase claimed the original accident had wiped a lot of the navigation, the maps, the charts. Even if Arden existed somewhere in the Archive, it surely wasn't the same Arden that Cullen had come from, three hundred years later.

And the war, if it had ever had a reason, now had a hundred reasons, in names like Arden, and probably others. It didn't need Reunion to give it another.

"Are you a good man, Mr. Cullen?"

A blink. Cessation of the combing. "Am I—what?"

"It's a serious question. Do you view yourself as a good man?"

"Hell if I know." Cullen took a moment, then resumed combing. "Are you?"

"Hard one to answer, Mr. Cullen. I try."

"Try? To do what? You called yourself a negotiator. Negotiating for what? What are you doing here, if not because of me?"

"To find a way for atevi and kyo to live peacefully in the same universe. That's my job: to find a peaceful solution, cure problems, find mutually acceptable paths through sticky situations. In my own experience, if you can get enough *good* people together, no matter how different they look, they really want much the same thing—the sort of things that good people naturally give each other. Things like respect, and common sense, and communication. But those things are really hard for some people. Particularly the communication part."

"Communication. With *them*?"

"Among good people, it's hard. With bad people it's fairly well impossible. So I ask—are you a good man, or a bad one?"

The comb stopped. Cullen stared at him as if he'd changed colors.

"It's very basic," Bren said. "There are some *very* bad types that are clever with words. But they make up their own meanings . . . and in situations like this made-up meanings really don't get very far. Good types work until they understand what the other person meant, rather than investing in winning. What kind are you, Mr. Cullen? Are you a *good* man? Are you invested in winning, from here? Or are you willing to take a chance?"

"What kind of chance?"

"Talking to them. —You have an uncommon opportunity to do that, Mr. Cullen. There's one kyo who's really interested in talking to you. A kyo who seems to be a pretty good fellow—it's hard to judge on a very limited dealing, but there's a good chance he really *is* a good fellow. Enough of a chance that I wouldn't suggest he take a chance with you, except I have the impression you might be a man of some character, yourself: intelligent, I think—certainly resilient. You've been a long time with just your own thoughts, here. I'd like to leave you in a far, far better situation. That begins with someone to talk to."

"Interrogation? Not interested."

"Do you know anything, after all this time, that they *don't* know?"

"No. But they don't know that."

"Oh, I think they can guess. Time's passed. Quite a lot of time, by that tangle you've got. Whatever you know is obsolete, if it ever was that important."

"It wasn't. It never was."

"At this point, then, you have no real usefulness to them—except to this one kyo, who has taken an interest in talking to you. I don't know his rank. I don't know how high up he is. What I do know is that his function is a little like mine: negotiation; and that his people regard him highly. Whatever he is among his people, there's one asset that could make him very important—and that is his having someone like *me* at his elbow when he talks about ending this war."

"Is *that* why you're here? To end the war?"

"Not *me*, Mr. Cullen. I said someone *like* me."

"You're not making sense."

"You. You could be that person at Prakuyo's elbow. *You* could help bring an end to your war. *You*, performing exactly the same office for the kyo as I do for the atevi. I'm the translator. The bridge between opposing forces. I find a way to talk instead of shoot. I find out the enemy's opinion, and I represent it fairly. I convey my employer's opinion to them. I work with both sides until I can find a way for them not to shoot at each other. That's what I am. That's what I do. So, what do you think? Can you make a try at talking to these people?"

It was still hard to see anything of Cullen's expressions, just the mad dark eyes. The stare.

"People?" The tone was harsh, defensive—challenging the notion.

"Absolutely, Mr. Cullen. Absolutely they're people. Different as they come—well, different as I've yet seen, but they have kids, they laugh, in their own way. They have emotions such as humans have, possibly very close to what humans have."

"Even if I accept that, I *can't* talk to them. I don't know how."

"I can teach you. I can teach you enough in three days that you can express yourself, ask questions, and convince these people that you're worth talking to. After that, it's up to you. But I'll give you the tools for that, too. Is there a glimmer of hope in that? Absolutely. There's hope in that for a *lot* of people. *Become* me. *Become* what I am. Learn to speak the language, think the language, dream in the language."

"I can't do that."

"Not if you believe you can't. Believe that you *have to.* Figure that every word you learn is valuable. Three hundred words, and you can carry on a conversation. When you can carry on a conversation you're a person to them. And from that start, you can get *more* words, on topics that interest you. I don't know how much aptitude you have. But you're in luck on that point, Mr. Cullen. The one kyo who's interested in you *does* have it— so even if you can't do it all, he can meet you coming the other way, and the two of you can make it. This person has the importance to negotiate with *my* superiors—and *that* is power. He'd also like not to be at war with humans. He's said so. Does the thought of ending this war appeal to you at all, Mr. Cullen? Or had you rather just sit in this box?"

"I can't—" Cullen began to shiver—controlled it, tucking both hands under his arms. "Can't think at the moment."

"You *are* thinking. You're asking yourself if there's a way out. And if there *is* a change, is it going to be worse? I can't answer any of that. I can't fix your situation. But *you* can. I'll tell you this much, Mr. Cullen—you're potentially *important.* You're *so* potentially important I'm going to take several days off from a major diplomatic conference between the kyo and the power I represent, and I'm going to *teach* you how to teach yourself from here on out. *You* don't think you can do it. *I'm* going to show you that you *can.*"

"I don't know . . ."

"Comb the hair, Mr. Cullen. Easier to keep it controlled in a braid, and I don't think you'll find a kyo anywhere who knows how to cut hair. At least you can trim a braid. Let's get you cleaned up, for a start."

Cullen began to comb again, mechanically. Yanked without finesse. Hair broke, snarled in knots.

"I'm going to open the door, Mr. Cullen. Step back a bit."

Cullen didn't protest. He stepped back. Bren took the key card from his pocket and put it in the slot a little removed from the door.

It slid back. And there was no barrier.

Cullen stood there, looking at them, outnumbered.

"Sit," Tano said in ship-speak, waving Cullen toward the inbuilt bowl-bed that was the only furniture.

Cullen sat. Tano took the comb from him and, standing, began to work on the problem himself, with water from the tap. It was going to be a lengthy process.

"Let's start," Bren said, folded his arms and leaned against the wall. "Three days, Mr. Cullen."

Several hours made a difference. Cullen—shaven, damp hair combed and braided, enough of it surviving to make a very respectable queue, though without a clip—sat on his bed. Bren sat on a chair—Jago had brought that in. Banichi and the rest of them sat as easily on the floor as about a campsite.

And Cullen was trying. Hands clasped white-knuckled, elbows on knees, occasionally, despite the sweat beading up in the humidity and the heat, giving a small shiver.

It was easy to feel sorry for him. Easy to feel deeply sorry in the situation, that he had to turn off compassion, and tell Prakuyo never, ever, to let this man go back to his own people.

Am *I* a good man?

Good enough to keep the existence of those I protect as secret as it needs to be? Yes. In any way I have to.

Good enough to use what I know—in the best way, and help this man? And help the kyo? I hope so.

"The face," he said to Cullen. "They find our faces a little scary."

"Mutual," Cullen muttered.

"Until you know the kyo in question, wear just one comfortable expression, and try to keep it. Their faces can't move. The fact that ours do—spooks them and confuses them. Kyo faces do blush pretty much under the same conditions we do. Look for the speckled patterns in the skin to come and go. The eyes are expressive. Kyo we've dealt with know, now, that our facial shifts mean something specific. They'll be working to understand and adapt, but until they know you really, really well, try to keep your face calm, so they can concentrate on what you're saying."

"I get that."

"Sounds. I'm not sure whether it's more important than vision, but hearing is very, very important to them. Listen to the sounds they make. Learn to differentiate. The booms and thumps affect the meanings of words, the way if we smile or snarl while saying something, it changes 'Sure I will' into a joke—or a firm no. Just use your ears. The booms are startlement and happiness—except the really loud ones. I suspect those can hurt you."

"That—I know."

"Let them know if they hurt you. They can learn restraint, the same way you'll control your facial expressions. The thumps are disapproval, the louder the more definite. Pay attention to those. I'm sure there are finesses to them I don't remotely imagine. Over time, you'll figure things I don't know. And time is something I think *you* will have."

"You're terrifying me. I can't possibly—"

"You can, Mr. Cullen. Look at what you've learned in, what, three hours? You can ask to talk to someone, you can say what you need, you can understand instructions about this place. That's a lot—in three hours. Now I'm going to test your memory. I'm going to leave you for a while. Sit and think through all those expressions. When I come back—I'll see how much you remember."

Cullen nodded. "I'll be here."

Joke. A grim one. But a rise in spirits. Bren gave an appreciative nod, got to his feet, Banichi and the others got up, and very matter-of-factly Tano took the chair outside and set it down as they left. The key card closed the door, and locked it. Banichi tested it.

"We need some things," Bren said to them, walking away down the corridor. "I shall ask to talk to Prakuyo, and make some arrangements. I would like two of you to go back to the station and bring another change of clothes, a paper notebook, and several pens." He gave a signal that meant ulterior motive, without defining what it was, but likely his aishid could guess one primary reason was simply to establish that they *could* come and go without hindrance.

"Yes," Algini said.

"Be discreet in all this. No word of this prisoner to anyone, except the barest details to the dowager, in utmost secrecy: tell her Cullen exists, that I am negotiating, that I wish her to hold this matter to herself alone, and that I am requesting her help in maintaining deep secrecy. Do not give a hint of this to any staff, not even Narani. Nor to Jase-aiji. I shall ask Prakuyo to request this also of Matuanu and Hakuut, and only hope they have not at any point talked about Cullen or what I am doing on this ship. Discretion. Absolute."

"Yes," Algini said. It was a given that Algini and Tano, second pair in the aishid, would be the ones to go, leaving the two primary, Banichi and Jago, in attendance on him.

"I shall ask clearance for you," he said, and looking up, he said loudly to the walls of the corridor, "Prakuyo, please come talk. Want send Tano and Algini back to Alpha."

Prakuyo was not long in returning to the small conference room, and he brought two others with him. One was Huunum an Hus, whose mouth was a little undershot, and whose eyes were murky green; the other was Ukess an Am, whose face and arms were extremely freckled in brown and gray-green. What their authority was, or whatever their involvement in the question of Guy Cullen, one had no clue—they might even be there simply because Prakuyo was obliging the atevi sense of numbers.

"Hear," Prakuyo said in Ragi, as they stood in the small conference room. "Hear all talk. Bren stay. Teach Cullen kyo words. Good."

"Three days," Bren said. It was pure bargaining, pure assumption that he *was* going to leave when he wished. "Three days stay on ship. Tano and Algini go station now, bring clothes for three days. Give Cullen kyo words. Make Cullen peace."

"Ten day," Prakuyo said.

That was *so* much better than Prakuyo might have asked. But in a first bargaining session, surely one should resist a little, and test how and if the kyo dealt with it.

"Seven is fortunate number."

Boom. "Seven. Yes. Tano and Algini go station. Prakuyo send writing to Hakuut and Matuanu, say all good, not say human on kyo ship."

"Yes." He gave a little bow, inexpressibly relieved at that statement, and changed immediately to Ragi. "Clothes for seven days, nadiin-ji. Prakuyo-nandi also requests you tell our two guests that everything is going well over here, and that we are reaching agreement. He will send a written message."

"Nandi," Algini said, order accepted.

Prakuyo delayed to pass a hand over the lighted tablet, tap what might have been a keyboard on the screen for an extended message, and then extract a card. He held it out to Algini. "Give to Matuanu. Not Hakuut. Yes?"

"Yes," Bren said quietly and quickly. Algini politely, with a bow, took the card, tucked it in his pocket, and Prakuyo then instructed his own aide Ukess in a rapid and cheerful patter of instructions.

"Yes," Ukess said then, bobbed and bowed and motioned with both hands to Algini and Tano. "Come, come."

The station had indeed figured somewhere in the set of instructions Prakuyo had just given. Tano and Algini could speak to ops from kyo communications, at which point *Phoenix* would give orders, Central would give orders, and they would get Tano and Algini to the station and back without a problem . . . or, one hoped, too much inquisitiveness from ship command. Jase was the only officer who *could* talk to Tano and Algini. And Tano and Algini had their instructions, and the message to Matuanu.

Their departure brought their company down, now, to himself, Banichi and Jago, and Prakuyo and his two. Six, Ragi-honed instinct said, was an untrustworthy number, infelicitous two of felicitous threes, a number foreboding a division of interests—without mitigation.

There was usefulness in that stray superstitious thought.

"Atevi say six is not all felicitous," Bren said in Ragi. "But Cullen is our seven, which is a number of much greater happiness. Will *you* talk to Cullen now, Prakuyo-ji?"

"Yes," Prakuyo said with a deep thump, and added what seemed an entirely sensible request, considering the nerves on both sides: "Not open door."

Bren walked down the hall with Banichi and Jago alone, no kyo in sight, given the curve of the hall, and within his cell, Cullen stood up to meet them.

"Cullen talk?" Bren asked in kyo, the promised test. And for a moment Cullen looked frozen. "All good, Cullen?"

"Talk," Cullen managed to say, likewise in kyo, a minor triumph. Then Cullen went further. "Tano? Algini?"

Say they were off to visit the space station? Absolutely not. For all Cullen was to know, this was a meeting in deep space. "Tano and Algini sit, rest. Hear?"

"Rest, yes," Cullen said, then looked past him in alarm. "Kyo."

"This is that person I mentioned," Bren said in ship-speak. "This is Prakuyo. The one who wishes to talk. Be calm. Be polite. Talk to him. He actually understands a little of our language . . . and he *is* interested in you, which is good. Can you be calm?"

Cullen drew a deep breath. His lips made a thin line.

"He's been here before. With you. And before."

"I don't doubt. Has he ever hurt you?"

"No. He gives orders."

"Face," Bren said. "Just tell yourself that every time you deal with them. I've agreed to spend seven days here, teaching you, helping you. It's his idea. I think he might get you out of that cell, if you make a good impression. And if we can get you this far in three hours, think what we can do in seven days. Face. Face."

"Got it," Cullen said, and managed his expression, as Prakuyo came close to the transparent door.

"Face same Bren," Prakuyo said, looking Cullen up and down. "Yes." A wave of his hand about his own hairless head. "Good."

"Cullen," Bren said, "this is Prakuyo, Prakuyo an Tep. Prakuyo an Tep, this is Cullen."

"Cullen," Prakuyo said. With a little boom. "Good. Good see face."

"Talk," Cullen said in kyo. "Talk. Want talk kyo."

"Yes," Prakuyo said. "Understand. Prakuyo understand human talk. Not say good. Hear good."

"He's saying," Bren said, "that he understands far more of our language than he can speak. Our language has sounds kyo can't make and certainly the other way around. Pick words you *can* say. Say it in human language, then say the same thing in kyo. Prakuyo understands that way of working."

"What does he want?" Cullen asked.

"*Ask* him," Bren said.

Uncertainty. Panic. Cullen brought his face under control. "Want?" he asked. "Prakuyo want?"

"Peace," Prakuyo said, that simply. It was not a word they'd gotten to with Cullen.

"Peace," Bren translated it, and Cullen sucked in a deep, deep breath, then carefully, consciously pressed his open hand to the barrier between them.

Prakuyo did the same, hand to hand, on either side of the barrier. Stood that way a moment, two beings staring at each other, two open hands that didn't match, two faces each seeking answers.

Tano and Algini had returned—but without nand' Bren.

Nand' Bren, they said, wanted to stay seven days talking to Prakuyo, just talking. And *they* said they needed to talk to mani, in mani's rooms, with Matuanu.

How could they talk to Matuanu? And *why* should they talk to Matuanu and mani at once?

Cajeiri tried to concentrate on the board in front of him, the game mani had deserted to disappear into her room with nand' Bren's aishid—and Matuanu—leaving him and Hakuut to continue on their own.

It was Hakuut's move. Hakuut was probably asking himself exactly the same questions. Hakuut was *much* better at Ragi. Matuanu hardly talked at all. In either language.

It was secrets Tano and Algini brought back. Cenedi and Nawari were in that room. They would learn.

Secrets. Something important enough to go to the one place in the suite that was free of recording devices, but maybe not of Hakuut's hearing.

On the far side of the board, Hakuut's eyes flickered to the door, to the game, and back again. After that first game, Matuanu and mani, watching, had let the two of them make their own moves. Cajeiri had planned to let Hakuut win, being diplomatic . . . and discovered there'd been no charity involved. Hakuut had been winning without any help.

Suddenly, Hakuut reached out, moved his aiji-dowager recklessly close, then sat back, looking again to that closed door.

Cajeiri saw it. Hakuut had not. He had just lost the game.

Cajeiri said nothing, just reached silently to counter the move and check Hakuut's aiji . . . and discovered the board was trembling. His hand was trembling. He set down the piece, and as he did, it chattered against the board.

He pulled the hand back, and clenched his fingers together as that trembling reached deep into his gut. His ears began to make strange buzzing sounds, and underneath the buzz, a deep, deep hum, a rumbling that he felt more than heard.

"Haku-ji!" he gasped. "Face!" And as quickly as it had started, the strange hum ended.

"One regrets, Jeri-ji."

Hakuut's face slowly came back into focus.

He drew a deep breath. "Hakuut upset?"

"Many upset. Tano and Algini come. No Bren. Good. Not good."

He drew another breath, and gestured toward the board. "Draw?"

"Draw."

Silently, they began putting the pieces in their little case. Before they could finish, mani emerged from her room. Nand' Bren's two bodyguards bowed and took their leave toward nand' Bren's rooms, without so much as a glance his way. Cajeiri stood up in respect, Hakuut set the game box on the side table and stood up as well. Matuanu, with a bow to mani, told Hakuut to come with him, and the two of *them* disappeared into the kyo section of the suite.

The door shut. It never had until now.

Cajeiri stood, waiting for mani to sit and for the tea to be poured, neither of which happened.

"Young gentleman," she said, which she almost never called him. "I shall be in my suite for a while, with Cenedi. I trust you and Hakuut did not come to disagreement."

"No, mani. He was worried. One believes he was worried. He might have been listening."

Mani ignored the hint, pointedly. "You will be pleased to

know our guests will be remaining with us for a felicitous seven more days."

"Nand' Bren?" he asked, worried. "Will he stay there seven days?"

"The paidhi-aiji reports good progress. He sees the need for these seven days. His aishid is here to obtain more clothing and make the arrangements for his absence. I suggest you continue to work with Hakuut on the dictionary. These seven days should not be wasted in these premises, either."

"Mani," he said, uninformed, and dipped his head respectfully as she returned to her rooms.

And shut the door.

Seven days. He glanced at his aishid, standing silently beside the door. Seven days, with secrets passing behind closed doors all around him. He wished *he* had ears like the kyo, whose ears were hardly visible at all.

He wanted to know. He very much wanted to know . . . but when mani said it was secret, it was secret.

The door to the kyo suite slid open and two very sober kyo came out.

Not just Matuanu. Hakuut, as well. So Matuanu, having heard whatever it was, had told Hakuut not to tell whatever Hakuut might have heard, and probably whatever he might hear. And he did not think Hakuut would disobey that instruction.

Tano and Algini never even came back into the sitting room. They sat down with the tablets again, he and Hakuut, and at a certain point Hakuut looked up, toward nand' Bren's apartment.

"Door open?" he asked Hakuut.

"Open and close," Hakuut said. "Two."

So Tano and Algini were leaving by the servant passage, going back to the lift, and not going through the sitting room and foyer at all.

It seemed quite clear he would not learn *anything* from *anybody*, not for at least seven days.

*   *   *

Prakuyo sent gifts down, a plate of food, including sweets, and a new robe, a geometric pattern, blue and gold, and a very large tufted pillow, brown and gold. Ukess and Huunum brought them, and, the cell door being open, cautiously ventured in to set them on the floor.

"Stand," Bren prompted Cullen, and did that, himself. "Bow. These are for you."

Both kyo bobbed slightly, hands folded.

"Thank you," Cullen managed to say as they left.

Second bob, facing him, before they left.

"Furniture," Bren said. "Food. A sampler of kyo food, by the look of it. Generally—taste a very little of something new. If your tongue feels odd in a few minutes, don't swallow it. Let them know, not just what tastes wrong, but what you like. —They *do* have alcohol, by the way."

That drew interest.

"Be careful of it," Bren said. "Strict limit, when they do give it to you. Know your limit, and stay well inside it. One lapse can turn a conversation into a disaster. You can't afford that, especially now, no matter what the pressure. I hope, I sincerely hope, that you'll find them as tolerant and reasonable as atevi have been with my early mistakes. But don't make that one. You can't ignore their customs or their sense of limits. Boundaries, both personal and cultural. Accept them. If you can work them into your own thinking, you may find they're *not* barriers; if you look at them right, they're keys to the things you need the most."

Cullen looked at him the same desperate way he'd looked at Prakuyo. "How long have you done this?"

"Years. I was younger than you when I started, and I'd studied the atevi language and customs since I was a child, preparing for the job. And I'll tell you something. I wouldn't trade what I do. I've had the chance to quit, but I wouldn't trade it for anything, more so as the years pass. I wish you that kind of luck. I truly do."

"I'm scared," Cullen said. "I'm scared as hell."

"Better than over-confidence. Much better. Right now you can only anticipate. I've been in that situation—lately, with the kyo themselves. But once you're in a situation, you have a job to do. Do your best to prepare yourself, keep reminding yourself that both sides believe they're in the right, and when in doubt, bow. Be immaculately polite, and listen to what they're saying. Never, *ever* assume; if in doubt ask for clarification. Stay out of angry groups. The subsonics you know can hurt, if they're upset. I'm not sure how bad it can get, but I suspect it *can* be a weapon, even among their own kind, and very likely there are some individuals particularly good at it."

"There are." There was a slight tremble in his voice. "There's one real scary one."

"On the other side of the coin—be polite to him. Remember to control your face and your voice. Intimidation needs response, bait needs biting. If you do neither, the attacker has nothing to build on. Point of interest: the kyo say that connections once formed are permanent. *Exactly* what they mean by that I'm not sure, but possibly it's just that they stand by their relationships once they do make them, and consequently don't commit to them instantly or lightly. Do things their way. Respect them, take them as they are. There's only one of you, and it's their ship."

It was scary, how much a person yanked out of human culture unwarned, unschooled, and unprepared to deal with non-human instincts—wouldn't know. It had taken the War of the Landing and a lot of good intentions on both sides for Mospheirans *and* atevi to internalize it.

"Let me explain how atevi are, and how we adapt to each other, how we deal with the differences. It won't have a thing to do with how kyo are . . . but it's the best working example I have."

A deep breath. "I'm ready."

"All right. Let's talk about salads."

22

There was no letup. Tano and Algini came back with the clothes, with paper writing materials, which were a major asset with Cullen, and with a very large container of frozen teacakes which Bindanda had sent over for Prakuyo. Banichi left Cullen's cell to confer with Tano and Algini, then came back with a tiny hand signal to say everything was in order— meaning Tano and Algini had delivered the message to the dowager and given Prakuyo's written note to Matuanu.

So everything was stable over on the station, and secrets were locked down.

That was, Bren thought, a mortal relief.

He sat in the cell with Cullen, and, once given the resource of paper and pen, he wrote words and created a dictionary on the spot: no tablets, none of the elaborate work he had made to bridge the gap to the kyo . . . no pictures that betrayed the planet, or the relationship.

"Tablet has Mospheirans, Reunioners," he said to Prakuyo, during one of their periodic conferences. "Not give Cullen tablet. Pictures speak many, many word. Mospheirans. Reunioners. Atevi world. Not good give Cullen."

Prakuyo gave a series of little thumps and said, "Not give. Understand."

"Kyo write words. Show."

That had been an undertaking, a test of eyes and brain. It was, thank God, not word-dedicated characters, but a sort of alphabet with a few combination symbols, and interspersed with glyphs which—a strange revelation—represented the booms and thumps. There was a happiness glyph, as best one could figure it, and an unhappiness glyph. There was a warning glyph, an encouragement glyph—fourteen of them, and possibly more that Prakuyo didn't consider as basic.

He took notes for himself.

And he presented the system to Cullen, who just dropped his head against his knees and stayed that way for a time, before he sat up, rubbed his face, and propped his head in his hands.

"It's not easy," Bren said. "I'm not saying it's easy. You have time."

"I have a *lot* of time." Cullen laughed, a thready, desperate sort of laugh, rubbed his face hard, and then said, "I'll work on this. I don't know if my brain can handle it, but I'll try."

"Don't expect to learn it all at once. But writing is another key to dealing with the kyo. Literacy is *also* a way for you to take notes that don't fit in our writing. You'll rapidly reach a point you'll think thoughts you can't think in our language. You'll know names of things you can't think of except in kyo. That's when you'll start living in the language. But before that— let me warn you—you may reach a whiteout. Total panic. Inability to think of any word in any language. You may break down in tears. That's all right. Many do. I have. It'll pass, usually in less than an hour. Think of it as a gateway, one you'll learn to pass, back and forth—and the better you do it, the faster you get out of that no-words moment." He didn't want to linger on the problems of that gateway, the possibility that Cullen might fall far out of practice with his own language, his native thought patterns—a loneliness more extreme than he'd ever had to deal with. What Cullen had ahead of him was—total.

He'd always been able to make periodic visits to Mospheira. He'd always been able to renew his human way of thinking. Of being. He could talk to family. Visit familiar places.

Even so, he'd long since lost track of the Bren who had first crossed the strait, naive and completely without a map.

"Make the kind of relationships kyo can make," he said to Cullen. "*Find out* what relationships they can make. They may meet you on your own territory, to a degree you can't imagine now. There'll be individuals you want to attach to, individuals you want nothing to do with, and some that may take a while to get to know—but turn out something different than you thought. People, in other words. Good ones and bad ones."

Long silence. "What if," Cullen asked, "I went over to your atevi? What if I went—wherever you come from?"

He'd dreaded a repetition of that question—profoundly dreaded it.

"No. Right up front. No. Don't hope for it. The government I represent won't allow it while this war goes on."

Cullen looked at him, just stared, with feelings too muddled and disappointed even to read.

"But," Bren said, "the kyo *do* want you. *They* want you."

"What if I don't want *them?*"

"They *need* you. *You* have the history with them. You're much closer to understanding them than I am. What you have to do is stop *your* war."

"Stop the war." Another grim laugh. "*How?*"

"That's something you have to figure out, Mr. Cullen. I can't. I *have* a job. You're the one who has to figure out the kyo, and live with them, and figure out what started this war, because that may be the key to why it continues. It's pretty certain the kyo in charge of this ship don't want it, and probably people in your government don't want it, either. Look at all this vast space where you might be, and, instead, you're locked together killing each other. Figure out how to stop that. Figure out why it started and convince both sides to back off, because there are plenty of territorial alternatives, and a lot of room out there, if you don't trek across sensitive territory, which seems to be what somebody has done. It may be just that simple. And unfortunately just that complicated. Because you won't be dealing with common sense and common goals. You'll be dealing with personalities—on both sides—with their own agendas and their own phobias, who've maybe done some very bad things they won't want to admit were a mistake. It's your job to straighten that out, or maneuver to give power to people who'll make a different choice."

"How the hell do I do that?"

"Pick and choose *who* you talk to. This is vitally important. Pick the best people to talk to. And be accurate. Give accurate warnings. Give the people that work with you results that make *them* important to other people. You may not know a thing about kyo politics. But you have at least one potential ally, if you'll work with him. If you want to resign it all and live out your own life taking no chances, that's on you. But I'm telling you right now . . . there's no one else in your position. *I* can't do it. I won't desert the people I work for."

There was a long silence then, Cullen staring at him with anger evident, then at his hands, maybe thinking it over, maybe refusing to think at all.

He could lose Cullen, he thought. He could have Cullen leap up right now and declare he'd had enough, and wanted no more to do with him or his help.

But what did a man do, who'd not seen another human being in—long enough to decline to the state he'd been in?

What did a man do, presented with a chance to end that isolation, and what did a man do who might never in his life see another human being, whether things went right or wrong?

Cullen would someday find out what he had kept from him, and hate him for it. Prakuyo knew. Everybody on this ship knew. So someday Cullen would know . . . everything.

That was as it had to be.

"I'm not sure I can do it," Cullen said.

"If you *were* sure," Bren said, "I'd say you weren't bright enough to do it. There's no guidebook. I can't predict what you'll meet. I don't know. If I tried to advise you, I'd be wrong. You only know when you see the situation in front of you. That's how it's done."

Cullen spent a while in a disconsolate knot, arms on his knees, head resting on his arms. Bren waited, leaned all the way back in the chair and waited. Banichi and Jago, never leaving him but what Tano and Algini took their turn at watch. The cell door stayed open. The whole corridor was quiet, the whole territory given over to them.

Was it safe to sleep in the cell with Cullen? It was as safe as his aishid made it. And Cullen had never made a try even to walk out the open door, not that there was much to gain in that direction.

Bren got up very quietly and went back to the conference room, as he did now and again. He had lost all awareness of time passing, of day or night.

This time he did, unintentionally, fall asleep in the conference room, tucked up in a large padded chair, and he waked to find Banichi and Jago doing much the same in the chairs over against the wall, which meant that Tano and Algini had gone on watch with Cullen. He got up very quietly, with no illusion that he could move softly enough to avoid waking Banichi and Jago, but he tried; he availed himself of the facility adjacent to the conference room, washed his face in cold water, and went back down the curving hall to the cell, where Tano and Algini were awake and on watch.

Perhaps, he thought, he might call his bodyguard back, quietly lock the cell door and let them all catch a few hours of sleep, hoping that would draw them back from the edge they'd been on. But Cullen was not asleep. Cullen hauled himself to the edge of his seat as Bren arrived, sat crosslegged there, hands locked on his ankles—tense.

"Thought you might not come back," Cullen said.

"I fell asleep." Bren sat down in the chair he used. "I wish I had easier answers. I wish I had a happier situation for you. I don't. I can't. It's going to be hard at first, damned hard. But I hope there'll come a time when a few more humans join you, to learn from you, to become translators in their own turn. I hope so. That's for you and Prakuyo to figure out. I'll say only one thing on that matter: *if* that happens, you have to have some sort of authority over others. You will *have* to have. You and Prakuyo . . . what you can build between you will be unique. This opportunity to immerse yourself, one human partnering with this one kyo may never happen again. More than one human living among the kyo, learning from you—that's something for you to explore, when it happens; and it may. It has advantages. Mental health, for one. Multiple minds, multiple talents working on the problems, for another. That's all on you to develop, within whatever framework you can work out with Prakuyo."

"That's—"

"What?"

"I don't know. It's a long way from where I am. It's not real to me."

"Make it real. Dare to dream. And have the practicality to make it happen."

Cullen carried a shaking hand to his head, rubbed his brow. "I'm nobody, actually. Not—not a government sort. Electronics."

"That's all right. I trained to write dictionaries. You'll get it. The language? Three-year-old kids manage to learn *one* language. *You* did. It's all practice. Names of things around you. Things you want to eat. You learn the things you use. *Then* you move on to the big things."

"Seven days."

"Plenty of time for what I have to offer. I can't give you the language on a plate. I'm still learning that, myself. What I can give you are the keys, the structure, as much of it as I've figured out. A technique for learning, and enough words to ask questions. After that . . . I've nothing more to give you. You're the one with the chance to become fluent. One day, with luck, you'll be teaching this to another human. Telling another human what you know. Keep that in mind as you learn. Realize you're going to have to explain as well as use it."

"And after seven days, you'll go back to—where?"

Question repeated. And maybe a chance to make sense to Cullen—with caution.

"A place we have," Bren said quietly. "A group of humans and a world full of atevi. We didn't start out so well. We had ourselves a war. But a few humans and a few atevi figured out how to stop it and do something different, two hundred years ago. We gained that expertise. That's the thing I'm trying to pass to you—*how* to do what I do, as the appointed contact. And it all starts with two reasonably ordinary, smart individuals learning that their way isn't the only way. You've got a potential partner. Don't lose him. Don't mess it up for him. Or for you. It may not be the work of one lifetime. It wasn't for us. I'm one of a long, long string of translators, who've finally gotten wars stopped. Not conflict. We've still got that. But wars—no. We don't do that."

Long, long stare. "I hear what you're saying."

"Good."

Another pause, then: "You said two hundred years? You named, that first time we met . . . what? A ship? Two? *Phoenix*? *Reunion*? Never heard of either of them."

"Probably a footnote in the loss column of some long-forgotten company ledger. Likely not the only one. The universe is a big place. I suspect humanity's shed itself in more than a few odd spots in space, not all of which are connected to your lot, not all of which want to be known to your people, especially while you come with a war attached. That war of yours did spill over into our area. The kyo mistook us for you, mistook an exploratory mission for, well, a reconnaissance mission not, I suspect, unlike your own, and attacked. When we didn't fight back—and this is important—I think the kyo tried to talk to this one lot of strayed humans, a splinter off our group. Prakuyo's team was killed. He survived, locked six years in a room like this one, unable to talk to anyone, damned near starved to death on the diet. He was half his current weight when we got him out, whether or not it was intentional, or just food he had trouble eating. So I suspect your case interested him for very personal reasons. I don't know enough of the language myself to ask him that. But you haven't starved here, whatever else."

"No," Cullen said soberly. "I haven't."

"He brought you to me—posing me a question, perhaps. Atevi were the first to really talk to him, atevi I work with. I think he wanted me to talk to you, to make *you* able to talk to him. He saw my function with the atevi—at least he's got a notion what I do. He understands my sort of humans aren't yours. And I'm not sure yet that he has a clear idea what the possibilities are, but I do know. I know that if you attach yourself to him, and the two of you manage to understand each other, the both of you, together, can do much the same that the first of *my* office did, two hundred years ago, when they stopped a war neither side could understand. What we built is something neither of us could have done alone. That's what I'm handing you. That's what I want you and Prakuyo to do."

Long silence. "I don't even know where to start."

"You *have* started. So has he. You'll figure out the rest."

"God. I don't know if I even believe you."

"That's all right. The language is real. The chance to stop your war is real. Anything else is . . . irrelevant. In seven days, you'll have enough words to ask for things and say please and thank you, and for you to talk to Prakuyo. He sent you a *pillow*, for God's sake. What more do you want of him?"

Cullen began to laugh, tucked up a knee, leaned his head on it, and folded his arms about his head, laughing, then crying, quietly, the two intermingled.

Tano and Algini, a little removed from where they sat, looked worried.

"It is not a concern, nadiin-ji," Bren said quietly, and just waited, while Cullen regained control, and wiped his eyes, and went on wiping them.

"All right?" Bren asked eventually.

"Fine," Cullen said.

"You understand me."

A nod. "Not wholly sure. But—yes. I just—it's crazy."

"Nice pillow," Bren said. "I'm sure he'd like to have had one, in his situation. He didn't have a bed."

"I get it," Cullen said. "I do get it." His voice shook, steadied. "I'll take care of that damn pillow. I will."

"I think we could both do with a few hours of sleep. The brain processes things in your sleep. You'll wake having forgotten some things you thought you knew and remembering things you can't even remember learning."

A weary chuckle. "Not that different from engineering, then."

"Not that different. I'll show you how to manage the alphabet, next lesson. I need to figure that myself. It will give you a feeling for how I approach a problem. Reading is real helpful, when you're trying to immerse yourself in the language. The more hours you can spend using the kyo language, the better."

"When you go—that's *all* I'll have."

"That's all there'll be," he said, "until you can talk to Prakuyo. And until you can rescue more of your people. But two cautions on that score. One: don't spend too much time in the human way of thinking. It will undermine your connection to the kyo."

"Makes a strange sense. And the other?"

"It was *after* we got to talking, after we were sure we were friends, humans with the atevi, that *we* went to war with each other."

"*Why?*"

"That's another thing I need to explain to you, tomorrow. We solved our problem. But it's real helpful for you to know, and for Prakuyo to know, why that happened. I can't tell him right now—I don't know what the touchpoints are with the kyo. But between you, you can figure it out. You'll discuss it with him. You'll come up with your own ways to solve it." He stood up with the weight of hours on him—too many hours, no sense of day or night, too much kyo tea and nerves at raw ends, but over all, it was a good time to quit. "See you at breakfast."

Four days. Four days since nand' Bren had departed for the kyo ship. Four days spent trading words and playing board games with Hakuut, at hours that mani's orders kept regular.

Four days in which one's thoughts wandered back and forth between the ship and the game and the words and pictures of the tablet, which changed *only* with what Hakuut was doing and what he was doing—not the way they did when nand' Bren was also working on the dictionary. Maybe it was because the tablets' messages could not reach the ship. Reports came in on com, every ten and a half hours from Tano or from Algini, reports that satisfied Cenedi. Antaro and the others talked with Cenedi, quietly, properly, asking his questions that were not useful to ask mani, and Cenedi's word was simply that nand' Bren was safe, and that nand' Bren was where he wished to be.

Nand' Jase was not entirely happy. Nand' Jase spent time in nand' Bren's apartment, but nobody knew any more than what Cenedi relayed to them, that said nand' Bren was safe, and that "things" were progressing. Not even Narani knew any more than that, or admitted he knew it, and nand' Jase frowned a great deal, and went back and forth between Lord Geigi, and the guests in Lord Geigi's apartment, and Gin. His aishid said that Cenedi suspected nand' Jase was under pressure from the ship-aijiin, who were not getting any more information. At one point, nand' Jase directly *asked* mani, which was because nand' Jase had no aishid capable of asking Cenedi, and Cajeiri somewhat held his breath, because that could be said to be pushing, on the part of the ship-aijiin.

But mani was patient with him, and had tea with him—to which Cajeiri was also invited—and told nand' Jase only that there were regular, scheduled reports to assure their continued safety and ability to communicate, but that was all they knew.

Nand' Jase said, too, that Bjorn's household was being moved from Lord Geigi's apartment, that there were questions Gin-nandi wanted to ask Bjorn's father, that there was an investigation into the company Bjorn's father worked for, and that Bjorn's father had gotten his papers back, and that he would get title to his portion of them, and that the others who might have title might get it by his voluntary sharing, or by lawsuit. Bjorn's father said he *would* share—Gin worked that out—and Asgard Company, that Bjorn's father had dealt with, would find itself in legal trouble regarding the rights for which they had gotten Bjorn his tutoring—somebody might file on them in the Mospheiran way, which was not Intent, but Mospheiran law was involved, and *maybe* Tillington was. So the company was going to give up the rights to Bjorn's father and continue Bjorn's lessons and Bjorn's father and other people were going to have a safe residency Gin was providing—while Tillington and certain other people were going to have to explain things to the investigators.

It *was* a lot of news. Gin-nandi was not a patient sort of person, and the people who had gone with her on the ship were just like an atevi household. If Gin wanted something done, people did it and gave each other orders, everybody trying to be quick about it.

So yes, Gin was a not a person who was going to be patient with Tillington.

And he hoped Bjorn was going to be all right.

"The Andressen house will go down to the planet," Jase-aiji

said. "They will have to pass the same tests as other people do to go up and work on the station."

"Is Andressen-nadi to be respectable?" mani asked. "Shall he be disgraced for his dealings?"

"Under the circumstances, nand' dowager, one expects he will gain respectability: his dealings were with property he rescued, the existence of which he declined to reveal to *Phoenix* command, and to his fellows, but he did preserve the materials. He used them in illicit barter, but he did so in the constraint of the situation, to help his family survive and gain status that might save them being shipped to Maudit—never a good plan. Gin-nandi will protect him—she will certainly protect Bjorn's interests. I have spoken to her about that."

It was good news. It was very good news.

But it was not news about nand' Bren and the situation they all were in, even Hakuut and Matuanu.

The ship-aijiin were growing impatient, asking Jase what was going on and what nand' Bren might be saying and promising.

"He will promise only such things as he must promise," was mani's judgment, "to secure a safe outcome and a fair relationship. The ship should do *nothing.*"

"Ship command is being very cautious," was Jase's answer. "They ask. I have told them—when you have information, I shall know it and relay it."

"That is the case," mani said.

Very possibly, Cajeiri thought, Hakuut and Matuanu were listening to all of it. They were not taking pains to keep it otherwise.

But Hakuut did ask, once he and Hakuut resumed their session at the dining table, "What Jase-aiji say? Ship-aijiin upset?"

"Not upset. Worried. Think-this, think-that. Ask when Bren will come back, what kyo ask, what nand' Bren say."

Hakuut said: "Matuanu and me worry same."

Oh, there were questions he could ask . . . questions about

what Matuanu had told Hakuut. Ever since that day, there were moments Hakuut would fade away from whatever they might be doing and stare across the room.

Listening? Trying to hear secrets that might pass beyond the walls?

He wished he could hear all the way into that ship out there. He wished mani would volunteer whatever Tano and Algini had had to say to her and Matuanu, when they made their visit.

But if mani wanted to say that, she would, and she had not.

We—remained a hard word. *We*, even *I*, was problematic—as if whatever *we* might be was so enmeshed with *I*, or vice versa, that kyo just felt—intruded upon if someone assumed it.

Ragi had an impersonal *one*. And kyo had an impersonal. It finally came clear, dealing with Huunum and Ukess. They were *we*. One boomed, the other did—it was that simple. But get a mob together . . .

"Many, many kyo are not a good *we*," as Huunum put it. "Crazy. Two, three, good. Kyo choose two, three learn, report, talk to number one kyo. Much more fast decide."

Well, it was *not* the way atevi decided things, unless one counted clans, but it appeared that agreement-groups among the kyo were not by birth, gender, or political rank. They were somewhat by personal affinity. They were, in fact, whatever kyo wanted them to be.

"I think," Bren said to Cullen, in the long sessions which, a day ago, had moved to the conference room, "that it expresses what we call affection, and consensus, what atevi call man'chi, and clan, and their decision-making may be something we had rather approach the way they do, in small groups that build into a network of little groups. Quiet that way. Easier on human nerves."

"Can they get anything done that way?" Cullen asked.

"Clearly they do, don't they? You can work with it. You're smart. You adapt. Thank God."

"You say—tomorrow we'll start using just kyo. Just kyo."

"You have to."

Long pause. Bitten lip. Cullen was struggling with something. There'd been more than one such moment.

"Going to miss human language," Cullen said in a shaky voice. "Haven't heard it for so long. Don't want you not to use it."

"And you want to make sure you don't lose touch with it," Bren said. "You're going to need it as much as the kyo language if you're going to negotiate a peace. Prakuyo can use it. Not easy for him to pronounce the lip sounds. He makes them somewhere inside. But you can talk to him when you have to." He understood the loneliness. He'd been there, in the early days. And he'd started using Ragi with people all around him— because he couldn't be like his predecessor, perpetually silent, solitary, withdrawn, communicating only in writing. He *had* to talk to people. He was that way. It had caused him a lot of trouble, in the Department of Linguistics.

Cullen wanted to talk. Cullen hadn't had the skills to learn more than a handful of expressions, and his captors hadn't helped him—Prakuyo could have, but hadn't wanted, Bren strongly suspected, to compromise the test he was running: to bring the two of them face-to-face and find out whether they were the same species, the same culture, the same political entity. Prakuyo had needed to know that, and now Prakuyo did have his answer, and Prakuyo, who had spent his own time with nobody to talk to—a very terrible thing for a kyo— definitely wanted to talk to Cullen.

Prakuyo had set up a meeting—because Prakuyo was *not* the highest authority on the ship. There were two higher, two from whatever shape Prakuyo's government took. Their names were Kokrohess an Ye and Heyyen an Crus, and they were, Bren began to suspect, part of an attempted "we" involving Prakuyo, a situation that had yet to work itself out, in kyo terms—and persuading them was important . . . to everybody.

Understand it all? Learn the kyo mindset? He had two days

left of the seven he'd promised—and yes, he very likely could change that. He could volunteer another day—another seven days—but there would never be an end of things to learn, mysteries of behavior, mysteries of concept. There would never be a time in any near future he could unravel anything without uncovering another mystery, in a species so different.

No. What he discovered along the way, he passed to Cullen. He gave Cullen as much as he could. But the first paidhi among atevi hadn't been a linguistics expert, only a man who'd fallen into the right place to learn, and who'd understood what atevi wanted and who'd done the best he could, making it all up as he went along.

Cullen at least had somebody to show him how to make tables, how words built other words, how minds differed, how to show respect and how to show good will—how to utter those important words, whatever they really meant in kyo, to say that one had meant better than had just seemed, and that one was happy with what had just happened. That was where it started.

Beyond that . . .

"I'll talk in human language tomorrow," he said, ceding the point, because he could. "I wanted to help you as much as I can—but you'll have long enough to practice in kyo. We'll do as much of it as seems useful."

"And then you'll leave."

No equivocation. "And then I'll leave."

23

The sixth day. The sixth day, there was the usual message, called in—so Antaro and the others said. And it was the day before the last day.

Cajeiri had learned words until his head felt stuffed—but he hoped nand' Bren would be happy with what he and Hakuut had added to the dictionary. He was particularly eager to show him the kyo writing system he was rapidly committing to memory. He wished that he could be cheerful. He tried to be. But he worried. He worried that something might be wrong, aboard that ship, that nand' Bren and Banichi and the rest might be in trouble. He would not expect Hakuut knew anything about it, but he could believe it of Matuanu, who in all these days had said very little, that only to Hakuut, and spent a great deal of time sitting in a chair near the kyo apartment door, watching.

Just watching. And maybe listening . . . to absolutely everything that went on in the area.

"What is Matuanu doing?" he had asked Hakuut once, and Hakuut had just bobbed and hunched his shoulders, which seemed to be a kyo sort of shrug.

Nand' Bren had told his aishid, who had told Cenedi, who had told his aishid, that Matuanu might be something like Guild.

And Guild sitting and watching and watching for hours with his principal absent was not a happy situation.

Matuanu was watching. And listening. He could probably hear the lifts going up and down and Jase coming and going and all the staff going about and Cenedi having meetings with people who did not talk out loud.

Matuanu was mapping the patterns of the station, what was normal, what was not, the noise of staff at work, the lack of noise when Guild met Guild. That was how Antaro described what Guild did when *they* were set to watch a situation—like hunters in Taiben forest, listening, learning from everything that moved and failed to move. Matuanu watched and listened. Cenedi watched and listened through the eyes of staff as well as Guild, and maybe with things that Guild was not supposed to talk about. And meanwhile the Guild Observers sat and watched everybody, mostly inside their own quarters, speaking only to other Guild.

There were regular things to observe, like clockwork—despite nand' Bren being gone. Staff had duties. Jase-aiji came and went, but he was absent for most of every day, dealing with Gin-nandi and Lord Geigi: they knew that. Maybe he was talking to Sabin-aiji and Ogun-aiji and station security.

And when Jase-aiji was out, so that nand' Bren's staff had nobody to wait on, they helped mani's staff, and polished and cleaned things, whatever they could find to do.

And Bindanda cooked and baked. Teacakes never stopped. Bindanda had sent a great many of them over to the ship with Tano and Algini, and Algini's call had asked for more, frozen, to be sent down for somebody to deliver to the kyo ship, so *somebody* over on the kyo ship had to be enjoying them. That seemed a hopeful sign.

But one still worried. And the sixth day was shaping up to be like the third or the fourth or the fifth day, only with Matuanu grimmer and more silent, saying not a word at breakfast.

Six was a mixed sort of number—unfortunate two of a fortunate number, or two very infelicitous numbers—and he was down to figuring numbers like the 'counters. He told himself again and again the numbers were only for superstitious people, which he had not been brought up to be, but six was *still* a chancy sort of day and he wished it were over and that today were the seventh, which was moderately fortunate.

"Such faces," mani said at breakfast, at a table which had their two kyo guests, and him and mani—*four* at table, which was how much great-grandmother made of the numbers. "Such faces. There has been far too much study, too much chess, too little noise."

He had never in his life thought mani would complain of too little noise.

"Let us summon your guests," mani said with a wave of her hand. "Let us see if there is cheer to be had in their company."

"Yes," he said, but he worried as soon as agreement was out of his mouth, what mani was up to, and whether there was any problem on the ship that mani knew about, because Cenedi was always the one who took the messages from Tano and Algini.

Mani would not bring his guests into danger. He was sure of that much. So they were safe here.

And mani wanted noise.

It was another sort of chess game. Matuanu would sit and listen to everything going on. He was scary, in Cajeiri's view of things.

But mani intended to make a little noise.

Prakuyo leaned back in the conference room chair, legs crossed, arms clasping a prosperous belly, issuing a faint thumping sound as his head bobbed. "Six days," he said. "Six days, Bren-paidhi, great change. Should we-on-this-ship trust him? This is the question."

"He-unassociated can go this way, that way," Bren said honestly, "but Cullen wants to learn. He-unassociated wants association, wants not to be alone. Cullen wants to see the war stop. He-unassociated says—these words—too many dead. He-unassociated understands the loneliness at Reunion. He-unassociated believes you-associated with many understand his loneliness on kyo ships."

"True," Prakuyo said, bobbing his head, his whole upper body. "Is association safe, Bren-paidhi? You know what we-wider-association want."

"A paidhi. A translator. A bridge. Cullen wants the same, wants to build from his end of the bridge. Kyo build from the other side. *Prakuyo* builds from the other side."

"One understands. Cullen wants build bridge. We-association trust Cullen use hammers?"

Prakuyo made a joke, a very little one. They had reached that point of understanding.

"Someday you-association have to," Bren said. "Yes."

"Tomorrow seven day. Kyo day? Atevi day?"

"Prakuyo decides."

Boom. Thump. "Atevi day is fair," Prakuyo said.

"Fair," Bren said.

"Atevi ask a treaty," Prakuyo said. "Tonight Cullen will meet the aijin over this mission, and one will urge—" Thump. "—agreement to Cullen, agreement to treaty. Important that this happen. Important that Cullen speak well. Very important. The authorities will ask his name, will expect him to make a bow, and if he does well, they will give him water and food. He should drink and eat. Then he may sit down. Be welcome. You remember."

"I remember." Kyo had offered them the same, back at Reunion.

"Good we meet," Prakuyo said. "Good we meet, Bren-paidhi. Say same to the dowager, to the boy. We shall go tomorrow."

"You-Prakuyo will not go to the station to bring Matuanu and Hakuut."

Thump. "No. Matuanu will come, bring son."

That . . . took a moment to process.

"Hakuut is Matuanu's son?"

Boom. "No, *Prakuyo's* son. Fair. Tabini-aiji sends Cajeiri.

Hakuut comes wait on the station. Good that Hakuut sees Cajeiri. Good for atevi. Good for kyo . . . some day." Prakuyo uncrossed his legs, gave a triple click deep in his chest. "Together-we talk to Cullen now," Prakuyo said. "Be sure Cullen uses the right words for the kyo aijiin."

It was good to see Jase-aiji arrive in the foyer, and good to see Irene and Gene and Artur, who entered very quietly. The whole day had felt chancy, and Cajeiri had been locked in court expression for so long his face felt numb, all the muscles reluctant to respond as he met his guests.

There were, of course the courtesies, the bows, the address to mani, with Jase-aiji and mani being polite to each other—but solemnity affected everybody, except Matuanu, who was just—whatever he was.

Mani had ordered a party, setting lunch with a variety of refreshments, including those Hakuut greatly favored. Hakuut had far more Ragi now, not as much as Irene, but he was willing to use it, and he kept trying until he could be understood. He asked Gene to laugh again. Gene tried, and then did, and then Artur started, and then Irene . . . which made everyone much more relaxed, and a bit silly, and by the time lunch was over, they found themselves trying to explain why people ate things in order, with dessert last.

He had never even wondered that. He thought now it was peculiar that humans did and atevi did. Maybe one had learned from the other, or maybe it was that, if one ate sweets first, one would fill up on sweets and miss the meat dish.

It was the first time that day he had wondered about something that silly, as opposed to whether nand' Bren was all right and why nand' Bren was taking so long and whether Prakuyo would come back when nand' Bren did . . .

Hakuut asked where they lived, and Irene answered that: she said they lived upstairs. And Hakuut asked what they did on the planet when they visited.

Cajeiri opened his mouth to divert that question, because he really did not want his guests to explain about Lord Geigi's neighbor and the Assassins . . .

But Irene said: "We saw a storm, with lightning."

"We rode mecheiti," Gene said.

And Artur, from his pocket, pulled a handful of pebbles, one of which he showed. "Water did this," he said. "Years and years in this rock. Take. You have."

Hakuut took the pebble into his gray, large hand, held it, looked at it. "Bone of the planet," he said, which Cajeiri noted with some interest. It sounded like something he should remember, something nand' Bren would want to know.

"You keep," Artur said.

Hakuut closed his hand. Then bobbed a little, with a soft set of booms. "Thank," he said, and got up and took it to Matuanu, who, indeed, took it in his hand and looked at it, then handed it back.

There *should* be gifts, at a long parting. Cajeiri excused himself, and went to his room very quickly and found two of his good collar pins, not a well-thought gift, certainly not as good as Artur's, but he brought them back all the same, and gave one to Matuanu and one to Hakuut. Craftsmen had made them, each.

Hakuut then, got up and went to *his* rooms, and brought back a small box, which he opened, and shook out a set of little metal beads. He gave one to Cajeiri, one to Irene, one to Gene, one to Artur. The carved box he gave very solemnly to mani, with a little bob and bow.

"Thank you," mani said in kyo.

Which surprised absolutely everybody.

It was court dress for dinner—atevi style, and kyo. Bren had his best coat, lace that was damned hard to manage at table. Cullen's robe was a gift, a design like a wire diagram in gold, on a blue fabric. He was clean-shaven, scrubbed, hair braided in a simple queue.

And tied with a white ribbon. "Atevi gave me this," Bren said, as Tano was securing Cullen's braid. "The white is the paidhi's color, his badge of office. Wear it."

"Are you sure I'm ready for this?" Cullen asked, and the anxiety was utterly readable.

"Face," Bren answered quietly, in full control, then, humanly speaking, "Yes. You have to be."

It was only Cullen's second venture up into the heart of the ship. The first had been this afternoon, in a working session, where they'd met with the Authorities, the two who'd come with Prakuyo, who apparently sat in judgment. *That* had been daunting, a test of his aishid's nerves as well as his own and Cullen's. It was the scenario he'd imagined: a number of kyo in one place all arguing, with the subsonics at full bore. Noisy, to say the least. And there'd been only five of them: the two Authorities, Prakuyo, and his two aides. He didn't, personally, want to know what it would be like with ten or twenty of them going at it in the heat of argument.

Cullen might find that out someday—unsettling thought. Though kyo must be as capable of feeling pain—must have some sort of restraint in mass encounters, be it manners, rules, or just reluctance to gather in large arguing groups.

"You've survived the hard part," Bren said, as Tano stood back, task finished. "Prakuyo said they were impressed. And always remember: you'll have Prakuyo with you." For a moment, he was back on a windswept balcony, having his first breakfast with Ilisidi, freezing to death . . . Ilisidi's challenge to a human whose influence on her grandson was not always down a line she approved. Had she stopped such invitations? Not in the least. *She* liked the cold air. "You'll make your own way. You'll learn things I envy you."

"Wish you could stay. Even a few more days."

"You don't need it. You don't need me. You have everything you need."

"Not everything I need!"

Emotion. Out of control. He let his silence speak for him, and a moment later:

"I'm sorry. Chalk it up to nerves."

"Prakuyo will remind you. He'll take care of you. He's promised. Be fair to him. Learn what he can teach you, which is everything. Forget, for all practical intents, that we ever met—because you're on your own."

"I don't *want* to forget."

"I'm gratified. But I'm no use to you, beyond this. You've got a war to stop. Lucky for you—the kyo want to talk. I hope you can find some humans who do. Or that you can teach another human and pass the job on. Somebody has to do it. What's happening now makes no sense. My advice—don't expose yourself to risk. Don't go into human hands. Talk for the kyo, from a distance. Unless humans have changed in the last several hundred years, you'll become a high-priority target, somebody some humans won't believe, and will want to silence. Expect that. Just be smarter, more apt at getting contact, and listen to the kyo's advice. Work with them to disengage. Be damned careful about who you empower, and who gets in power on the human side."

"Who *I* empower?"

"The white ribbon isn't purity. It's no color at all. It's *neither* side. You represent the kyo honestly and accurately. And when you speak for humans you represent the humans honestly and accurately. That requires *you* be both honest *and* accurate, which means understanding the kyo beyond anything you imagine. That's how you get power. And that's how you use it."

"I'm not sure I'm that smart."

"You'll get there. It all starts with your willingness." He made a conscious gesture, one he didn't make with atevi, and clapped Cullen gently on the shoulder. "You'll do fine."

Cullen made one he never made, and threw both arms around him, one strong hug, startling his bodyguard. "Thanks. Just thanks."

"Come on." He patted Cullen on the back, headed him for the cell door. "Say your good-byes to this place. You won't be back. They're moving you to better quarters."

Cullen stopped. "I want my pillow."

"Let Prakuyo know. I'm sure he can arrange its relocation."

A nervous laugh. "I'll do that."

And he walked out into the corridor, and down toward the lift, never looking back.

Prakuyo had called—and Hakuut and Matuanu were packing. That was one thing.

But Banichi had called, and talked to Cenedi, and to mani, and Cajeiri had not been able to hear a thing, except mani had arranged her own gifts for Prakuyo, which she was sending with Hakuut and Matuanu—the tablets they already had in their possession, and one more; and a large, a very, very large package of orangelle teacakes.

He could stand it no longer. He went to mani's sitting room, while staff was scurrying around with mani's orders. "Is nand' Bren coming back, mani-ma? Is he coming back now?"

"He is coming back," mani said. "He is coming back with a very important document, which important kyo have signed and sealed, and which he has signed, in your father's name, with his authority."

Mani in fact sounded very pleased.

"So will Prakuyo come back?"

"No," mani said with a wave of her hand. "The mast is highly inconvenient, and the kyo cannot deal with the air or the cold there. Prakuyo bids us farewell from the safety and comfort of his own ship. He is anxious to recover his son . . ."

"His son! Hakuut?"

"Hakuut is his son. Hakuut, it appears, is sixteen years old. For much of his life Prakuyo was a prisoner on Reunion, and Hakuut came aboard the ship after we rescued Prakuyo from Reunion. Prakuyo called it *fair* that he bring his son, since we brought you. It was, in his way of thinking, reciprocity. It meant different things, for different reasons, his son, my great-grandson. But the kyo's reciprocity has let us explore the differences, and find agreements. It has not seemed unwise. And in the same reciprocity, nand' Bren and his aishid will traverse the mast at the same time Hakuut and Matuanu make that passage. And once they are all in their proper places, the kyo will take their ship from dock and go back to their own place."

"Will they come back?"

"No. The document, to which nand' Bren set your father's agreement, and his own with his seal, says that no ship from here may enter kyo space, and no ship of the kyo may come here."

It was, overall, very good news. He had a little difficulty thinking he would not see Hakuut again, that when he parted with him in the foyer, they would never meet again. Never was not a word he had much experience of, where it regarded associates of his. He did not know how to give them up.

He was already having to put a pin on the edge of his map for associates on the station.

He was going to have to put another, perhaps up in a corner, for places much farther away than Reunion.

It was a short stop at the residency, with the dowager preparing to go upstairs, and the kyo quarters now deserted. Geigi's people and Gin's would move in, collect whatever information might be left in those premises—for science.

What might remain on the other side, the atevi side, was off-limits to Gin's crew, and simply would be moved out, sent to the cyclers, and otherwise stripped back to the simple set of panels that had combined to make the semblance of an atevi residence. It was over, mission accomplished.

But there was no rest to be had here, in an artifice rapidly collapsing. Rest would come when he reached his own apartment, upstairs, and settled into his own bed, in the reasonable expectation of not having the place blown to oblivion.

"Nand' Bren!" Cajeiri didn't quite run. He walked like the young gentleman he was. It was obligatory to exchange courtesies with Cajeiri, to thank his exhausted staff, and to pay respects to the dowager, who had held up amazingly in the odd hours and the long effort to achieve—whatever they had achieved. He had two of three documents in a cylindrical case, each written in kyo script, with numerous glyphs of emphasis, and in atevi symbols, and in the Roman alphabet, in three languages, in such equivalency as he and the kyo could manage, in an impressive assortment of colors of ink, and with various seals, including his own ring, which he had used three times on each document, for aishidi'tat, Mospheira, and the ship-folk—he did need to inform the captains on that score, but it would be binding, for the very practical reason that its captains *would* agree, none of the four having any interest in seeing another Reunion situation, all of the four having no reason to object to seeing Reunion's survivors find a place on an atevi-ruled planet, out of their hands.

There was one thing left he *could* do, having some fluency.

"I shall go up to ops," he said to his aishid—they were equally as tired, equally thinking, surely of a chance to rest, which they had gotten only by turns, for what had been a long, long effort. "If I stop, nadiin-ji, I think I shall be too tired to walk any further. I need to be in ops, with Jase. I need to be there, if any question comes from the kyo ship. I cannot answer the technical things, but I can translate."

"Yes," Jago said, which was absolute, for all of them. The determination was there to finish it, do the job—and *then* get to their own residency, because this one was already in pieces.

"Advise the staff," he said. "Tell them we are absolutely too tired for festivities, even deserved ones. We shall simply arrive and sleep, if you wish, nadiin-ji."

"No reports to be made," Banichi said. "We have told Cenedi: we shall make our report tomorrow."

To the Observers—that was a question, what to tell them,

how far to rely on their good sense. He had to rely on his aishid to make that judgment, and he was not sure what that would be.

Tell Jase?

He was still asking himself that when he got into the lift, bound for ops.

He was asking himself that when the lift let them out again in that heavily securitied corridor, near that massive door, beyond which one of the station's essential nerve centers gave orders and regulated processes.

Tell the captains the truth?

Truth had done damage within the ship, after lack of truth had roused massive distrust. Lies and secrets had been the rule.

And aboard that kyo ship was one devastating secret, the existence of which threatened—everything.

Outside of himself and his aishid, the dowager knew. Cenedi knew. Tabini would need to know. He had to ask himself whether even Shawn Tyers, sitting in the Presidency of Mospheira, should be privy to a secret that, if ever whispered in the halls of government, would hit the streets and rouse—God knew what reactions. Panic. Anger. Conspiracy theories would run wild inside the hour.

He didn't know about Shawn's security. He didn't know whether Shawn also had people *he* would feel obliged to tell, and if he did, and *they* had people—the damned thing was endless. How many degrees could the information go out, before *someone* talked to somebody in a hallway in Mospheira's power structure and somebody else overheard?

Tabini knew how to keep secrets. The dowager had taught him.

There would come the day Cajeiri had to know.

But right now—he was missing a razor and a comb which he had to make some excuse to replace, and a guilty conscience said that telling staff he had accidentally left them aboard the kyo ship was just—a question he didn't even want to raise. A comb was one thing. A razor had to come from Mospheira. It could be gotten on the station, on the Mospheiran side. Atevi didn't use such a thing.

He could ask Gin. But that was one more person he was asking himself should he tell. Should he tell Geigi? Should he tell—when he got down to the world—his brother Toby?

But at some point, he had to draw the line and stick with it. At some point, he was going to have to choose to lie to someone who had a *right* to know. Because at some point, the risk became too great. It was a weight he had to carry. He had talked to Cullen about the hard parts he'd have to deal with; *he* had his own. He couldn't share the responsibility.

Secrecy. As heavy as that knowledge was, it went along with the strong likelihood that at some point—*Cullen* was going to find out. Prakuyo knew, and Prakuyo's crew knew, and the whole kyo hierarchy had to know. At some point they'd have to trust Cullen with the truth of the atevi and that the entire time he'd been with Bren, he had been a shuttle-ride away from another human civilization. They'd have to tell him someday—or Cullen would find out someday. Such things were ticking bombs, waiting until some point of stress to blow wide and do damage. But he couldn't control Cullen. Cullen had to figure for himself. And maybe if any human could understand why he'd had to keep that secret—by the time he figured it out—Cullen might.

"Bren." Jase caught sight of him as he walked in, as guards passed them through. Jase welcomed him, nodded to his aishid, and beckoned them on into the narrow aisles of techs and screens.

Two big screens showed the kyo ship, with the umbilical still attached, or at least as much as the cameras could take in, a confusing pattern of reflected sun, red and blue working lights from the station structure, and absolute, unremitting black of shadow.

"How was it?" Jase asked. "You look exhausted."

"Pretty tired," he said.

"What took so long? Agreement, your message said. Have we got one?"

"Pretty good one. The kyo are keeping Reunion alive. Re-making it, I suppose, in their own way. They don't want contact. They want ships to stay out of their space. But if we need to contact them, we can go to Reunion. We can contact them there. That's in the document." Deep breath. "I had to sign it for the captains. It seemed expedient. I know what that's worth, technically, but it was that or lose the momentum. And they were agreeing. They just don't want to be contacted right now. Maybe never, but certainly not until they've ended their war. They wanted to be sure they didn't have a situation with us on the other front. I convinced them we're peaceful, and as anxious for privacy as they were. They were glad. We all signed. I brought you one of three documents. It's in the things I'm sending up to the apartment. I'm just not up to an interview with Ogun and Sabin right now, if you understand."

"I do. So will they. We're all, *all*, grateful."

A voice on com said, *"Uncoupling."*

The screen didn't appear to change. The umbilical was still out there.

"Confirmation on uncouple. Clear."

A schematic flashed up on the second large screen, simply a set of dots, moving to the right.

"They're moving."

The dots vanished in favor of the second ship image, a white structure slowly, slowly moving in relation to the station structure. The umbilical separation became clear, the end just left, motionless, while the ship, at the speed of a train leaving station, eased itself back and back.

"Moving with authority," Jase murmured. "But they pretty much do as they want to do. Scared hell out of ops coming in."

"All booms clear," came the word from com. *"Clear to go."*

The ship moved more definitely now, straight back, at increasing speed.

"Were you all right with them?" Jase asked with a critical look.

"Short sleep. Long sessions. But we're fine. We're all fine. More than fine. Good outcome, Jase. Very good outcome."

The ship kept accelerating. Backward—forward—who among them knew which end was the bow, or whether the kyo much cared?

"Cajeiri kept asking, had I heard, had I heard. Ogun was worried about you. That's a first."

"Gratified," he said.

Jase just looked at him. Second brother, Jase. Jase, who *did* carry a paidhi's burden—the power to decide, the power to inform, the obligation at times to take a stand against his own superiors.

"Jase," he said, and lapsed into Ragi. "Come upstairs. We need to talk."